# TAMING MR. WALKER

## LONDON MISTER SERIES BOOK 1

### Rosa Lucas

# FOREWORD

Disclaimer: The material in this book contains graphic language and sexual content and is intended for mature audiences.

The vocabulary, grammar, and spelling of Taming Mr. Walker is written in British English.

# 1

**Charlie**

**Where the hell are you? Mike's on the warpath. You're the target, by the way.**

*Thanks, Stevie.*

I fire the phone back into my bag and barge through the glass doors of Dunley Tech, doused in the perfume of the London underground.

Jackie, our darling receptionist, looks up from whatever influencer's Instagram she's trying to imitate this week. She's packed so much powder on her face that she looks like a cake.

"Morning." I nod curtly.

"Wow." She drags her eyes from the screen. "Your skin looks really…"

I raise my eyebrows, waiting.

"Grey." She screws up her face. "Were you boozing last night?"

"Thanks, Jackie," I reply, fumbling to find my security pass in my bag. "That's almost as nice as when you asked me if I had washed my hair with conditioner. I was up until 3 a.m. sorting out the server outage if you must know."

"Fascinating." She turns back to Instagram.

"They've started without you. Mike's raging. He says you better be ill or dead, arriving this late."

Damn.

I look at my watch. It's 10:20 already.

Mike Chambers is our Head of I.T. and has been since the company started a decade ago. An absolute dinosaur in the workplace. He hates change and any ideas that don't come from him. Greasy, uptight, and in desperate need of a good seeing to. We're convinced he's a fifty-year-old virgin.

I brace myself and push the doors of the boardroom open. It's our weekly management meeting where we sit through Mike's dick swinging, with a slideshow in the background. For an hour, he rants and stomps his feet while the rest of us wait patiently for the peacocking show to draw to a close.

Everyone has strategically chosen seats away from Mike. I walk to the only remaining seat next to him. "Sorry, Mike, I'm running late this morning."

He leans over and breathes directly into my face. Any closer and I'll dry retch. "I can see that. We're discussing why the India office was offline for two and a half hours last night. Thirty staff members were unable to do any work. Not one line of code written!"

"I understand your frustration, Mike—" I start.

"That means horse shit, Charlie." He slams his fist onto the table, making everyone in the room wince. "Can you explain what happened? Can you explain to the board why our most critical software release won't be out on time?" He juts his finger in my face as he leans over the table. "Can you explain what the fuck went wrong?"

I draw in a sharp breath and refrain from vomiting profanities at him. "It was a problem with the network again. Once the problem was established, I logged a severity one call. This was the fastest they could do it."

"The fastest?" he scoffs. "Don't be ridiculous. Who fucked up here? I NEED ANSWERS."

With every word, he jabs his finger on the table. He likes using his fingers for effect; we suspect he's read it in a *Management for Dummies* or *Control your Workforce* book.

"Contractually, they can take up to twenty-four hours for these types of problems. Those are our SLAs."

He blinks furiously. "How are you going to make sure it won't happen again?"

"I can't," I reply through gritted teeth. "Unless you let me move us to the cloud, we'll never have the resilience you want."

"Bullshit!" he howls. "We are not creating a bloody cloud, Charlie!"

I open my mouth and close it again. I drew Mike basic diagrams, but he didn't get it. "We don't create the cloud," I say slowly. "Amazon has already done that."

Mike is Head of I.T. but doesn't understand I.T. He believes a company's software and hardware should run by pressing a large green 'Go' button. He can't understand why the button sometimes stops working, and because of that, he gets mad.

Very mad indeed.

If a bug was found in the Operating System—it was my fault. If the payroll software had bugs in its latest version, again, my fault. His printer running out of paper, my fault; his mate sending him an email with a virus attached, my fault; and the company firewalls blocking his porn sites were all my fault.

The last one was *actually* my fault.

None of us took Mike seriously, but we had to go along with the charade.

After five years of dedication and hard graft, I had reached the soaring success of lower-middle management.

My eyes scan the table for support. Dana shrugs her shoulders. Tim picks his nose subtly by pretending to remove fluff from his cheek. Everyone else is staring at their phones or out of the window.

I glance over at Stevie. He gives me the blowjob sign by pushing his tongue into his cheek.

*Fuck off*, I mouth back. Great bloody comradeship in this office.

"Can we talk about the acquisition, Mike?" Tim interjects, breaking our standoff.

Everyone sits up, interested.

Mike shifts his weight and sucks in air like Tim has said a naughty word.

"They still won't tell us who's buying the company?" Tim continues. "I heard it's one of the tech giants."

Mike's eyes dart around the room. He's nervous. "I expect we won't see any changes." Translation: I have absolutely no fucking idea.

"Will our pay stay the same?"

"Will our jobs stay the same?"

"Can we still get the Costa Coffee discount?"

"Will there be redundancies?"

Redundancies. *Shit.*

I haven't paid attention to the subject of the company takeover these past few weeks. I'll have to find out from Stevie what he knows.

Mike raises his hand to quieten us. "It's business as usual, as far as we're concerned. Nothing will change."

There are a few murmurs.

"Comms will go out in a day or two," he says firmly.

Comms. I hate that word. Comms, vision, strategy, strategic vision, all words that got Mike licking his lips. "There will be comms" is what he says when he has no clue what's going on himself.

Our barrel of questions is interrupted by a knock at the door.

"Excuse me, Mike." Jackie smiles with fake sweetness. "I have an important message for Charlie." She looks stunning, but that's because she uses the reception as a salon.

Mike nods at her to continue.

"It's your sister. She says it's an emergency."

Oh, God. My stomach heaves.

This is bad.

Someone's dead.

Dad's dead.

There's been news from Ireland that he's had a heart attack ... or he finally overdosed on drink?

No, Mum's dead. Someone crashed into her when she was driving too slowly.

Both are dead.

"That's fine." Mike waves his hand to dismiss me.

Shakily, I stand up. Be strong, Charlie. You must be strong for Callie.

Although why does Callie know before me? Surely it should be the older sibling that delivers bad news. Why isn't Tristan calling? Is there something wrong with Tristan?

I follow Jackie out to reception, getting out my phone. Sure enough, there are ten missed calls from Callie. Shit!

"Did she say who it's about? Is it Dad?" I ask in a high pitch.

She shrugs. "Not in my job description to ask."

Bitch.

I grab the phone. "Callie?" I stammer. "What is it?"

"Charlie!" she shouts over the noise of traffic. It sounds like she's on a busy road.

I'm right; Mum's been in a car accident. "Yes?" I shriek. "What is it? What's going on?"

"Thank God." She exhales heavily. "I'm in *such* a dilemma. I'm just outside Selfridges with a hundred bags, and I can't move! You'll have to come here and help me carry them to the train."

"What?" I hiss in a lowered tone so Jackie can't

hear. "You got me out of a management meeting because you have too many shopping bags to carry home? *That's* the emergency?"

"Yes!" she exclaims. "I'm stranded, and Mom says I must be home in an hour! It wasn't until I went to the shoe section and bought the three pairs of boots that I realised I couldn't lift everything! I had to call for a security guard, and he helped me get to the door with the bags but with an appalling attitude considering how much I'd bought, complaining that it wasn't in his job description—"

"Callie," I cut in, furious. "Do you realise I'm working? You cannot call one of your shopping sagas an emergency and demand I leave a meeting for it! It's 10:30 on a Monday morning. Why the hell are you not in school?"

"Keep your knickers on, it's not like you've got an important job like Tristan." She yawns. "So, how long will you be then?"

"You'd better pray that I don't come down there, Callie. Because if I do, you are going to find a stiletto lodged deep into your arsehole. Now fuck off!"

I slam down the phone.

Unbelievable.

Jackie coughs behind me.

I whip around to face her.

"That sounds like quite the dilemma," she purrs. "Your poor sister."

I shoot her a venomous look. "It's not in your job description to listen in on private calls."

"And it's not in yours to take them," she fires back.

"Go back to your hashtagging, Jackie."

She rolls her eyes. "I doubt you even know what that means."

"I am very aware of the usage." Snatching a sheet of paper from her desk, I scrawl furiously. "Have you forgotten that I'm the head of I.T. Support?"

I place the paper on her keyboard. "Hashtag this, Jackie."

#GOFUCKYOURSELF

# 2

## Charlie

"Hello?" I call out from the hallway, flinging off my sneakers. It's 7:30 on Monday evening, and I'm already waiting for the weekend.

Cat, Julie, Suze, and I have shared a flat in Kentish Town, North London for five years. We would have preferred if the mice hadn't moved in at the same time as us, but hey, you know what they say about London—you're never more than a metre away from a rat.

Cat teaches drama at a school in Highgate. She said the kids have their own drivers and the school is so posh that even doctors can't afford to send their children there.

Julie is a lawyer for a publishing firm in Liverpool Street and is flourishing due to her sociopathic personality. We made her take a test once, and let's just say, from the results, we will *never* cross her.

No one really understands Suze's job, something to do with logistics?

It's Julie's flat, a fact she never lets us forget. It's even woven into her chat-up lines. What do you do? *I'm a lawyer and a landlord.*

We've never been able to figure out how she owns a four-bedroom flat in North London on her wages, even if it is outdated and riddled with mice. You need old money for bricks like this.

When we first met Julie, she dazzled us with her welcoming charm. *Sit down, girls, welcome to your new home. Cat, don't worry about washing up, dear, I will do that. Of course, it doesn't matter that you spilt your tea on the carpet, Charlie, let me clear that up for you.*

The honeymoon period lasted five days. After that, there were plates smashed, daily screaming sessions, and a hole kicked in Cat's bed when she took longer than six minutes to shower.

We continue to live here because we're too scared to hand our notice in to Julie. The same reason she's never been dumped by a bloke.

Suze is sprawled on the sofa watching a cooking show.

"Hey," I say, throwing myself into the armchair. "I thought you were supposed to be at yoga tonight."

"I was, but I didn't want to overexert myself," she explains between mouthfuls of scone and clotted cream. "I booked into spinning tomorrow, so I didn't want to ruin that by doing yoga tonight." She waves the scone in the air. "And this is a Keto scone, so no harm done!"

"But you didn't go to Pilates last night because of yoga tonight." I frown, confused.

She waves away the question. "Like faffing about in leggings trying to find my inner beauty is going to do me any good. Didn't you hear? I'm going spinning tomorrow! That's six-hundred calories burnt in an hour! I need the energy for it."

I give her a blank look. "Sure."

"Hey, Charlie." Cat breezes out of the bedroom with a post-coital glow, with Stevie trailing after her. They've been hooking up ever since Cat tagged along to my last work drinks. Loudly. She's become a lot more adventurous in the sex department. They have gadgets and devices that require manuals.

"It's a bit early, isn't it?" I raise my brows.

She shrugs. "It's the only time we get to ourselves."

"With Suze in the flat?"

"If we don't have some sexy time while she's here, we'll be celibate," Stevie replies.

That's true. Suze books a lot of gym classes but never leaves the flat.

Cat eyes me. "You look stressed."

I pour myself a large glass of wine from the bottle Suze has started. "No, I'm not." I sigh. "This is the most chilled I've ever been in my life."

"So, have you thought any more about your birthday?" Cat asks excitedly.

"I told you this topic is not open for discussion."

Suze looks at me. "Twenty-nine ... nearly thirty ... that's frightening. Speeding towards forty now."

"Yes, Suze." I give her a filthy look. "I am very aware of the fact I'm aging. Can you please stop emailing me that picture with all the cats at the door saying that they've heard I'm nearly forty and not married?"

"But it's funny. At least you have some love interest this year, better than last year." She tilts her head, studying me. "Although I never hear *you* having sex."

"Suze," I say, gritting my teeth. "Stop keeping tabs on my bedroom routine."

"You need to do something regularly for it to become a routine."

I suck in sharply. She has a point.

"It's hard to make time. I'm working such long hours," I snap defensively. "After a while, the sex goes on the back burner, doesn't it, Cat?"

Cat frowns. "Not for me. I mean, you two are still in the honeymoon period; it's been about eight months, right?"

The three of them study me from the sofa.

"Why, Charlie, how often are you and Ben having sex?" Cat asks.

The question rattles me. "Oh well, you know, as often as we can …" I trail off, trying to remember the last time.

"Once a week?"

"It depends. I've been exhausted recently with work and everything."

She stares at me. "OK, so when was the last time?"

I gulp. "Maybe four weeks ago?"

"Four weeks." Stevie shakes his head, laughing. "He's definitely getting it elsewhere."

"He is not," I shoot back defensively. Mind you, if he is, then it would mean I wouldn't have to when

I'm tired.

What am I saying?

"I haven't wanted to lately," I admit.

"Bloody waste of cock!" Suze snorts. "Ben is damn gorgeous. If you don't want it, I will!"

"You don't want to?" Cat shrills. "Charlie, you need to have sex with your boyfriend. That's the difference between a boyfriend and a *friend.*"

"I know that!" I wail, slumping into the chair. "I just don't want to anymore. I wish I could. I used to be good at pretending that I liked it every now and then, and I did that at least once a week. Maybe twice if I was drunk enough, but recently I just haven't been able to." I gulp a large mouthful of wine.

"But why don't you like it?" Cat asks.

I think for a second. "I get distracted. And bored. Now it kind of feels like a chore, like hoovering."

"Distracted?" Cat repeats, distraught. "Hoovering?"

"Doesn't your mind ever wander when you're having sex?" I ask.

"Not really. I'm pretty much always thinking about the task at hand." She smirks at Stevie, and I grimace. "So what do you get distracted by?"

I think back. "The last time we had sex, the Seattle office had an open issue that I just couldn't get resolved, so I—"

"You got distracted by work?" Stevie interjects, laughing his head off. "That poor bloke. It must be like having sex with a cardboard box."

I narrow my eyes at him.

"Charlie," Cat hesitates, "is it sex, or ... sex with Ben?"

"What do you mean?" I return dismissively. "I love Ben obviously, so it's nothing to do with him. It's me."

"Yes, but if you think about it, you also love Barney."

I can't believe she just compared my boyfriend to my old dog. "Cat, that's the worst comparison I have ever heard. I know you and Stevie are being adventurous in the bedroom, but—"

"Why, why would you think that?" she snaps defensively.

I never told her about the whip I found in her room when I went in to borrow her purple top. "You seem like the adventurous type."

"I wouldn't say that!" she answers too quickly.

"Ben is coming over tonight." Thinking about it, I take another large gulp of wine. If I get pissed, maybe I'll get in the mood.

"Maybe you just need to spice things up a little," Cat muses. "You're right; couples can't do the same old boring things all the time and not expect to get complacent."

"But what can I do?"

"Why don't you try talking dirty to him?"

I'm listening. I've never talked dirty to Ben before; just a few 'oh's and 'ah's thrown in for good measure. I reach for my phone. Google will know what to do.

\*\*\*

There's a knock on the door, and Cat answers it. We have devised a cunning plan of seduction. I'm draped across my bed, wearing a fluffy pink underwear set that I got on sale at Ann Summers. I hear Ben come to the bedroom door and adjust my bra so my nipples peek out.

Ben knocks. "Charlie?"

"Enter," I answer, huskily.

Coming in, he flops onto the bed, head in the pillows. "What a day! I'm exhausted."

Great, he hasn't noticed. I'm wearing my sexiest come-fuck-me outfit, and I feel like I have the sex appeal of a slug.

"Hey." He looks up and laughs. "Why are you dressed like that?"

I stare at him, appalled. Must I point out that I'm seducing him?

I persevere. This must pay off. Right now, I can't afford to introduce objects into the bedroom. "We haven't been together in a while, Ben." I thrust my breasts out and smile at him pointedly.

"I know." He gives me a dark stare. "You had that freak period that lasted for two weeks, remember?"

OK, so I did tell a little white lie about having my period. But surely all girls do it when they're feeling tired? After the roast dinner, I was *so* stuffed. Excuse my crudeness, but you really couldn't have fitted anything else into my body.

"It's finished now." I tug at his shirt and try to rip it off as sexily as possible, but his head gets stuck and he has to help me.

What I don't understand is that Ben is an attractive guy; I know that because I see other women looking at him in the street. It's just that I've lost the spark to fancy him anymore. It's that feeling of excitement in the pit of your stomach that makes you hold in your farts around them. I began releasing my farts within a few months of dating Ben.

"OK." He grins, his mood suddenly picking up. He rips his clothes off in a hurry. Poor guy, I guess I have sexually starved him these past few months.

He scrambles onto the bed, and I climb on top, ready for the rodeo.

His dick isn't ready for me yet, so I take him in my hands. With my best glamour puss pout, I start stroking.

He groans a sigh of approval.

*Yes,* this bitch has still got it.

I can't stop thinking about my credit card bill, though.

I must pay it tomorrow, I keep forgetting. Maybe I should pay it immediately after the sex. Yes, that's what I'll do. When we finish, I will pay the £200 that I owe Barclays. I should never have let it get this high.

Those bloody jeans I bought don't even fit me, and I have thirty days to return them, and this must be what, day twenty-six? I'll need to do it tomorrow at lunch, but Mike has called that goddamn meeting about the company takeover at lunchtime tomorrow. Who is buying us? Stevie's right. Maybe I should pay more attention. Why can't they just tell us, why all the secrecy?

"Charlie!" Ben sits up, shouting my name.

I snap back to the room. "Yes?"

"I feel like I'm a cow being milked." His voice is strained. "You're just a milkmaid hurrying on to the next job."

I smile suggestively. "Well, *that's* a fantasy I haven't been in before."

He's not laughing.

I look down.

He's flaccid.

*Oops.*

He pushes my hand off him and sits up in the bed. "This isn't working, Charlie."

"Don't worry, we'll get it back up again," I coax, rubbing his back.

"Not my dick," he snaps. "Us. These days you have the sex drive of a cardboard box."

"You've been chatting to Stevie about our sex life?" I hiss indignantly.

"About our non-existent sex life." He scrambles for his T-shirt. "Let's just leave it for tonight, your mind is clearly elsewhere."

"Ben," I whine in his ear. "I'm sorry. Next time, yeah? I'll even do a motorboat the way you like it … although it's very ticklish."

He nods, pulls the covers up, and turns to face the wall.

At least I can pay my credit card now.

# 3

## Charlie

"Thanks for being my date, Cat."

We examine our handiwork in the mirror.

I'm wearing a black top with a killer low back that doesn't allow for a bra. It's paired with tight black jeans that hug my ass. My face is painted with red lips and smokey eyes, and my dark brown hair cascades down my back in layers.

I look good, and I know it.

This is the most effort I've put in since Ben and I started dating, and he's not even here to see it. I couldn't ask him to be my date after the milkmaid saga. We needed some time to cool off.

"Like a femme fatale." From behind us, Stevie blows a slow dirty wolf whistle. "You polish up well, Miss Kane."

"Thanks," I grudgingly reply. Stevie isn't one for compliments, so I'll take it.

"I feel sorry for the poor bugger that'll chat you up tonight, though," he continues, "once he finds out you give terrible hand jobs."

*There he is.*

I whip my head around to glare at him. "I do *not*

give bad hand jobs! And will you stop talking to Ben? You're not even friends. You're supposed to be my friend, not his."

"Stevie!" Cat gasps. "Don't be hard on Charlie. Ben should guide her better rather than go mouthing to you. How will she improve otherwise?"

"Can we stop!" I hiss. "That is not the reason we are having problems."

They nod at me, smiling.

"My hand jobs are so good I could be a professional prostitute!" I yell in their faces. How dare they.

I rummage in my bag for my phone. Tristan texted the address of the party. No doubt it'll be one of London's most pretentious bars.

It's Saturday night and my big brother Tristan's fortieth birthday. Sometimes I wondered if he was switched at birth, snatched from his real parents who are politicians, royalty, or Nobel Prize winners, and given to the Kane clan.

This would explain how he became not only one of the most powerful lawyers in London, but the managing partner of a prestigious law firm in the city. By the time he hit my age, he was absolutely loaded. High-profile international cases have elevated him to minor celebrity status and pin-up guy.

He's got a townhouse in exclusive W8, one of Britain's most expensive postcodes, holiday homes in four other countries, and if the rumours are true, a new woman every night of the week. Apparently, representing clients in the International Criminal Court is quite the turn-on.

A fact I didn't need to know.

The reason I've put so much effort into tonight isn't Tristan turning forty.

Or why my stomach is doing somersaults.

No, that is because of Tristan's best friend.

Danny Walker, financial tech tycoon, self-made multimillionaire, and my arch nemesis.

Tristan's right-hand man. They met at university, both penniless and hungry for success, and carved out their fortunes together.

Both were from new wealth, which is one of the reasons why they had so much in common. It made them all the more exciting to women. They had the roughness of men from the council estates done well. Julie said they looked like dirty sex.

The Nexus Group, the fastest growing I.T. company in Europe with a dominant presence in Asia and the States.

Enterprise resource planning, accounting, sales, supply chain, content management—it wasn't the sexiest of software, but with Danny Walker owning the majority shares, it made him a very rich, powerful man and *that* was sexy.

His aggression in business won him consistent headlines and cringe-worthy nicknames like '*Dirty Danny*' and '*Danny the Destroyer.*' My favourite circling social media is '*Wanker Walker.*'

Social gatherings with Danny Walker fill me with dread. It stems back to when I was twenty and drunk out of my mind at one of Tristan's house parties. Tristan had naively allowed Cat and me to attend, so we started drinking cider on the train there to get us in the mood.

That night I made a critical judgment in error. I misread Danny Walker's attempt at conversation as flirting.

When he asked me what I planned to do after university, my natural instinct was to climb onto his knee, wrap my legs around his waist, and dry hump the hell out of him.

My memory of that night is sketchy, but I do recall that he outright rejected me. That part has been imprinted in my brain ever since.

I remember him snapping at me to get off him like he thought I was a stupid, irrelevant college student. He wasn't far off the mark.

The next morning, I woke up hanging off the sofa in Tristan's apartment, with Tristan yelling at me. Danny was nowhere in sight.

Thinking that Danny Walker would ever be interested in me was the most naïve mistake I've ever made.

I can only blame the booze and that it was my first time tasting oysters. I rammed those suckers into me, not realising they were making me as horny as a bonobo in the jungle.

It's Tristan's fault, really, for providing oysters.

The guy has barely smiled at me since, but that's fine because eight years later, I still can't look at him without going scarlet.

To this day, I can hardly keep up with what he's saying. As he discusses IPOs and other acronyms and jargon with Tristan, I have to pretend I'm not looking them up online. It means Initial Public Offering, for reference.

My contribution to the conversation is nodding repeatedly like a pigeon.

"So, where is it?" Cat peers over my shoulder. "Kensington? This is definitely a free bar, right?"

"Of course." I roll my eyes. "Tristan always puts his hands in his pockets."

"Let's have one for the road so I have the guts to mingle with all these city suits."

"OK, just one," I warn. "You know you're a lightweight. I'm not propping you up all night."

One wine each transitions into finishing the bottle.

I become more sophisticated after a bottle of wine, *slimmer too*, I think as I pass the mirror on the way out.

Ten minutes later, we're in the taxi and I realise that polishing a bottle of wine off was a big mistake.

*Big.*

*Huge.*

Cat is a bad passenger sober, never mind after guzzling a litre of cheap corner shop wine.

The taxi driver has met people like Cat before. An intimidating 'spew and I'll sue' sign glares at us from the back of his seat.

In a matter of minutes, she turns to me, eyes bulging. I see quick swallow movements in her throat. Then a silent spray of vomit splatters on my feet.

I stare dismayed between my feet and the sign. Having already gotten some on her seat, we can't ask the driver to stop, or he might see it and sue us. I would be guilty by association. Luckily, he hasn't noticed yet.

"Do it quietly," I whisper.

To her credit, she is a quiet vomiter, despite the violent heaving of her shoulders. A pool of yellow liquid builds up on the floor around our shoes, and I pray that the driver doesn't turn around.

I babble on, having a monologue with myself that doesn't require answers from Cat, to distract him from the retching sounds.

As we drive around Hyde Park, the vomiting thankfully subsides.

We come to a halt outside a *very* lavish bar. I spot some of Tristan's friends mingling outside.

"Are you done?" I grit out, facing her.

Her lips wriggle but she doesn't respond. She swings the taxi door open aggressively, narrowly missing a passing car.

"Bloody hell, Cat!" I hiss, clambering out of the taxi.

"I'm so sorry, sir!" I say to the driver, chucking a few twenty-pound notes through the window to cover the cleaning.

Cat runs around to meet me on the pavement, then opens her mouth and ejects the dirtiest, loudest and most offensive burp I've ever heard.

I put my hands to my mouth in shock.

Friends of Tristan stop talking abruptly and spin their heads around.

"Jesus, Cat," I snarl at her. "Talk about making an entrance."

"I'm sorry," she wails, eyes wide. "It wouldn't stay in."

"Are you done *now*?" I bark.

She nods her head meekly. "That's the last of it."

"Never again," I mutter, regretting my date selection.

She looks up at the bar, ignoring Tristan's friends still eyeballing us, and lets out a slow whistle. "Champagne it is then."

The bar is as prestigious as they come. Two beautiful hostesses stand at the door with clipboards, their sole purpose in life to make me feel inadequate and unworthy of entry. Four burly bouncers surround them, looking suspiciously at us.

It looks like one of Tristan's private member clubs. He must have rented out the entire bar for the evening.

The largest bouncer puts his hand out to block us as we ascend the steps. "Sorry, we have a certain type of clientele here. Ones that do not belch at the door."

"This is my brother's party," I retort, trying to look dignified. "My name's Charlie, and my brother has paid a small fortune for this venue, so let us in."

One of the clipboard chicks flicks through the list then looks up at us in disappointment.

"Fine," she snaps. "But keep her under control."

She wiggles a finger in disgust at Cat.

Cat pouts. "I'm actually a teacher in a very prestigious school in Highgate."

"Lady, I don't care if you're a teacher in Buckingham Palace." The bouncer shakes his head. "I've met builders with better manners than you."

I couldn't argue with that.

"Just come on." I hoist her up the last step, and clipboard chick #2 reluctantly leads us through the velvet curtains into a haven of London's richest and finest.

*** 

Tristan's parties are sex immortalized. This one is no exception. It's a menagerie of beautiful people dripping in designer labels, sipping decadent cocktails while discussing how rich and successful they are.

It's true what they say, money attracts beauty. It is difficult to tell who is naturally pretty and who has plastic. I mean, what are the chances that out of one hundred women, every single one has big breasts *and* full plump lips?

With their tailored suits and extravagant accessories, the men are equally lavish creatures, trying to prove they have the biggest dick through their watches, cufflinks, and anything else that will inform their fellow partygoers of their net worth.

It's bottomless free drinks on tap. We are handed a Bellini at the door. Every table is stocked with bottles of Moët champagne and Belvedere Vodka. I better keep an eye on Cat.

These parties would be so fun except for two invitees—one, Danny Walker, and two, my Irish mother. Being the model son, Tristan invites my mother to every birthday party. It's equally sweet and cringeworthy. He doesn't want her to feel left out.

It's been a hang-up of his ever since Dad disgraced us to go running back to the Republic of Ireland into the arms of another woman, leaving us with a load of debt. For the first time in Mum's life, she had to work out how to pay the mortgage and bills. She was a woman scorned; still, to this day, we cannot talk about the *adulterer* in her presence.

We've had sporadic contact with him, the occasional birthday card or drunken Christmas call or, in Tristan's case, a plea for a loan of cash that will never be returned.

I glance over to the corner of the bar and see the perfect storm for humiliation. Tristan, Danny, their friend Jack Knight, and a waif-like blonde bombshell are talking to Mum.

Mum is dressed like she's at a 90's wedding. Big hair, big shoulder pads, and talking at a hundred miles an hour.

Danny listens, oblivious to the women circling, falling over themselves to be noticed.

Asshole.

Hot as hell, drop-your-pants gorgeous asshole but still an asshole.

At 6'4, he's taller and broader than anyone else

in the room, even Tristan, who's a close second. His thick biceps are folded over his wide-set chest, the white shirt straining under the pressure of muscles, and his chunky legs are spread in a manly pose. He is a massive Adonis of a man, the opposite of what a tech tycoon should look like. Thick black hair, sharp square jawline, the roman nose that I want to punch, and full luscious lips.

What chance did I have?

All that beauty wasted on such a moody obnoxious prick.

Cat visibly wilts beside me. "The level of testosterone in that corner should be illegal. How are we supposed to function as women with that sausage fest? I'd definitely be the stuffing in a Tristan-Danny-Jack sandwich."

"Can you not include my brother in your sick fantasies, please?" I narrow my eyes at her.

"You have to admit it, they are so damn *masculine*," she gushes. "Men's men. Not just pretty faces either, all dripping in cash. How come we aren't that lucky?"

I roll my eyes. "It's hardly luck, Cat."

"I suppose I've chosen a vocation over cash," she muses like she's a martyr. She looks down at her phone and starts typing. "Danny Walker, CEO, and founder of tech giant The Nexus Group, estimated net worth £700 million. In recent years, Danny has become known for his aggressive acquisitions in an attempt to monopolise the UK tech industry."

I dig her in the ribs. "Can you stop stalking him

online? Tristan's friends are milling around us!"

"It gets more interesting." She ignores me. "The court case between Danny Walker and a previous employee, Sam Lynden, has finally concluded. It was confirmed that Sam Lynden received a significant financial pay-out after accusing Mr. Walker of physical assault."

"He has a temper," she swoons. "Dangerous." She clicks on the images. "Wow. He has been with a *lot* of hot women."

I snap the phone from her hands.

"Charlie! Over here!" I suck in through my teeth at the voice. Mum has spotted us and is frantically waving us over.

Tristan beams at me, beckoning us over, and I give a little wave.

I lock eyes with Danny. He stops abruptly in his conversation with Jack.

*Oh, God, those eyes.*

My stomach does a somersault. The brown penetrating eyes bore into me, cruising my figure before landing back on my face.

His eyebrows join in a deep frown as if even the sight of me displeases him. Where did he acquire this inane ability to make me feel inadequate?

"Charlie!" Mum yells, waving her arms wildly. Several people turn to look at her strangely.

"Yes!" I mouth back. What's the woman doing? I can clearly see her, yet she's causing a massive commotion.

"Let's do this," I mutter to Cat, who needs no

invitation to go over.

"Hi, all." I flash a forced smile at the group as I lean in to kiss Tristan. "Happy birthday, old boy."

He sweeps me up for a hug.

"Hi Mum," I greet her.

She leans in for an air kiss on each cheek; that's her thing at these parties.

Jack, the most charismatic of Tristan's friends, pulls me in for a hug. "The stunning Charlie, always a pleasure to see you."

Tristan jolts him as Jack shoots me a grin that could melt my pants off. "Behave, Jack. Sister. Off-limits."

I flick a sideways glance at Danny to find he's observing me warily. Like I might be mildly contagious. The flashbacks hit me.

*I climb onto his knee and wrap my legs around him.*

"Danny," I choke out.

"Charlie," he responds in his low Scottish drawl. He stiffens as he calculates whether he has to hug me.

That voice. Why does it make me think of sex? My name rolling off his tongue makes the hairs on the back of my neck stand up.

I hate how he affects me. I must have a disorder. Asshole Arousal Disorder where I'm only interested in men who ignore me.

*I grind my body against his thighs.*

Stop it!

I snap out of it.

"You've all met Cat before." When I turn around, I see her smiling like a simpleton and doing the little jig she does when she's nervous.

"Hiya," she says in a high pitch.

Tristan clears his throat and looks at Danny pointedly, who is ruffling his hands through his hair like he's agitated.

"Charlie, Cat, this is Jen." Tristan places his arm on the blonde stunner's back.

She has poker-straight long blond hair and is super skinny with beach balls stuck to her chest. Just the type my brother likes.

"Hi, Jen." I smile.

"Hi, Charlie, Cat." Jen leans in for a kiss. "It's great to meet the little sister!"

I stiffen. I'm not *her* little sister. She looks five years older than me, max, not qualified to be talking like my new stepmom.

"Jen is a human-rights lawyer," Mum announces, clearly a fan.

"I don't like talking about it too much, but yes, I'm the youngest human rights lawyer in London." Jen flutters her eyes around the group. Satisfied with the murmurs of approval, she moves on. "What do you do, Charlie?"

"I.T. Support." My lips curl in a permanent fake smile, knowing she's only asking because it's never going to be as good as the youngest bloody human rights lawyer in London.

"That's wonderful." She clasps her hand to her

chest as if I've just revealed I'm a heart surgeon. "Turn it off and turn it on again!"

"At your service."

Pathetic.

"The I.T. Support people in our company are rubbish," she adds unnecessarily. "I'm sure you're *much* better, though." She stares at me like she doesn't believe that for a second.

"Right." I give her a death stare.

"Oh." She places a well-manicured hand on Danny's bicep. "Danny could get you a job at Nexus! I'm sure he could find you a job doing *something*."

"No, that's fine, I'm not looking," I fire back quickly as Danny stiffens. Not a hope in hell would I beg that cut-throat, ruthless, all-round bastard for a job.

Aside from the obvious shame of trying to maul him, the other glaring issue is that he will never hire me. I'm not the 'Nexus calibre.'

I need to move off this topic. "Cat's a drama teacher in Highgate. Since we're going through our CVs."

"That's right," Cat cuts in, looking at Tristan intently. "Mine's a *vocation* rather than a career."

"How lovely. I live in Highgate," Jen says. "Got a little maisonette there. Bought it a few years ago. The garden is small, but it has a little summer house I can use as an office, and the view of the heath is nice from the balcony."

I watch her as she talks about what is definitely a multi-million-pound house like it's a cute cottage.

"It sounds very ... quaint."

"Charlie and Cat live the bachelorette life in Kentish Town." Tristan's eyes wrinkle in amusement. "Party girls. Although you rarely come to my parties anymore unless I force you."

*That's because I tried to dry hump your hot best mate.*

"Kentish Town?" Jen looks at me as if I've just been released from a maximum-security prison. "I guess property prices are lower there, since it's up and coming!"

"We're renting," I mutter.

She has a mortgage, and what do I have? Mice.

"Charlie knows I'll help her out when she wants to buy," Tristan jumps in, overcompensating in case they thought he was a tight git, with his poor penniless sister living in squalor.

"No," I fire back in dismay at my charity case persona. "When I buy, I'll do it myself."

We are *not* broaching this topic here. Tristan is forever trying to give me free money.

"How long have you been dating Tristan?" I ask Jen politely. I don't like this girl so I'm hoping it won't last. It never does with Tristan. I reckon I'll have to play niceties for three months, at most.

"Oh, no!" She laughs. "This gorgeous one is mine." She pokes a finger into Danny's ribs.

He shifts uncomfortably from foot to foot, with his hands shoved deep into his trouser pockets. He has remained silent throughout the conversation.

My stomach clenches and I force my happy face.

*"No, Charlie, I'm not doing this. I'm not interested,"*
*he says as he pushes me off his knee.*

So this is Danny's type.

The opposite of me. Blonde, highly successful, waif-like, feminine.

"Where's Ben?" Tristan prompts.

"Charlie and Ben are on the rocks. She might be single soon," Mum announces. "Again."

"Mum!" I glare at her in horror, as the men mumble their apologies.

"Oh, poor thing," Jen purrs as she rubs Danny's arm. "Boys, do you have any nice friends for Charlie?"

"No," Danny replies with unnecessary force.

I shoot him a look and meet a dark gaze. So I'm not good enough for any of his friends now, either?

"Before Ben, Charlie had loads of men," Cat cuts in unhelpfully. "She has no problem on the pull." *You're welcome*, she smiles at me.

Tristan splutters on his whiskey.

A deep blush soaks into my cheeks spreading outwards until my ears are red.

"Over my dead body is Charlie going out with any of our sleazy friends." Tristan laughs, but we all hear the steeliness in his voice. "Not happening. They'll keep their bloody hands to themselves. I've already noticed a few eyeing you already this evening."

"Well, I like Ben," Mum interjects sorrowfully. "It's time you stopped flitting from boyfriend to boyfriend."

I roll my eyes. "Then you go out with him."

They all laugh. Yippee. Charlie's love life is hilarious.

"How's work, sis?" Tristan nudges me. "You get that pay rise you were after?"

As they lean in to hear, I'm tempted to lie.

"No," I reply with a heavy sigh. "My boss is a prick."

"You've been working really hard in this job," Cat nods in a second attempt of support. "Remember in your last one you used to take naps in the toilets and call in sick all the time? You don't do that in this job."

"That was years ago," I growl. After tonight I'm submitting an application to the Guinness World Records for Cat as the worst date ever. "And I was bored at that job."

"Don't worry, Charlie." Jen places a hand over mine. "If you ever need any career advice, I'd be happy to help."

"Thanks, Jen," I simmer. "Sounds like I can turn to you for any type of life advice."

My eyes snap up to see Danny staring at me, frowning.

"There's the girl who belches like a builder," I hear behind me loudly.

For fuck's sake.

Jen's mouth drops open.

"Excuse us," I grab the arm of Cat, the belching builder, and flash them my most dazzling smile. "We're going to the bar."

# 4

## Charlie

I keep Mum and Danny at bay for an hour by hiding Cat and I among a group of investment bankers. We're sampling the bar's most exotic cocktails to the delight of our financial friends.

There is the 'bacon-me-angry' cocktail made with bacon fat-washed vodka, the 'butternut-old-fashioned' cocktail with spiced and sweetened butternut squash infused into Bourbon, and the plain nasty 'bloody-tampon' with whiskey, tequila, vodka, and cranberry juice for a splash of fake menstruation.

Nothing that should ever be in a drink, but that's why they charge you double, and, hell, this is on Tristan's tab. A girl must know when to keep her dignity versus when to freeload, and I certainly won't be paying twenty-two pounds for butternut squash bourbon with my mother hovering in the background.

Tristan was right; he does have a lot of pervy friends. The bankers aren't my cup of tea, but they serve the purpose of a confidence boost after Jen's passive-aggressive roasting.

"You'll sing, Charlie," Mum announces as she approaches behind me. "Excuse me, gentlemen."

I turn around to see her elbowing her way through the bankers. She's red-faced from too many sherries. Now my own mother is cockblocking me.

Tristan saunters behind her, his eyes filled with mischief.

"What? No!" My mouth falls open. "This is not the time or the place for music from the old country. It's Kensington, for God's sake."

"It's tradition, sis." Tristan grins. "I've made sure there's a guitar here."

"Tristan!" I wail. "Why would you do this to me? It's not even a fucking funeral!"

"Language, Charlie!" Mum tuts. "Stop this nonsense. You have a beautiful voice. It's the only reason I come to these shenanigans."

My eyes narrow. "You come here for the free sherry, Mum. Tristan, please." Looking at him pleadingly, I clasp my hands in prayer. "If you have any love for me, you'll stop this car crash."

He shrugs his shoulders as if it's beyond his control. As if he had nothing to do with it except deliver the instrument to make it happen.

I whack him on the chest.

"Hey!" He rubs the attacked area. "I actually like your singing. Besides, I couldn't live with Mum's nagging if I didn't."

That's easy for Tristan to say. The rest of the guests might not appreciate the interruption. He may not have anyone turn up on his forty-first birthday after this.

I glance up at the sexy stage and flinch. It's designed for soul, jazz, or burlesque, not for an Irish fiddly-dee session.

"Singing at Aunt Mo's funeral is one thing. I can handle that. Singing Irish covers at an exclusive members' club—not so much!" Looking up at the ceiling, I let out a tiny wail. "Oh my God, why is this happening to me?"

He cocks a brow. "Stop being dramatic. Anyway, the band is waiting for you."

"Charlie?" Mum calls.

"What?" I flip around to glare at her. "I've given in, damn woman. I'll sing one song."

She purses her lips into a thin line. "Maybe you could put on a bra before you go on stage?"

*Argh.* I growl loudly and storm off, walking straight into Danny Walker.

A flicker of amusement crosses his face as he steps aside. "Good luck," he says in his low, dry voice. The voice that makes my breath stall.

I grunt and move towards the stage.

Ten minutes later, and two bloody-tampon cocktails down the hatch, I'm waiting at the side of the stage. I look down at my breasts. Perhaps the chicken fillet bra is a mistake? I'm well-endowed in that department. The inserts are meant to make me appear sultry under dim lighting and sexy lampshades, not naked under a stage spotlight, like some sort of sex show.

It's too late to inspect them further. The band beckons me on stage and introduces me on the mic.

As I walk onto the stage, a deep blush spreads outward from my cheeks and reaches my ears. The walk is always the worst part.

With a sympathetic smile, the lead singer hands me an electric guitar. It's a tough transition to make, going from sexy jazz to old Irish country.

"Thanks for giving us a break." He grins. "They're all yours."

He's not bad-looking.

As I put the guitar strap around my neck, stage nerves rumble through my stomach. Since I was eight years old, Mum had wheeled me out at every wake and wedding to sing her traditional Irish favourites. I was the Kane singing sensation. Audience members are usually old Irish women who toe-tap their feet in appreciation. Not bloody Kensington brokers and lawyers whose idea of a piss-up is a weekend in Monaco with bottomless champagne aboard a chartered yacht. This is a more difficult crowd to please.

The crowd becomes uneasy with the lack of jazz. I clear my throat. "Sorry, folks," I say into the mic in my huskiest stage voice. "My mother is forcing me to do this. Since my brother is paying for all your drinks, you're expected to be nice to me. I promise I'll only make you listen to one song. But please don't cheer because then my mother will make me do it again."

There are a few laughs and cheers in the crowd.

"Also, I'm used to doing funerals, so my main audience is mourners and the dead."

There's more laughing. That's it, funny girl. Now they feel sorry for you and won't boo you off the stage. Or the 'brother paying for drinks' line nailed it.

I start strumming, trying to channel Celtic rock vibes. I've chosen an upbeat Irish jig adapted for the electric guitar. It's quite funky, like old traditional meets new rock.

It's got a fast tempo, and the crowd sways in response.

The first line is a belter. My stage show's success depends on this first line. If I don't do a Sinead O' Connor, it's a flop. I breathe in then blast the opening.

The crowd responds with whoops and whistles.

I've nailed it.

The upscale Kensington club transforms into a rowdy Irish pub. Who am I kidding? Eventually they all do, no matter how stiff the suits are.

A few Chelsea types attempt to river-dance at the front of the dance floor. Cheers erupt from the audience, and I sing louder while strumming on the guitar furiously. Performing Irish music is like a workout. I'm sweating down my back and chest.

When I sing, I just lose myself in it. Once I get the first good reaction from the crowd, I can ride the adrenaline wave and own the stage.

The song's a long one, about six minutes or so. Traditional Irish ones always are. I'm exhausted by the end, and my black jeans are sticking to me with sweat.

"Thanks, folks." I give a little wave to show I'm done.

Claps and whoops erupt from the floor.

"One more!" a voice booms from the crowd.

I smile and shake my head.

"More!" The shouting continues, becoming louder as it propagates throughout the room.

On the side of the stage, the lead singer raises his eyebrows encouragingly. "One more?" he mouths.

I look down at the crowd.

Danny Walker stares at me, not smiling. I've grown accustomed to his rigid body and unfathomable stare over the past decade.

What *is* this asshole's problem?

"OK, just one more," I say into the mic. The next one I do isn't a cover; it's one of my own. It would be too much pressure for me to admit that to the crowd. I'll let them think it's another cover. It's still Irish traditional but sultrier. I was obsessed with Amy Winehouse when I wrote it.

Mucking around with songs is just a hobby. I think some of my creations are pretty cool, but of course, I'm biased, as are my friends and family. Even Julie goes easy on me when it comes to my own creations.

I've never received constructive feedback, so the reality is that I probably sound like a banshee and get sympathy votes. I've even secured a few shags from doing gigs. Again, maybe sympathy shags, but I'll take them. It's nice to pretend you have groupies.

Mum thinks the songs are too sexy for funerals, so I never get to sing them.

With my eyes closed, I start strumming and singing. It would be too off-putting if people walked out during one of my own. I'm blessed with a decent vocal range that I can demonstrate in this song. I sing the last verse, deep and husky, then open my eyes to look down.

The first pair of eyes I lock onto are Danny Walker's. While the crowd moves around him, he stands rigidly. His hands are buried in his pockets, as if this is the most uncomfortable situation he's ever encountered. His dark gaze makes me stumble on the last line, and I curse him silently for controlling my vocal cords.

The crowd cheers in appreciation, and I hear someone shout my name. Likely Mum.

My eyes scan the room.

Cat's mouth hangs open and her hands are laced over her chest. She's my biggest fan.

Tristan beams up at me, and Mum looks chuffed despite the lack of an appropriate bra.

In my sweaty jeans, I trot off stage, waving.

"Sensational." Mr. Lead Singer winks at me as I pass him the guitar.

I wink back, talking the language of flirt. At least someone appreciates my singing. Danny Walker and his rigid square jawline can go to hell.

As I walk through the crowd, I'm patted on the back like a D-list celebrity.

"Amazing Charlie!" Cat rushes forward to hug me. "It's like Riverdance meets soul."

"Wow!" From behind, strong arms lift me off my feet, and I tilt my head to see Jack Knight grinning at me. "Charlie, what are you doing to us? You broke everyone's heart up there."

I roll my eyes but bask in the compliment. Cat's right, he's easy on the eye. He can leave his arms around my waist.

"Very good," Jen says, her lips forming a thin line. As if marking her territory, she has one arm around Danny's waist and the other draped across his chest. I don't blame her, women are circling. "I assume you *only* do covers?"

Bitch.

"The second one was one of her own," a low, dry voice replies before I can, and I look up at him, surprised. How did Danny Walker know that?

"Uh, yeah, actually, it's one of mine."

A drunken bloke pushes me from behind. "Dolly Parton! Do Dolly!"

"I don't do Dolly requests," I snarl at him, creating distance between us.

"Dolly!" he roars again. "Come on, you've got the jugs for it."

My mouth drops open.

"Back off," Tristan growls behind me. "Who the fuck is that guy?" he mutters to Danny.

"Come on, Dolly bird," the guy continues, misreading Tristan's wrath.

People are staring now.

"It's not American Country, it's Irish Country, you moron," I bite back. "Now back off … you Dolly loving dick." It was the best insult I could muster.

Tristan steps in. "If you talk to my sister again like that, I'll rip you a new asshole. I don't know who you are but fuck off out of here before I do something I regret."

I smile. Sometimes having a bad-tempered big brother is great.

*\*\**

**Danny**

Get a grip, man.

I down the rest of the glass like it's cheap scotch rather than one of the world's oldest single malts. My knuckles squeeze the glass so hard I might break it. I had been saving that malt for a special occasion, but tonight called for it. I needed something to take the edge off.

I jerked off twice in the dark, in my office.

Ridiculous. Not my typical end to one of Tristan's parties.

I wonder what she's doing now. Did she go home with anyone? There were enough rich fucks trying. Is she having sex with one of them right now? The jazz singer looked like he fancied his chances.

My dick's been throbbing ever since I clocked that she wasn't wearing a bra. Her naked back, the subtle outline of her breasts in the sheer top … what chance did I have after that?

My eyes close as I relive the swell of her breasts as

she sang. Her jeans were so tight around her ass that they could have been painted on. Those lips, *fuck*, those full sexy lips that I can only get away with staring at when she's singing. Imagining those lips wrapped around my cock, drinking me up. My cock twinges at the thought of her kneeling before me, eyes staring up at me as I hit the back of her throat.

On stage, she was so sassy and in control, I nearly came right there in my trousers. I had to keep readjusting myself like a dirty old man.

For such a possessive brother, I don't know why Tristan encourages her on stage at those parties. I'm pretty sure I wasn't the only one there with his hands in his pockets. She had us all captivated. All drooling like idiots.

The type of girl who can make a man fall on his knees and beg for a taste of her.

I was just another man in the audience lusting over the younger girl. So now I'm a fucking cliché. This is what happens past forty.

If Tristan knew, he'd beat me senseless.

It's one itch I can never scratch. I've been warned enough times by Tristan to know that the friendship would end if I took a crack at his little sister. Not surprising since he knows me so well. After a few nights of passion, she would be gone from my system, and I would lose the best friend I've ever had.

I can't put my finger on why she gets under my skin. Yes, she's beautiful, but I'm not exactly lacking in options. Perhaps it's because she looks at me with such venom, there's no doubt about how much she despises me.

Perhaps it's because she's one of the only women in the city I can't touch.

Her mother was videotaping her tonight.

I need to get my hands on that video. I wonder how I'll wrangle that from Tristan without making it look suspicious. I smirk at the thought of asking Mrs. Kane for a video of her daughter singing so I can add it to my wank bank.

The knots in my shoulders tighten. I should have sorted a plan by now. Having her work under me isn't a viable option. I'll offer her an obnoxious sum that she can't refuse in exchange for quitting.

Before I start something I immediately regret.

I laugh out loud. Am I losing my game in old age? There's an acquisition worth twenty million pounds in the works, and my number one concern is that my best friend's younger sister, who I'd like to fuck, is an employee?

First thing tomorrow morning, I'll call Tristan and explain what I need to do. He's a businessman; he'll understand my justification.

Let's hope he doesn't smell the bullshit.

# 5

**Charlie**

There's a bustle around the office that isn't normal.

It's Monday morning. Everyone should look depressed and tired. No one should be perky. They definitely shouldn't be exchanging *niceties* with each other like they are in this parallel universe.

Jackie sits on reception with a full head of smokey evening make-up, dressed like she's about to walk down the runway.

We must have a *really* rich client visiting the office. She's too distracted to even take a swipe at me as I walk past.

I walk onto the fourth-floor open-plan office.

This is so wrong. People should be eating breakfast, scrolling through social media and talking loudly about the weekend. Anything but actual work. This morning, there's not a single social media page being browsed.

I walk past each desk, and it's the same body snatcher scene. My colleagues have been replaced with polite clones executing work activities and whispering in hushed tones.

Terrifying.

On my way to my desk, I pass Mike. He has what looks to be all the reports from this quarter scattered across the floor. He's never read those reports before despite us sending them religiously. How did he even find a copy by himself?

"Stevie!" I grab Stevie's arm. "What the hell's going on?"

He looks at me like I'm a moron. "The buyout's done. Today the new diggers come in, i.e., the new CEO and his management. Get ready for the bulldoze."

"Oh." Last week, I hadn't paid attention to the updates. So that's who the new suits milling around are. "But they've said not much will change, we'll just have a parent company. Mike called them a friendly passive owner. They'll just leave us alone, right? Why does everyone look so uptight?"

Stevie rolls his eyes. "They always say that. *Nexus* have bought us. They don't just leave companies alone. They buy the company, trim the fat and suck the best bets into Nexus."

"What?" I stop walking. "Nexus?"

No.

Stevie has it wrong. There's been a mistake.

The blood drains from my face down my body and accumulates around my ankles. There is no way that Danny Walker would have bought our company.

"Bullshit," I spit out.

"No bullshit," Stevie replies. "You'll see for yourself when they come in. Get your CV together because that CEO guy of Nexus will annihilate half the company. He cherry-picks only the best, and the rest of us will be on our arses down at the job centre."

Suddenly, there is not enough oxygen in the room.

"It doesn't make sense. They don't operate in the insurance sector." I collapse into my chair, flapping my hands.

"They changed their minds, they do now." He shrugs, leaning against the side of my desk. "They've taken over all the other markets. It was just a matter of time."

I swallow air and choke. "OK, but surely they'll leave us alone?"

"Not likely. From what I've read, Danny Walker is ruthless. My mate works at ETech. Nexus bought it last year. Fifty percent of the team chopped. The people that kept their jobs now work ten-hour days. It's hell, he said."

"Are we the fat?" I squeak. "I've only been in my promotion a year."

He grabs my hand, irritated. "Stop drumming your fingers on the table like that; you look like a basket case."

"Sorry," I whimper. "It's just that this is really bad news."

"I don't know why you are so worried." He points at himself. "*I'm* fucked. I've been doing three hours of work a day since I got here. I can fool Mike, but these guys will sniff out my slacking a mile off." He frowns. "Wait. Isn't your brother mates with the main man, Walker?"

"Yes." I sigh.

"So, you're fine? He'll never get rid of his friend's sister."

"I'm not fine." I slump forward in my chair. "For the past eight years, I've barely been able to be in the same room as Danny Walker out of shame. He thinks I'm a hopeless desperado who he prefers to ignore, and now, thanks to Saturday night, has fresh in his mind the idea that I'm a useless employee who doesn't deserve a pay rise and spends her day sleeping in the toilets at work."

I inhale sharply. "So, no. I'm not fine."

"OK." He stares at me. "I didn't understand any of that. You're going to have to explain it in more detail."

Dare I tell Stevie? He knows about every other aspect of my life. He even accompanied me to the pharmacy to pick up thrush medication, for moral support. At least I'd get a bloke's perspective.

Mike knocks his fist against the pillar in the middle of the room, so I don't get a chance to elaborate. "Main boardroom in fifteen minutes," he bellows, shuffling from foot to foot. He looks even twitchier than I do. He must be afraid they'll ask him what I.T. stands for and find out the truth; he's got no clue.

"The end is nigh," Stevie declares ominously.

I attempt to swallow the giant lump in my throat.

"Gotta do emails." He turns to walk towards his desk but not before pointing his finger at me. "But I'll be back later to hear this story."

People are already loitering around the boardroom even though we've got a quarter of an hour left. There will be zero productivity until this meeting is done.

I squint to see through the glass.

There he is.

Danny Walker leans against the boardroom podium, talking to some other blokes in suits.

My skin prickles at the sight of him.

The dark blue tailored suit fits perfectly over his athletic figure. Just a little bit of dark chest hair peeks out of the crisp white shirt, and he has a few days' worth of stubble growth, giving him a rough edge. He looks sensational.

Smug arrogant bastard, swaggering around like he owns the place. Because the motherfucker does now.

I don't know whether I'm turned on or traumatised. Likely a bit of both.

So *this* is the CEO version of Danny Walker. I'm used to seeing him in social environments. I'm even more rattled than I usually am when he's in a room, which I didn't think was possible.

I feel so stupid. Why the hell didn't he mention this on Saturday evening?

Am I so insignificant to him that he couldn't muster the common courtesy of saying, "By the way, Charlie, you know that company where you've worked for five years, and haven't yet been given a raise? Well, guess what, it's mine now."

My heart pounds at the thought of entering the

boardroom. Maybe I can sneak away, and Stevie can tell me what he said.

No, I'll need to face Danny Walker sometime. Besides, why do I care what this man thinks of me?

When those intense brown eyes catch my gaze, my breath hitches. I duck down behind my monitor. Very mature. Is this what work will be every day now? Hiding under my monitor?

"Time to face the showdown," Stevie calls over to me, getting up from his seat.

I nod and fall in line with him as we shuffle into the boardroom with the rest of the team.

I slump into a seat near the door and drag Stevie along with me. I need physical and moral support if I collapse.

Tension circulates through the air like it's being pumped out the vents. About fifty of us squeeze into a boardroom meant for thirty people max. The Seattle and India offices are on video link.

People line the walls, standing up.

My knees bounce up and down as I rock from side to side in my seat. I'm claustrophobic. I need to leave this room. My fight-or-flight response tries to kick in. But what can I do? I can't punch him in the face. Equally I can't run from the room, I'll cause a scene.

Someone shuts the door.

With his sleeves rolled up, Danny Walker leans against the podium. He looks the opposite of me—relaxed, confident and breathing easy. This is just another day in the office for him, another takeover. He swirls coffee in his hand and laughs easily with

ROSA LUCAS

another guy.

There's no question about who owns the room.

He looks up, and his eyes search the group looking for something or someone.

I sink further into my chair. Eye contact in this close proximity will induce a panic attack.

The room is filled with dull chatter as Danny talks to the other guy, not in any hurry to greet us.

Finally, he clears his throat, and the room quietens.

He doesn't have to shout or bang fists like Mike. Danny Walker is dominant at his core. Cat was right. A man's man.

Silence descends as everyone awaits his first word. I hear my heartbeat loud in my ears and wonder if anyone else can.

"Hello." The low guttural voice makes everyone sit up straight. "I'm Danny Walker, founder, and CEO of The Nexus Group."

Like we needed that introduction.

I hear someone's ovaries explode.

"By now, you have been told the news of our partnership between Dunley Tech and Nexus." He smiles around the room, flashing perfect white teeth.

"It's hardly a partnership," Stevie mutters under his breath.

"I'm very excited about our new venture together," Danny continues, slowly pacing across the floor. "At Nexus, we've been watching your journey for a while now, and I see a lot of potential in your software."

I cringe, sinking further into my seat. He's been watching my company and said nothing. Did he tell Tristan? Did they talk about how I would react? Am I the *last* to know?

I've worked here for five years. I know the weaknesses, and I have ideas on how to improve them. Being on I.T support is like being verbally slapped in the face every day. Everything is your fault, even when it's not. No one ever calls support to say *well done, good job*, do they? As the team leader, I take the full verbal beating to the face when a particularly nasty call comes in.

Is my opinion so irrelevant to Danny Walker that he barely thought it was worth a quick: "Hey Charlie, you know the company you've worked at for years, what's it like?"

The deep baritone interrupts my inner rant. "It just needs a little more drive, more innovation to take it to the next level and truly dominate the insurance sector. Nexus is the company to do that." Every word is spoken with the confidence of a man who has no doubts about his abilities.

With my hand resting on my stomach, I take slow deep breaths.

Beside me, Stevie gives me a funny look.

This is pathetic. Danny Walker's presence is turning me into a hot mess.

It looks like I'm not the only one. As I glance around the room, I see all the girls in the office staring up at him like they want his babies. They're all flicking their hair, touching their lips, smiling, re-crossing their legs, and other desperate attempts to bring his focus towards their body parts. In the front row, Jackie leans forward to offer a bird's eye view of her breasts.

My heart plummets.

I zone out. I can't listen to his words. Sitting here, one of many, I realise just how much we are worlds apart and how ridiculous I was for trying to dry hump the guy. I'm surprised he didn't call the police on me.

"I plan to get to know all of you, what you do and what the company stands for," he continues in his dry Scottish voice. "The company has been operating at a certain level, good but not exemplary. I will personally oversee the smooth transition of Dunley Tech, so you'll see a lot of me around the office over the next few months."

What?

No, no, no. I'll never survive sustained exposure to Danny Walker.

He stops in the middle of the room. "In the meantime, there's nothing to be worried about, just go about your day job as normal. Later today, the team will send out the information you need to understand any changes over the next few months while you become employees of Nexus."

Stevie shoots his hand up. What the hell! I'm supposed to be camouflaging myself.

Danny squints to see who has their hand raised. "Yes?" He nods for Stevie to ask his question.

He tilts his head to see me over the shoulder of the guy I'm hiding behind. Our eyes lock for a painful moment before he turns his attention to Stevie.

"How do you see the team size changing when we merge with Nexus?" Stevie asks.

There's a communal intake of breath around the room.

The million-dollar question.

*Are we going to keep our jobs?*

"Some of the departments will need restructuring," Danny replies, straight to the point. He props a foot up on one of the podium steps and rests his elbow on his knee. Even in his suit, he looks more like Special Forces than a tech CEO. "It may mean role changes or even redundancies. I can assure you if that happens, you will be rewarded fairly for your time with Dunley. We'll start with offering voluntary redundancies."

The group collectively stiffens.

Some of us will lose our jobs.

Murmurs resound around the room and on the video conference. The remote offices look even more freaked out than us.

"Think heavily about what you want to do," he continues, unaffected by the tension in the room. "Nexus is a highly rewarding but competitive environment. We recruit only top calibre. If you are not willing to put in one hundred percent, then it is not for you. We'll also be suspending the lease on this building and moving the company into the main Nexus headquarters. Still London Bridge, so your commute time will remain the same. Although hopefully, you'll find the new offices a little more," he pauses, searching for the right word, "interesting."

That's an understatement. Dunley Tech office is a funeral parlour compared to the swanky, sexy Nexus headquarters.

Tristan gave me a tour once. It features a rooftop lounge overlooking the River Thames, a gym with a jacuzzi, multiple restaurants and cafes, and a yoga studio. It is designed for staff to never leave the building and never dream of leaving the company. If you make it past their gruelling recruitment process, you're a lifer.

A babble of excitement flows through the room. If we make the cut, we get to leave our depressing drab office.

"That's all for now." He nods, informing us our time is up.

Most of us pile out of the boardroom while some loiter. The loiterers fall into two categories: the Jackies who want airtime to practice their art of seduction, and the arse-lickers who want to stand out to the new boss man.

I'm in my own category, the fool that dry humps the boss without his authorisation.

Mike stands beside the podium, jutting his chest out in an extreme show of peacocking. "Any questions, let me know!" he shouts.

Everyone ignores him.

Danny Walker shifts his gaze to Stevie

and me and raises his eyebrows slightly in acknowledgement.

I nod briefly in return and burst out of the doorway, barraging my way through the bottleneck.

"So?" Stevie nudges me when we return to our desks. "Spill the story."

"Fine." I slump into my wheely chair. "Eight years ago, I was at a party at Tristan's. Danny always attends Tristan's parties, so of course he was there. He never talked to me much at them, I was just the young silly sister at college, and he was the CEO running his big shot company. He was talking stocks, and I was taking shots."

"And?" Stevie makes a motion for me to hurry up and get to the good bit.

"I was drunk at the party. Back then, that was nothing new. Cat and I brought this rocket fuel spirit to Tristan's house. Let's just say it gave me the illusion of grandiosity. I misread Danny Walker's signals, climbed onto his lap, and began manhandling him. But he rejected me and pushed me away."

"You what?" Stevie roars. "This is brilliant. You just made my day. You basically indecently assaulted the new CEO."

"Glad someone is happy about it." I tut, crossing my arms. "I've been so embarrassed that I've barely spoken to him since then. It's a lose-lose situation. Either I stay and hide from him in shame, or I quit and try to start over somewhere else. I can't face seeing him in this office for the next few months."

Stevie looks over at Danny, who is still in the boardroom, a strained look on his face as he talks to Mike. Mike throws his arms around excitedly. "It was eight years ago." Stevie shrugs. "He's had so many women grab his dick since then, he must have forgotten it."

I shake my head. "He doesn't like me. He never talks to me. He just grunts and frowns. He thinks I'm Tristan's silly little sister," I continue, logging into my laptop. How the hell can I concentrate on work now?

"Shit." Stevie looks at his watch and jumps up. "Look, all you did was grab your boss's boss's boss's dick. It could be worse."

"How could it be worse?" I mutter, putting on my glasses.

"It could have been Mike's dick." He waves dismissively and hurries back to his desk.

I breathe out loudly, and absently check our open support tickets. I can't focus with this hanging over me. I need to take matters into my own hands. In the browser, I type London's main job page and press return. Let's see what this city has to offer.

Someone clears their throat behind me.

Tilting my head around, I stare into his masculine, sharp face. He stands too close, towering above me. So close, I can smell his scent.

"Charlie." He fixes his detached stare on me.

"Mr. Walker," I reply, my throat dry.

Annoyance flickers over his face. "There's no need to call me that here. I'm still Danny."

"Why didn't you tell me on Saturday?" I ask, my voice faltering. "You knew that I work here."

"Yes, I knew that." His lips disappear in a tight line. "I couldn't announce it before today. Legalities."

I smell bullshit.

With a dark stare, he looks over my shoulder and then back at me. "Looks like you're busy."

Shit.

The job site.

I bite down on my lip. "Just in case you no longer need an I.T. Support lead." I swallow the hard lump in my throat, feeling my cheeks burning.

He hesitates but doesn't correct me. He's about to speak when a blonde lady approaches, beckoning him to follow her. Cheryl, I think her name is. "If you'll excuse me, Charlie."

"Oh," Stevie calls out while Danny Walker is still in earshot. "You could cut the tension with a knife."

Danny hears it because he cocks his head slightly at Stevie before walking on.

"Behave," I snap back.

*** 

It's Monday evening, and we've moved our Thursday flat dinner date forward. It was called for after my nasty little surprise today.

The girls are talking about the mice situation in the flat while I'm typing away on my work phone.

Julie watches me. "What drama is it this time? Someone's lost a cable?"

I glare at her. "It's the Seattle office. They've lost

connectivity to the London server that hosts the invoicing application."

She rolls her eyes. "Please stop talking. I'm bored."

Cat pats my hand. "You have to tune out, Charl. It can wait until tomorrow. There will always be some problem you need to solve." She smiles sympathetically. "You just need to try to relax and not think about it outside of work hours."

I give her a strained smile. "It's out of work hours in London. But in Seattle, it's morning time. Then in another few hours, Singapore will be waking up, then India."

"You can't be on call all the time," says Cat.

"Besides." I sigh, taking a sip of wine. "Danny Walker already has it in his head that I'm useless at my job. I don't want to give him an excuse."

My phone beeps as messages come in thick and fast.

I type my response to the Seattle Support team and hit Send.

"Jeez." Julie's eyes widen. "You're a freak. You can actually type without looking at the screen."

I smirk. "Don't you have to type in work, Julie? Or do you just bully your paralegals into doing everything?"

"Of course," she replies deadpan. "I talk. They type."

"Why do you have so many issues, Charlie?" Cat asks.

"Mike thinks we have a big lever for the company that we pull up and down to get online." I use air quotation marks for emphasis. "He won't let me move us to the cloud."

Cat nods, her eyes glazing over slightly. "The cloud."

I've drawn Cat the same diagrams as I've drawn Mike. Even her knowledge surpasses his now. She nods sympathetically, and I decide it's time to change the subject.

Sometimes I wish my friends understood the pressure on me. While Cat and Julie meet for Legs, Bums and Tums twice a week, I'm busy working round the clock trying to support dodgy systems. Any time of day, I can tell you what time it is in any time zone. Cat has a running joke about my 'clock watching.' All applications have to be running and available twenty-four hours a day.

"Why are you bothering?" Julie questions. "It sounds like you'll be out the door soon if Danny Walker despises you so badly."

"Maybe it's time to move on, Charlie?" Cat asks.

She's right. Why am I bothering?

My belly lets out a rumble, and Julie looks at me in disgust. "Control yourself, woman, will you?"

"I haven't eaten lunch today," I complain. "Where's Suze?"

Suze was supposed to meet us thirty minutes ago, and the waitress is getting twitchy since we only have the table for another forty-five. If we have to go somewhere else for food, I'm going to throttle her. This is very unlike her to be late for a dinner date.

"She must have fallen under a bus." Julie looks at

her watch in disbelief. "Unbelievable."

"Hey, girls," Suze rushes over to the table, flustered, flapping leaflets in her hands. "Guess where I have been?"

We wait.

"Here!" She lays the leaflets with a zen like model bending backward on a mat down in front of us.

"Bikram Yoga," Cat reads aloud. "That's the yoga you do in thirty degrees?"

"Forty, actually," Suze corrects. "It's amazing! The difference it can make, honestly, girls, this is it for me."

"Have you just come from it?" I ask.

We look at her in surprise. Suze has signed up for more fitness schemes than I can remember, but she rarely manages to start them, never mind follow through the course.

"Uh-huh." She nods. "I bought a twenty-day introductory pass. I thought I'd be cautious. I didn't want to purchase the yearly pass just yet, but I reckon I'll be going at least three times a week."

"Let's not get too carried away," I jump in. We've been here before when Suze tried to get a refund for her zen-do kickboxing outfit. "So ... did you like this yoga?"

Suze laughs. "Oh, tonight was just an introductory chat and filling out the registration form. I didn't actually take the class!" She shrugs dismissively. "I know it's the sport for me. I've tried yoga before, and I liked it. Only thing I didn't like was all the stretching and lunging. But in forty degree heat, you can bend more easily."

"But you look really ..." Cat tries to search for a word nicer than sweaty, "flushed?"

Suze nods enthusiastically. "Even the reception was boiling! I probably lost weight just sitting in the reception area."

"Forty degrees is pretty hot." I frown. "Suze, I don't think this class is meant to be relaxing. If just sitting in reception made you sweat, God knows what it's like in the actual yoga studio."

"I don't think I've ever stood in forty-degree heat, never mind exercised in it," Cat muses.

"Well, now is your chance," Suze replies happily. "Because I have signed you both up with me," she says, facing Cat and I fully now.

My mouth drops. "No, no, no, we are not doing this again."

I shake my head firmly, ready for a fight.

She pouts. "What about our 'try everything once' pact?"

"It sounds like my idea of a nightmare. That's the last place I want to be. I already pay to stand and sweat on the tube. I don't need to pay anymore. And I'm too busy with work," I add quickly as my get-out clause.

"I already have a gym membership, Suze," Cat points out. "And it's hard enough to use that. At the rate I attend, I'm paying about twenty pounds a class."

"Ah, come on, girls," she whines. "Everyone is talking about it! It's amazing. It gets rid of all your cellulite."

"Really?" I snort. "NASA would have a better chance of filling the craters on the moon with Poligrip." I can't even look at a goat's cheese tart without the cheese shooting straight through my system and landing on my butt.

"Actually, Charlie." Cat looks at me thoughtfully. "She does have a point. Jenny in the Maths department has better legs now than our gym teacher. She has been preaching about Bikram Yoga for months now. And a few other people I know have been raving about it." Her brows lift. "Don't you want to look your best with Danny Walker roaming around the office?"

"I suppose, since I've lost all dignity, I should try to look half decent," I reply, through gritted teeth.

"Come on," Suze whines. "It's in London Bridge. It's literally around the corner from your office! Please, please, please."

"Fine," I snap, knowing it's easier to give in and go to the one and only class Suze will ever attend. "I'll do one class."

"Yeah!" Suze claps her hands. "Now, let's celebrate."

I call over the waitress.

"Caesar salad, please," Julie shuts her menu, uninterested. She would have been as excited ordering sawdust. If it doesn't contain nicotine, she'll take it or leave it.

The waitress looks at Suze, who hasn't opened her menu.

"I'll have the steak burger with blue cheese and onion rings as extra, with the mayonnaise and chilli dip and a portion of mini wedges with guacamole."

"Jesus." Julie's face distorts in disgust. "Do you know that off by heart?"

"I have a good memory," she snaps defensively. "And I'm allowed a treat every now and then. It's going to evaporate off me at Bikram!"

My phone buzzes again, demanding attention.

"I'm going to smash that bloody thing," Julie grumbles, and the others don't argue with her.

I look down.

**Charlie**
**Meet me in my office. 8am**
**Danny Walker**

*Shit.*

# 6

**Charlie**

I didn't sleep a wink last night worrying about this meeting. Why did he have to be so vague? Could he not have given *some* indication as to what it's about?

He has some nerve. Emailing me at 9 p.m. the night before and expecting me to be on call at all times to check my emails. My contracted hours don't begin until 8.30 a.m. I am under no obligation to see this git before then.

Even his emails are devoid of manners as if every word is too much effort. An automated messaging service would have more charisma.

Of course, I didn't have the guts to say that.

It's 7:59, and I've been pacing in circles outside his office for ten minutes. It's an office he's commandeered for the acquisition.

I'm wearing my most professional-looking grey skirt and white blouse, ironed for the first time since I bought them.

I take a deep breath in, smooth my hair down and knock on the door.

Nothing. Did he hear me? I know he's in there. Is he making me stew?

I knock again.

"Come in," a gravelly voice responds after a minute.

I wish he didn't have that deep Scottish voice that triggers my heart to beat double time.

As I enter the office, I close the door and stand awkwardly in the centre of the room, shifting my weight between my feet. I don't want to get too close in case he can smell fear.

Behind his desk, he stares at his laptop and scowls. He doesn't even look up. "Sit down."

Suddenly I'm irrationally nervous. I take the seat opposite him, pulling my grey skirt down to my knees when it creeps up. While he's frowning at his laptop screen, I sneak a glance at him. Even at 8 a.m., the bastard looks sensational.

Something on the screen causes his thick Roman nose to flare. He always seems so angry. I wonder if anyone gets to see a softer side.

I rehearsed the scenario over and over in bed. I was going to walk in self-assured and composed, look him dead in the eye, and make sure he knew I was a confident, powerful woman unaffected by his presence.

Instead, I'm just sitting here, gormless, watching him ignore me. To kill time, I pick at imaginary fluff on my skirt. The silence is killing me. Maybe it's a CEO intimidation tactic. Or maybe he's just an asshole.

"Hi." My voice comes out louder than I expect it to. "What do you want?"

His eyes snap up to mine as if taken aback. "Good morning, Charlie." He leans forward in his chair, folding his large arms across his chest. His sleeves are rolled up to his elbows showing his muscular forearms.

I avert my eyes from his distracting bare arms.

"I hope that's not how you greet clients."

"I'm Support, not Sales," I reply bluntly. "I only talk to clients when they're already annoyed. Anyway, you've never seemed one for niceties. Not with me anyway."

"Very well." He cocks a brow. "We'll skip the niceties and get down to the reason I asked you here. Listen," he starts in a smooth voice, rolling up his sleeves further. "I wanted to tell you as soon as possible given our ... common connection."

Unease rolls through me.

"As you heard in the intro yesterday, we'll need to streamline some of the company's departments into our parent company, Nexus."

*Streamline.* Cutting the fat.

"It's simply not economical to keep the team structure as it is," he continues, scanning my face. "I've secured you an excellent position in another tech company with the same package. And of course, your leaving package here will be very generous. More than any other pay-out, so I'd advise you to keep it to yourself."

I stare at him aghast. He's fucking firing me?

"You're firing me?" I blurt out.

"No," he replies, his eyes steely. "You're being

offered a very generous redundancy package and a new job elsewhere. This is special treatment given the circumstances."

I blink at him, confused. "How have you decided this so quickly?"

"What with our connection to Tristan, I wanted to secure you a decent package quickly ..." he trails off, searching my face for comprehension.

*This is about me being Tristan's sister?* I feel my temperature rise. How dare he.

"Special treatment?" I explode, glaring at him. "You think you can fire me and decide where I work?"

His eyes flash with anger. I guess no one talks back to Danny Walker.

He pushes his chair back and moves to the front of the desk, towering over me. "You'll do well to treat me with some respect, Charlie. No one talks to me like that," he growls, his hands gripping the desk hard. "If it hasn't sunken in yet, I own this company. I say who stays and who goes."

I draw in a sharp breath. "This can't be legal! I've worked here for five years, and you fire me after day two of—"

"You are not being fired," he cuts me off. "It's a very generous redundancy offer. I can assure you our lawyers are very comfortable with this." He lets out a harsh breath. "I can't play nice here. We don't need both support teams going forward. There will be forty percent redundancies, minimum. See reason."

My eyes narrow. "You haven't even looked at my credentials or what I've done."

"What about what you haven't done?" he responds, his voice strained. "There are constant outages. Development is crawling. Your department is inadequate."

"I know that!" I'm fuming. I can't believe Tristan is friends with this asshole. I can't believe I ever found him attractive. "I'm up all night trying to resolve the outages," I splutter. "If Mike didn't veto my proposed cloud solution, we wouldn't have any outages. Instead, all I can do is paper over the cracks."

"And you just gave up trying?" he barks back at me.

"Yes," I snap. "After six months of trying. Have you met Mike?"

"That's a defeatist attitude," he retorts.

"Seems like I'm easily defeated by pompous men in suits who don't listen to me," I fire back.

His eyes darken. "Careful, Charlie."

I meet his unrelenting stare head-on, not backing down.

"Listen to me," he says, emphasising every word. "You can accept my generous offer now, or you can try to convince my HR team to keep your job."

"Do I have a choice?" I ask, trying to keep my voice steady.

His lip curls in displeasure as he studies me like I'm a petulant child not eating my porridge. "Right now, yes. I've put an informal agreement on the table to make sure you are looked after. You have about ten days to mull it over. After that point, it's up to my team to decide who to keep. We'll be cutting 40% of the workforce. I can't offer you as good a package if you walk away from this offer now."

"And you think I won't make the cut on my own merits," I reply, with a sharp bite. "I'm not just Tristan's silly little sister. I've done a lot for this company this past year. I've saved us twenty percent in support costs this quarter."

His square jaw clenches. "I'm not saying you won't make the cut, however, be warned the calibre of the Nexus team is exceptional. I'm giving you a chance to walk away, so you don't have to try. Tristan knows that and understands."

"Wait, what?" I jump from my seat to face him head-on. Or at least chest on since he's at least a foot taller than me. I'm going to have to buy higher heels for the office.

"*Tristan* knows?" I shriek. "You told Tristan before me?"

I stare at him incredulously. This guy is an absolute snake.

He bites his lip and has the decency to look guilty for a fleeting second. "I didn't have to tell you personally, but I wanted to because of our history and ..." He pauses. "Connection."

"How lovely of you," I deadpan. "A real saint."

"Less of the attitude, Charlie," he growls through gritted teeth. He's pissed now.

"It's Charlotte to you," I snap, crossing my arms

over my chest. I need to bury my fists, or I might punch his stupid, gorgeous, arrogant face.

"Just read the package. It's already in your emails. You'll be happy. Lots of people would love to be in your position. The new company has very—"

"You don't get to dictate where I work," I interrupt.

I'm done here. I can't listen to this guy any longer.

I storm out the door, slamming it so hard anyone already in the office turns around to stare at me.

Seconds later, the door flies open as I'm halfway down the aisle, and I hear angry footsteps advancing on me.

My arm is yanked backward by a powerful hand, and I flip around dead in my tracks.

"That's the last time you slam a door on me, Charlie," he snarls, staring down at me. He's so close I can feel his breath on my cheek with every angry word.

Staring back at him defiantly, I jerk away from his grasp. Everyone in the office is watching the showdown.

I can't think of a good comeback. Turning my head, I storm down the aisle, hoping he only saw the anger and not the hurt in my eyes.

***

**You OK, sis?**

I stare down at my phone.

Great.

Tristan knows already. That means Mum and

Callie likely know. I'm eighteen again, and they all know my business. Mum is probably telling it to Father Murphy in confessions.

I don't reply.

**It sounds like a fantastic opportunity. Danny is offering a brilliant package. You can take some time off if you want, with your pay-out!**

The dots indicate he's typing more.

**I'm great x** I respond, trying to close the line of questioning. I don't want to talk to Tristan about this yet. It's too fresh.

I stare at my phone, sighing heavily. I know he's right. I read the package, and it's decent, better than any redundancy package I've ever heard of.

It didn't make Danny Walker any less of an asshole.

I joined the company straight out of university, and for five years I had worked my way up to a mediocre middle management position by working long hours and putting up with Mike's shit.

The truth is, despite all my complaining, I *like* working here. I have friends here. It's my comfort zone. People respect me here. I've just been promoted, and now I'll have to build myself up all over again somewhere else. Now all my long hours mean nothing. If I move to a larger company, they'll never give me the same responsibility with my level of experience. It'll be an instant demotion.

Sure, it isn't the best company to work for. We don't have a restaurant or gym like Julie's office, and the offices are more skanky than swanky, but it's my world.

Now within one day of taking over the company, Danny Walker destroys all that by sauntering in, swinging his dick, and informing me I need to pack my bags.

The whole thing just leaves a bad taste in my mouth.

He just *assumes* I'm rubbish at my job and that I'm not serious or intelligent enough to meet his standards. Not like Jen.

I know that's why he never offered me a job at Nexus. When I was looking for work all those years ago, he was willing to get me an interview at any other company, but never his. Never Nexus. Even when I saw jobs advertised at Nexus.

I'm just an irrelevant and inferior pawn in his game of acquisitions that he needs to remove to save an argument with Tristan.

Then he implies I should be grateful for him setting me up with another job I didn't even agree to? I'm not a charity case.

Truth be told, I'm hurt more than angry. After ten years, he still sees me as a silly little girl.

He never even gave me a chance.

"You're the talk of the office," Stevie announces, sliding his chair over to me. "There are two camps, the people who think you are brave talking back to Danny Walker and the people who think you are an idiot."

"Great." I snort. "Everyone knows about our little

tete a tete."

"Look, if it's killing you this much, just ask him outright, why?" he suggests. "Just keep calm, no flying off the handle."

He's right. I need to manoeuvre this calmly and rationally. Prove to Danny Walker that I'm a mature woman.

My jaw tightens with determination as I open my emails and start typing.

**Dear Mr. Walker**
**How dare you ...**

I delete the typing.

**Dear Mr. Walker,**
**I would like to understand the rationale behind my redundancy offer. Can you elaborate with specifics on why I was narrowed out to be removed from the team?**
**Kind Regards,**
**Charlotte Kane**

There, that'll do. Before I can talk myself out of it, I hit send.

The response is instant.

**Charlie,**
**Please set up a meeting with HR to discuss any outstanding questions. Rest assured that the team will take you through everything and ensure you are supported throughout this process.**
**Read the package first. It's an extremely**

**generous offer.**
  **Regards,**
  **Danny Walker**

I snort, and a few people beside me look up.

The atmosphere in the office is like a funeral home. We regard each other with suspicion now that we realise we're competing against each other. People traipse in and out of meetings with the Nexus HR team like a counselling clinic. This may be the highest level of productivity our company has ever seen, as we all fight for a place.

I hit reply and hammer on the keyboard.

**Dear Mr. Walker,**

**As you personally made the decision of removing me from my job and you personally notified me of this decision, I'd like you to explain why I was chosen.**

**Is this A) because you think I'm incompetent after doing zero research and relying on your own prejudices about who you think I am, or B) because I made a stupid mistake eight years ago that I bitterly regret?**

**Which one is it?**
**Kind Regards,**
**Charlotte Kane**

I suck in sharply. I've never broached the dry hump incident before. It's always been the elephant in the room.

I wait.

And wait.

No response. Spineless.

Forty-five minutes later, an email pops up.

**Charlie,**

**It's C) the company's new operating model requires streamlining, and we do not need two IT departments.**

**I made you a personal offer. The decision to accept it or not is yours, however, if you choose not to, you will be subject to the same redundancy selection process as the rest of your colleagues, whereby we will assess whether the job still exists under the new structure.**

**For what it's worth, I am disappointed that you have regrets from eight years ago.**

**Sleep on it. You'll come round and realise it's the best outcome.**

**Regards,**

**Danny Walker.**

I read it again, blinking. Then again, more slowly. He's disappointed that I have regrets? What the hell does *that* mean?

# 7

**Charlie**

"Legally, he can do it," Julie confirms as she scans over the document I had printed. "He's offering you voluntary redundancy."

She flicks through it, searching for something. "I don't get it. It's a bit strange that the CEO of the Nexus Group is getting involved in low-level details like this. He's got hundreds of employees. Doesn't he have bigger things to worry about?"

"I'm the pathetic little sister. I'm an inconvenience," I mutter, taking my anger out on my wardrobe. I'm searching for an outfit for dinner with Ben, and with the force I'm yanking the hangers, I'm likely to break the pole. "I'm not the right calibre for his company, and he needs to get rid of me quietly, so I'll be a good little girl at Tristan's parties."

"It would appear like that, yeah." She shrugs.

I shoot her a look. "I didn't want you to agree with me."

"Then don't ask."

"So, what do I do?"

She pauses. "Do nothing yet. You have ten days to think about this. Get your anger out with angry sex.

Then you'll think straight. In the meantime, let him sweat."

Ben and I are going to dinner tonight with some of his friends. It's a great opportunity for me to get out of my sex slump and stop festering over Danny Walker.

One of the perks of having a stinking rich brother is that you get freebies like access to exclusive restaurants and private members clubs. Usually, I decline because I can't be bothered with the ordeal of getting dolled up for these places, but it's time Ben saw me for the vixen I am. It's make or break time.

We've been put on Tristan's guest list for the new sushi restaurant in the Shard, meaning we get fifty percent off the bill. He would pay for my entire bill without blinking an eye, but I'd rather not feel like a charity case.

Reliable Ben is at the door promptly at 7 p.m. and does a double-take when he sees me.

"Wow." His mouth hangs open. "I forgot you could dress like this."

I open my mouth to tell him off, then falter. When *was* the last time I'd dressed up for Ben?

Any time there is mention of a restaurant, I'm diving into my elasticated stomach-expanding trousers. The priority has always been food over fucking.

"Wait until you see what I'm wearing under this." I wink at him and grab my coat.

\*\*\*

We are guided through the restaurant by a beautiful creature, and I silently thank myself for finding the willpower to dress up. Waitresses are never just waitresses in these bars; they are models with a canny ability to make you feel as attractive as a stone.

The restaurant is typical Tristan, a sky-high terrace with river views of the Thames through floor-to-ceiling windows while a live jazz band serenades in the background.

London's most gorgeous people have been gathered in red velvet booths. It's a beautiful scene. You need to be rich, beautiful, or an oligarch to make the cut, or in our case, freeloaders of the rich.

At the table sit Mikey, his girlfriend Sarah, John, Bernice, and a couple I've never met. They look chuffed. I've clearly earned major points for landing us a table when getting one is notoriously difficult.

Ben wraps his arm around my shoulder and beams. "Tony, Andrea, meet the missus."

My shoulders stiffen. A flood of panic, fear, claustrophobia, and nausea wash over me. When did I become a missus instead of Charlie?

"Hiya," I reply shakily, taking a seat next to Sarah.

The men are gathered on one side of the table, and the girls on the other. A tactical move by Mikey and John, no doubt.

"We were just talking about how beautiful these are," Sarah says as she points to the white flowers in the middle of the table. "They would be perfect on my two side tables in the marquee."

I brace myself for a long night.

Sarah is talking about her wedding. Apparently, she is frenzied with preparation even though the event is over a year away.

Feigning interest, I smile.

"Gorgeous," Bernice gushes. "Mixed in with lilies, right?"

John has been getting heavy hints from Bernice that she would also make a wonderful bride.

"Naturally," Sarah replies with a chuckle. "You know, finding the right wedding florist is an absolute nightmare. I've had five interviews already, and I still haven't found a satisfactory one. Five! I keep having these recurring dreams that I arrive at the marquee, and the flowers are sitting on the wrong table lopsided."

Honestly, if you are going to have a nightmare about wedding flowers, at least imagine killer weeds suffocating the groom.

"You're so lucky," Bernice says loudly, throwing eyes at her boyfriend. "I'll be a pensioner by the time John proposes."

"You're only twenty-eight," I point out. "Plenty of time."

They laugh between themselves.

"Charlie, you never change. Such a free spirit."

"What about you Andrea, how long have you been going out with Tony?" Sarah excitedly leans towards Andrea, hopeful for an extra number for her hen party.

"Six months," Andrea replies shyly. "I guess it's early days."

"Six months! Mikey and I moved in together after six months. We just knew it was right."

Bernice nods in agreement. "Although I had to wait nearly a year for John to take the next step."

"I think we'll take it slowly," Andrea gets in quickly before they invite themselves to her and Tony's home-warming.

"Ben and I have no plans to move in together any time soon," I tell them bluntly.

Bernice waves her hand dismissively at me. "You'll change your mind soon. Just you wait."

The talk teeters off to a discussion on Andrea's blue shoes and what a great bargain they were but inevitably veers back to weddings.

"... I said to her, are you having a laugh? Brown rolls with the goat's cheese salad?"

"... sometimes they just don't appreciate how much work goes into a wedding. Do they think the corsages just magically arrange themselves?"

"... the chairs are going to be wrapped in white linen with gold rimming, and NONE of the legs can be seen."

"... waitresses can't be too pretty."

"... was I being mean when I told Shelley to lose some weight to be a bridesmaid?"

"... but bridesmaids can't upstage the bride so she can't lose too much weight."

"... I think the priest actually fancied her a little."

They blather on for about an hour and a half

while I quietly get drunk by myself, nodding and murmuring at suitable moments. At the other end of the table, Andrea does the same. I have a feeling Tony is going to be dumped after tonight.

I excuse myself to go to the bathroom. If I time it right, they will have moved onto the digestives before I return.

I'm walking back from the bathroom, staring at my phone, when my face crashes into a wall of warm, hard muscle.

"Sorry!" I start, but stop abruptly when I meet the familiar cold stare.

"Charlie." His eyes drop down to my ankles, then follow a path up my bare legs, waist and breasts, before settling back on my face with a frown.

"Danny," I choke out, ignoring the somersaults in my stomach as he says my name.

He clears his throat. "I wasn't expecting to see you here."

"Likewise," I fire back. "Why are you here?" I glare at him. "I specifically asked Tristan if he was coming here tonight."

"I'm not here with Tristan."

I turn my head to see leggy Jen watching us. She flashes me a fake smile.

"Excuse me," I say, narrowing my eyes at him. "I need to get back to my table. Unless you want me to move tables? Or restaurants if I'm too much of an inconvenience?"

We stare at each other, the tension flowing between us like a live wire.

Such a damn pity I want this jerk's hard cock inside me.

I wrench my gaze from him and step around him.

"Wait." His hand engulfs my lower arm, and I feel myself stiffen under his touch. "Can we start acting like adults? All this melodrama is giving me whiplash."

I look at him flatly. "Maybe when you start treating me like one? You failed to tell me that you were planning to buy my company and get rid of me. We even talked about Dunley at the party! How embarrassing. So excuse me if I feel a little put out. You had this planned for ages, didn't you?"

His pause gives me my answer.

To my left, a camera phone clicks, and we both turn to see a Walkie groupie taking photos for the 'gram.

"Don't fucking start this here in the middle of the restaurant, Charlie," he growls, his arm tightening around mine.

"Don't you fucking start." I jerk my arm away from him. "You don't have to worry about me embarrassing you here, Danny. Or in the office or at Tristan's parties. It was much nicer when we ignored each other."

I march towards the table without looking back.

"What's he doing here?" Ben asks when I return to the table.

"Eating. Exactly like us," I snap, and immediately regret it. "Sorry."

Ben's brows furrow. "I don't like the way he looks

at you."

"Like he's going to kill me?" I mutter.

"No." He scowls. "Like he's going to eat you."

His scowl deepens as he stares over my shoulder. "He's watching you right now."

I'll give Danny Walker something to watch.

"Ignore him." I lean into Ben and slide my legs between his. Then I wrap my arms around his neck and pull him in for what might be the longest, most passionate kiss of our relationship.

Grinning, Ben releases himself from my lock. "Let's get the bill quickly." He signals to the waitress.

She walks over, smiling. "It's your lucky night. Your bill has already been paid by the gentleman on the corner table. As an olive branch to Charlie, he said?" She raises her eyebrows hoping we'll understand what that means.

The others look equally confused and ecstatic.

As I flip around in Danny Walker's direction, he raises his glass with a curt nod.

Incredulous, I stare back at him.

"Is that ... Danny Walker?" Bernice gasps. "*Danny Walker* is buying our dinner?"

"Prick," Ben says, grimacing.

The waitress's jaw drops. "*The* Danny Walker?"

There's a barrage of questions about why Danny Walker is buying our six hundred quid dinner.

"How do you know him?"

"What did we do to deserve this?"

"Aren't we going to thank him?"

"No," I reply through gritted teeth as I restrain

Andrea from running at him.

If this arrogant git thinks he can throw money at the situation, he has another thing coming.

"Excuse me, Miss?" I turn to face the waitress. "How much is his dinner bill so far? I'm going to repay the favour."

"About three hundred pounds, give or take." She looks at me blankly. "You want to pay for his dinner?"

This is going to be an expensive night.

"Charge it to my card." I plaster a smile on my face as I hand her the card. "Can you give the gentleman a message, please?"

"Of course." She beams, delighted to have the excuse to talk to him again. They always are.

"Tell him that, unlike all his other women, I won't be bought."

\*\*\*

"Did you have a good night, honey?" Ben whispers in my ear as we snuggle up in bed.

I smile at him fondly and lie. "The best."

"Sorry the girls were wedding mad. I hope it wasn't too boring for you."

"It was fine." I run my hand down his manly jawline affectionately, and he kisses me softly on the nose.

Ben really is a great guy. He is good to look at, good to me, and good to old ladies crossing the street. The man is a catch, and I don't deserve him.

"Are you happy, Charlie?" he asks softly, his eyes

full of fear and hope.

"Yes, Ben, of course." I pull him close, and we share a comforting embrace. Why do I feel so guilty?

Ben drifts off to sleep quickly, content with my answer. I watch him sleep, wondering why I'm feeling so restless myself.

I finally fall asleep at 4 a.m., and I dream of a white wedding where I'm walking down the aisle, and everyone is smiling at me, but something's wrong, and I can't figure out what it is. Is my bra too tight? Is my tan too orange? Ben is waiting at the end of the aisle.

"It's the missus," people are shouting. "It's the missus."

I jerk up in bed as I wake up in a sweat.

I look down at Ben's beautiful silhouette under the blankets, and panic rips through me.

A missus wears rollers, large support bras, cashmere jumpers with pearls on them and carries tissues in their pockets. My mother is a missus. I am most definitely not.

\*\*\*

**Danny**

"You're late," I mutter, watching the stunning hostess take off Tristan's coat.

"When am I early?" He grins, handing her a twenty.

She purrs back at him, and I roll my eyes. Tristan has women hanging off him everywhere he goes;

bars, offices, gyms, churches …. He even had the audacity to pick up a nurse when I was having shoulder surgery.

He nods to the three empty glasses. "I see you've started without us."

"Long week," I grimace, downing my third scotch.

I nod curtly to the waitress for the same again. Unlike Tristan, I'm not charming.

"Here's Knight." He nods to the club door where Jack is being led in through the curtain. "I can always rely on him to be later than me."

"I heard that," Jack responds as he flashes a large smile at the hostess. With her heels, she's at least six feet and almost face to face with Jack. Looking sheepish, he sits down. "I did a quick pit-stop at Yoga Teacher Sara's."

"You dirty dog." Tristan laughs loudly. "I hope you've washed your hands."

"Pale Ale, please." Jack smiles at the waitress and winks at us. "Better wash my mouth out too."

"Jesus, Jack." I shake my head. "It's not even dinner time yet."

"What's up with you, Walker?" he asks as he loosens his tie. "You seemed really uptight on the phone."

"Is it Jen?" Tristan raises his eyebrows at me.

I stare at him. It takes me a second to register who he's talking about.

"No." I almost laugh. Jen is not a problem at all.

"The acquisition then?" he prompts, looking at me in confusion. "I've never seen you this unnerved before."

I grind my teeth together. *Why am I so uptight?*

I lost a sale worth ten million a year in revenue last week, and that didn't faze me. What the hell is wrong with me?

"It's not Charlie, is it?"

I give him a double look. Why's he bringing up his sister? It's day three of being in the office with her, and I'm wound up so tight I'm exploding at everyone. They think I'm a monster, just like she does.

"Mate, you don't need to worry about how I'm reacting. I get it," he says when I don't respond.

"She didn't take it well, Tristan." I sigh, wondering why I'm straying into this conversation. "Has she spoken to you?"

"No, not really." He shakes his head. "I'm getting radio silence which is why I know she's upset."

He stops talking, distracted by the waitress placing our drinks tray on the table.

"You did what you needed to do." Tristan shrugs. "She'll come round. She's just proud. It's the first company she's ever worked at, and she's been at it a long time, so she's emotionally attached."

"She'll snap your offer up when she realises what a dick you are to work for." Jack laughs. "Doesn't she read the papers?"

Tristan smirks. "To Danny the Destroyer."

They raise their glasses in a toast, and I roll my eyes.

"'*Walker wipes out another competitor in his quest*

*for domination*' was the headline last week," Tristan chuckles.

"Don't start." I grimace. With every takeover, my reputation gets dragged through the mud further. I'm the poster boy of the evil tech industry. "And quit with that fucking name," I add. "It makes me sound like a comic villain. Which I am, according to Charlie. She's furious. No employee has ever talked back to me like she has."

"That's Charlie, hot-headed." Tristan chuckles.

Hot-headed? More like downright fucking difficult. Spurting out whatever is in her head without thinking, doesn't she know how to act in an office?

"I saw her at the restaurant last night." My jaw tightens. "You didn't say she would be there. She nearly burst my balls in the middle of dinner."

"She can burst my balls anytime." Jack gives a low whistle. "Sorry, Tristan, but the girl gets hotter every time I see her."

"Careful, Knight," he growls. Tristan would send both of his sisters to a convent in the mountains if he could. Since Tristan's dad did a runner and left Tristan with the three Kane women, he took on the dad role, which involved vetting boyfriends. The minute there was even a whiff of any of us going near Charlie, he would have our balls in a vice.

"As a peace offering, I paid for her and her friends' dinner," I explain. "It backfired," I continue through gritted teeth. "She threw it back in my face. When I went to pay my bill, she had already paid it. She said something about me trying to buy her."

Tristan throws his head back, laughing. "You just can't seem to win with Charlie. What did you do to rub her up so much the wrong way?"

I squirm in my seat as I recall the look she gave me after she crushed her breasts against my chest. It was as if I was the worst man in the world. I can do no right with the woman. I pay for her and her friends' fucking cocktails, and she takes a strop?

His brows lift. "Want me to talk to her?"

"No," I reply, too quickly. The less Tristan talks to Charlie about this, the better.

I know I was harsh with her over the redundancy offer. I thought giving her the offer myself would make it better, but it made it too personal. She knows exactly how to push my buttons, and I handled the situation like a jackass.

She'd been right, Mike was useless, and that wasn't her fault.

I figured she'd be happy about the generous pay-out. I had her new company write an open start date into her contract, so she could take some time off and travel. Why wasn't she happy?

Of course, Tristan knows that too, which is why he's been acting so reasonable.

"Mate, I know I'll get lynched for saying this," Jack says. "But as a red-blooded male, I think you should keep Charlie out of your cesspit of a friendship circle. Half of the city's financial district tried their chances at that party."

My eyes widen. *Drop it, Jack.*

"They wouldn't fucking dare," Tristan growls, narrowing his eyes at Jack. "That goes for you too, Knight, get any ideas of my sister out of your sordid mind."

Jack laughs. "I wouldn't go there. I like having my balls attached to my body. It's just a warning, Kane." He shrugs. "She looks good. Every dick in that party was standing to attention. If you insist on inviting her to the same parties that you invite your sordid lecherous mates to, well, you only have yourself to blame."

"Fuck's sake, Knight." Tristan glowers at him.

I need to steer this topic away before I'm exposed as a sordid lecherous mate.

"You've made your point, Jack," I say. "Don't make him as uptight as me, for God's sake."

"Maybe you're uptight because the waitress is eyeing me rather than you." Tristan grins.

"I can soon change that," I respond, raising my glass to her suggestively. She gives me a flirty smile.

"She's all yours." Tristan smirks at me. "You and Jen aren't exclusive then?"

I shake my head. "No. I've made it very clear; I'm not interested in commitment."

Jack tips his head back and laughs. "You're forty-one now, Walker. You have a beautiful young human rights lawyer who wants to have sex with you every night despite you having the charisma of a cockroach and you still don't want to commit? What exactly do you want?"

"Variety." I grit my teeth.

"He's got the right attitude," Tristan says dryly. "No commitment, no chance of a fucking bitch ex-wife to deal with."

"Hear, hear." I raise my glass, thinking of my own disastrous divorce. "What's the latest?" I ask.

Marrying Gemina was Tristan's most financially and emotionally expensive mistake, eleven years on, and he is still paying for it. As far as divorces were concerned, his was as hostile as they come. The woman was pure toxicity, letting him think Daniel was his son while she was shagging behind his back. He spent four years believing that he was Daniel's father, only to find out it was some bloke she met in a Monaco nightclub.

Now Daniel is six, and Tristan still treats him as a son but has few rights. He hasn't a leg to stand on legally, meaning Gemina can demand extortionate amounts in spousal and child support to fund her diamond fetish.

Tristan's brows form a deep frown.

I don't know why I brought it up. It pains me to see how much stress the situation puts on him; it's like a dark shadow over him. He needs to deal with it.

I know he lies awake at night worrying about never seeing Daniel again, that she'll just take off with some geezer.

"She's demanding I buy her a holiday home in France," he replies flatly. "Says she needs to be near her sister."

"You've already bought her two houses," I seethe.

"How many does she need?"

"If it's not a house, it's a boat or a car or a fucking island," Jack says. "How do we sort this bitch out once and for all?"

"No, Jack, we can't have her offed." Tristan rolls his eyes. "I just have to keep paying if I want to see my son." His face darkens. "I can't lose my son."

"You won't," I say quickly. "We have enough cash to keep paying her until we find a better solution. Like death."

"Glad I chose a rich godfather." He chuckles as I beckon the hot waitress over to us.

She sashays over.

"Now, if you'll excuse me." I drain the rest of my scotch glass. "Hi." I flash her a smile. "What's your name?"

# 8

**Charlie**

Ben answers the door to me with a kiss and a glass of wine.

"Hiya, honey, it's nearly ready." He wipes his hands on his apron to gather me up into a hug. "I made you pigs-in-blankets. I know you like them."

I do. In fact, I had a sneaking suspicion those buggers were the deciding factor in me coming over.

He ushers me into the living room where he has the table set with nice little napkins and sauces.

I slump onto the sofa, stomach churning in anticipation. Ben is an excellent cook. It's one of the reasons we work well together.

"Voila!" He emerges from the kitchen carrying two gigantic plates of yummy, stodgy food. Yet another night of lying on my back and groaning for the wrong reasons.

"This looks delicious." I smile happily at the feast.

He leans forward to kiss me. As his tongue enters my mouth, I close my eyes and try to focus on the moment.

My tongue responds, but my head isn't behaving.

I imagine I'm in another mouth.

The mouth of an obnoxious, arrogant Scot.

I'm a terrible person. Damn you, Charlie, focus!

When we emerge, I look at Ben and see our relationship clearly for the first time.

My chest tightens. I can't do this anymore. I can't just go through the motions. Don't get me wrong, the guy is one in a million. He is one of the warmest, kindest boyfriends I've ever had.

But not for me. I want to have the fear of wanting someone so badly that my heart rate spikes when I see them. Fear that makes my throat clam up, so I forget how to take in air when they speak to me.

Julie says this is typical of me. I stay in relationships far longer than I should because I feel guilty about ending them.

"Ben," I start in a small voice.

"Yes, honey." He smiles back between forkfuls of mashed potatoes.

Oh hell, it's pointless to waste good pigs-in-blankets. I'll try again after dinner. "This is delicious."

I shovel the food into my mouth as if the government had just announced a shortage.

After dinner, we settle into the couch to watch a movie. Ben bought my favourite dessert, a sticky toffee pudding with whipped cream.

My stomach gurgles in protest as more food is shoved into it than it can handle.

He snuggles into me, either ignoring or not caring about the noise.

I sit upright. I can't procrastinate anymore.

*Do it, do it, do it.*

"Ben, we need to talk," I frantically say while taking a big swig of wine.

He puts down his plate. "Damn, that's a serious statement. Why am I hoping that you just want to talk about the plot?"

I smile sadly. "No, it's not about the film. It's us. I just don't think—"

"What?" He stares at me blankly.

"That it's working anymore." I gulp mouthfuls of air. "I think we'd be better off as friends."

There. I said it.

"What?" He rubs his face. "I don't understand. Why?"

"I'm sorry," I whisper, my eyes on the carpet. "I still love you, but it's more sisterly or motherly now if you get my drift."

Small whimpering sounds come from him as he puts his head in his hands. I can't stand this. I wish I could retract my painful words now.

"I don't want to hurt you. We can still be friends, of course, but—"

Yes, perhaps we can be good friends! Without sex, we are more like friends now anyway. He can still cook for me if he wants. I'll even let him cook the pigs-in-blankets.

"You have to work at a relationship, Charlie," he replies in a clipped voice. "You can't just magically keep the spark without trying."

"I know. I should have shaved my legs more. I stopped putting in effort. This is my fault." I watch in despair as his face contorts with threatening tears.

"Eight months, Charlie. Did it not mean anything?"

"Of course, it did! But sometimes relationships just run their course," I say, rubbing his shoulder.

He shakes his head. "This is so unexpected."

Is it? If I'm honest with myself, the relationship was over months ago. I just didn't read the signs.

He sits up. "Is there someone else?"

"No!"

"Is it Stevie?"

"No," I reply, taken aback. "You know Stevie is a mate. He's seeing Cat, for Christ's sake!"

"Is it to do with my Mum? I know she is full-on, Charlie, but she only wants—"

"No!" I interrupt sharply. Although his Mum did act like …

"I don't know what else to say," I add softly. "I'm sorry, Ben." I fixate on the carpet. "You're right. I'm a terrible girlfriend. I put work before us. I'm always tired. I can't stop farting. And you, you are amazing —"

"Don't tell me I'm a nice guy," he cuts in gruffly. "Just leave it."

"I'll get a cab home," I offer.

He nods, a trickle of tears dripping down his chin.

There is something niggling at me, though. The thought of going back to a room full of Ben's sweaters and underwear. Before I leave, I have to dot the I's and cross the T's.

"Ben," I start. "I'll return your sweaters and underwear."

He stares at the floor without responding.

"I can separate the clean ones from the dirty ones if you like?" I add helpfully.

"For God's sake, Charlie, as if I bloody care about my pants!"

"I really am sorry, Ben."

He responds with a strained smile. "I know. It's not your fault."

"It's not?" I ask hopefully.

"What do you want me to say? That I understand and you shouldn't blame yourself?" He wipes his tears, a hardness in his eyes. "Fine, don't blame yourself. Don't feel guilty. Go home."

"I do feel guilty," I protest. "But we can't keep going out of guilt. It's not a very good basis for a relationship."

He nods and touches my cheek gently. "I just need some time."

I shuffle around the flat, hoovering up my belongings in a daze. My fluffy slippers, my elasticated trousers, my pink hot water bottle.

All evidence of the rut we have fallen into.

Tomorrow I'll go out and buy some saucy hold-ups and lacy knickers. I'm 28, when did I start acting 78? It's time to reclaim my sex life.

***

It's Friday morning, so I should be in a good mood.

I would be, if I wasn't standing in the rain outside

a Bikram Yoga studio at 6:15 a.m.

I'm already panting from belting across London on my bicycle to get there on time.

Suze chose the lazy option, the underground. When she sees me, she exhales heavily.

I look at my phone. "Where's Cat?"

"She couldn't make it. She's snowed under at work."

"Cat?" I ask in disbelief. "Do you realize Cat spent three hours on Monday rearranging her knicker drawer by colour because she was 'so on top of things'? The little bitch, if I have to go through this, she bloody well has to also."

"You're right!" Suze becomes indignant. "All I asked her to do was stay in one class for ninety minutes. That's not too much to ask."

"Come on." I fling open the door to the reception and am hit by the smell of sweat. "Let's get this over and done with."

After registering, we walk to the studio and peer inside the glass window while waiting for the last class to end. As I glance around the room, I begin to wonder if Suze and I misunderstood the dress code. There are girls wearing bras and shorts so tiny, I'm sure you can see internal organs when they bend over. There is more muffin top on Kate Moss than in this studio.

As the door opens to the studio, I'm greeted by a heatwave that rivals a cremation.

Suze stares at me wide-eyed, a bead of sweat forming over her eyebrows.

We trudge hesitantly into the studio and find an area to stand as near the door as possible.

About twenty people are already lying on their backs on yoga mats with their palms facing the ceiling, taking long deep breaths. At least ten more people pile into the room.

What the hell? How are we all going to fit in here?

I open my mouth but no oxygen goes in. It's hard to breathe in this heat.

My feet start to cook on the ground, and I hop from foot to foot.

This isn't pleasant heat, like my juicing retreat in Sardinia. Or standing on a beach in Jordan.

It's *way* hotter. Boiling. Record-setting extreme climate conditions. A room unfit for human habitation.

It's taking all my strength not to bolt out of the door.

"Are they fucking serious?" Suze hisses at me, becoming more frazzled by the second. "This isn't right! It's inhumane!"

Usually, I dismiss Suze's dramatised accounts of sporting activities, but I couldn't argue with this one. I wouldn't heat a hen house to this temperature.

The door closes, and I feel my heartbeat accelerate as waves of panic wash over me. There is no way I can stay in this room for ninety minutes. But there are so many people between me and the door.

Beside me, Suzy moans softly.

I close my eyes and tell myself I won't die from spontaneous combustion.

"Good morning, ladies. Welcome to Bikram Yoga." A short lady with an Eastern European accent smiles around the room. "This is going to be an intense session. You may experience discomfort, panic, nausea and the feeling that you want to run out of the room. It's a challenging class. Regulars will already be familiar with the great benefits this class offers. For new starters, I ask you to bear with it. Do not overexert yourself for the first few sessions."

Suze nods her head feverishly, either in agreement or as part of a fit.

The instructor paces up and down the front of the room. "Your main aim this morning is to stay in the room for the entire ninety minutes. If you do that, you'll do extremely well."

"Stay in the room," I repeat to myself quietly. "Just stay inside the room."

I've never been one for confined spaces. If someone tells me the toilets are out of order, I immediately have to go. If someone tells me to be silent, I'll get a parched throat and be choking to cough. Bikram lady is telling me I need to stay in this Saharan heat for ninety minutes? My brain is ordering me to get the hell out.

"We have a few new starters this morning. Where is Melissa?"

A lithe girl in a catsuit wiggles her hand in the air.

"And Charlotte and Suzanne?"

"Oh, that's us!" I rasp, raising my arm in the air. Hearing my voice is strange, it's dry and breaking.

"OK, ladies, take it easy. If you feel nauseous, just

stop the exercises, sit down on the mat and breathe through your nose."

She clasps her hands together. "Right, let's begin the first posture!" Her hands stretch above her head. "Bums up to the ceiling. Follow the ceiling to the back wall with your eyes."

"How many postures are there?" I throw Suze a desperate look.

She can barely answer me. "Two, I hope."

We watch as the instructor and most of the class stretch and bend in the heat. I tentatively follow, trying to work as little as possible. Beads of sweat gush down my arms and soak through my shorts and underwear. On my feet, sweat droplets collect in the vein grooves.

"Keep pushing through, ladies. This is the final warm-up posture." The instructor bends to the right and my classmates obediently follow. "Well done! That's the warm-up over."

"Warm-up." I scratch the beads of sweat tickling my arm. "Can you believe it?"

I turn to Suze and watch open-mouthed as she picks up her soaking towel and trundles towards the door stepping over the sea of sweaty bodies.

Ignoring the instructor's call, she flings the doors open, letting in a gush of glorious cold air, and with that, she is gone.

The instructor watches in bewilderment. "OK." She laughs. "Hopefully, the rest of you will attempt to stay in longer than the warm-up. Bikram's not for everyone, as we can see."

Sniggers reverberate around the room, and the girl next to me shoots me a sidelong glance.

I bend over into the frog position and hope that Suze has passed out from the heat, because if she hasn't, I'm going to knock her out when I get out of here.

"Just enjoy the deliciousness of this pose, ease your back into the beautiful arch that your body is craving."

I snort as sweat rolls up my nose from behind my ears.

"Let your eyes follow the line in the ceiling and breathe out and smile. Hold it … Hold it," her voice trails off. "And relax."

I fall onto the floor in a heap, flinging sweat at the girl beside me.

"Now down into the toad position. And release. Be taken by the breath filling your lungs …"

Sweat gushes down between my breasts like a dam breaking. I'm sliding in my own damn sweat.

I see the crack of the door and feel pangs of despair.

But most of all, I'm angry.

Angry at the instructor who is prancing around like a mad woman practicing labour breathing techniques, who won't let me leave the room.

Angry at Suze for giving up on everything she has ever attempted because she's spineless.

And angry at myself for having a less elasticated bum than the pensioner springing about in front of me.

The instructor's voice drills into my brain. "Lock your knees. Reach down, fingers under your feet, push and LOCK your knees. Elbows straight, forehead to the floor, LOCK YOUR KNEES." She walks past me pushing my knees out.

"They don't bend any more than that," I growl at her, and she smiles serenely.

# 9

**Charlie**

I get a guilty message from Suze with three kisses, saying she's waiting in Starbucks a few doors down. As the cold air outside hits me, I've never felt so happy to live in a country with shite weather.

I walk into Starbucks to see her enjoying a Grande latte with cream on top and a large carrot cake.

"I'm so sorry, Charlie." She has the good sense to look guilty. "Are you mad at me? I couldn't breathe. I thought I was having a heart attack. I thought the walls were closing in. I just had to get out of there. I was drowning in my own sweat."

"Tell me about it." I shoot her a filthy look. "You had ten whole minutes. I had to endure ninety minutes of sweat going into cracks where sweat shouldn't be. Not just *my* sweat either."

Suze screws up her face as I lean over the table. "I wouldn't have minded waiting for you to take a shower. You look absolutely drenched. Your hair—"

Seeing my expression, she trails off. I know how my hair looks. It's like a soaking floor mop stuck to my forehead.

"The shower queue was too long," I reply, gritting

my teeth. "Now I'm going to have to sneak into work like this and shower there."

"Oh." She chews on her lip nervously. "Did it get easier?"

"No. It was horrific. I'd prefer to stick chillies in my eyes."

"So, you didn't enjoy it?"

My eyes narrow.

"No. Did you enjoy Starbucks?"

"Ah come on, Charl," she whimpers. "I'm sorry. If I could physically stay in there, I would have. I'm like a big heat sponge. And I'd eaten an omelette before I came out. My poor bowel was quivering."

"You aren't going to make any progress if you only stick at it for ten minutes," I snap and immediately regret my harsh words.

"Perhaps next time, try it without the heat first," I offer more softly.

"Uh-huh." She nods. "You wanna share a muffin?"

I shake my head. "I need to shower before the Starbucks staff throw me out."

\*\*\*

I sneak in through the office doors at 7:45 a.m., getting some sideways glances from the security guards.

Thankfully at this time of the morning, few people will be in the office, except for the hardcore developers who don't sleep.

The showers are on the lower ground floor, meaning it's unlikely I'll be spotted.

My shorts and T-shirt are moulded to me like a wet T-shirt competition. My shorts are offensively short. Porno short. They were never supposed to be worn outside of a gym.

I look like a prostitute who has swum in a river.

I fumble around in my bag between my work clothes and laptop.

Shit! I don't have my towel.

How the hell did I forget that? Now I have to go up to the fourth floor and get my spare.

Stealthily, I enter the elevator at the lower ground reception. So far, so good. There's no life around yet except for the security guards.

My reflection hits me in the elevator mirror. It's worse than I thought.

I'm *soaking.*

My shorts and T-shirt cling to every bone and bump in my body. There's a full outline of my bra and pants.

The elevator pings open, and I run to my desk, bending my knees to stay low.

A few developers sit with headphones in their ears, eyes glued to the screens. They don't acknowledge me. It would take a hurricane to distract a coder.

I make it to my desk and hunker down to open my drawer. Yes! The blue towel is still here from when I brought it in last year.

There's a slow whistle behind me. I jump and bang my head on the desk.

My eyes snap up to find Dylan Anderson smirking

at me. As he evaluates my outfit or lack thereof, his eyes balloon. Dirty Dylan, we call him for his lechering on anyone with a pair of ovaries.

"Aren't I glad I came in early this morning? That is one glorious sight."

I cross my arms over my chest as his eyes move from breast to breast. "Piss off, Dylan."

"Come on, Kane, you don't walk around the office like that without expecting a little attention."

"I'm not after your bloody attention," I spit out the words. "If I could spoon out your dirty little eyes, I would. Go and slide back under the stone you crawled out from under. I'm just here to get a towel."

He leans in and places a hand on my sticky arm. "If you need a hand scrubbing your back ... Oh shit ..."

He jerks away, his eyes popping.

I flip around to see what has distracted him.

Danny Walker storms towards us, eyes blazing.

I recall Tristan saying he did a few years in the military when he was younger, and now I can see why. He approaches like a tank, ready to go into combat with his enemies.

His intense eyes lock with mine.

"Mr. Walker," Dylan stammers, retreating backward.

## Danny
### Ten minutes earlier.

"How do we stop it from getting to press?" I bark down the speaker-phone.

There's hesitation on the other end. "I've made all the calls I can, bro, but they want to run this article. It's too hot to pull."

I run my hands through my hair and scan the article again in disgust. I've had many smear campaigns against me these past few years, but this is beyond scandalous.

Sam Lynden.

The prick that took me to the cleaners for shoving him when he was threatening his girlfriend, my own employee.

It was nothing more than a jostle. Of course, she backed his side, left the company, and they both went skipping into the sunset with a big lump of cash.

Now they're back for more. The article talks about how I sleazed over his girlfriend and tried to force her to sleep with me, then how I attacked her boyfriend when he confronted me.

It's a crock of lies, but the public won't question the evidence. Because it fits my ruthless sleazy businessman image, I am guilty de facto.

"Danny?" Karl prompts. There are sirens in the background, and I can tell he's on his way home from a bar. "Are you still there?"

"Yes."

"It'll hit the papers tomorrow," he says firmly. "We need to do damage control. The lawyers are prepped and ready to hit him with a libel defamation case."

I eye my scotch glasses in the drinks cabinet. No, I need to wait until at least midday.

"Fine." I exhale hard, half-listening as he explains the plan.

I glance through the floor-to-ceiling glass walls of the office. I'm probably shouting so loudly; the story has already broken in the press.

What the ...?

"I have to go, Karl." I slam down the phone.

She has got to be joking.

She's bent over her desk in tiny shorts and a T-shirt giving some guy an eyeful of her rear. Her T-shirt is sticking to her, exposing the curve of her breasts. There's a clear outline of her nipples.

Despite my rage, my cock unhelpfully springs to life.

My company, my office, isn't a strip club. What's she playing at? Wearing tiny shorts so that everyone can eye-fuck her?

Is that what she wants, this geezer's eyes crawling over her skin, her curves?

Is she deliberately trying to get a rise out of me?

Is she trying to fucking seduce me?

The moron at her desk slides his hand up and down her arm.

I fire open the glass door, banging it against the wall. My fists ball up like angry stones as I pace down the centre aisle of the fourth floor.

"You, get the fuck back to your desk," I snarl to the guy when I'm still at least four metres from them.

My blood pressure is off the scale.

He scuttles off like the rat he is.

Her eyes grow large as I storm towards her,

stopping inches away from her face.

"What are you playing at?"

Sweat is beaded everywhere on her body, between the crevices of her breasts, on her forehead, down her legs, *there* between her legs.

I try not to get hard. Focus, Walker.

My eyes snap back up to her face.

"What?" With a horrified look on her face, she steps backwards.

"You flirt on your own time, not my time," I growl down at her. "Do you think this is appropriate office attire?"

She stares up at me like I'm insane.

Then she snaps.

"How dare you talk to me like that," she shrieks, pushing me in the chest. "I'm sorry that my sweaty body brings such offense to the office. You see, I forgot to bring my nun's habit to Bikram Yoga. I'm sorry I forgot my towel and subjected poor Dylan to the torment of seeing my damp skin. I'm sorry that it caused him such distress he felt the need to offer a helping hand in the shower. I'm so sorry I'm forcing that on him."

Her jade green eyes flicker with fury.

"In my office, you don't walk around dressed like a stripper," I snarl back, struggling to control my breathing.

She blinks. "Are you calling me a stripper?" Her hands flap at her side, and I wonder if she's going to slap me.

"I'm saying you're dressed like one."

Our eyes lock, neither of us backing down.

She waves her hands around the isolated office. A few coders bang keys on keyboards with their heads down. None of them look up, despite the commotion.

That's coders for you.

"There's no-one here! It's not like I'm going to sit in my own sweat all day. I'm grabbing a towel and running to the shower. In fact, I would be done by now if you hadn't ambushed me. What is your problem?" Her eyes thin into slits. "You think you can dictate where I work, now how I dress? Jackie wears short skirts to the office every day!"

What *is* my problem?

My problem is that I'm out of control. What am I playing at? We're a tech company, not a library. I let my staff wear whatever they want. Many of the developers wear jeans with holes in them and frayed T-shirts.

Why do I care what she wears?

She stares at me, demanding an answer.

I need to reign it in. I'm 6'4 and ranting at a girl over a decade younger than me and at least a head shorter. If HR saw me now, they'd be calling in the lawyers. Again.

I clear my throat. "Look, wear what you want, but you can't just strut around with barely more than a bikini on."

Hurt flashes across her face. "Excuse me," she says, her lips in a fine line. "I'm going to take a cold shower."

She turns on her heels, giving me a view of that glorious backside and those toned legs.

I'm going to need a cold shower too. And anger management classes.

# 10

## Charlie

"He said what?" Stevie asks too loudly. Curious, Dana and Tim lean forward in their seats to listen.

"Shush, keep your voice down!"

"Let me get this straight. Danny Walker informs you that you no longer have a job, but he's got you a job somewhere else, bearing in mind you might not even want to work there and didn't go through an interview, so God knows how he pulled that one off, then he reprimands you for what you are wearing?"

"Don't forget he called me a stripper." I grimace, my knee bouncing up and down. After this morning's episode, I'm like a basketball.

"I don't get it." His brow furrows. "This must be personal. Jackie sits out there in a mini skirt so short I can see what she's had for breakfast."

"Exactly." I roll my eyes. "Of course, it's personal."

"It sounds like a libel case. Is he allowed to do these things?"

We stare over at the main boardroom where the asshole is holding a meeting with Dunley senior management.

Danny talks, and the others nod like pigeons.

Pathetic.

Does anyone ever question this guy?

"Mind you, are you gonna try and take on one of the most powerful men in tech?" Stevie shrugs. "I guess he's used to people taking the cash and running. It doesn't matter how he treats them."

"I nearly slapped him." I giggle, remembering his angry face.

"Damn, Charlie, reign it in. Are you trying to get fired? Fired ... or fucked?" he adds sarcastically, and I hit him on the arm. He wheels his chair closer. "Let's check the employee contract. See what it says about dress code."

I nod. "I should have my contract in my emails from when I started."

Stevie peers over my shoulder as I filter my emails from my first year at work.

There it is. I click to open, and we scan through it. Bingo! The proof that Danny Walker was way out of line, and I hadn't violated any company policies.

*Dress Code. Between the hours of 8:30am and 5pm, employees shall maintain a dress code of smart casual. Clothes with slogans, or graphics that display profanity are not permitted. Notwithstanding, no employee shall be discriminated against because of dress.*

"It specifically says between 8:30 and 5," Stevie points out. "And it doesn't mention anything about shorts." He looks at me. "What are you going to do?"

I smile. Choke on this, you obnoxious prick.

## Danny

"Listen," I snap, "We've been over this. I want every employee to be assessed and scored in the next two weeks."

"Danny," Cheryl, my head of HR, pleads down the phone. "It's not enough time."

"It's not up for negotiation. I want this project done quickly."

"OK, but can I ask what the rush is?" she prompts softly. "You've never rushed a takeover like this before." Cheryl would be on shaky ground if she hadn't worked for me for a decade. I'm not a man who likes to be questioned.

I sigh. I don't have an answer for her. Can I tell her that my dick isn't playing nicely, and I need to get this wrapped up because I'm a walking erection?

I close down the questioning: "I need redundancy packages to be issued in ten days' time. Understand?"

"Perfectly, sir," she responds in a clipped tone.

I hang up fuming and instantly regret it. It isn't Cheryl's fault.

I'm doing the right thing even if Charlie can't see it right now.

What would Tristan prefer? Me giving his little sister a very generous redundancy package and a new job elsewhere or me fucking her senseless? That's what would happen if we were in the same office every day. It would end in tears, likely hers. I simply can't have her as an employee. Despite my reputation, I've never fucked an employee.

Merging Dunley Tech's I.T. department into the central Nexus department makes perfect sense. Tristan's a man of business. He will forgive the first but not the second.

So will she, with time.

I wonder how long she'll walk around sulking. She looked like she wanted to murder me this morning.

My cock clenches at the memory of her standing defiantly in front of me, hands on hips, chest moving angrily up and down.

She's lucky she didn't slap me. I wouldn't have been able to control the urge to fling her over my shoulder, carry her to my office, slide those wet shorts down and fuck her out of my system.

Unfortunately for both of us, her fury turns me on even more.

I twirl the ice around my scotch glass.

I need to get rid of this tension before the awards ceremony at 7 p.m. They probably won't take too kindly to me presenting awards with a tent in my pants.

I check my watch. Twenty minutes until the car arrives. I'll take matters into my own hands.

Literally.

I laugh out loud to myself as I roll down the blinds. I've never masturbated in the office before. Haven't needed to.

No woman has ever gotten me so worked up that I couldn't just put my lust aside and continue with business.

I lock the door and pull down the zipper of my trousers to release my hard cock.

Fuck I'm so ready. What a waste.

This is what I've resorted to. Instead of focusing on a multi-million-pound acquisition, I am hand fucking myself in a shitty, make-shift office.

I wrap my fist around my poor aching cock and start stroking.

I need something to get me there quicker.

*The video.*

In the end, I didn't have the guts to ask Tristan. There was no plausible reason I could come up with as to why I'd need a video of his sister singing. He knew when I was on the chase, and he'd see right through me.

No, like a true stalker, I gained access to the CCTV from the bar that night, citing I had my watch stolen. They knew it was a ten grand watch. They gave up the footage with no argument.

With my dick in one hand, I scroll impatiently through my phone with the other.

*Bingo.*

There's that beautiful face. I could stare at those green eyes forever.

I turn down the sound and stare at the soft mouth with the luscious lips. What I wouldn't do to bite down on that lip.

I imagine my hands running up her body, cupping those breasts, my mouth biting and sucking those glorious nipples. Pulling her legs apart, reaching my hand down into her warm core; pushing my fingers into her. Imagine finger fucking her until her legs give in. Hearing her moan as she screams my name. *My* name.

*Yes.* I'm close.

I pump my cock hard, watching it swell in my hands, my climax building.

The door handle rattles from the outside.

*What the fuck?*

How is it turning?

I locked it.

Except it's not locked.

The 2D vision on my phone turns into a 3D version as she storms through the door, flapping paper in front of her face.

She stops abruptly, the papers falling to the floor as her eyes travel downward.

"Don't you knock?" I growl, breathing hard.

She doesn't answer me. Instead, she just stands there, watching me with my hand on my cock.

Her jaw hangs open.

Her flushed cheeks and dilated pupils tell me she likes what she sees. She wants it.

A small whimper escapes her, pushing me over the edge.

It's too late. I'm too far gone. I can't stop this train wreck.

I climax hard, groaning as my juices spurt out into the tissue.

Her eyes travel upwards and lock onto mine, shocked.

"This is a private office," I snarl as I wipe my semen on the tissue. "You can't just waltz in whenever you feel like it. Didn't you see the fucking blinds down? Do you think you have special rights?"

She opens her mouth to speak then closes it.

I'm furious. With which one of us, I cannot fathom. Her for storming through my office uninvited or me for not being able to stop myself from erupting in front of her.

She bends down to fumble with the papers she dropped, and I realise just how nervous she is.

"Sorry," I say softer as she scrabbles with the paper on the floor. I fix myself back in my pants. "You weren't supposed to see that."

"I wanted to talk about my employment contract," she stammers, staring at the floor. "I'll come back when you have your hands free."

I laugh despite my compromising situation. The girl is sassy, I'll give her that.

The door slams shut.

I freeze. The car will be outside now for the awards ceremony. Did I really just finish myself off in front of an employee? In front of Tristan's little sister?

I breathe out sharply. I've been in hot water before, in situations where HR had to intervene, and had one too many libel cases brought against me, but this is a whole new level.

I laugh hard.

This could be the biggest fuck up of my career and yet the most arousing.

## Charlie

I close the door and hear him fumble with the latch behind me.

*Did that just happen?*

Did I really interrupt Danny Walker's most private moment and just stand there and watch?

Michelle, his PA, looks at me questioningly from behind her desk. "Anything else you need?"

Yes, please, a tub of ice to submerge myself in, to stop burning up.

I must look strange, standing here frozen to the spot clinging to documents.

"No," I respond in a jerky voice, walking off. I need to steady my breathing.

*He saw me and didn't stop.* He kept his gaze on me and kept going until he ejaculated, right there with me watching.

I can say, without a doubt, that was the most sexually charged experience of my life despite the fact I wasn't directly involved. I never took myself for a voyeur before.

I'm slick between the legs. Watching him come undone in front of me has turned me into a bitch in heat.

I need to get out of the office. My vagina is throbbing.

The *look* on his face. His orgasm face. Something I never thought I'd get to see.

Watching his liquid spurt out, so much of it, I wanted him to empty inside *me*. Every last drop. It was so damn thick, so angry looking. Like it could tear me apart. I wanted to run and grab it in my hands and bury it deep in me.

And those *eyes*. How he stared at me with such conflicting anger and lust. No man has ever looked at me like that before.

No wonder women fling themselves at him.

He's destroyed me. I'll never be able to have sex with another man again without being disappointed.

I take a slow, deep breath as I get into the elevator.

The employment contract shakes in my hands, the ends of it saturated in sweat. I'll have to print another one.

Mr. Big Shot Danny Walker, multi-millionaire CEO, so in control of every part of his life and everything around him, caught with his hand down his pants masturbating to a video with me in it.

I smile to myself like a fool.

He thinks I didn't see the video. It was from the party; I recognised the blue lights of the stage. I don't know who took it, though, it seemed to be from a bird's eye view.

Was it me that he was masturbating to? Or Jen?

I look down to see soaking patches under my arms. Same as between my legs.

At least I've time to change before the speed dating event Julie has bullied me into this evening. Although how I'm supposed to make light conversation with a load of dudes after witnessing *that* is beyond me. I need some serious advice and hard liquor to navigate through this one.

# 11

**Charlie**

"We need to distract you, Charl. This will be good for you." Cat looks at me encouragingly. "You might actually meet a decent bloke here."

I've been in a daze ever since I closed the door to his office.

We're in a bar in Leicester Square, central London, waiting for a round of speed dating to start. Technically, Suze, Julie, and I are speed dating, but Cat and Stevie have tagged along to observe the mating rituals from afar.

We've spent the past hour dissecting the scene I walked into in Danny Walker's office.

"Are you sure?" they kept asking.

"*Yes, I recognise a dick when I see one,*" I confirmed.

They're sceptical.

I get it; it's unbelievable.

Even I'm starting to think I imagined it. For five years I've worked in that company, and the most gossip we had was Jackie shagging the intern in the photocopier room.

Within one week, Danny Walker has bulldozed in, bribed me to leave, said I remind him of a stripper, and accidentally masturbated in front of me.

We change the conversation at the insistence of Stevie, who is sick of talking about Danny Walker's beautiful dick.

God damn, that dick could be the star in a TV series.

"What about the Swedish guy?" Suze nudges me. "Focus, Charlie. Stop thinking about Danny Walker."

I shake my head. "Nah. He's gone silent."

Stevie sniggers. "What did you do this time?"

"I'm not sure." I take a sip of my wine, thinking. "He asked me what I wanted to do on our date, and I sent him a link to a taxidermy class in East London. Haven't heard from him since."

There's silence.

"Taxidermy?" Cat repeats slowly.

"As in what the guy did in Psycho?" Stevie chimes in.

I nod. "Yes, that's it. Taxidermy, stuffing animals."

"Oh. What would you be stuffing?"

I shrug my shoulders. "A mouse. I spotted it on Timeout. I thought he would think I was adventurous. Remember our 'try everything once' pact?"

Cat frowns. "You never told me you're interested in taxidermy."

"You told the Swedish guy?" Stevie shakes his head.

I sit up defensively. "If I can't be honest, there is no point pursuing it. If he's not man enough for it—"

"Probably best to keep a bit of mystery

sometimes, Charlie," he butts in. "Considering you haven't met the guy yet. For the next guy, just say that drinks are fine. Stick to the script. Best not to mention anything about your hobbies."

I release a snort. "So, one little dead mouse frightens blokes away?"

He looks at me like I'm a moron. "Most blokes aren't into women who dissect things. Makes them think there is a possibility of the woman going nuclear and one day chopping off their penis in a rage."

I pause. "It might not have been the taxidermy."

"There's more?" Julie barks.

The four of them look at me tentatively. "Sweet Jesus, you didn't tell him about the haemorrhoids, did you?"

I glare back at them. "No! Anyway, everyone gets haemorrhoids once in their lives!"

Cat turns to Stevie. "Not me, only Charlie."

He humours her by nodding then turns back to me. "Your pulling techniques are terrible."

"If he met you, he would realise how great you are." Cat rubs my arm. "But Stevie's right, when a guy chats over text, maybe you should just talk about going for dinner or something. Don't let him see what you're really like."

Suze nods in agreement. "You do better in person."

I tut. "That's if people would follow through and meet me. I swear, in this day and age of online dating, people are disposable. All these men make plans then don't follow through. I've had so many guys on Tinder contact me, and we'll chat for a few days back and forth, then boom! Nothing!"

Stevie looks at us knowingly. "That's because men are using the probability factor. They don't just say yes to who they like, they say yes to everyone. If their success rate is twenty percent, they need to say yes to four women."

"That's disgusting," I say, outraged. "And you can't count."

"Perhaps you're not filthy enough?" Suze asks. "Have you considered uploading nude pics? You could cut off your head, so no one knows it's you."

I choke on my wine. "I'm not taking nude selfies, Suze."

Cat shakes her head. "I don't understand. What happened to the old days of meeting someone in a pub? Now people would rather search through pictures than talk to someone in the flesh."

"We are living our lives online, and I'm sick of it." I sigh. "Would it have been as romantic if Richard Gere found Julia Roberts on a porn app?"

Cat giggles. "Or Ryan Gosling found Rachel McAdams through Snapchat?"

"It's too much! The guy I was talking to over Tinder, we haven't met, and he asks me if I want to become friends on Snapchat. Why, I ask? Because we can send each other pictures. But what good will pictures do? I can't talk to a picture."

"Speaking of apps and hobbies, tomorrow we're putting your songs on OpenMic," Cat says firmly.

"We've been talking about it for too long, Charlie. And that's something you say on a date, not taxidermy."

I roll my eyes. "Fine."

We've been talking about putting my songs on OpenMic for a year. It's a new app where people can rate your music. Ratings scare me. I don't want to be judged and rated. My target audience, friends of my mothers, aren't on OpenMic. But I need to shut Cat up once and for all.

Maybe we could put the songs up, then I'll take them down on the sly a day later.

*** 

Thirty minutes later, Suze, Julie and I share a bar table, waiting for the first round of speed dating to commence. The women sit in allocated seats while the guys rotate. We've been given score cards where we write the blokes' names down and an area to add comments, and we all have to wear name badges.

So clinical.

The first guy sits down in front of me. He's short, suited, and wearing glasses. Not my type, but I'm happy to have a chat for two minutes.

"Hi." I smile.

He peers at my name badge instead of meeting my gaze. "Sorry, I can't read that. Could you move your arm?"

Is this guy for real?

"You could ask me my name instead?" I suggest.

He tries to see past my arm, which I refuse to

budge.

I watch him write down 'Charlie' in very clear handwriting.

"Charlie." He sits up straight, pushing his glasses up his nose as if he's doing an inspection. "What do you do for a living?"

I'm bored now, and it's not even a minute in. "I work in I.T."

He nods approvingly and writes down 'IT' on the comment section beside my name. Clearly, I've ticked a box on his checklist.

"Great, and what's your favourite colour?"

I stare at him. "Why? What can you do with that information?" I don't have a favourite colour, it depends on my mood.

"Let's move on. Favourite animal?"

Sweet Jesus, I'm being interviewed by a four-year-old.

"My favourite animal? To do what with, eat? Breed? Ride? Taxidermy?"

He looks at me, waiting.

"You want a definitive answer? Fine. Rat."

His eyes narrow.

A phone bleeps.

"Is that the bell ringing?" I ask with feigned regret. "Times up, I think."

"No, it's a phone," he deadpans. "Do you like travelling?"

I glare over at Julie, who forced this on me.

"Twenty-five fucking quid," I mouth when she catches my eye. "Yes, I like travelling."

I turn back to my date. I need this bell to ring.

"Where have you been?"

"In my life?"

He nods.

"You want me to list all the countries I have been to in my life?"

He's waiting.

"Right, well how about I'll decrease the scope to this year, shall I? India and Seattle."

Our vibrant conversation is interrupted by the bell to signal we move on to the next date.

I glance over at the guy leaving Suze to join me. He looks about eighteen.

Jesus Christ.

We have twenty men to get through. It's going to be a long night.

*** 

Despite our best efforts, speed dating doesn't deliver us the men of our dreams, so we head home empty handed at 11 p.m.

It wouldn't have mattered if a Hollywood movie star had rocked up for a date; seeing Danny Walker in all his fierce, naked glory has now ruined my future love life. Every dick past this point will be sub-optimal.

My mind is still racing from the bizarre events of the day.

I hiccup loudly. I'm drunk after resorting to a round of shots to get me through the last five speed dates.

We turn the corner to our flat and I stop abruptly on the pavement, making Cat walk into the back of me.

"Jeez, Charlie, watch it."

There's a black Aston Martin parked across the road from the flat. On our street, it sticks out a mile.

My heartbeat races. I recognise the number plate from Tristan's house.

*He's here.*

Why is he on my street? Does he know that I live here? He is breaking so many rules in one day; it's a tabloid's wet dream. My wet dream too.

Thankfully I'm wearing the black dress.

I climb the steps to the flat with the four of them chatting gibberish around me, oblivious to my heart palpitations. I can't focus on a word they're saying.

"Cat," I mutter without moving my lips. "Get your keys out NOW."

"Alright, keep your knickers on," she huffs, fumbling in her purse.

I stare tunnel-visioned at the flat and ignore the Aston Martin.

I'm not brave enough to look over at the driver; my knees might give out. This is *my* territory. He's not supposed to be here. I can handle him in glitzy bars or talking on stage at events, not here outside my flat.

Once we are in the hallway, I slam the door closed, collapsing up against it.

What now? Knowing he is metres away is bringing on an angina attack. What the hell is he doing here?

Is he here to issue me an injunction order to stop me talking about what I walked in on? Or personally deliver a P45? I've never been in this situation, but I'm pretty sure this is his fault. OK, I did just barge in, but I wasn't expecting a naked dick to be on display.

It's a tech company, not a titty bar.

Is it even legal to masturbate in an office? Regardless if he owns the company? I've no time to consult the resident lawyer, Julie.

He knows I'm here. *I'm so not prepared for this.* Everything I said before was Big Girl Talk, empty bluffs, shit-talking.

Sure enough, the buzzer goes. He doesn't waste time.

I freeze, gripping the inside of the door.

"Did you order a takeaway?" Cat walks into the hall and stares at me questioningly. "It doesn't open by leaning against it, you know."

"Cat," I hyperventilate. "It's *Danny Walker*."

She halts mid-step. "Here?"

Both of our eyes widen when we hear another persistent buzz.

"How do you know it's him?"

"The car was outside."

"Oh." Her mouth falls open. "Are you going to let him in?"

"I don't know." I swallow, staring back at her. "My head's spinning from the shots. I can't think straight."

The bell buzzes again.

Julie charges into the hallway. "Who the hell is buzzing?"

Cat looks at her meaningfully. "It's Danny Walker."

"Here?" Julie barks.

I nod, biting my lip.

"Interesting." She smirks. "Dammit, girl, you have him by the balls! Take them!"

"I don't know what that means," I hiss back.

"It means take control, Charlie," says Julie incredulously, yanking a button open on my black dress. "This is your territory. Seduce him."

Before I can stop her, Julie leans over me and presses the button to open the door.

"And take off those massive pants, for Fuck's sake!" she snaps. "He'll see you have no VPL. Works every time."

I hear the outside front door of the house open and slam shut, then heavy footsteps climb the stairs.

There's a loud knock on our flat door.

Cat scuttles down the hall, grinning, followed by Julie mouthing 'take them off.'

In the absence of a well-thought-through strategy, I whip my underwear off and stuff them behind the radiator.

On the other side of the door, he clears his throat with more than a hint of impatience.

I stealthily retreat a few steps into the hallway to pretend I haven't been hiding behind the door, then take loud deliberate steps back towards the door.

Trying to slow my breathing, I swipe the latch

and open the door, meeting his gaze head-on.

"Danny?" I say, my voice pitched too high.

He's wearing his tailored blue suit from work minus the suit jacket. The white shirt is rolled up to his elbows, showing his gorgeous, tanned arms layered with dark hairs.

His eyes rake down my body and back up again, a cynical smile reaching them as he fixes his stare back on my face.

I feel it in my gut.

"Nice dress. Suits you."

"What are you ... why are you here?" Standing in the doorway, I shift my weight from one foot to another.

He looks taken aback. "I'm here to apologise."

Not a single speed date came close to making me quiver like that dry Scottish voice does.

His brows rise. "Can I come in?"

"I guess." I open the door wider, and he follows me down the hallway.

Stevie and the girls are sitting transfixed on the sofa, blatantly eavesdropping. They might as well have popcorn in their hands.

"Mr. Walker," Stevie mumbles, eyes like saucers.

He greets them with a curt nod then turns to me. "Can we go somewhere private?"

"We only have one living room. So it will have to be my bedroom?"

Hesitance flickers over his face, then he nods his consent.

"OK," I shrill, mentally visualising the state of my

bedroom. "This way."

He follows behind me, the scent of his cologne filling the hallway. Damn, that's delicious.

I push open the bedroom door. It's worse than I imagined. "I wasn't expecting visitors."

I flinch as his eyes scan the room. There are clothes and underwear mixed in with shoes and books all over the floor. As if I'm boycotting wardrobes.

"Take a seat." I beckon to my pink armchair in the corner.

He lifts a collage of large underwear from the armchair, holding them out in his hands. "What would you like me to do with these?"

Shit. My time of the month pants. Nobody on this earth should be exposed to those except for me.

"I'll take those," I say, snapping them from him and bundling them under a pillow.

He squeezes into my dainty chair, looking entirely out of place, his thick legs spreading outwards.

He's too big, too manly, too overwhelming for my room. It dawns on me that this is the first proper man I've had in here.

I perch on the side of the bed, facing him, very aware of my pantyless state. *If I move my legs at all, he'll see everything.*

"Drink?" I ask, trying to sound casual.

"No. I'm OK. I've got a work call after this. I can't drink any more this evening." He smiles politely, leaning back in the chair.

*After what?*

I watch him, not knowing where to go from here, then break the silence. "Have you been out this evening?"

His shirt looks crumpled, and there is a faint smell of scotch coming from him. "I did the opening speech at a start-up awards ceremony," he explains casually. "Over in Canary Wharf."

Of course, he did.

Presenting at an awards ceremony is just another night for him. No different to the movies or a takeaway.

"See any companies you want to take over?"

"A few," he replies deadpan, my sarcastic tone wasted on him. He studies me with a hint of suspicion. "Where were you tonight?"

"At an eighteen-to-thirty-something speed dating event," I admit.

"Eighteen to thirty," he repeats slowly. Something flares in his eyes, annoyance, perhaps? It's gone before I can decipher it. "What about the Ben bloke?"

"We're not together anymore." My stomach flutters. "I'm single," I add for the avoidance of doubt.

"I see." He looks at me with an unreadable expression. "See anyone you liked ... at this speed dating event?"

"No. No one interested me." *Not like you*, judging by the growing slickness between my legs as my bare flesh creates friction with the bed.

"I prefer older men," I announce with bravery

fuelled by Tequila. "Someone harsh, rough, bossy. Someone who will put me in my place."

Take the hint, man.

His eyes darken.

"You're better off with someone your own age."

I squeeze my legs tight together to hide my arousal.

I know I'm not imagining this. The sexual current in the room could be sliced with a knife.

He's just as unhinged as I am.

A sound comes from his pocket and we both look down at the interruption as he grapples to retrieve his phone.

"Sorry." He switches the phone to silent mode. "There's a critical call with the States tonight."

"Take it if you want," I offer, but he waves at me dismissively.

"It's OK. I'll leave soon and deal with it."

*If this is a fleeting visit, why is he here?*

"I get it." It dawns on me. "You've come here to shut me up about today. To make sure I don't report you to HR."

He frowns, cocking a brow at me. "I'm not worried about that. You came into the CEO's office unannounced." A smirk threatens his lips. "In fact, I could give you a warning."

"To stop me telling Tristan then," I say, huffily.

"Obviously, it would be preferable he didn't find out, but no, that's not the reason I came here."

My eyes follow his jawline as he runs a hand over his stubble.

"I'm here to apologise. I shouldn't have put you in that position. My actions were inexcusable. I just want you to know that's not something I do in the office. It was a one-off."

His fists clench around the sides of the armchair.

"I never meant for you to walk in on that." His voice is strained. "I locked the door. Or rather, I thought I had."

"I shouldn't have barged in," I admit, crossing and recrossing my legs. I can't keep still. Not when he's here in my room.

"In my defence, you could have immediately shut the door." His lips twitch slightly. "If you tell Tristan, you'll have to explain to him how you stayed until the end."

"I wanted to see what part of the video you would finish to," I fire back.

He swears under his breath. "I didn't think you saw that."

For the first time since I've known him, I see a flush rise in his cheeks. Not so sure of yourself now are you, Mr. Walker?

"It was me, right?" I probe, needing to be certain.

His eyes darken to almost black as he looks back and forth between mine. "You know it was you."

I swallow the lump in my throat. "How did you get the video?"

He pauses for a long moment. "I lost my watch and asked the bar for footage. You happened to be on it."

I look down at the expensive watch safely on his

wrist and raise a brow.

Now I'm confident I'm not imagining this. The chemistry charges between us, and he feels it as much as I do. He wants me as much as I want him.

"Why were you watching a video of me?" I whisper, already knowing the answer. "That footage was of me, and I'm not a watch thief."

His square jaw clenches. "I think you know why, Charlie. Do I need to answer that?"

I squirm, creating friction with the bed against my exposed clit. Wearing no underwear has tricked my core into thinking I'm getting fucked by him tonight, and I'm so ready, so swollen with need, I could explode just by rubbing against the bed.

He hasn't even touched me yet.

Our eyes lock, and I *know* he's having the same carnal thoughts as me. He wants to fuck me right here as hard as he can.

"Say it," I whisper.

He stares back at me through hooded eyes, the room so quiet I can hear his laboured breathing.

I part my thighs slightly. Just enough to give him a teaser, basic instinct style. I've never been this brazen before, not even with boyfriends.

His eyes drop downwards, and a tortured groan erupts from his throat. "Stop it, Charlie. You're drunk."

"Stop what?" I pout innocently, noticing with delight his trousers straining with an increasing bulge.

I swing my legs innocently over the side of the

bed.

"What the fuck are you playing at?" he whispers hoarsely, squirming in the seat. "This won't end well."

"Answer me," I demand, my eyes big. "Why were you watching that video?"

He glares at me, his knuckles clenched around the chair.

I glance down at his large, calloused hands and think about what they could do between my legs.

"Because I was imagining bending you over my desk, deep inside you, giving you the best orgasm you've ever had in your life."

I stop breathing. The words send an electric shock straight to my clit.

I want him buried deep in me *now*. I need him to fuck me so hard I beg him to stop. I need him to make me orgasm so loudly the entire street hears me.

The phone lights up on his knee as another call comes in.

"Put some underwear on, Charlie," he orders, his eyes almost begging me. "Before I do something I regret."

I smirk back at him. "It's my bedroom. I don't think your authority extends to bossing me around here."

"Don't push me," he growls, his lips drawing into a thin line. His mouth says one thing, but the massive tent in his trousers says another.

I get up from the bed and take a step towards him.

Before I can lose my nerve, I take his hand, prizing open the clenched knuckle.

"It's not fair to deprive me of my best ever orgasm," I say softly, trailing his hand up my bare leg.

"Stop, Charlie." He freezes as his hand approaches my inner thigh. "This isn't happening."

I ignore him.

"I mean it, stop," he repeats, his voice strained, making a half attempt to remove his hand.

His body disagrees as he widens his legs so I can stand in between them.

I lift my dress up so it bunches around my belly, and push my thighs against his knees as wide as I can. Now he can see everything. I'm pink, swollen, and soaking wet.

"You're soaking," he groans, running his tongue over his teeth.

"I've been wet ever since seeing my boss in a compromising position today," I whisper as he stares mesmerized at my slit. "I've been fantasizing about it ever since."

The tent in his trousers strains against the fabric, and he shudders, closing his eyes in an attempt to compose himself. "You're going to be the death of me."

When he opens them again, he looks at me with such pure carnal need, a gasp escapes me. "Open your pussy wide," he growls. "Let me see."

I'm so needy I obey without objection, stretching my slit open with my fingers.

"Yes," he groans, unable to tear his eyes away. "That's the most beautiful sight I have ever seen."

My pussy muscles clench as I imagine myself wrapping around his thick cock, swallowing it up.

"Charlie," he whispers darkly, his eyes holding mine. "You're so ready for me."

I'm so ready for him, it's embarrassing. I've never been this overly sexual, this desperate for a man. Nothing else matters but my need to come hard here and now, to leave him no doubt about how he leaves me a horny, quivering, hot mess.

His phone buzzes again angrily on his knee.

"Piss off, Karl," he mutters, firing it on the floor.

With one hand, I hold up my dress while my other hand tentatively runs over my slit. "I've never done this in front of anyone before," I whisper in a moment of insecurity.

"*Fuck.*" His jaw clenches hard as he tries to repress the indisputable lust holding him in turmoil. "That's the sexiest damn thing I've ever heard."

I slide my fingers in and out of my wetness, letting out a soft moan as I imagine *his* fingers exploring me, fucking me.

"Good girl. Do it for me," he growls. "Push your fingers deeper into your pussy."

I thrust deeper, my breath becoming shorter and faster as my head rolls back.

"No. Look at me," he scowls. "You need to look at me when you come."

I focus my gaze back on him as I thrust two fingers into my swollen flesh again, moaning loudly.

He looks at me like he's just been given the gift of sight.

I part my thighs wider, going deeper with my fingers, the sound of my slickness becoming faster and heavier in the air, consuming both of us.

My fingers find my swollen clit, and I rub my most sensitive spot in such a way so that he can see how pink and aroused it is. How much it is swelling for him.

His eyes stay fixed on my opening.

"Danny," I beg. "I want to see you. I want to see how turned on you are."

He sucks in a breath and closes his eyes. "If I take my cock out, it's going inside you." The threat in his voice makes me shiver. "I won't be able to stop."

My legs shake as my circular movements grow frantic and furious, my moans quick and desperate. "I want to feel you," I say breathlessly. "I'm so close."

He exhales heavily and jerks in the seat, his length bursting to be let out of his suit trousers. "I want to," he whispers, placing a hand over his hard cock. "So damn badly."

The look in his eyes of raw, animalistic lust tips me over the edge.

"Fuck me, Danny, please," I cry out, on the verge of breaking. "I want you inside me."

His eyes squeeze into thin slits as he struggles for control.

The sound of his phone repeatedly buzzes on the floor.

I let out a final cry as my arousal bubbles out of

control and collapse on top of him. I close my eyes, breathing hard.

Buried under my hair, I hear him attempting to steady his own raspy breathing.

"You've just ruined me forever," he growls from below me. "I'll never fucking recover from this."

I straighten up, grinning, with a post-orgasm rush.

"Charlie." He sighs, running his hands through his hair as the phone never stops. "I need to answer this."

Lifting the phone up, he gets to his feet and pushes me away gently.

I hear the furious voice of Karl down the phone. "What the fuck, man?" Karl roars. "Where are you? You were supposed to be on the call ten minutes ago. Are you trying to blow this fucking five million quid deal?"

Danny's eyes connect with mine as he grimaces. "Cool it, Karl, I'll be on in five minutes. I'm going to the car now."

"You're taking this conference call in your fucking car, Danny?" I've never heard Karl so angry, and I've definitely never heard him shout at Danny before. "Why are you not in your home office? The awards thing finished two hours ago! Where the hell are you? Do you know how unprofessional this looks?"

"Give me a minute, Karl." He switches onto mute, his expression pained and flustered as he locks eyes with mine. His voice switches to a soft tone: "I really have to go, Charlie."

"It's OK." I smile. "But in case you forget …"

I take his hand and trail it along my opening, still wet with arousal.

He groans, then his hands grip the back of my hair and pull my mouth onto his, attacking it furiously with his lips.

I open my mouth wide in response, my tongue meeting his with the same hunger he pushes into mine. I feel his hard length up against my stomach, and he pushes a finger deep into my core, making me cry out in his mouth.

"Seems like you've broken your promise of no touching," I moan softly.

He releases his wet finger from between my legs. "Seems like I have."

Then he's gone through the door with a furious Karl berating him down the phone, leaving me a sticky mess.

# 12

**Danny**

I wasn't lying when I told her she had ruined me. I almost blew a five-million-pound deal so that I could sit in a small girly flatshare, squirming in my own pre-cum watching a girl too young for me and completely off-limits, get herself off. Like a horny schoolboy.

Karl is still livid with me even though, by some miracle, I managed to salvage the deal. He was too furious to pull the details from me of why I was AWOL.

I couldn't explain it to myself, never mind Karl.

I take a swig of coffee. I was on the conference call until 2 a.m. and then had Karl bust my balls for thirty minutes after that. Telling me how reckless I was, how we had been working on this deal for months.

It was worth every minute.

Watching her get herself off was the biggest turn-on of my life.

The bloody simpleton Mike is droning on when I enter the boardroom. He thrusts his chest out to show me he has control of the room.

Compared to any of the Nexus offices, this place is a joke. The boardrooms are filled with dying technology that wastes half the meeting trying to establish a video-link and plastic chairs that look like they belong in a school.

I'll be glad to see the back of this pokey dump when we move them into the Nexus headquarters next week. Although half of them won't get to enjoy it for very long.

I scan the room, and all eyes are on me with one exception.

She stares intently at Mike like he's the most interesting man she's ever heard. I'm almost jealous. A flush creeps across her face.

I exhale hard as I sit down. My eyes drop to her long, toned legs. She must be about 5'7, still short compared to me. At 6'4, everyone is short beside me.

I take in every detail of her appearance, banking it in my mind for later. Up past her tight jeans hugging her thighs to where her long brown hair curls around the curve of her breasts.

*Fucking delicious.*

Mike clears his throat. "Boss, we were just recapping on what has gone well this quarter."

"Why?" I ask, frostily.

"Why?" he repeats less confidently.

"This is supposed to be a crisis meeting," I snap, leaning forward in my chair. "Not a meeting where you pat yourselves on the back saying what a great job you've done. Bluntly, these products are failing."

The room collectively inhales a breath.

"Sir," he stammers, "against our stats, we are—"

"Your stats are wrong," I cut in. "From now on, you measure against the Nexus stats. And against those, your products are failing."

"Mr. Walker," he braves again. "We've received positive feedback from all our major clients through the questionnaire we sent out."

I run my tongue over my teeth. I don't have the patience for this garbage. Together with spending half the night on calls to the States and a certain brunette keeping my dick awake, I'm tired as fuck.

"No new customers in three years. No increases in the current customer usage. Constant outages. High support calls. Bad reviews in the press," I list out through clenched teeth. Do I have to do their jobs for them? "This is where you can set yourself apart from others. Where is the initiative in this room?"

Now, none of them meet my gaze.

Mike clears his throat so much that he seems to be choking.

"Has *anyone* tried to address any of the issues rather than bury their heads in the sand?"

Tumbleweed.

The only sound is me angrily drilling my fingers on my laptop, trying not to punch a wall.

Why do I fucking bother? I should sack all of them on the spot. Most of them stare at the floor. I scan the room, demanding them to make eye contact with me.

My eyes flit to Charlie again.

Her cheeks redden as she looks up, then she turns

away.

As I glare at Mike, I let out a heavy breath. This is his fault, he's buried any last hope of innovation in this team.

"The software is ten years old with no proper design behind it, there's no strategic thinking. It's been a mismatch of add-ons and hacks over the years with not a single coherent design or vision," comes a strong voice from the other side of the room.

My eyes travel back to Charlie, surprised.

Her knuckles grip the side of the seat. "It's expensive to maintain, and we can't push new features fast enough. We do no user research on what our customers actually want. No new customers in three years because we've added so many hacks. It's an over-engineered system," she continues. "People are scared of it."

"Nonsense," Mike barks. "Charlie, I really don't think this is help—"

"Let her finish," I cut him off, raising my eyebrows for her to continue.

"The lack of increase in the current customer usage is because we're not adding the features they want." She pauses. "Constant outages are because we have an unsustainable hosting platform."

My attention is drawn to her mouth, but I find myself listening to what she's saying.

"High support calls because of our constant outages, obviously." She stops to take a breath. "I have a number of suggestions for quick wins that we could add that would cut development time but, ultimately, this software is built on aging technology. If we want new clients and to keep our existing clients, we need to redesign it top-down not bottom-up as we are currently doing."

I arch a brow. "Good, Charlie. I'd like my designers to hear your ideas."

A flash of annoyance passes over her, and I can't nail why. Is she pissed off at my surprise?

"I wholeheartedly agree with you," I reply firmly. "We need to invest in re-engineering this product from the top down. Remember, you have the backing of a global tech company now. I want to hear ideas on how we will make this happen."

I grit my teeth and wait.

Finally, they start talking, so I know they're not puppets, and ideas start bouncing around, tentatively at first, then boldly.

My attention drifts back to the leggy brunette.

She's facing me, but her gaze is on everyone but me. Is she embarrassed? Does she regret it?

It was obvious she'd been drinking. She isn't known for being so overtly sexual; such a tease. Then again, it was the first time in years I had been close enough to her to find out.

Her breasts rise up and down in her white shirt, triggering arousal in my groin.

She fidgets in her seat and uncrosses her legs, bringing the glorious memory flooding back.

The girl is sensational, there's no doubt about that. Karl and Jack have both said it themselves, although they somehow aren't as affected as me. A stare from those green eyes under their dark eyelashes and I turn to goo.

Seeing her play with herself was the hottest fucking turn-on of my life.

Pleading with me to take her, to have her. That pink, swollen, beautiful pussy; it could have been all mine. Knowing I'm the only man she's ever done that in front of.

*And the only man she ever will*, a small voice pipes up in my head out of nowhere.

My eyes rake over her body. I can tell she senses it; she bites her bottom lip, clearly anxious with the attention.

I should be motivating this group but instead, I want to order them all to leave so that I can rip her jeans to shreds and fuck her right here on the desk. Mount her like a fucking animal.

She felt so tight.

Feeling her wet flesh has left me harder than ever. She was soaking. I wouldn't last long the first time, not if she's that wet.

I watch her lips from across the room, those full pink lips, and they remind me of her other lips. I want both around my cock, sucking me dry.

Taking my length as I come inside her again and again.

She wants me sexually. I know that for sure now.

I put my laptop over my erection and silently command her to look at me.

Finally, our eyes lock, and her lips slightly part, a

glorious flush rising to her face as I eye-fuck her. I smile softly as our secret passes between us.

She stares down at my laptop. She knows *exactly* what I'm thinking. That I'm replaying the image of her fingers satisfying her swollen pink pussy in my head.

She's the most captivating woman I've ever seen.

"Mr. Walker?" I force my eyes off her and return to Mike.

"Say it again, Mike," I ask, irritated, forcing images of a naked Mike to calm my erection.

"What's our action plan?" he stammers.

What *is* my action plan? Where does this end?

Karl has been ranting to Jack and Tristan about my behaviour, and they are asking questions.

**She must have been a good lay,** Tristan joked in a text message this morning.

Tristan.

To him this would be the ultimate betrayal. I'm Daniel's godfather, for Christ's sake. The boy is named after me.

She won't tell him. I might get away with it. There's not a hope in hell she will want Tristan finding out about last night's events.

Besides, I haven't slept with her ... yet. Last night was all her doing.

But what happens if HR tells her she hasn't made the cut? She's so feisty and unpredictable.

Why am I kidding myself? She is in control. She is metaphorically leading me by the cock wherever she wants me to go.

## Charlie

Oh. My. God.

There's no return from this. No salvation.

Life imprisonment would be a better option than working under a guy who I threw myself at, begging him to take me, only to be rejected.

*Forced* myself upon.

Offered myself on a *plate*.

Who the hell does that?

Do I have *any* self-respect left? After living as a prude for the last twenty-eight years, I have now morphed into some desperate horny exhibitionist.

Of course he had an erection. He's a bloke. When the shots wore off, the reality and facts of the evening started to emerge. He tried to stop it. *Find someone your own age. You're drunk.*

How drunk was I? Every time I recall the events in my mind, they change.

When I finally got to sleep at 5 a.m., the sick dread had ravaged my mind so much I woke up sobbing.

He hasn't contacted me. Then to have to sit in that meeting with him ... my stomach was in knots the entire time to the point I thought I might be sick.

He looked so tired and irritated throughout the entire meeting. Why the hell did I think I could seduce a moody CEO who thinks his new child company has the collective intelligence of a gnat?

My hands shake as I adjust my glasses and try to focus on the screen. After Danny Walker's tongue lashing, everyone in the office is quiet and sullen.

I have four hours and twenty-three minutes until I can pick up my coat and run out of the building.

Mike sucks his teeth loudly beside me, stabbing at my nervous system. *Every time.*

"Fuck's sake."

I turn my head to see what he's complaining about and see Danny Walker advancing towards us, his face taut with tension.

Dark shadows circle his eyes, and his hair sits in an unruly mob on top of his head, but he's still devastatingly handsome.

He slams paper down in front of Mike's desk, and in a battle of teeth, bares his own to Mike.

I can't cope with this. I shrink into my chair, covering my face with my hand.

"A whole day, Mike?" Danny barks from my peripheral view. "The software was down for a whole day?"

My heart gallops. The damn outage. Mike knows nothing about it.

I spring to standing as if someone lit a match up my ass.

"Just a minute, Charlie," Mike barks, annihilating my escape.

I turn to them both, my stomach fluttering with unease. "Yes, Mike?" I ask softly.

"It's Charlie's responsibility to ensure we suffer no outages." He smiles triumphantly. "Charlie, please explain how this mistake was made."

I stare at him in disgust. Talk about throwing me under a bus.

My eyes dart from Mike's to Danny's to find he is watching me warily.

"Configuration changes weren't applied correctly to some of the servers," I say feebly. "I'm working on a report explaining the root cause and how to ensure it doesn't happen again."

We stare at each other, my skin pricking with embarrassment.

Danny runs a hand over his jaw. "Two days ago, and you haven't done the report yet?"

My entire face is on fire as I drop my head in shame. "We've had to resolve other critical issues since. I didn't have time."

"I'll make sure Charlie understands the repercussions, Danny," Mike sneers, and my eyes rise to glare at him. "This won't happen again."

"It's Mr. Walker to you," Danny growls, his jaw tight. "Don't blame your staff. You are Head of I.T., correct?"

Mike's face drops. "Yes but—"

"I'm sick of hearing excuses. Do your job and take accountability." Danny lets out a tired breath and turns his focus to me, wordlessly. For a horrifying moment, I think he's going to reprimand me for what I did last night. Who can tell with this man?

I fight back tears.

"Charlie, I want that report before you leave today," he says flatly, rapping his knuckles on the side of my desk as he starts to walk off.

"Yes, sir," I reply in a whisper.

He falters briefly in his stride, just enough so that

I see something dark flash across his face.

Four hours and ten minutes until I can hide from the world.

I've never felt so incompetent, as a female, as an employee and as a person.

# 13

**Danny**

**I believe you have my coat.**

"Danny? Did you hear what I said?" Jen leans across the table to shake my hand.

"Just a minute," I say, staring down at the phone. I can see her typing.

**I'm assuming this is Danny. Yes, it's here.**

The typing dots start appearing again.

**Do you want me to give it to Tristan?**

I sit up alert. Hell, no. What's she playing at? Is she threatening me?

**Definitely not. I'll collect it this evening.**

I could have told her to bring it to work. Or give it to charity. I have a hundred other coats.

**I'm busy this evening.**

I stare down. Jealousy spikes through me. What's she doing? Is she with a bloke?

**Busy all night?**

She types, then stops, then types again. Nothing comes through.

**Will you be home at 10pm?**

"Danny?" Jen says louder, pouting at me across the table.

The phone pings, and I exhale heavily, satisfied with the response.

I type back.

"Sorry," I reply sheepishly. "I'm distracted. I need to swing by the office after dinner this evening. I'll get you a separate car home."

Her eyes widen. "But you'll come back to mine afterwards, right?"

I sigh. What the hell am I doing? "Sure."

## Charlie

I pull open the shower door and step out into the steamy bathroom. The long shower has done nothing to quieten the shame. Wrapping my wet hair up in a top knot, I wipe the steam from the mirror. My bare, pasty face stares back at me.

I dry off and pull on my shorts and sweater. I couldn't have put in less effort if I had tried. The last thing I want him to assume is that I'm trying to maul him again. That ship has sailed.

My phone bleeps.

**I'm downstairs.**

Let's get this over and done with.

"Good luck," Cat mouths from the sofa as I walk past, grabbing his jacket.

He doesn't buzz. I guess he doesn't want to come anywhere near the flat. I open the door and trundle down the communal steps of the house we share with the lower ground flat.

Taking a deep breath, I open the front door to the house.

He looks down at his phone, a scowl covering his face.

"Hi," I greet softly as our gaze connects.

His expression softens slightly. "Charlie."

"I have your coat," I say quickly, offering it to him.

He takes it, a mild frown crossing his face.

"Listen, Danny," I start my prepared speech. "I have to apologise for how I behaved last night. It was completely inappropriate, and I deeply regret putting you in that situation. I'm starting to look for other jobs. I've even applied for a job in the Cayman Islands."

"Cayman Islands?" His mouth twitches as he looks down at me. "Isn't that a little extreme?"

"No, it's not," I snap, not appreciating the interruption. "I would also like to plead with you to kindly forget my indiscretion. It was totally out of character for me, and I am quite mortified."

Until I said it, I didn't realise how true it was. Tears swell in my eyes.

"It only happens with Tequila then?" His eyes crinkle with amusement. "No Tequila tonight?"

I don't find it very funny. *Don't play with me, you teasing bastard.*

"Don't laugh at me," I whisper angrily, facing the floor. A single tear rolls down my cheek, and I wipe my cheek quickly, thankful I'm not wearing make-up.

"Oh, Jesus, Charlie." He bundles me up in his arms, pressing my head against his chest. "The last thing I want is to upset you."

"I'm just embarrassed I threw myself at you." I sniff into his chest, feeling his heated breath on my forehand. "And now I have to see you in the office knowing you think I'm an imbecile who can't even write a report."

He lets out a heavy sigh on top of my hand. "I was cranky today. I didn't get much sleep. Perhaps I was a little … sharp with you."

"It's OK," I sniffle. "You were right to be angry."

He puts his hand under my chin and forces my head up. "Charlie, I can't treat you differently at work." His brows pinch together as he stares down at me. "But you don't need to be embarrassed. I'm just as much to blame."

I scrunch my eyes shut. "You rejected me."

He snorts. "You mean I used every ounce of willpower not to fuck you."

His hands clamp possessively around my lower back.

When I open my eyes, I see conflict raging through the intoxicating dark eyes.

"You have no idea how attracted I am to you, do you?" he whispers hoarsely. "If you haven't noticed, the sexual attraction between us is making me a little crazy."

A smile escapes my lips. "Really?"

"Really," he replies dryly. "You were close to getting fucked in the boardroom today."

*Shit.* My eyes widen.

"Damn, I'm regretting not putting on make-up, and brushing my hair tonight."

"Yeah, that makes me feel even guiltier." He laughs wryly. "Since you look about twenty without make-up."

I close the distance between us, pushing my body against his, and tilt my face upwards, my lips parting slightly.

*Kiss me, you damn fool.*

The internal battle in his head rages on across his face, and I know what side I'm on.

My hands clench tight around his waist so that his now-erect length presses hard against my lower stomach. With no shoes on, I need to reach up on my tiptoes.

He lets out a slow, tortured groan, then crushes his lips against mine, forcing my mouth open.

*Yes.* Exactly what I've been craving.

The coat drops to the ground, and he takes my head in both his hands, holding me in a grip.

My hands are all over his body, in his hair, over his firm pecs, his thighs, that washboard thick stomach.

I can't touch it all fast enough.

I reach down and wrap my hand around his hardness, and a low guttural moan erupts from his chest.

"I shouldn't be doing this," he says hoarsely, breaking free from the kiss.

My hand wraps defiantly around his cock.

"So you keep saying," I huff. "But you also said you could give me the best orgasm of my life. Bloody prove it."

He chuckles, his dilated pupils darkening to

almost black.

Without warning, he sweeps me up in his arms and pushes my legs around his hips so that I'm straddling his groin.

I let out a surprised yelp as he starts to ascend the stairs. "Put me down! We're going to fall."

Ignoring me, he continues until we reach the top step. "Open the door," he demands gruffly, his breathing laboured.

"It would be easier if you put me down." I giggle, pulling my keys from my pocket.

After a few tries, the door opens, and he jolts it wider with his foot, walking down the hall to my bedroom, carrying me like I'm the weight of a book.

He throws me down onto the bed and climbs on top, forcing my legs open with his knee. With the same aggression, he takes the hem of my shorts and underwear and tugs both down together so that I'm naked from the waist down; my heated, swollen pussy exposed.

Panting, I lift out one leg at a time, and he fires the underwear on the floor.

*Fuck.* Heat pools in my stomach with the anticipation that this is finally happening.

I grind against his knee, creating a damp spot on his suit trousers.

"Widen your legs so I can look at you." His voice is thick and throaty.

I push my legs against his knees as wide as I can, and he hovers over me.

My lips part, and I let out a small moan as his

fingers explore my wet slit.

"Fucking hell," he groans as his fingers slip. "You're so tight I'd break you."

I clench around him.

"Charlie," he hisses as his eyes grow massive.

His lips crash down on mine, and I wrap my arms around his neck, holding on like my life depends on it.

I moan into his mouth as he circles my opening, teasing me. I grind against them impatiently, wanting them inside. I need his fingers to be deep inside me. I arch my back upwards, thrusting myself into his hand.

"Please, Danny," I pant, looking up at his giant frame.

He pulls away from my lips and looks down at me. "Yes, say my name, sweetheart."

The bedroom door creaks slightly as Cat or Julie walk down the hall, and we both look up momentarily.

"Danny," I cry louder, grabbing his hair with my hands.

Using one hand to keep his weight above me, he widens my legs further with the other so that I'm spread across the bed. Then, watching my face, his index and middle fingers enter deep, thrusting in and out of my wet opening.

I cry out as his strong fingers fuck me again and again, my insides growing wetter with each penetration.

My hands fall back above my head on the bed. I'm

incapacitated. I need him to make me come hard. I moan loudly as my pussy clenches around his fingers.

What the hell is happening? I never made noise with Ben or other blokes. Now I'm wailing like a banshee.

"So tight," he groans, hot breath on my face. "Do you know how good you feel, sweetheart?"

I stare into his beautiful face, his mouth hanging open, any remnant of composure gone. In all his speeches and talks, I've never seen him more focused than he is now, never seen this carnal determination on his face.

He catches my stare and pushes his lips back onto mine again, his harsh stubble razoring my face.

My breath quivers as he pushes a third finger into me, quickening the rhythm.

Then he pushes up onto his knees, and his other hand makes its way to my throbbing clit, dying for attention.

"*Oh, God,*" I whimper, pushing my head backwards into the pillow as he caresses my bud.

The sound of my dampness echoes through the bedroom with his strokes, making him release a low growl.

I'm drenched.

"I've been wanting to hear this for a very long time."

"We're so loud. Someone will hear us," I rasp through broken pants.

"Let them hear." He strokes so furiously a sheen of

sweat forms on his forehead.

Aching to explode, I claw at his biceps to push his hands deeper into my core.

"Come for me, baby," he whispers as my body jerks and spasms against his touch.

"Danny!" I cry out. "I can't take it." My voice is so high pitched I barely recognise it. My core is so close to explosion it hurts. "It's too much."

He kisses my forehead gently. "It's OK, baby, let it happen. I need to see you come." He sounds almost begging. His eyes bore down on me, hard and determined, "Scream my name."

Our breaths quicken together as I feel the eruption of my orgasm bubble to the surface. My legs jerk as I come harder than I ever have before, screaming his name loudly—no longer caring if the whole damn street can hear—and release my juices into his eager hands.

"Yes." He collapses on top of me, a boyish grin spreading across his face.

My legs engulf his waist, my open wet sex rubbing against his stomach.

I stare up at the ceiling, stunned, as he tries to steady his breathing. We haven't had sex and he just gave the best orgasm of my life with his fingers. I am so screwed.

There is no point of return from this. No other man's fingers can compete.

Lifting his head from where it was buried in my hair, he strokes my cheek, and I feel my juices on his hands.

We stare at each other for what seems like an eternity as I wonder what the hell just happened.

"You kept your promise." I smile softly as he traces a line across my bottom lip. My lips feel swollen and used.

"What do you do to me, Charlie?" He frowns as his eyes scan my face. "I can't seem to keep control when you're around."

My hands trace his sharp, square jaw. "Do you always have to be in control?"

A smirk hovers on his lips. "Yes."

I open my mouth to give a witty comeback but instead, a nervous giggle comes out. Something about his tone told me he meant it.

"Now, if you'll excuse me." He smiles crookedly. "I've been bursting to go for an hour. Where's your toilet?"

"Next door on the left," I reply, lying back contentedly on the bed.

"Ok." He climbs off the bed and gives me a loaded wink. "I'm just getting started with you."

He stops when he gets to the door and turns around. "There's no coming back from this, Charlie. I've opened a floodgate that I won't be able to close."

"I know," I whisper back from my position on the bed.

His eyes travel down my body, naked from the waist down, and he flashes a boyish grin I've never seen until tonight.

As he leaves, I lie back in a post-orgasmic trance. Danny Walker's fingers have been inside me. It was miles better than my fantasies, and I had fantasised about it A LOT.

I stretch my hands out on the bed and hit something hard.

His phone. There's a message flashing on the screen. I wonder if it's from Tristan. If only he knew.

It's from Jen. I sit up, suddenly alert.

I read the message, then read it again … and again.

**Thanks for a lovely dinner tonight. Drop by when you're finished in the office. I'll be waiting up x**

# 14

## Charlie

I jolt upright in the bed.

*No, no, no, what have I done?*

Danny was with Jen before he came here, and now he's going back to her? What was this, a quick finger fuck visit?

Suddenly I feel stupid ... and dirty. It's not like I expected us to be exclusive after our brief interlude this evening but surely bouncing between two women on the same day is against the rules?

Sleazebag.

Yet I can't even blame him. Once again, I've thrown myself at him. Of course, he wasn't going to stop me.

His words echo in my head. He warned me, but I ignored him.

*There's a reason why Tristan warned me to stay away from you. He knows me too well.*

My eyes well up with tears. I need to compose myself before he comes back. I hear the toilet flush and grab my shorts, fumbling to get them up my legs.

I don't want to have this conversation. What

would I say? It wasn't like I didn't know he was with Jen. He never lied to me.

Before he can enter, I yank the bedroom door open.

"Hey." He tucks a strand of hair behind my ear and smiles.

"Look, you need to leave," I reply hurriedly. "This is a mistake."

He freezes in the doorway, bewildered. "What happened while I was in the bathroom?"

I move into the hallway sidestepping him, but not before he grabs my arm.

"Charlie?" His brow furrows into a deep frown. "I don't understand."

Of course he doesn't, he's a pro at casual flings. Trying to explain why I have a split personality would involve admitting feelings that have been bubbling for a decade. But I can't do that. I'm *not* letting Danny Walker see me cry.

Untangling my arm, I walk down the hall. "Let's forget it happened, Danny."

I hear his footsteps following me into the living room.

Julie, Cat, and Stevie freeze mid-sentence.

"Can we talk about this in private?" he demands, staring at me and ignoring the others. "What the hell is making you blow so hot and cold?"

I cast my eyes downwards. "I got caught up in the moment, but this is not a good idea. Can we just leave it at that?"

"Could you say that to my face rather than the

sofa?"

"Can you please just go?" I look up at him pleadingly. If he doesn't go, I'll break down in front of him.

Danny watches me with a deep scowl on his face as the room becomes awkwardly quiet.

Julie and Cat sit upright on the couch holding their breath, like if they don't move, we'll forget they're there. Even Stevie sits timidly at the corner of the sofa. They exchange glances between them.

"Is this about the outage report?" Danny asks in a level tone. "You want me to go easy on you?"

"What?" *Seriously?* Does he really think I'm that childish? I look at him incredulously. "No." My lips form a thin line, not backing down.

After an eternity, he exhales harshly. "Fine. Whatever you want."

The other three stare at me gobsmacked as he storms down the hallway to my bedroom.

"What the hell hap—" Cat shrieks, stopping mid-sentence when he reappears with his suit jacket slung over his shoulder and his phone in hand.

"If you figure it out, you can enlighten me," he mutters, his dark eyes trying to make contact with mine. "Rather than this mindfuck."

Fidgeting with the drawstring on my shorts, I force a smile. "Bye Danny, sorry about this evening."

"I'm not sorry," he replies through clenched teeth.

I fixate on the armrest.

*Leave.* Just leave.

The room is frozen in a weird pose. Julie and Cat

stare at the TV even though the sound is off. Stevie sinks into the sofa in an attempt to disappear from his boss's boss's boss.

Danny stands with his arms crossed in front of me, demanding that I look at him. "Is this seriously it, Charlie?" he finally asks in a strained tone. "What the fuck just happened?"

"A mistake," I croak.

"Bullshit," Danny barks back, slamming his hand against the wall and making the four of us jump.

He breathes out angrily. "Charlie?" he growls as he opens the door. "Contact me when you've grown the fuck up."

***

"Let's nail this fucker."

"I'm not sure, Julie." I slump into the sofa. "I just want to forget the whole ordeal."

She smacks her lips in dissatisfaction. "You do realise that dirty dipshit is fucking her right now?"

"Don't," I whimper, clutching my chest tightly.

She tuts at me. "You're letting him treat you like a whore. Didn't he tell you that you looked like a stripper?"

"She's right," Cat chimes in. "He tries to get rid of you from the company, then he plays you for a fool, stopping by for a quick bootie call."

"To be fair, I got more out of it tonight than he did," I point out meekly.

Cat groans. "We know, we heard."

"Sorry." My cheeks colour.

"Nonsense," Julie snaps. "If he had the chance, he would have fucked you, but you saw the message. Do you want to be the one-hour booty call? Do you?"

"No," I reply in a small voice as I stub my toe into the carpet.

Stevie shakes his head. "Honestly, Charlie, there's no dressing it up. It sounds like you were a stopover. You have to admire the guy for his stamina. Two in one night at his age."

"Thanks, Stevie." I poke him hard in the ribs. "Nice to see you admire your new boss so much."

I'm so stupid. What did I expect? To lift my skirt, and he would be mine forever? I know his reputation. From Tristan, from the *media*, for Christ's sake. From my own eyes. I've seen him at parties. So why did I ignore the facts?

"What if he tells the management team?" Stevie asks. "I better not be implicated in this; I'm an accomplice."

My eyes widen. "He wouldn't do that."

Julie sneers, "Oh, please. He wants a side fuck. Now you've consented, he'll disclose whatever it takes to cover his own back. It's always the women that end up being disgraced. You'll be known as the girl who slept with the boss, and he'll be the stud."

*Would he?*

The small voice in my head reminds me of his reputation.

"You might never work in this town again!" Cat adds dramatically.

I throw a cushion at her.

Staring between the three of them, I open and close my mouth. "What would we do? You know, just to scare him and show him I'm not a pushover?"

Julie sits up in business mode. "I'll go after him for indecent exposure. You caught him masturbating in public. The grey area is that you burst in through his door, so we might have a hard time arguing that it was in public. Also, we need to prove intent to cause distress by the act."

I grimace. "I wouldn't exactly call it distressing."

"No." She exhales briskly. "You stayed to watch the show, which weakens our case."

"Also, you invited him into your bedroom and up your skirt," Cat points out.

"Irrelevant," Julie snaps. "His act of exposure left her vulnerable, and he seduced her. Look," she says impatiently, "when I'm at work, I'll send you enough ammunition to prove that you're not a soft touch. Think of it as a legal rough up from the heavies."

I nod. I'll read it for entertainment value. I doubt I'll act on it.

Groaning, Stevie shakes his head. "Keep me the hell out of this. Some of us want to keep our jobs. I still get paid for eight hours a day, even if I'm useless and only work three."

"So, what's his deal?" Cat looks at me curiously. "He's always so moody. At the party, he had a permanent scowl on his face."

"I feel a bit bad sharing this," I start, rubbing the rim of my wine glass. "It's quite a sad story. He grew up on a rough council estate in Glasgow. His father was a proper scallywag. Disappearing for days then when he did come home, he would be so high on drugs that he'd beat Danny's mum. One day, when Danny was about fifteen, he came home to find his mum lying in a pool of blood in the kitchen. His dad had shot her then shot himself."

They stare at me, transfixed.

Stevie exhales. "Christ, no wonder he's so … dark."

"His teens were pretty fucked up," I continue. "He went to live with his gran or someone in a remote village in Scotland. Then he went to university in England and met Tristan. They became close, and he started spending weekends at our house. After what happened, Mum felt sorry for him and was happy to get to cook for someone else. He was always there when I was growing up. He became a bit of an extension of our family. Tristan even made him godfather."

"And you are godmother," Cat muses.

"Kinky." Julie smirks. "So you've known him since you were ten, huh? I dread to imagine the wild teenage dreams with *that* walking around the house."

"I wouldn't say I *know* him," I reply. "I only know his backstory from eavesdropping when I was younger and Tristan telling me the tame snippets. I was never allowed to ask Danny outright."

"But you used to fantasise about him, right?" Julie questions.

"Of course." I roll my eyes. "Mega crush."

I shudder. "When I was thirteen, he brought a

girl to our house for dinner. I stormed off to my room and threw a massive hissy fit. The whole house could hear it from the dinner table. Danny had to come up and tell me I was still his favourite girl. Thinking about it, we had a better relationship when I was thirteen," I add wryly. "He used to buy me little gifts. After the dry humping debacle where I made a total tit out of myself, he grew distant with me. The majority of his communication with me the past ten years has been grunts and monosyllables."

Julie shakes her head. "You've liked this guy for nearly twenty years. You're supposed to move on from your first crush."

"This is why your love life is suffering now," Cat adds. "You compare everyone to him."

I take a large gulp of wine. "I can't seem to act rationally when he's around. I turn into a quivering emotional nutcase."

My phone bleeps on the sofa.

**Don't play games with me, Charlie.**

I read it out loud.

"Is that a threat?" Cat shrieks. "What does that mean?"

I save his contact in my phone, not that I needed it to know it was him. No one else speaks this bluntly. No '*Hi*.' No '*It's Danny, by the way*.' No kisses.

"Look at this." I show them my phone so they can see the contact picture. Danny is sitting in a plane cockpit wearing a pilot headset. There is a glimpse of a smile on his face.

Cat grabs the phone, moaning softly. "Are you

kidding me? Tell me that's fake before my ovaries explode in a hot mess. Tell me he's not an actual pilot. Can the guy get any more orgasm-inducing?"

"Every woman's wet dream." I screw my face into a grimace. "He has a small aircraft licence. I think he even owns a plane up in Scotland."

"Send me this picture before I go to bed tonight."

I stare at Cat. "That's not helping. So? What do I reply?"

"Nothing," Julie answers, snatching the phone from Cat. "Not a damn thing. If you reply, he'll know he's got you. Just leave it. Don't forget he's with Jen right now, texting you. What an asshole."

My heart sinks. I didn't need the reminder. I know one thing for sure. Danny Walker will never fully be mine.

"Forget dirty Danny Walker." Cat lifts out her laptop from under the coffee table. "So what if he's a zillionaire CEO pilot with a body like Satan? *You*, lady, are going to be a superstar."

She beams as she turns her screen to face me. It's got OpenMic launched on it.

"I'm not sure about this, Cat." I chew on my bottom lip. "Haven't I had enough humiliation for one week?"

"Just one song as a tester," she pleads. "Something to add to Danny Walker's wank bank."

"Fine." I sigh. "But that is not the reason I'm agreeing to this."

# 15

**Charlie**

It's Wednesday morning, and I'm staring at the email from Julie rather than the mountain of support calls. Danny Walker has ignored me all week, acting as if I don't exist. Clearly, Jen had serviced him sufficiently, so he has no further need for me.

There have been zero messages after I failed to reply to the '*don't play games with me*' message.

Who does he think he is, for Christ's sake? Al Capone? Who talks like that?

I hate that he affects me so profoundly that he consumes most of my thoughts. Such wasted effort.

Everyone else in the office gets a nod of recognition or even a hint of a smile. Me? The one time we walked past each other, getting in and out of the elevator, he looked straight through me as if I was a ghost. I'm starting to think the guy is a sociopath.

Julie was spot on. I can't trust him.

I'm paranoid every time I hear someone whispering in the office, and I swear Michelle, his PA, is laughing at me when I walk past her.

It doesn't help that everyone else in the office is as pathetic as me. People are tripping over themselves to be in his eye line like he's some sort of god. Jackie's skirts are so tight now it takes her ages to shuffle anywhere.

Even the men are flirting with him.

To make matters worse, Mike has been raving to anyone that will listen about his 'night out with the big boys' this evening. Danny is treating the leadership team to an all-expenses-paid night at the swanky new bar in the hotel beside the office. I have visions of them laughing as Danny regales tales of his Friday bed-hopping activities.

A small part of my head knows he's better than that.

I scan the email again and flinch. Julie doesn't mince her words.

**I am writing to express my concern over your inappropriate use of nudity in the work area and inability to follow your own company's code of conduct....**

**...my misconduct concern is related directly to you, as CEO....**

**....Your lewd, inappropriate sexual act has brought on unwanted anxiety for me in the workplace. Please confirm how you intend to rectify the situation.**

I chuckle to myself, imagining Danny's face when this pops up in his inbox.

No, I'm not sending that.

**Please note that I will not accept bribery or pay-out to be silenced for your sexual indiscretions.**

I quickly close the email. Danny Walker would hit the roof if he caught wind of this.

When I open my phone, ready to text Julie to warn her to cool it, I see five missed calls from Mum. Great.

If I don't call back, the calls will continue all day.

I hit redial.

"I wouldn't like to imagine what would happen if someone passed away, Charlie. We would have the funeral before you picked up your phone." Not 'hello' or even a 'how are you?' That's my mum.

"Has anyone died?"

"Of course not!"

"Well then, is there any need to call me so many times when you know I'm working?" I snap. I don't have the patience for this today.

"If you answered the first time, I wouldn't have to call the other four times," she bleats in her faded Southern Irish lilt. "Charlie, I'm not well," she continues at great speed.

I'm not alarmed. "What's wrong?"

"Janey Davidson is stressing me out." Poor Janey Davidson. Ever since Mum moved into the new house Tristan bought her in St Albans, she hasn't been able to acclimatise to the hip neighbours.

"What has she done now?"

"What has she done?" Mum squawks so loudly I flinch. "I'll tell you what she has done. She has taken up piloting in her front garden! She's been strutting around in a bra with her fat arse and these great big jugs bouncing around, trying to do the splits. Right in front of me! I can't even enjoy my own garden without her getting naked. It is a complete disgrace on the street!"

"Do you mean Pilates?" I question incredulously.

"Sure, isn't that what I said? She's driving down the bloody value of the properties in the street. You wouldn't get that in Cork, I tell you what, this country ..."

I hear this line almost every day of my life, in supermarkets, parks, bus stations, houses, planes, dentists, any open space you can imagine. *You wouldn't get that in Cork.*

"Pilates is a very normal way of keeping fit," I explain. "Janey has every right to do it in her garden."

She sucks in a breath. "That strip show isn't normal at her age! It's immoral. Who deals with these types of matters, the council?"

"Do not call the council, Mum," I warn. "They'll tell you off for wasting their time. Again. Just ignore it—"

"Betty, get out," she roars down the phone. "Charlie, I have to go; the rabbits have broken out and are running riot."

I stare up at the ceiling. Why doesn't Tristan get these critical calls?

"But before I go, I have more news."

"Oh yeah?" My ears prick up. I sense I'm not going

to like the sound of this.

"I'm coming to visit you this Saturday before Tristan's fortieth dinner party."

"We just celebrated Tristan's fortieth. How many parties does he need?"

"Don't be childish, Charlie," she tuts. "This is for family and close friends. He barely got to speak to us at the last one. Expect me at 10 a.m."

The phone goes dead before I can retaliate.

*Family and close friends.* So not only do I get to spend the workdays being iced by Danny Walker, now I get to spend my Saturday night doing the same.

Everything is too closely intertwined. I need to move cities and change my birth certificate.

My phone buzzes again. It's Cat.

"I just checked Mark out on Facebook," she announces breathlessly. "You have to see this."

Mark is my online date for this evening in an attempt to stop obsessing over Danny Walker.

"Oh, God." I groan. "What is it? Is he married? Girlfriend? Gym selfies? Skinny jeans? Satanist?"

"No, nothing like that!"

"Is he a chav?" I ask. "Sometimes, I don't mind a bit of chav."

"No, listen, it's not that," she says excitedly. "Charlie, he is *gorgeous*. I mean, drop-dead gorgeous. Stop dead in the street and wet your pants gorgeous."

"Really?" I ask suspiciously.

"Look, the class is going crazy here. I need to go."

"You rang me in the middle of teaching?"

"That's how gorgeous he is. You need to hear. I'm sending over his profile link. You need to do some serious prep for this date, and I am not talking about a simple leg shaving. Gotta run."

I zoom into his contact photo and sit up.

*Oh.* This guy is smoking hot.

An email flashes in my inbox from Suze. "Cat told me he was a HC?"

I smile to myself. Yes, definitely in the *hot-cock* category.

Maybe I can kill two birds with one stone tonight.

I'll have to leave work early, nip to the shops then home before our date.

If Danny Walker thinks I'm going to sit around pining after him, he has another thing coming.

***

I self-administer every possible beauty treatment I can in the timeframe.

Hairs are threaded, plucked, bleached, waxed, and tweezed. Skin is toned, cleansed, moisturised, exfoliated, and sandpapered.

I am as hairless as a Sphynx and smell like a branch of The Body Shop.

I'm wearing a fitted nude colour dress that I spent a fortune on that gives the illusion of nakedness. It screams sex.

My lip liner is painted to maximize my full lips, and my eyes are dark and smouldering.

The dress curves around my breasts in just the

right places. It's my best come-fuck-me look ever.

"If you can swing a second date out of this one, Charlie, I'll be impressed," Julie says as the girls inspect my 'natural' tan.

"He's 6'3. You need to wear tall heels," Cat adds.

I turn around. "So he says. He could be lying on his profile."

"I looked at his profile pictures on Facebook and 'gram. He looks 6'3." She inspects my new bra that pushes my breasts to my chin.

"Isn't that a little stalker-ish?"

The girls roll their eyes.

"Nonsense," says Julie, "you never go on a date without checking every form of social media first."

"Sounds worse than the government. What else did you find out about him?"

"Not much." Cat shrugs. "He owns a farm of foxes."

"What?" I snap. This is worse than I thought. "Why would you farm foxes?"

"I'm joking," she giggles. "Why are you so on edge?"

"I'm waiting to find out the catch," I explain.

"Don't be so negative," Julie tuts. "There doesn't have to be a catch."

"There's always a catch," I grumble.

# 16

**Charlie**

I walk into the Regency hotel feeling more confident than I have in weeks.

It's the latest London hotspot for suits, models, and influencers, dripping in decadence and drenched in dark lighting that could make anyone look seductive.

It also happens to be the venue of choice for this evening's management team outing as it's conveniently on the next street over from our office.

The hostess smiles at me. "Who's your reservation under?"

I smile back. "Mark, table for two."

She reads down the list then nods. "Right this way. Mark is already here."

Thank God. I follow her. At least Danny Walker won't catch me all dressed up sitting alone.

I stride across the bar, my heels clicking, and do a mental high five as some of the men's heads turn.

I dare not look around the bar in case Danny and the senior team are here yet. I'm not supposed to know they're here.

She leads me to a candlelit table where a dark-haired muscular guy is seated, and I inhale sharply.

His photo wasn't lying. The guy is gorgeous.

His eyes go wide as he gives me a slow once up and down.

"Hi." He beams as he jumps up to give me a bear hug.

"Hi," I return, my mouth dry.

As he stands up to pull out my chair, he towers above me, proving that he is *not* lying about his height.

"Thanks." I smile shyly, sitting down.

There's a button in the booth called 'Press for Bubbles.' Don't mind if I do.

"Do you always look this incredible?" He grins. "I couldn't believe my luck when the girl that all the guys were staring at walked over to my table."

I laugh and roll my eyes. "Do you always know the right things to say?"

"Seriously." He leans into me so that our arms are touching. "Do you feel heat at the back of your head right now? You have at least forty sets of eyes on you."

I don't know whether to swoon or retch. The guy is laying it on thick. Is this his tried and tested panty removal method? If so, I'm down with that.

I opt for swooning. "You know how to make a girl feel special, I'll give you that. Is that an Australian accent I hear?" I can't stop smiling at his beautiful face. He's about the same height and build as Danny and just as handsome with one obvious difference—his face is open and welcoming. It's the opposite of the cold hard one I see when I lie awake at night.

"It is." He grins. "I came over here for medical school then never left."

"Yes, you work in Guy's hospital around the corner?" I administer my most dazzling smile. "What do you do?"

"I'm a cardiologist." Collect six points!

He continues, "I also teach a kickboxing class a few nights a week, but that's more for fun." Advance to go!

"Fixing people's hearts must be pretty intense," I say, trying to hide my pathetic swooning.

I need to up my game here.

"What about you, Charlie?"

"I.T. Support for a company around the corner," I reply in a husky voice. Did I just try to make I.T. Support sound sexy?

"Damn, if I'd known I.T. support desks were this hot, I'd have broken my laptop a long time ago."

I laugh too loudly at his joke, flicking my hair over my shoulders.

It's working. He's responding to my amateur flirting.

He watches my lips as I speak and gently nudges my arms and knees every so often. Maybe I.T. Support *is* sexy.

I like this guy.

*Shit.* Did I really think this through?

How will I concentrate on Mark knowing Danny Walker is metres away?

It dawns on me that I don't want to blow this

date with Mark. In the short twenty minutes that I've known him, I can confirm that he is a perfect specimen of a man.

The champagne arrives as if by magic. This button is awesome.

I hear Mike before I see him.

The calming ambiance of the bar is interrupted by his obnoxious bellowing. He always talks too loudly, even when he's standing next to you.

They have arrived. I daren't look around to check if *he's* with them.

They have clearly been somewhere else first because Mike is slurring his words as if he's had a bucketload.

"Charlie?" Mark looks at me with his eyebrows raised.

My eyes search his. "Sorry, can you repeat that?"

"Ouch!" He laughs loudly. "I've lost the focus of my girl already."

My girl. It sounds much sexier than the missus.

I'm talking, but Mark is distracted by something over my shoulder. Is he looking at another woman?

"Now, who's lost focus," I say in a clipped tone.

"Sorry." He strokes my arm reassuringly. "It's just there is a group of men staring over at us. One looks like he's going to kill me." He chuckles, focusing on whatever is happening on the other side of the room. "Jesus, do you always get this reaction? Good thing I can defend myself."

"Really?" I play dumb whilst my heart pounds hard in my chest.

"I think I recognise that guy." He squints over my shoulder. "The tech guy, Walker!"

Panic engulfs me. "Danny Walker," I rasp. "He's actually my boss. Well, my boss's boss's boss. We work around the corner. They probably just recognise me."

He shoots up an eyebrow. "You work for The Nexus Group? You must be an I.T. whizz."

I shake my head. "No, a small company they have just bought over. Ignore them," I add quickly. I need to get his focus away from that side of the room. The last thing I need is Mike coming over drunk out of his skull.

Mark smiles as he runs a finger down my cheek. "The only person I want to pay attention to is right here."

I beam and lose my basic hand-to-mouth coordination, spilling champagne down my dress. "Ahh!" The coldness seeps through the silk fabric of my bra.

Mark jumps up and grabs napkins from the table beside us. "I'd wipe you down, but that's probably too familiar for a first date."

"A little." I grin as I take the napkins. I wipe at the growing stain on my chest. "I'm only making it worse." I sigh. "Excuse me, Mark. I'm going to pop to the ladies."

As I glance around to find out where the toilets are, I meet the icy stare of Danny Walker blazing across the room. His scotch glass pauses mid-air.

He's at the furthest corner, and still, his gaze

manages to suck the wind out of me.

My stomach twists. How does he manage to make me so uncomfortable? I'm sitting with a handsome guy that is openly interested in me, and it's the sadistic moron across the room that makes my stomach tense with nerves.

Thrown off my game, I give a brief nod of recognition and divert my gaze.

"Do you know where the toilets are?" I turn back to Mark.

He points behind me to a wall at the other side of the bar. "Just there, do you see the split in the wall?"

"Not really." I frown, confused. "There's no door." All I can see are dark blue walls, no door or bathroom sign.

"It is over there, I promise." He laughs. "It's just very subtle; there's no handle. You have to just push the door."

"Why are they hiding the toilets?" I grumble.

Damn these bars trying to camouflage their bathrooms because going to the toilet isn't sexy.

"OK, I believe you," I say, not convinced. "Be right back."

I get up and stroll as casually as possible across the bar, clutching my bag against my champagne-soaked tits.

"Charlie," Mike bellows as he spots me, his nose and cheeks an unattractive alcohol-induced glowing red.

There are ten of them, mostly men, sitting around a table with enough bottles of champagne to service the entire bar, never mind them.

I give him a curt nod of recognition and a brief wave at the rest of the team.

Karl Walker, Danny's brother, shoots me a brilliant smile and beckons me over. We've met at a few of Tristan's events. I hadn't realised he was in town. He runs the New York branch of Nexus and is Danny's number two. They share the same physical traits, but that's where the comparisons end; Karl is the polar opposite of Danny, charming and charismatic. Not an arrogant, cold prick.

I give him a sly nod to the table where Mark is waiting and shake my head politely as I try to push forward on my shaky twig legs.

Karl's not taking no for an answer. He moves towards me, stopping me in my tracks.

"Charlie." Karl kisses both my cheeks. "So good to see you again. You're not getting off that lightly."

I can't believe this man was birthed from the same woman as his brother.

Ignoring my protests, he pulls me along with his hand on the small of my back.

Their table is loud, the rowdiest in the bar as they all talk over each other and jump between seats in a drunken state of restlessness.

A few of them shout my name excitedly like I've descended from heaven or a similar miracle. I'm nowhere near their level of drunk.

"Are you coming to the strip club, Charlie?" Mike jumps up and down excitedly like a little kid with new toys.

"Not tonight, Mike." I cringe. "I would prefer to stick chopsticks up my nose."

My eyes float to Danny as he leans against the table, holding a beer. The sleeves of his shirt are rolled up, and he's loosened the top three buttons revealing a tanned chest.

With his cold eyes locked on mine, he takes an aggressive swig of his beer.

"You look sensational, Charlie," Karl says, oblivious to the tension.

I smile at him. I had always warmed to Karl. He was the life and soul of every party. If I had any common sense, it would be Karl that I would be lusting after.

"I'm actually trying to hide champagne stains." I laugh, jutting my chin down to my breasts. "I'm not called Clumsy Charlie for nothing."

Karl nods to the table. "Who's the lucky guy?"

"Ah." I look over where Mark is sitting, looking a little bored. "He's actually a blind date." I blush. "He's a doctor."

His eyebrows arch. "I thought you had a serious boyfriend. Shane?"

"Ben," I correct him, tucking a stray hair behind my ear. "We split up."

"How do you know this guy?" a deep voice growls beside him.

*None of your fucking business, mate.*

"It's an online date," I say after a pause.

He glares back at me without blinking. "Does Tristan know about your blind date? You know the security concerns he would have."

"I'll bear those concerns in mind," I respond through gritted teeth. "If you'll excuse me."

"Lovely to see you, Charlie." Karl grins at me flirtatiously.

I make my way to where the toilets are and stand, confused. This is the spot where I saw someone push the wall a minute ago, and the door opened. There's nothing here but a blue wall.

Do I have to say Open Sesame or something?

I push at the wall. Nothing budges. I move along the wall and push harder. Still no movement.

I feel across the wall, and the tables around me stare. This is getting embarrassing. I look like I'm trying to push the wall down.

A waitress stops to watch me. "Can I help you?"

"I'm trying to find the toilets," I reply.

She points to a section of the wall further down.

I push the wall, and low and behold, it moves. It's like trying to enter fucking Narnia through the wardrobe.

"Is it male or female?"

She rolls her eyes like I'm a moron. "It's gender-neutral."

It's as confusing inside the bathroom as it is outside; dim lighting and mirrors make going to the toilet a sexy, but difficult experience.

An environment more akin to a brothel than a bathroom.

"Look at the state of you," I scorn my reflection in the mirror. The stain makes my breasts look obscene like I'm applying for a wet T-shirt competition.

The door crashes open and slams against the wall.

I whip round to see Danny Walker standing in the doorway, face like a bull about to charge.

My eyes widen. "What the hell are you doing?"

"Me?" he snaps. "What the hell are *you* doing?"

"What?" I stammer, taking a step back.

He slams the door shut, and I jump, dropping my lipliner down the sink.

"Are you trying to fucking tease me? Parading some prick in front of my face?" He storms forward into my personal space. "I told you not to play games with me, Charlie. Playing me like a pet."

My mouth drops open. "*What?* What an arrogant git you are."

Even if he is right.

I square my shoulders, stepping towards him.

He's drunk, I realise as I watch his erratic breathing. "My date is none of your business."

His stormy eyes tell me he doesn't like my answer.

I turn to retrieve my lipliner in the sink, but he grabs my arm and pushes me against the wall, his hot breath on my face.

I feel his hardness slam against me like a volt of electricity, and I gasp.

Before I can stop myself, I'm widening my legs and pushing my hips into his, so his dick is hard between my legs.

My head weakly protests at my actions but is no match for my traitorous body. All willpower goes out the bathroom window. I need him so badly.

I grind against his erection.

He lets out a low guttural moan and grabs my ass, clenching me against him so hard I think I'm going to bruise.

"You're going to ruin my date," I stammer.

"I'm going to fucking ruin you," he growls as he hitches me up in his arms and walks us both into the nearest cubicle.

Inside, he slams the door and pins me against the wall with his legs. He pushes his tongue into my mouth, and I respond furiously. I wrap my left leg around his hips to push closer into his hard cock. I need skin on skin.

*This man.* He'll be the end of me. When did I become one of those girls that fucks in a toilet?

His hands roughly pull my panties to the side, and he pushes a finger deep inside me. I yelp at the shock then warmth circles between my legs.

I cry out as he starts pulsing in and out.

"Do you have any idea what you do to me?" he breathes against my lips. "This wetness is for me."

I moan into his mouth, grabbing onto his biceps to stop from sliding down the wall since my legs can't do their job.

"Double standards, Danny. I don't share," I whisper as my hand travels down to rest on his hardness. "If you want me, it's only me."

He flashes me an arrogant smirk. "You want me all to yourself, Charlie?"

I fight my urge to let him bring me to climax right here in the cubicle. Instead, I yank down his trouser zip and release him from his boxers. I need to be in control for once.

He hisses in response as his cock snaps up against his stomach. *So so ready.* So angry. So massive.

For a second, I stare at it in awe.

"Like what you see?" he whispers with a dark smile.

Instead of answering him, I push my hand down and give him a hard stroke from base to shaft.

He lets out an appreciative moan, and I wrap my hand around his large length and stroke with intensity. He's so engorged, so ready to explode, and I've barely started.

"*Fuck,*" he mutters through clenched teeth, gripping the walls to steady himself. "I won't last."

I stroke faster and harder, my own arousal deepening as I watch the control I have over him.

He rests his forearms on the wall on either side of my head and closes his eyes, pressing his forehead against mine.

"Keep going," he whispers against my face.

"Still trying to buy me out?" I pant.

"At this rate, I'll give you the damn company." He draws in a stuttered breath. "I'm close."

I stroke, watching his face contorting in pleasure. His tongue hangs down over his bottom lip. He shudders and lets out a groan that echoes throughout the toilets.

Without stopping to think, I aim his cock at his custom-made designer trousers and feel the warm liquid squirt out into my hands and all over his trousers. It explodes out, thick and fast. I release it and wipe my hand on his shirt, smearing his jizz over himself.

"Now I need to go back to my date, Mr. Walker," I whisper in his ear.

I push him away from me, and he falls against the opposite wall of the toilet, surprised.

"Charlie," he snaps, steadying himself.

With a wink, I open the door and leave him underwear down, jizz on his trousers and jaw hanging open.

# 17

**Charlie**

"I'm so sorry. It took *ages* to get the stain out." I sit down at the table again, my eyes darting everywhere but Mark's. I'm a terrible liar. He'll be able to detect I was touching another man's dick just from my face.

He smiles and looks pointedly at my chest. "It's still there."

*Oops.*

He doesn't seem to notice my twitchy behaviour, or perhaps he just thinks I've got first-date nerves, for he leans over, grabs my traitorous hands, and gives them a kiss, the poor unsuspecting bloke not aware of where they have just been.

"Don't worry, you're still the sexiest woman in here, stain or no stain."

"Uh-huh," I stammer.

"Fancy an obnoxiously priced cocktail?" he asks, gently rubbing circles on my slutty hands. I force a smile.

"Sure." I sneak a glance at the far side of the bar as Mark stands up. Danny Walker thankfully hasn't returned from the toilets, probably still trying to get his stains out.

Karl catches my gaze and smiles back quizzically. *He knows.*

I must have an arrow pointing to my head with the word 'hussy.'

I can't be here when Danny reappears. "Wait, Mark?" I call after Mark, and he turns. "Let's go somewhere more fun."

\*\*\*

Two hours later, and I'm drunk. I don't mean tipsy, giggling like a little girl drunk. I mean off your head, eyes-rolling-back-in-your-head *intoxicated*. For the past hour, I think I've been having a delightfully intelligent conversation with Mark. I'm not sure if he agrees.

He asks if I want to go back to his for a nightcap.

"Why not?" I squint at him. What a slut I am. I can't handle two penises in one night. I'll just have a nightcap, then get a cab home.

My head is really spinning.

He looks delighted. "I'll order a cab."

Thirty minutes later, I have slightly sobered up, and the cab pulls up outside Mark's house a few streets away from Notting Hill station.

"The entire house is yours?" I ask, bewildered, eyeing the huge Victorian semi-detached house.

"It is," he responds casually.

For a second, I think he's joking. This house is the size of Tristan's house, and he's a multi-millionaire.

"Charlie, are you coming in?"

I suddenly realise I am standing in the pathway

with my mouth open, and Mark is waiting with the front door open.

Inside the house is even sexier than the outside. It clearly has had every detail professionally designed, from the radiator valves to the art deco pieces scattered casually through the hall.

There's a stonking collection of art lining the hallway, which seems to expand into every other room.

What did I do to deserve this? I mean, I'm okay looking, but this guy is seriously out of my league. He could have collected a model- or influencer-type in that fancy hotel bar.

If I rounded up all the blokes I'd been with in my lifetime, and aggregated their looks, wealth, and brains, this guy would still be more intelligent, handsome, and wealthy. With the exception of Danny Walker, of course.

I relax into his cinema-style sofa, which has more appliances than my kitchen with its built-in fridge compartment and speakers. He flips a button, and I yelp as the sofa reclines ninety degrees. OK, so we are moving to the next base quickly.

He tops my glass up to the brim with wine before I have a chance to say no. I'm not sure that's such a great idea. I feel a little queasy after the concoction of banana and vanilla vodka cocktails. Now this syrupy wine. Bah.

"Charlie." He sets my glass down and leans over me. "Am I allowed a kiss?"

I laugh nervously. "I've no objections." One kiss

won't hurt. I mean, I'm single, right? Danny Walker isn't beating down my door asking for commitment.

This is it. I've really got to pull out my best tricks here. This guy is used to models swinging off his chandeliers, not drunk I.T. Support girls.

His tongue enters my mouth, and I carefully edge mine into his. Ah, this is a bit of a deep throat! This guy has got a seriously long tongue. A bit too long … my stomach lurches. Oh no, this is not good. Not good at all. I feel wine waves in my stomach.

Mark tries to get on top of me on the recliner sofa, and a hiccup escapes me into his mouth.

"Sorry." I cover my mouth with my hand as his brows furrow slightly. "I think you will have to excuse me one moment."

I struggle up from the sofa.

"Of course, if you want to …" He looks at me suggestively. "Freshen up."

I nod, banana very much to the core of my throat, and rush out of the room down the hall to his ultra-luxe bathroom.

The door is barely closed before the wave of winey bananas spurts out, like missiles hitting every surface available. Hitting the toilet. Hitting the bidet. Hitting the white marble spa bath. It's as if someone has set off vomit sprinklers from the ceiling.

Cherries from the bourbon cocktails, lime from the Long Island, mushrooms from my pizza before I left; my stomach is emptying out across Mark's lavish bathroom. Oh God, it's *everywhere*. A yellowy red tsunami has hit the bathroom. In my hair, on my top! Ahhh! On the shower curtain! And the shower mat! Frantically I grab a towel, but even they look like they were purchased in Harrods.

I rub down the shower curtain and stop in dismay. The stains have only rubbed deeper into the pattern. This guy is going to strangle me when he sees his bathroom or, even worse, make me pay for the damage.

What am I going to do? This is past the point of no return.

I can't go back to him; I can't own up to destroying his entire bathroom with vomit. There is only one logical plan of action.

As quietly as I can, I open the bathroom door and creep down the hallway. The front door is only metres away. One step at a time, trying not to breathe, I push forward towards the door. Slowly I turn the wooden latch and creep out into the night.

The huge door slams behind me. Gasping, I sprint down the street until I am sure I'm far enough away he can't find me.

Panting, I drop down to the ground to catch my breath.

I can't believe it. I've committed a sick-and-run.

# 18

**Danny**

"How's the hangover?" Karl pushes open the door and swings his head around, grinning. "You look rough."

I stare at him, deadpan. Doesn't anyone knock around here?

I've had three hours of sleep. I'm supposed to be prioritising our releases for next year to give direction to the product team, and my skull feels like it has been shattered into a million pieces.

Last night was stupid. I never drink so much I can't focus the next day. I always sneak off before it slides into debauchery at some strip club. Last night, all restraint went out the window. Seems like I've been doing a lot of stupid things recently.

Is this what a mid-life crisis looks like?

Karl ignores my glare and saunters into the room. He's too chirpy for my liking considering the night we've just had. Mind you, the guy is five years younger than me, so hangovers don't hit him as hard.

I eye the coffee in his hand. That better be for me.

"Why are you so happy?" I growl.

"I was right. You do need coffee." He places the espresso and an energy drink down on the desk in front of me.

"Thanks," I grunt. "I'm so fucking dehydrated my balls have shrivelled into prunes."

"What did you do with my sensible CEO brother?" He laughs. "It's not like you to fraternise with the staff."

"I'm showing them my fun side," I reply dryly.

He leans against the wall, grinning. "Did you show that model your fun side?"

He's talking about the Brazilian brunette that spoke five languages and told me what she wanted to do to me in each of them. Just my type.

"No," I answer truthfully. "I went home by myself."

"Opportunity missed. That guy Mike's a lunatic. I don't think he gets out much. Where did he end up? He was trying to go to another bar after the strip club closed. Some East London lock-in."

"In a gutter for all I care." I snort. "Mike's a prick."

Spraying thousand-pound bottles of champagne around on the company's money. I should dock it from his fucking salary.

"He'll be gone soon." Karl shrugs. "It was interesting seeing Tristan's little sister, Charlie." He looks at me closely. "Did you know she worked here before we started the acquisition?"

"Of course, I did," I return. "I'm executing a plan so that she's looked after. She's just resisting the offer right now. She'll come around."

He cocks his head, his mouth twisting into a smirk. "Did some of this *execution* happen last night?"

I slam my laptop shut, giving him my full attention. "What do you mean?"

He raises his arms animatedly. "I knew it! You could cut the sexual tension with a knife. So?" His voice hitches. "Is there something going on between you two? I'm assuming this is the reason why you're barking at all your staff and rebuffing models."

"There's been a few," I flounder, searching for the right word. "Incidents."

"Incidents?"

I exhale a heavy sigh. "She barged into my office one evening when I was, uh, sorting myself out."

Karl frowns in confusion then his eyes widen. "She caught you jerking off?" He throws his head back, letting out a disbelieving laugh. "Man, you cannot be serious."

"Deadly," I grimace. "I thought the door was locked. And my employees don't usually have the audacity to barge into my office uninvited."

My chest tightens. "That's not the worst part. I was watching a video of her at the time."

He stares at me, not blinking. "Damn, Danny. That's the creepiest thing I've ever heard. Are we going to be hit with a lawsuit?"

I slump in my leather wingback chair. "Let me worry about that."

His mouth twitches into a smirk. "Did she offer to give you a hand?"

I look at him flatly. "No. She didn't leave, though," I add, "she stood there ... and watched."

His jaw drops. "You kept going?"

I wince. "It wasn't something I could stop."

"Christ, man." He breaks into hysterical laughter, and I wait for the fit to end. Yes, very funny. "And they say I'm the reckless Walker. This is the most cliché porn movie script ever. Big bad boss seduces young junior employee. Did you fuck her in this office?"

"No. But I finished in front of her." I let out a joyless chuckle. "I was too out of control. The person I imagined stroking my dick rocks up midway through. I didn't stand a chance."

"Did she enjoy the show?" Karl sniggers.

"It would appear so because I went to her flat that night to apologise, one thing led to another, and we went too far..." I'm not willing to give away details.

"You slept with her?" He grins. "I knew it. I could smell the sex hormones a mile off from both of you last night."

"No," I say quickly. "She's volatile as fuck. She hates me. She wants me. She hates me. She's like a pendulum. We had a nice moment in her flat, then she flipped and kicked me out. The drama is fucking insufferable."

He slaps his forehead. "You two need to sleep with each other and get this out of your systems."

"I can't just sleep with her." I frown. "There's too much at stake. I might have already fucked up my closest friendship. Man, if he found out..."

I shudder at the thought of losing my best pal of twenty years.

Karl nods. "Tristan would go absolutely nuts. It's his one rule, stay the fuck away from his sister."

"Never mind the fact that she's an employee. I don't dip my nib in the company ink."

"But damn, she's hot. I'm just gutted you got in first. *I'm* not friends with Tristan. I'll happily fuck her."

I narrow my eyes on him. "Don't even look in her direction."

He gives me a devilish grin. "Damn, you do have it bad this time. What happened last night?" he probes. "You disappeared for ages."

I lean forward and place my elbows on the desk. "That would be the reason behind my expensive dry-cleaning bill in a dry cleaner's three miles away."

His eyebrows shoot up. "In the bathroom? Christ, Danny, any of the team could have walked him."

I don't indulge him with an answer.

"Is it purely physical?" He studies me. "Do you want a relationship with her?"

I run my hands through my hair, aggravated at the interrogation. "It's physical. She's too young and hot-headed. We aren't suited."

"Then keep your dick in your pants." He rolls his eyes. "There are a million beautiful twenty-five-year-olds out there that'll happily oblige you."

"Twenty-eight," I correct.

"Look, she's beautiful and feisty and sexy as hell. I get it. You've known her for years, and she's off-limits. You want what you can't have. But just don't stir up shit. You can't sleep with Charlie then walk away without repercussions."

"I bloody know that," I snap. "I've been trying to tame my cock ever since she drunkenly straddled me when she was at university. Now I have to watch her waltz around the office teasing me."

"At least in the Nexus HQ, you'll be separated by floors instead of this pokey office."

"I'm hoping she will have seen sense by then and accept my voluntary redundancy payout." I stare out the window. "He'll know, Karl. Tristan's already starting to ask questions about what's eating me."

He nods. "This is heading for disaster, bro. Quit before you break her heart and severely fuck things up."

*I'm screwed.*

## Charlie

They say hangovers get worse as you get older. People in their forties talk about this, and you laugh. *Of course, that won't happen to me*, you think.

But then you find out it is one hundred times worse than all the forty-year-olds were moaning about.

Why did they have to dress it down?

I wake up and can't feel my feet. It's as if someone is sitting on them at the bottom of the bed. I look down and try to wiggle them, then realise I'm still wearing my shoes from the night before, and they are hanging off the bed.

I move them and feel a million pins and needles stabbing me as they wake up.

My brain has dissolved, and a stone has been put in its place that is too big for my head.

*Thank God* I booked today as a holiday, or I would have to call in sick, and everyone would know it was hangover-related.

I shut my eyes tight, but the banging inside my head continued. I open them. It's still there.

My brain cells scream, gasping for water, but I am too weak to lift my body to go and get a glass.

Drunk memories flood my brain like a bad horror film.

They aren't in the right order, and I can't quite put all the scenes together.

The hotel. Hot Doctor. Kebab. Danny Walker. The nightclub. The sick and run.

Did I really puke all over someone's bathroom then do a runner? Is it vandalism? Can Mark call the police on me?

I'm in the paranoia stage of the hangover. I have nausea, reformation, and hunger stages still to progress through.

I lift my head to look in the mirror. There is dried dribble at the corner of my mouth. Mascara is still on one eye but not the other. I look like a depressed clown.

The flat is quiet. I've got no one to act as my priest for confessions. Suze isn't working today, so where is she? I go to message her and see loads of messages and missed calls. That is *not* what I need to see in the paranoia stage.

Two missed calls from Danny Walker, one at 11 p.m. then another closer to midnight. Two messages from him.

**Where are you?**

**Stop fucking around. You better be at home.**

There's one from Tristan.

**Charlie, are you OK? Danny said he saw you drunk last night with a strange guy!?**

That bastard ratted me out. That's all I need, Tristan breathing down my neck about personal security.

**I'm fine, Tristan, it was just a date, stop worrying!**

I'm not replying to Danny. My whereabouts are not his concern. He can find out through Tristan if he's that bothered.

There's an alarming gargle from my stomach. *Uh oh.*

My intestines twist in painful knots like someone is squeezing water from a dishcloth.

I leap out of bed and make it to the toilet with seconds to spare.

\*\*\*

Six hours later, Suze, Stevie, and I are vegetating in the local cafe, reliving my moments of shame. Stevie has bunked off work early.

We've just finished a taxidermy class; I wasn't joking when I told the Swedish guy I was going to do it. Suze signed us up months ago as part of our 'try everything once' flat charter.

In hindsight, I wouldn't have gone on a massive bender last night if I realised that stuffing a small mouse is actually a very labour-intensive four-hour process.

Whilst I'm not particularly squeamish, scooping out the eyeballs of a mouse can take its toll if you've spent the morning emptying your stomach.

"It's bad, don't get me wrong, it's bad," Suze says, slurping her double Snickers milkshake.

"He may have shagged you anyway if you had stuck around," Stevie adds as he chews with his mouth open. "It takes a lot to put us off, more than a bit of pee, shit, vomit, snot ..."

I wrinkle my nose. "Oh, great. That's something. I don't think I was really in the mood after my little explosion."

"I just wouldn't kiss you." He shrugs. "But everything else is fine."

"Typical!" Suze snorts. "Typical bloke. They don't care if they don't kiss you. They don't even care what your face is like. In fact, you could be headless for all they care, providing you have an available vagina."

"And yours is always available, isn't it, Suze?" he teases, and she fires a napkin at him.

"What happened at work today, then, Stevie?" I ask, casually changing the subject.

He rolls his eyes. "You mean what's happening with Danny Walker. No point trying to be subtle."

"Well?" I ask.

"You may not be the only one regretting last

night. He looked pretty haggard this morning. Most of the leadership team are walking around like zombies today," he says whilst shovelling beans into his mouth. "I heard Mike being sick in the toilet this morning."

"I'm going to be sick again if you keep eating with your mouth open," I snap.

"If you want me to be your spy," he continues with his mouth open, "you'll be nice to me."

"I don't need a spy." I sigh, pushing food around my plate. "The guy is haunting me. He's at work. He's on my dates. In my fucking dreams. And now tomorrow night, he's at my brother's house. Again."

"Just stay away from his dick," Suze warns. "What with your mother being in the house."

That's easier said than done.

Stevie chews on his lips.

"Spit it out," I grimace.

"Apparently, he got a *lot* of female attention last night. The rest of the team were jealous. Some half-famous Brazilian model cuddled up to him, and he may have taken her home. That's the rumour."

I retreat three stages in my hangover and resist the urge to vomit again.

One minute, I'm excited that this might be the start of something new, mainly when those startling eyes are staring into me like I'm the most important woman on the planet.

The next minute, I hear that he's tomcatting his way all over town.

That's it over. No more fumbles, no more

fantasies, and certainly no future. I move on.

# 19

**Charlie**

I'm waiting outside Kentish Town tube station at 10 a.m. on Saturday morning. It's going to be a long day.

I hear them before I see them.

"To the right! Stand to the bloody right, woman," Callie bellows.

I hear Mum tutting. "If they want to pass me, they can ask."

Their two heads appear at the top of the escalator. Mum's is rollered to within an inch of its life, and Callie has on a crimson (is that food colouring?) crop.

Callie grins when she sees me, but Mum looks tight-lipped, and I groan silently as I spot the bum-bag fastened tightly around her midriff. One hand clasps it with an unyielding grip for fear of dirty Londoners stealing her loose change.

At the barriers, Mum makes a great scene of stepping aside to face the wall while she opens her bum-bag to get her ticket. With a look of triumph, the ticket is produced and placed in the ticket slot in slow motion.

I watch as she places the ticket in the wrong gate's

slot. The barriers to her left bang open, waiting for someone to walk through them.

Mum frowns at the barriers she is standing in front of and tries to push them open. "These ones aren't working."

"Go to the other one." I beckon furiously to the open gate, waiting for someone to come through while Callie sniggers behind me. "The *other* gate. That's the one you opened with your ticket. The one that's open. The OTHER one."

I point at the barriers she put her ticket into like I'm doing a ridiculous mime show. "You're supposed to walk through THAT one."

She tuts but finally moves to the correct ticket barrier. "Well, that's annoying. Why don't they all open when you put your ticket in? Then you could go through any."

Exasperated, I stare at her. "What?" Half of me wishes I hadn't explained how to get out of the barriers so they would be stuck in there.

"You should have seen her trying to open the toilet door on the train," Callie moans. "And then the screams when the train started moving!"

Mum is out of touch with modern transport. She only started to visit London when Tristan moved here, and he usually sends a driver for her. This time she decided to go rogue and slum it.

After the barrier ordeal, Mum announces that she wants to go back to mine for a cup of tea before sightseeing. I know what she's up to. She's mad with nosiness and wants a poke around my flat to see how clean it is.

We stroll back through Kentish Town to the flat.

"Hello," I shout tentatively through the flat door. No reply, great! "Cat's in bed, so you'll have to be quiet."

"At this hour?" Mum's lips purse into a thin line. "And I was looking for a tour of the bedrooms."

"Why don't you sit down, and I will make a nice cup of tea?" I bundle them into the living area where they can do minimal damage and give it a once-over for signs of drug abuse or sexual activities. Thankfully I had remembered to hide Julie's '101 Amazing Sex Games' book.

Mum glares at our sofa in disgust and hovers above it like she is afraid of catching fleas.

I come back with three cups of tea and, proudly, a jug for milk.

She gives it a quick sniff before reluctantly accepting.

"I've got your post for you." She rummages through her bag, hankies and tissues flying everywhere as she hands me a pile of crumpled letters. I've still got letters going to Mum's house as Julie is doing a council tax dodge.

I glare at her. "These are all open?"

"Yes." She shrugs as if she hasn't committed any crime. "You owe an awful lot on that credit card."

"You shouldn't be opening my mail!" I snap.

"Someone needs to keep an eye on your finances since you're obviously not doing it."

Argh. She has been in the house for five minutes,

and my blood is bubbling.

"Callie, what are you doing?" I demand.

Callie wriggles on the sofa like it has fleas. Maybe we do have a problem. "Your sofa is uncomfortable," she complains, reaching her hand under the cushion. "Wait, I have found something."

Her right hand reappears with two objects. "What are these?"

My heart falls into my bladder and crushes it as she waves the chlamydia test that the chemist forced on Julie when she got the morning-after pill. I'm going to kill Cat for her stupid hiding place. I told her to hide any items that would bring my reputation into dispute.

Worse still, in Callie's other hand is the postcard that Cat bought in Amsterdam with two dicks going into a mouth, one black, one white with the slogan 'no racism.'

Callie's mouth drops open.

I snatch them from her before she can wave them in Mum's face.

Luckily, Mum is too engrossed in the pizza marks on the carpet to notice. She looks up, never missing a trick. "What are those?"

"It's just Suze's weight loss device." I walk as casually as possible to Cat's room and fling them both in. There is a muffled "hey" as I slam the door. What else is lurking in this living room to trip me up?

"What's up with you, Callie?" I attempt to change the subject yet again.

She shrugs.

Mum's face turns white. "I'll tell you what's up with this young pup. She's been suspended from St Mary's."

"Suspended?" Now here is a bit of news. I look at Callie, who breezily flicks through a magazine she has found on the coffee table. She's in her final year and only has six months to behave.

"She's brought the family into disrepute, this young missy has." Mum covers her mouth and looks around in case any of my neighbours have glasses to the walls.

"She tried to summon the dark side." It comes out as no more than a whisper.

"She did what?" I ask, confused.

Callie looks up from the magazine, bored, and sighs. "The Ouija board. I was caught doing the Ouija board."

Mum shakes her head. "The nuns are in uproar. They're holding a special mass to cleanse the school, to undo the damage that Callie has caused!"

"Why did you do that, Callie?" I turn to her. "Do you even believe in the Ouija Board?"

She laughs. "As if. But stupid Bernice O'Hagan does, so we wanted to prove to her that it's all shite. Then Sister Tessa came in and saw us and started foaming at the mouth in shock." She yawns. "It's my last year anyway."

"That's terrible behaviour, Callie," I scold in the way a dutiful older sister should. "Getting suspended from school isn't going to get you a very good job, is it?"

She looks at me, deadpan. "If you can get a job, anyone can, even though it did take you a million attempts."

"Piss off," I bite back. I'm a little sensitive about the number of interviews I had to endure.

"I can live off Tristan's allowance anyway." She rolls her eyes like I'm stupid.

"Tristan is giving you an allowance?" I stare at her, disgusted. "That's how you can afford to go shopping in central London!"

"Enough bickering, for God's sake," Mum barks, putting down her cup of tea. "I have had enough of this bad tea. Let's see your bedroom."

"Fine." I put down my tea and lead them to the bedroom, which thankfully has the bed semi-made and underwear tidied away.

"Could do with a bit of Shake n' Vac." She sniffs the air while Callie goes through my make-up. "And this carpet. When was the last time it was hoovered? Is it supposed to be this colour?"

She bends down for a closer inspection. "Weeks of dirt on this. What's this?" She picks up a Smint that has rolled under the bed at some stage in its life and has hairs, and other gooey bits from the carpet stuck to it. "You've been doing drugs!"

I gawk at her flabbergasted. "It's a Smint."

"A Smint!" she shouts, narrowing her eyes at me. "Don't use your drug jargon on me, young lady. Is it one of those dancing pills?"

Callie guffaws behind her and gets a slap around

the head.

"It's a mint," I repeat slowly.

"A mint, heh? So would you let me lick it then?"

I look at the Smint with the multi-coloured arrangements of hairs, probably some of mine, some of Ben's, and maybe even whoever lived in the flat before.

I stare at it pointedly. "I wouldn't advise it."

"I bet you wouldn't." She gives the Smint a lick, waiting for me to stop her before she needs her stomach pumped. Her face changes from anger to surprise to disgust as realisation dawns. She starts picking hairs out of her mouth.

"Oh, it is a mint."

"See?" I roll my eyes. "Now, can we please get this sightseeing over and done with?"

One hour later, we are on the sightseeing bus touring Trafalgar Square. I thought it was the best way to keep them quiet for a while.

By 4 p.m., I am exhausted and ready to go into witness protection so I can hide from my family. Big Ben wasn't big enough, St Paul's wasn't holy enough, and Shakespeare's Globe was a fake.

I'm *so* not ready to go to this dinner party of Tristan's. Why am I deliberately entering a scenario of being in the same room as my mother, my sister who spills all my secrets, my boss who wants to get rid of me, and a guy I jerked off in the toilets, who coincidentally happens to be my boss?

\*\*\*

Six hours of Mum complaining is too much. I don't know how I survived being with her so long in the womb.

I've gone for a casual look; jeans, sneakers, and a sweater that hangs off one shoulder. It's an outfit that often causes me to get ID'd, so I must look younger in it.

Tristan sent a car to collect us and take us to his house, which meant I didn't have to brave manoeuvring Mum through more public transport.

He opens the door of his townhouse in Holland Park, beaming at us. "My three favourite ladies."

If the rumours are true, that's not correct.

It's a Grade II listed building with three floors, big bay windows, and an entire glass wall of floor-to-ceiling doors opening onto a landscaped garden.

Every Londoner's wet dream.

Julie and I stalked it on YourMove, and it went on sale for twenty million, although I would never ask him how much he bought it for.

We don't talk about money in the Kane house.

Every time I visit, he's had something new done. A new jacuzzi bath, heated floors, surround sound. Last time he had converted one of the bedrooms into a cinema room.

"Come through, ladies," he says, taking our coats. "It's a full house."

The deep Scottish voice assaults my ears from the kitchen.

We walk through to join the party. In the kitchen,

Jack, Tristan's law firm partner Rebecca, and her husband Giles sit on barstools around the marble island.

Danny is propped against the fridge while Karl attempts to make cocktails at Tristan's bar. Tristan has a kitchen the size of mine, Julie's, Cat's, and Suze's bedrooms combined.

My throat dries up as I take in Danny.

He's in jeans and a blue cashmere sweater that fits his body in all the right places. I want to run into his arms and wrap them around me.

His eyes find mine, then drop brazenly down to my midriff. His hands tighten around the counter. It's subtle, but I see the movement. *He likes what he sees.*

His face is warmer this evening. Maybe being around close friends in a home environment makes him less hostile.

Even through their schoolboy teasing and jostling, they exude an undeniable air of dominance.

They are all late thirties, early forties, with Danny being the oldest. Jack's younger, maybe thirty-five. While the rest of us are just trying to get through the week, they make success look so easy.

Rebecca wears a gorgeous tailored trouser jacket suit and open-toe heels. Now I feel childish in my ripped jeans and running shoes.

Can Tristan not see how the dynamics change when friends and family mix? These two worlds don't belong together.

Tristan demotes Jack from cocktail making and

prepares drinks as everyone welcomes us. Besides Mass, Tristan's events are Mum's social life. She's in her element as the men tell her how young she looks, and Rebecca compliments her rollered curls held tight against her head.

"Sherry for Mum, small wine for Callie, Old Fashioned for Charlie." Tristan serves our drinks, and I look on impressed. His cleaner/house help Natalia usually does everything for him. He must have given her the night off.

"What did you get up to today?" Rebecca politely asks us.

"We started off with a look around Charlie's flat," Mum responds, happy to be the centre of attention.

"It was more of an inspection than a tour," I grumble, jumping on a barstool. "Who looks under someone else's bed, for Christ's sake?"

"Tristan, can you send your cleaners to Charlie's?" Mum pipes up.

"Mum!" I snap indignantly, my cheeks flushing.

I turn to Tristan, smirking. "Although at least it's not tidy enough for them to spend the night."

I've officially handed responsibility for Mum and Callie over to Tristan. It wasn't a difficult choice for them, with options being topping and tailing Julie's sofa or a wing of Tristan's mansion.

He opens the fridge and takes out a batch of tiny canapes.

I eye the yellow jellylike substance suspiciously. "What are these?"

"Golden beet and elderflower jelly," he explains as

if it should be obvious.

Don't be fooled; these are no shop-bought canapes. These have been bespoke designed for Tristans's tastes by an exclusive caterer.

Mum prattles off every detail about our day, explaining things she learned about Big Ben, Houses of Parliament, and the St James' Park swans as if these people didn't live in London.

They politely listen and murmur approval and disapproval at the right times during the storytelling.

Callie and I hang back, relieved Mum is taking the limelight. My eyes stray to Danny, and as if he can feel it, he moves his focus from Mum to me, his eyebrows rising.

I feel my cheeks heat and avert my gaze.

"You have to try these lobster rolls," Rebecca gushes, passing the plate to us.

Mum shakes her head at Tristan. "When are you going to find a nice woman to cook for you, Tristan?"

"I already have two." He smiles in amusement. "My lovely mum and my delightful cook, Natalia."

"No," she replies crossly. "Someone you don't have to pay. A wife. I'm never going to get a day out."

"You've already had a day out," he mutters darkly. "It didn't work out, remember?"

No, it didn't. If God made a new person from a serial killer and the girl from the Exorcist, that would be Tristan's ex-wife Gemina.

"Isn't that a bit sexist?" I point out, spearing a piece of lobster and shoving it into my mouth,

"What if Tristan's new mystery wife is a terrible cook?"

"She couldn't be any worse than you." Mum shakes her head at me, and Tristan grabs me around the neck for a hug. "Your cooking drives them all away."

"That's true," Callie pipes up. "If Charlie had a dinner party, everyone would leave in coffins."

"How rude," I mutter, fixing my hair from the bird's nest Tristan created with his jostling. Honestly, I'm not five years old; you'd think he'd realise he can't play the same games with me.

"When *are* you finding a wife?" Jack's eyes twinkle in amusement at Tristan.

"Don't start this in front of Mum," Tristan moans, shooting him a warning look. "I'll never hear the end of it now."

"It's hard to believe that London's most handsome eligible man is still single." Rebecca smiles. "And you too, Jack." She prods him in the ribs.

"Make it a hat-trick," Tristan says. "Walker too."

My mouth falls open in surprise, and I snap it shut before anyone can notice.

Danny Walker is now single? The air feels weighted as we all study him with interest.

"No, Danny!" Mum slaps her hands over her mouth like this is the worst news she's ever heard. "What about beautiful Jen? Surely, you didn't let her go? Please say no."

Way to go, Mum. Great wingwoman.

He clears his throat. "Sorry to disappoint, Mrs.

Kane."

"When did that happen?" I ask quietly.

His eyes lock with mine. "Last Friday night," he answers me coolly.

The corners of his mouth quirk into a light smile as my mind ticks over and a silent acknowledgement passes between us.

He split up with Jen on the night we made out. I have so many questions.

Did he split up with her over me? Was it before or after we made out? Was I wrong about him?

"Oh," I whisper. "Sorry."

"Don't be," he says darkly.

"What are you looking for, Danny?" Rebecca asks curiously.

He turns to her. "When I find it, I'll let you know."

They laugh even though it's not particularly funny.

I don't laugh. I knew what he's saying.

*It's not you.*

I'm a fumble in the toilet, not a serious proposition. Not a girlfriend. Or a wife.

"Do you want to get married again, Danny?" Mum asks. "Nice chap like you must have all the ladies after you."

"Careful, Mrs. Kane." Karl chuckles. "He has a soft spot for you."

"How could I not?" Danny flashes her a grin. "She's like a second Mum."

I frown. That makes our fumbles sound a bit incestuous. Not to mention a shrewd tactic of question avoidance.

"I know!" Rebecca pipes up. "This is *perfect* timing. One of our senior lawyers has been begging me for a date with *the* Danny Walker. She couldn't believe her luck when I said I knew you! She's six foot, beautiful, and extremely sharp. Mara. Thirty-five, just the perfect age for you, Danny. Shall I set it up?" She looks at him excitedly.

My breath hitches, and a surge of jealousy soars through me.

*No. Don't do this in front of me.*

Tristan sucks in sharply. "I don't know about this, Becks. She's one of our best lawyers. I'm always nervous about mixing Danny's pleasure with my business. I don't want it to end in tears."

"They are *perfect* for each other, Tristan," Rebecca scolds. "Don't stand in the way."

"Mara is very hot," Tristan agrees as he hands Danny a scotch. "You'll fall for her as soon as you see her. She's your ideal woman."

I stare transfixed at my jellied lobster canape concoction. Humiliating is not a strong enough word for this situation.

Danny takes the scotch and raises it to his mouth, lingering over it. "Sure," he replies.

"Fantastic." Rebecca squeals, getting out her phone. "I'll text her now."

Damn you, Rebecca. I put down the lobster tail. My appetite is ruined.

I have my answer, he didn't split up with Jen over me. What an absolute bastard. How could he do this in front of me?

Now I have to sit through dinner in agony.

"What a lucky girl," Mum swoons. "Rebecca, you must help our Tristan also."

"Right, now that we've sorted a wife for Danny, it's time for dinner." Tristan makes gestures for us to move out of the kitchen.

I force a smile and get up from my stool. Karl falls into step beside me.

"Hey, gorgeous girl." He puts his arm around my waist. "You OK?"

"Of course," I lie.

His face says he knows. He knows everything. Of course, he knows. Danny and Karl are close. How embarrassing. He must think I'm pathetic.

"It's good to see you, Karl." This time, I'm not lying. We take seats at the table, and I'm glad that Karl sits beside me. Tristan takes his place at the head of the table, and the seats fill up, leaving one empty directly opposite me, which Danny takes.

The caterers have not only made the food, they have also prepared the table in advance. Four sets of cutlery rest on cut slabs of stone and three types of glasses, one for water, one for wine, and the third is anyone's guess. There's an elaborate centerpiece made from roses and other flowers I don't know the name of.

The napkins were made from a material that would be better suited to a designer dress. There's a monochromatic theme going on that I know is not by accident; he has paid a lot of money to make it appear casual, probably for Mum's benefit.

Tristan brings out the venison starter. It looks suspiciously like the food in the fancy restaurant where Danny paid for our meal.

We chorus our 'Oh's and 'Ah's.

"A toast." Tristan stands at the head of the table, beaming. "To my amazing friends and family who have supported me these past forty years."

"I'm not even twenty!" Callie yells.

"To the next forty!" Jack shouts, raising his glass.

"To amazing friends." Danny raises his glass.

We all take a drink.

"Did you get any nice presents, Tristan?" Rebecca smiles.

He winks. "Your weekend in Florence, of course."

"Don't forget your six-month membership to Stringfellows from me." Jack grins as my mother's lips form a tight line.

Tristan looks at Jack dryly as he takes his seat. "Thanks, Jack. And Charlie's present, of course." He raises a glass to me.

Rebecca turns to me. "What did you get him, Charlie?"

"What do you get the brother who has everything?" I laugh. "I got him a joke tie because I can't afford where he actually shops and some aftershave that he'll definitely put down the sink when we leave."

"Oh, come on," Tristan cuts in excitedly. "She's leaving out the best bit."

He looks around the table, building suspense.

"She wrote me a beautiful song called 'Brother.'"

I blush as I become the centre of attention.

"How sweet!" Rebecca gushes, clasping her hands together. "We have to hear it."

"So you did find something for the brother that has everything," Karl muses. "That's a pretty cool gift."

"It's silly," I murmur, fiddling with my knife. "It was the only thing I could think of that would be unique from me to him. I churned it out pretty quickly."

"And after dinner, we'll get to hear it," Tristan adds.

"No." I groan. "In that case, I'm going to get so drunk you can't possibly let me play it."

"Absolutely not." He pokes a finger in my direction. "I was worried sick on Wednesday when you didn't reply to my text. You need to reply to me, Charlie." He berates me like he's scolding an impotent child. "Let me put a tracker on your phone for safety."

"Absolutely not!" I gasp.

Mum's ears perk up. "What happened on Wednesday?"

Callie sniggers. "Charlie got drunk, went back to some dude's house, and vomited all over his bathroom."

"She did what?" Mum barks as I fire Callie a nasty look.

Out of the corner of my eye, I see Danny stiffen.

"Ignore her." I continue glaring at Callie. "Callie,

stop listening to my conversations."

I turn to Tristan. "Tristan, I'm not a child you need to protect, and no, you are not putting a tracker on my phone."

His brows knit together. "I don't like you being out on blind dates. It leaves you exposed."

"At least Danny can *look after you* on work nights out. You can stay close to him." Karl's eyes dance.

I choke on my wine. "Good thing he was out on Wednesday evening looking after you."

I wipe wine from my chin as Karl leans back in his chair, trying to hide his smirk.

Grass.

What the hell is he playing at?

"Yes." Tristan nods approvingly. "Make sure you go home with Danny, Charlie. The Nexus crowd drink too much, and there's a lot of random attacks happening in London these days."

Danny puts his scotch glass to his mouth, his granite expression focused on Karl. The drink hovers over his lips before he takes a large slug.

"Danny?"

Fuck the Michelin star food. This isn't worth the torture.

He looks between Tristan and me. "Of course, Tristan," he replies, his gaze settling on me rather than Tristan. "I'll look after her."

I'll never get through three courses of this.

# 20

**Charlie**

We are tipsy and talking loudly over one another by the table that sometimes cross over each other.

Even Danny is relaxed and laughing.

A few times, his legs brush against mine under the table, and I wonder if it's by accident.

Tristan has served up or, more precisely, paid someone else to serve up a storm. The extent of his work was letting the caterers in and showing them where the kitchen was.

Dinner was a complicated, decadent beef wellington with trimmings followed by an even more labour-intensive baked Alaska that Mum turned her nose up at. I could read her mind. Too fancy.

I'm so full that I have to subtly open the top button on my jeans without anyone noticing.

"Fucking hell!" Rebecca screams, looking at something under the table.

Everyone abruptly stops talking.

"Honey?" Giles jumps into action beside his wife.

"Tristan, you have a mouse!" she shrieks, leaping up from the table, pushing her chair away so that it falls to the floor.

Callie jumps on top of her chair. Mum knocks over an entire bottle of wine, spilling it across the table.

Karl jumps up from his seat and leaps back two metres, looking unexpectedly shook up for a man of 6'2. Giles tries to console Rebecca, who wails like a banshee, and Tristan and Danny are under the table. Jack sits back, laughing his head off.

It's mayhem.

"I see it!" Danny yells from under the table. "Fuck, it bit me!"

That's enough to set Rebecca off again. Rebecca, Callie, and Mum have formed some sort of demon choir, standing on their chairs wailing.

I peer under and spot the culprit.

"It's OK!" I shout. "That's my mouse."

Danny comes out from under the table, holding the mouse from my taxidermy class.

"What the hell is this?" His jaw slackens as he studies my creation, suited in its teeny tiny waistcoat. A trace of blood trickles from his finger. "That bloody sword it's holding pricked me. And why is it wearing a hat?"

"What do you mean, *your* mouse?" Rebecca queries, visibly shaking. "Is it a pet?"

"I taxidermied it," I explain as everyone looks between the mouse and me, confused.

Her eyes widen. "And you took it *here*?" she shrieks. "To a dinner party?"

I whither a little.

"I forgot it was in my bag," I mumble as they all lean in to inspect the mouse.

I grab the culprit from Danny, complete with hat and sword, and fire it back into my bag.

He bites his lower lip, trying not to laugh.

"He must have fallen out."

"I'm terrified of mice." Rebecca stares at me as if I've just declared genocide. "Can you put that thing outside?"

"It's dead, Becks." Danny laughs. "It won't hurt you. Except if you stab yourself with that little sword."

The men roar their heads off while Mum attempts to clean up the damage she has caused with the red wine spillage. Jack howls with tears coming down his face.

"Sorry," I gulp, pulling my bag close to me. "I'll just put him outside until I leave." I think it's a *him*. Although I don't remember seeing a little penis.

"You are so weird." Callie rolls her eyes. "No wonder you don't have a boyfriend."

"All this fuss over a dead mouse," I mutter. "Drama queens."

Rebecca gives me a death stare.

"I think it's endearing." Tristan chuckles as I escort the mouse out of the dining room.

"It's part of our flat charter to try anything once," I explain as I enter the room again. When I say it out loud to two CEOs and two world class lawyers, I feel a tad childish.

Rebecca eyes my bag suspiciously.

"It's a good motto." There's a hint of humour in Danny's eyes. The tension in his jaw relaxes for the first time, maybe since he was born. I swear he came out of his mother's stomach with a jaw that could cut steel.

Tristan slaps his hands together. "Crisis averted. Is everyone suitably full? Because we're ready to introduce the after-dessert entertainment."

My stomach sinks as Tristan smiles at me suggestively.

"No, Tristan," I groan, folding my arms. "I'm not entertainment. I'm not a bloody clown. Even if I do provide animals. It's not a circus."

I know what he's hiding.

He gets up and walks out into the hallway, then pops his head around the door, his eyes twinkling at me.

"No," I repeat firmly as he thrusts a guitar out from behind the doorway.

All of them cheer and yelp as I glare at the guitar.

"I've had too much wine to do this coherently." I sigh. "And my stomach is too full to lean a guitar against."

"Please, sis," he whines, giving me his best pout. "It's my birthday."

"You were forty, three days ago," I growl back, shooting my hand out to take the guitar. I won't hear the end of it until I've played the damn song.

The men whoop in appreciation like they are at a concert, and I realise just how drunk they all are.

I pull in a breath and strum the first few cords.

It's a soft, understated song, and I sing it in the low husky voice that it deserves. I lower my gaze to the guitar focusing on the strings. It's easier that way. I can get lost in the music and forget that they are here. I'm shy performing when people are so close, even if they have heard me lots of times.

I wrote the song as a thank you to Tristan for stepping in to support us when Dad left and for always protecting us. When I look up, his eyes are watering, and his mouth quivers as he tries to hold back his tears. Mum looks like she's going to blubber as well.

Get a grip, people.

It's partially the wine talking, but I know I've hit a nerve.

"Beautiful, Charlie," Rebecca gushes as I come to an end, and a round of clapping erupts throughout the table.

"I thought this was a party, not a funeral," Callie mutters as I shoot daggers at her.

"Tristan, are you actually crying?" Jack laughs, observing a sniffly Tristan.

"He didn't even cry when he lost the Hamilton case." Danny smirks. "Now he's blubbering like a baby."

"Piss off," he snaps, wiping his eyes a little.

Rebecca strokes his knee. "Ignore them, Tristan." She turns her attention back to me. "What a talent you have. It's such a unique sound."

"It's just a hobby." I shrug, picking at the hole in

my jeans.

"Well, I'm honoured." Tristan beams, stepping around the table so that he can gather me up in a hug. "To my beautiful, talented little sister, Charlie." He raises his glass as one arm snakes around my shoulders.

I roll my eyes. "The only guy I've ever written a song about is my brother. How pathetic am I."

"He's a very lucky guy," Danny says, his voice thick.

I look over, and something akin to pride flickers over his face.

*\*\**

There's an annoying buzzing sound demanding attention. I shuffle in the bed, ignoring it. It keeps going.

*What the hell?* I peel my eyes open, confused. Has Cat come home and started playing music?

It can't be my alarm; it's too dark to be morning.

I force myself up in the bed and look around for the source of the sound. My phone lights up on the bedside table.

Who is ringing in the middle of the night?

My bedside clock says ten past midnight. I must have fallen into a deep sleep as soon as I hit the pillow. A food coma from Tristan's.

I grapple at the phone, cursing the fucker on the other end. They aren't giving up.

Sharp green light stings my eyes, and the caller flashes across the screen. My heart goes from resting to racing in the space of seconds.

"Hello," I whisper, bringing the phone to my ear. I'm wide awake now.

There's a long pause.

"I need to see you." His voice takes the breath from my lungs.

"You saw me at the party."

"It's not enough," his deep voice replies. "Look, I don't know what this is, but I know I don't want to keep playing this game of cat and mouse with you."

I listen.

"I came over, we went too far ... but it was nice, then you flipped and kicked me out. Less than a week later, you're out with some bloke. I don't know where I stand with you."

"*You* can talk," I retort indignantly. "Says the guy who's tomcatting his way around London."

"Tomcatting? Seriously, Charlie?" He lets out a long sigh. "My reputation precedes me, don't believe all you hear."

"Oh, really?" I summon a deep breath. "In that case, when was the last time you slept with someone?"

"Jen. The night when you saw me in the restaurant."

"That was a few weeks ago," I calculate in disbelief. "You expect me to believe that? What about the girl on Wednesday?"

"The girl on Wednesday ..." His voice trails off. "I'm assuming you are talking about the Brazilian lady that took a liking to me at the after club. It seems the employees do talk."

"Yes. *Her*," I mutter dryly. "And yes, you were the talk of the office."

"Nope," he replies in a level tone. "I get hit on a lot. It goes with the territory. It doesn't mean I always act on it."

We fall silent.

"Can I get a car to collect you?"

I wonder if he can hear my heartbeat through the phone.

"Charlie," he repeats, his voice gravelly. "Did you hear me?"

"Yes," I choke out.

"Yes, you heard me, or yes, I can send a car?"

"Yes to both."

"Good girl," he growls, triggering a rush of heat between my legs.

"Oh, and Charlie?"

"Yes?"

"The offer doesn't extend to your little waistcoated friend this time." He chuckles. "The car will be outside in fifteen minutes."

The phone goes dead, and I collapse onto the bed.

# 21

**Charlie**

I eye the driver suspiciously in the rear-view mirror. He greeted me immediately outside my flat like he knew what I looked like and who I was.

Knowing Danny Walker, the guy has seen my dental, medical and financial records before collecting me.

Apart from the courteous greeting when he opened the door for me and offered me refreshments, we've been travelling in silence for forty-five minutes. Plenty of time for me to turn into a quivering wreck.

Is he at Danny's beck and call 24/7? Is that his job, collecting and dropping off random women at Danny's house? I wonder how many women have travelled in this car in the wee hours of the morning.

Danny lives in Richmond, across the other side of London. At this rate crawling through London on a Saturday night, it'll be morning before we get there.

The streets get wider and greener as we drive towards Richmond, with trees lining the pavements. Suddenly we are bumping along the road, and I feel like I'm travelling down a country road rather than a posh London suburb.

"Sorry for the potholes. The road is private. The residents own it." He smiles at me in the mirror. "They intentionally don't maintain it so that cars don't take shortcuts down it."

We pull into a private cul-de-sac, and he stops in front of a very intimidating house. "This is us."

I gawk out the window at a dwelling similar in size to Somerset House.

"You've never been here before?" He opens the door for me and watches me in amusement.

I shake my head.

"It's a Grade II listed building," he explains as I get out of the car.

It's a gigantic detached three-story Victorian mansion. No, scrap that. *Palace.*

I count three windows on either side of the magnificent projecting porch with fluted columns, six large windows on the second floor, and some sort of roof terrace on the top.

There's even a small *pond* in the immaculately groomed front garden.

Two cars sit in his driveway, the Aston Martin and a Range Rover.

This is the opposite of what I was expecting. It looks like a family home. Does he live with anyone? I've never asked. I realise I don't know much about his private life in London.

Maybe it's secluded for his loud orgies.

While I stand clueless on the lawn, Danny opens the door, a smile spreading across his face.

"Charlie." That deep sexy voice hits me, and a shiver runs up my spine. *Every time.* I want to bolt back to the safety of the car.

He's changed into a T-shirt with holes in it, jeans with paint on them and no socks. The T-shirt hangs over his sculpted chest perfectly.

He's never looked more handsome.

"Hi," I say awkwardly.

He raises his brows, signalling for me to come through the door. "Are you going to come inside?"

"I was expecting a butler to greet me."

"I'm your butler," he mocks, making the notion somehow sound filthy.

"Just a minute." He brushes past me, squeezing me around the waist, and strolls over to his driver.

They mumble something inaudible as I stand stiffly on the porch. Peering into the hallway makes me even more nervous. To no surprise, the interior is just as opulent as the exterior.

The hallway has huge ceilings, marble flooring, and artwork strategically placed on the walls. Everything flows together. A mix of country meets urban.

It's definitely the work of a professional interior designer.

There isn't a speck of dust.

The stark contrast in our residential abodes highlights just how far apart our worlds are. I'm reminded of who he is and who I'm not.

I can't believe I let him into my Kentish Town flatshare with charity shop furniture and wine bottle candle holders. He must have thought it was filthy. We have *mice*, for fuck's sake.

Why on earth does he want me here? He could have any type of professional model he wanted. Leggy, skinny, curvy, blonde, brown, redhead ...

If it's a conversation he wants, I can't talk about interior design, what race car to buy, or how hard life is for a CEO.

"You can go in, you know," his deep Scottish drawl whispers in my ear behind me, and I jump.

I bet Jen and his other ladies don't stand in the doorway like quivering wrecks.

"It must be a bitch to heat," I mumble as I take off my sneakers, realising they are covered in dirt.

He shrugs. "There's underfloor heating in most of the rooms. But the best thing is the two real turf fires. Nothing beats the smell of a real turf fire. I'll give you a tour."

He follows me in and gently peels off my jacket, his hand grazing my bare arm.

"You're nervous?" He arches his eyebrows, surveying me.

I chew on my lips as he brushes a lock of hair away from my face. In my bare feet, I have to strain to look up at him.

"A little," I admit.

"This is a first," his voice turns teasing. "I've never seen you nervous." His hand goes under my chin to drag my gaze up from the floor. "If it helps, you make me nervous too."

"I doubt that," I reply breathlessly. "Why would I

make you nervous?"

"Are you kidding?" He grins down at me. "You're fucking terrifying. You take one look at me, and I'm incapable of rational thinking."

I fight hard to prevent the goofy grin from escaping across my face. Inside, my heart does the bongo against my chest.

"Come on, I'll get you a glass of wine." He releases me and pads down the hallway. I follow him into a kitchen/breakfast room with beautiful, exposed brick walls and more state-of-the-art appliances than NASA. I bet only his cleaner knows how to use half of them.

"I've decanted a bottle of Pinot Noir. Does that sound OK?" he asks, bending down to get a wine glass from the cupboard, providing me with a view of that glorious backside.

"Sure," I reply, with fake confidence, cringing at the memory of asking him if he wanted a drink in my flat.

If he knew the crap my flatshare drank at this hour on a Saturday morning, he wouldn't ask me if I was concerned about whether my wine was decanted.

He hands me the glass.

"You live here alone?" I ask. I can't imagine living somewhere this size by myself. So far in my 28 years of life on earth, I am yet to experience living alone.

"Cheers." He lifts his glass to mine, and he anchors his attention back to me. "Yes. Just me."

My eyes widen. "How many bedrooms?"

"Five bedrooms, two reception rooms," he responds in amusement. "You were expecting me to live in some glass box in the middle of the sky in central London."

"With a swimming pool and strippers' pole." I smirk. "I didn't imagine suburbia. Don't you get lonely here?" I ask. Then I roll my eyes. "I expect you have a lot of company."

He shoots me a warning look. "I've lived alone since my marriage broke down. Over a decade now." He shrugs. "I'm used to it. Karl sometimes stays here when he's in town."

My brows shoot up. *Is Karl here?*

"Tonight, it's just us." He smiles at me suggestively, and a current of excitement flows through me.

Tonight, he's mine, *all* mine.

"Come, I'll give you a tour."

He takes my hand and directs me from room to room, explaining each room's quirks and history. It's minimalist but classic and stylish, like a show home. His cleaner must come every day.

"I can't believe I let you into my flat," I mutter, following behind him. "Into my squalor of a bedroom. How embarrassing."

He stops at the foot of the grand staircase, raising a brow in amusement. "I was delighted to see the inside of your bedroom. I wasn't there for the decor."

He nods for me to advance up the stairs. "I happen to like your bedroom. It's creative. It reflects your personality."

"Gee, thanks," I hit back sarcastically. "It's an attic room with a skylight for a window and furniture sourced from the local charity shops. What does that say about my personality?"

I walk up the stairs feeling uncharacteristically out of breath. Maybe it's because he is tailing me with a full view of my backside. Or the fact that there is one crucial room I haven't seen yet.

"How long have you lived here?" I babble as we reach the top of the stairs.

"Five years, give or take," he says, leading me along the top hallway.

"I bet you weren't living in an attic room when you were my age."

"No. I was living in the obnoxious penthouse apartment in Kensington. Exactly as you imagined." His deep brown eyes lock onto mine. "Tristan would buy you an apartment in a heartbeat, Charlie. Let him. You can live somewhere without mice, for God's sake."

"Is that what you think of me?" Bitterness fills my mouth. If I had a pound for every time someone said that to me that I'd be as rich as Tristan. "I'm useless without Tristan's money?"

He stops abruptly and turns to face me. "When did I ever give you the impression I thought you were useless? On the contrary ..." Danny leans closer, and I feel the warmth of his breath on my forehead. "I think you are sensational."

His eyes move down to my parted lips like a lion stalking their next meal. My skin tingles in anticipation as I rise up on my tiptoes to inch closer to his face.

*Enough word foreplay.* I'm aching for him to destroy me, to rip me to pieces.

"I need to finish your tour," he says softly.

He pushes open the door to reveal a vast country-style rustic master bedroom with high ceilings and an antique-looking chandelier hanging from the centre.

I gasp and do circles around the room.

My jaw drops as I look out onto the balcony offering unobstructed views across the River Thames. "This is your view when you wake up," I say to myself more than him.

"It's more homely than I was expecting," I murmur as I trail my slightly shaking hand over his oak furniture. "And so tidy. Do you even sleep here?"

I recognise the King size bed frame as a Chesterfield. I'm tempted to run and jump on it, but it's been made with such precision I don't want to ruin the work of art.

How many women have slept in that bed, I wonder?

Instead, I meander into an enclave of the bedroom.

"You have a walk-in wardrobe?" I stare at him incredulously, running my hand across the rows of expensive suits. He is a man of precision. All ties are neatly folded into position and colour coordinated. His shoes are lined up, each pair together. "This is the same size as my bedroom. Do you have a personal stylist as well as an interior designer?"

He leans against the doorway, enjoying my reaction. "I have a tailor that I go to."

"This is why your suits are moulded to you like freaking Batman. The ensuite?" I push open the second door beside the walk-in wardrobe, and he follows slowly behind me.

A freestanding white luxurious bath stands centerpiece, so clean it looks like it's never been used, and a walk-in shower to the side with enough room to host an orgy.

How many women has he had in the bath? In the double shower? Maybe not even one at a time.

It smells of him, but none of his products are on display. Where is all his clutter? Even the soap dispensers blend into the decor like art structures.

"Underfloor heating." I curl my feet on the warm floor.

Taking up floor-to-ceiling space on one of the walls is a deluxe mirror with lighting bordering it.

He appears in the mirror behind me, his dark eyes holding mine, and I remind myself to breathe.

"Do you like what you see?" he whispers behind me, making the hairs on my neck stand to attention.

I can't wait to have this man buried deep inside me.

"Yes," I rasp.

In the mirror, his eyes unashamedly watch my lips. "See how breathtaking you are," he says in a low growl, his breath tickling my ear.

I stand frozen, swallowing the nervous lump in

my throat.

His hands possessively tighten around my hips. "You're driving me out of my fucking mind." His voice is dark and husky, almost angry.

The mirror lighting throws shades on his jawline, making him look equally beautiful and predatory. This man is miles apart from any man I've been with before.

My breathing catches as he pushes away the hair from my shoulder and starts kissing my neck first softly, then with urgency and aggression.

He's so tall he has to hunker down to reach my shoulders. His touch burns a trail down my neck, and I squirm restlessly against him, moaning.

I feel him grow and press against my lower back. I grind my backside into his cock, and he lets out a low groan.

His hands roam across my chest, finding my hardening nipples through my sweater.

"Hands up," he murmurs against my neck, and I put both arms in the air as he pulls the sweater off. It tugs on his watch, and a thread unravels. "I'll buy you a new one."

I'm wearing a strappy top and a black lace bra. Watching in the mirror, he pushes the strappy top down to my stomach and unclips my bra so that my breasts fall loose.

His eyes bore hungrily into my naked chest in the mirror, a slow sexy smile lighting up his face.

His hands engulf my breasts, stroking and squeezing my rock-hard nipples, then travel down the front of my jeans. From behind me, he undoes my jean buttons. Gripping them in his hands, he slides them down, pulling my panties with them also.

I lift my legs up and out of the jeans so that I'm standing completely naked in front of him.

His jaw drops open as he takes in my complete naked form looking at me like he's never seen a naked woman. There's so much *hunger* on his face it terrifies me.

Has anyone ever looked at me this way before?

"This doesn't seem fair," I murmur through a nervous laugh. "I'm naked and on display, and you are fully dressed."

"It's fair. I've waited so long to see this. To see you."

His hands roam down between my inner thighs, and he pushes my legs apart.

Thank God I waxed. I flinch as he spreads my lips apart down *there* with his fingers, showing *everything.*

Something feral sounding escapes him.

"You shouldn't have waited so long," I whimper as he pushes a finger inside my wetness and starts exploring.

His jaw clenches. "We both know I'm not allowed to. I made a promise."

I cry out as he finds my clit. "Yes ... that's good ... keep going," I gasp through ragged breath.

He presses me up against him, and I roll my head back on his chest. He's a full head above me in the mirror. He breathes heavily against me, his jaw slack in the mirror as he watches. "I can't be around you and keep my distance."

He groans at the sound of my growing arousal. "Watch in the mirror, sweetheart. Every time you play with yourself, I want you to imagine it's this moment. That it's me getting you off."

I don't disclose that I already do that.

We watch his hands as he strokes faster and deeper.

He pulses his fingers against my clit, and I feel heat and chills simultaneously up and down my body.

I rock my head back against his chest, moaning as pleasure ripples through my core. My hands tighten around the arm holding me against him.

"Good girl." His eyes blaze with determination.

My legs feel like they are going to collapse. He holds me upright with one arm as he continues to relentlessly stimulate my clit with his fingers.

"Ah," I scream. "*Please*, Danny."

The orgasm crashes over me as my legs give in, and he catches my weight with his other arm. I cry out so loudly there's an echo around the bathroom.

Giving me no time to recover, he flips me around to face him, hitching me up in his arms so that my breasts are in his face.

I shriek as he pulls one of my nipples into his mouth, sucking hard. Then he carries me out of the bathroom, back into the bedroom, and throws me down on the bed.

I bounce then the mattress moulds around me. I could sleep on this baby for a week.

He advances on top of me, taking each breast in turn, sucking hard and aggressively.

I grab handfuls of his hair and pull as he pinches my nipple in his teeth. A mix of pain and pleasure.

My sex *aches* to be touched.

I wrap my legs around his still fully clothed body and moan. His hard-on grinds aggressively in the pulsing apex between my thighs, his face fighting impatience.

I grab the bottom of his T-shirt and tug. I need more. I need *him.*

He releases my nipples from his mouth and sits up, letting me peel the T-shirt off him.

His broad chest is how I imagined, better if that's possible. How does he maintain these muscles? His chest is sprinkled with dark hair and faded scarring across his chest. On his upper arm, there is a black and white mythical Norse tattoo, and the inside of the opposite forearm has a tribal design tattoo with writing. I stroke his chest, making a mental note to ask him about them later.

"These need to come off too," I pant, grinding my bare pussy against his covered legs. I fumble with his jean buttons, and he moves to help me, unfastening them at speed.

He pulls the jeans off along with his boxers, and his massive, hard cock springs free. It stands up hard and thick, just inches from my belly.

I'll never be able to take him.

He grins, watching my shock. "Scared?"

I gawk at it. "That thing will never fit."

He chuckles, bending down to put his lips on mine. "Don't worry, we'll start gently."

His head travels downwards, and he pushes open my thighs as far as they will go leaving me exposed and vulnerable.

"Wait, Danny," I stammer, trying to close my legs around his head. "I've never let a man do that before."

Jerking him off in the toilets was an anomaly. I'm actually a bit of a prude. Vanilla sex is my forte.

He looks up in surprise. "You've never had a man's mouth down here before?"

I shake my head, embarrassed at my lack of sexual experience. "You're probably used to women swinging upside down from the chandelier."

His mouth twitches. "Why not, sweetheart?"

"I've always been worried they wouldn't like it," I explain, blushing. "Like the taste of me, I mean ..." My voice trails off.

His jaw slackens. "You cannot be fucking serious? I've been fantasising about tasting you all night." He groans, his voice thick with arousal: "Every time I see you, I imagine what it's like to go down on you."

*Holy fucking shit.*

The way this man talks to me. Boyfriends never talk this dirty, this openly. I feel like a goddess.

He moves upwards and cups my face in his hands. "Do you have any idea how much I want you?"

I stutter, and an incoherent whimper comes out.

My mouth isn't connected to my brain.

"Do you trust me, baby?" his voice softens.

I nod, and he gently prizes my legs open. His lips press back against mine as he kisses me like he's starved. It's a wet, messy and urgent kiss, two people not holding back, devouring each other.

I close my eyes and grab handfuls of his hair.

His fingers travel downwards and stroke my wet opening. He slides two fingers deep inside me and pulses gently. I grind against him to push the fingers deeper as my arousal starts to build.

He slips them out of me and pushes them into his mouth, sucking them slowly.

"Best course of the day." He grins darkly as his head sinks down into my thighs. He lifts my leg over his shoulder, and I feel him gently widen my lips with his fingers.

I inhale sharply as his tongue dives deep into my opening with no warning. I resist the urge to close my legs as he eats me, licking and sucking relentlessly around my clit.

My pussy clenches around his tongue as it enters *again* and *again*, and I don't know if I will survive this.

I arch my back and let out a scream, pulling hard on his hair.

So *this* is why he lives in a secluded area.

As he sucks hard on my engorged bud with the skill of a man who has done it many times before, another earth-shattering orgasm bubbles up inside me as I spasm around his tongue.

The sound of my wetness slapping on his tongue fills the air, and he grunts in appreciation.

"So good," he growls into me. "Come for me, Charlie."

I've lost all shyness, all inhibitions. All that matters is that he keeps sucking down there. Consumed with unprecedented desire, I clench his head in a vice as his sucking intensifies.

I can't hold it anymore.

I gasp for air as my body takes over, and my arousal shoots through my swollen flesh, my legs shaking as I release.

Oh. My. GOD.

Why did I wait so long to let a man do this? Although I doubt any other man's tongue could do this to me.

He steadies his breathing, and he comes up again to my mouth, kissing me hard. I taste myself on his lips.

"Do you know what a turn-on it is knowing I'm the only one to have ever tasted you?" He groans into my mouth. "I could come just thinking about it."

He presses his body down on mine, and I feel every muscle, every curve of his perfect sculpture.

Truth to be told, I've never had multiple orgasms in one night.

With Ben, I'd become a bit of a faker. Now, here with Danny Walker, I'm trying to reign myself in. Everything about him reminds me of sex. How he stares at me, what he says to me, how he breathes.

Even offering that decanted wine turned me on.

His hardness presses against my inner thigh, and he kisses me, bearing his weight with his biceps.

I wrap my legs around his hips and push myself into his rock-hard dick so that it grows slick with my juices, making me shiver with the promise of what's to come.

We are skin on skin now, impatiently grinding against each other.

I can't get enough of this man, my thirst for him is *insatiable.*

My hand reaches down to curl around the base of his cock. I want, no, *need*, to taste him like he tasted me.

I push him off me, forcing him to rise from the bed then drop to my knees in front of him.

"Your turn," I murmur.

We stare at each other as I take him in my hands and slide my lips over the head of his shaft. He lets out a moan, and I take more of him in my mouth, inch by inch.

The shallow sucking becomes deeper, and he thrusts into my mouth with heavy breaths. I swallow the urge to gag as he grabs a handful of my hair and pushes himself in so deep that he hits the back of my throat.

His eyes fix on me as the moist sounds of my sucking fill the bedroom, along with his ragged breathing.

"Charlie," he growls. "Fuck, that feels so good."

My jaw aching, I resist the gag reflex and take him hard, again and again.

"No," he says in a strangled voice, pulling my hair back gently. I ignore his pleas and keep thrusting.

"Charlie," he rasps, pulling himself away so that he swings free from my mouth. "I'm too close already."

His length glistens at my eye line, coated with wetness.

I stare up at him in question.

"I want to come inside you." His voice is dark and raspy. "Are you on the pill?"

I nod.

"Good. I'm going to fill you up with my cum."

Holy God, this man talks dirty.

I smirk up at him. "You know, with chat like that, you'd make a good porn star."

He pulls me onto my feet and throws me down onto the bed, climbing on top of me. My legs clamp around him, digging my heels into his buttocks.

"I want you in me. *Now*," I demand, digging my nails into his back.

With our eyes locked, he strokes his shaft across my wet slit. My clit quivers as he teases me, and I arch my back into his groin. "*Please*, Danny."

I glare at him like I'm starved, and he grins back at me, eyes drowning in arousal, before pushing the head of his shaft into my slit, first gently before slamming into me with his erection.

I whimper as my core reacts to his size.

Cursing, he eases the pressure, thrusting gently, stretching me until I visibly relax.

"You OK, sweetheart?" he whispers.

I nod, unable to speak, grinding my knees against his hips.

He thrusts into me at just the right spot, and I moan hard against his mouth, feeling another orgasm rising up in my core. *It's too soon.*

"I've been dreaming about being inside you for a long time." Heat floods his eyes as he stares at me. "For my cock to fill your tight pussy."

I roll my head back, moaning. "Do you know how good this feels?" I press his buttocks into me so that he goes deeper.

"You want deeper?" he whispers hoarsely.

"Yes," I cry out.

He pumps harder. Until he is buried to the hilt, and he can't possibly get any deeper in me.

"That feels so fucking good," I moan.

A growl rumbles from his throat as my muscles clench hard and territorial around him.

"Damn," he moans, sweat glistening on his forehead. "I'm going to come quickly if you keep doing that."

I grab his hair hard as my entire body shudders with the pressure of him thrusting in and out repeatedly until I can't hold on any longer. Another orgasm rips through me even more powerful than the last.

His cock pulses furiously in retaliation, and I feel every movement as he comes deep inside me, his warm liquid pumping fast and furious into me.

We collapse back onto the bed, both panting, our skin sticking together with sweat and arousal. I melt into the bed covers, elated, exhausted, raw.

He runs a hand lazily over my sweat-soaked body, and I turn my head to face him. His dark eyes hold mine, and *something* passes between us. An acknowledgement, a recognition.

This wasn't just good sex. This was the best sex of my life. And the way he is staring at me right now? He agrees one hundred percent.

"Stop staring at me like that." I smirk.

He smiles, trailing a finger along my cheek and down my neck. The lights of the River Thames cast shadows over his masculine jaw, and I take in his features in awe. Without a doubt, right now, I'm the luckiest girl in London.

"You're heart-stopping," he whispers. "I'm not sure my poor heart can take this."

His large thigh shifts on top of me, crushing me as if he's forgotten how much heavier he is than me.

"Come on." He rouses from the pillow. "Before we fall asleep in this mess. Let's get you clean again."

"I'm not sure I can make it to the shower." I giggle. "I might need a walking stick."

I don't know what's happening between us, but one thing's for sure, I'll never be able to go back from this.

# 22

## Charlie

I wake in a bed so comfortable I think I'm floating and stare up at the ceiling, grinning like a lunatic. A bulky arm rests across my stomach and a thigh is wrapped around my hip. A sharp object pushes into the small of my back. It's the perfect cage.

He's heavy, but I can't bring myself to lift him. My bladder is bursting, but I'm not budging. I'll die in this spooning position, and they will just have to shape my coffin accordingly.

I cast a look over my shoulder to find him sleeping soundly, his face buried into my neck and his broad chest rising and falling.

I spent the night in Danny Walker's house.

In Danny Walker's bed.

Using Danny Walker as a blanket.

Twenty-year-old 'me' does a little victory dance in my head.

Somehow, this position seems more intimate than the endless sex the night before. We didn't drift off to sleep until at least 4 a.m. My inner thighs are still raw from being pushed apart, and my lady parts feel like they have done twenty rounds with a jackhammer.

His skin is warm against mine, and I know he's fully naked under the covers. I feel his breath on the back of my neck, and there's a sharp wheezing sound, like the sound of a goose being strangled.

I stifle a giggle to stop him from waking.

He stirs slightly, and I shut my eyes to pretend I'm still sleeping.

His thighs tighten around my waist as his cock hardens against my hip. He wakes himself fully with a giant snore as if someone has squeezed his airway shut, and I continue to act dead.

His mouth brushes along my neck planting soft kisses down to my shoulders. I'm wearing his T-shirt that goes down to my waist, and his erection digs into my bare skin.

Relief floods me that he doesn't scream with the sight of me in his bed.

"I know you're awake," he whispers in my ear as his hands travel down my stomach until he reaches my crotch and pushes two fingers into my sensitive slit like he owns it.

*Oh, God, that feels good.*

I inhale sharply and open my eyes. "Morning."

His face is inches from mine, and I hope my mascara hasn't given me panda eyes. I can't hide in the dim lights of night-time or under the excuse of alcohol influence.

*You're mine* comes a determined voice in my head as I stare into that handsome face.

*I'm not going to give you up.*

"Morning, you," he replies in his husky tone. "Did you sleep OK?" he asks softly as my insides begin to quiver from his strokes.

"Best bed I've ever slept in," I say, arching into his touch. "Although we've only technically been sleeping for four hours."

My breathing becomes laboured as his fingers tease my swollen clit.

This is embarrassing; I'm going to come quickly if he keeps doing this.

He'll think he is a god if all he has to do is touch for a few seconds and I lose control. I turn into him, wiggling my pussy against his crotch, and he groans.

"Hold it," he growls. "I'm coming inside you."

He gets on top of me and pushes my legs apart with his knees thrusting his erection up into my apex. "Spread your legs."

"Wait, Danny," I breathe, tightening my arms around his waist. "I'm tender. Go easy on me."

"Whatever you need, sweetheart. I'll be nice and gentle."

"You sure can fuck for an old bloke." I giggle.

"Cheeky bitch. I'm forty, not seventy," he grumbles. "I'll lose stamina if you keep talking like that."

His lips brush mine, and his tongue slides softly through my lips as he takes his length and runs it up and down my slit.

"Slow, remember," I whimper into his mouth as he pushes his tip inside me.

I wince and dig my hands into his back. I've never been this sensitive after sex.

"Relax," he whispers softly as he inches in and out until he feels my muscles let him in.

Our kiss deepens, and then he's fully in; I wrap my legs around his waist and push his buttocks into me.

My shallow moans are joined by his deep grunts and the sounds of boaters on the Thames. *Every* part of me is craving this.

"I'm not going to last," he growls and I know that I won't either. "I can't go slow."

Cursing, he thrusts into the deepest spot in my core again and again. His eyebrows knit together, and his mouth slackens into that gorgeous expression that tells me he's so close to coming.

"Fuck … you feel too good … I can't hold it."

Seeing him this turned on by me just accelerates my own climax, and I hold my legs tight around him as we race towards release.

With one final thrust, his liquid pumps furiously into me, and I feel every drop with such force a shudder of intense pleasure rip through my body.

"That's embarrassing," he pants. "That really was a quickie."

Our eyes lock, and he bends down to kiss me on the tip of the nose. "You're sensational, Charlotte Kane."

And you're unforgettable, Danny Walker, which is a big issue.

**Danny**

I have a full view of her body in the bright bathroom lights and take in every line, every curve like I've just been given the gift of sight.

She looks up at me, wet hair sticking to her forehead and water flowing over those plump lips. I stare down at that flushed, devastatingly gorgeous face, and my breath hitches.

*She's unbelievable.*

The sex was more than I could ever have imagined. Unforgettable mind-blowing sex.

The water forms waterfalls over the curve of her breasts, and my cock springs to life. The most minor thing sets me off.

"That thing always seems to be ready to go." She stares at my erection wide-eyed.

I grin down at her, washing every inch of her body with meticulous detail. I slide my hands up her inner thighs and circle around her opening, making her moan softly.

Will I ever get enough of this woman? Just looking at her drives me fucking wild.

I need to go easy on her. She was whimpering this morning.

I just can't control myself.

She raises a brow, amused. "I think I'm clean now."

She takes my cock in her little hand, and I'm putty; the girl owns me and my dick. A growl rumbles from my lips as she wraps her fingers around my shaft and starts pumping.

Then without warning, she is on her knees, sliding me in and out of her beautiful, soft mouth like she's starving.

"Fuck ... Charlie ... so fucking good," I rasp out. "Don't stop."

Widening her mouth, she slides me all the way to the back of her throat, and I wrap my fingers through her hair, fighting the urge to ram myself deeper.

Aiming my gaze downwards, I watch her swallowing my cock, and I'm hypnotised.

Her big eyes look up at me adoringly, and I know I can't watch this for long without coming. "I'm gonna come, sweetheart," I warn her, my eyes rolling up to the ceiling.

Ignoring me, she sucks deeper and faster, and I know I'm a goner. When I look down again, she stares up at me, cheeks flushed, eyes burning with determination.

Groaning loudly, my cock jerks as I empty myself into her mouth, and she drinks it down, never breaking my gaze.

"Thank you, sweetheart." I breathe heavily as I pull her up to standing and take her in my arms.

"You're welcome."

My lips take hers in a soft, lingering kiss then I pull back to stare into that beautiful face.

"OK, now I'm hungry," she tells me, releasing herself from my hold.

"What the lady wants, the lady shall get," I reply, opening the door of the double shower.

Standing behind her, I wrap a towel around her and squeeze her tight like she's a gift all wrapped up for me.

Her gaze meets mine in the bathroom mirror. "I've got no toothbrush with me."

"I've got some spare." I lean over and open the top cabinet taking out a toothbrush.

She frowns as she watches me. "One for every girl of the week"

"Not quite," I reply dryly. "I'm single, Charlie. What do you expect?"

I turn her around. "I want to spend the day with you," I say before I can stop myself.

Her face lights up.

"First, I'm going to make you breakfast, then I'm going to fuck you again."

\*\*\*

Thirty minutes later, she is perched on my breakfast bar in my sweater, five sizes too big for her and barely covering her underwear as her toned, naked legs swing out.

"Can you even cook?" She eyes me suspiciously as I add oil to the pan. "Tristan's like a giant baby waiting on other people to feed him. I assumed you were the same."

I turn to face her, indignant. "You assumed wrong. I can cook. Any more of that cheek, and you won't find out."

The sweater hangs down to expose a naked shoulder. Her dark brown hair tumbles loosely in waves over the curves of her breasts, messy and unbrushed, and the outline of her nipple shows she's not wearing a bra. I lick my lips, visualising those pink nipples underneath.

I might need to request she puts on a bra if she doesn't want burnt bacon.

I want her to wear this outfit for the rest of her life; hell, I'll even change the employee terms and conditions to allow her to walk around the office in my sweater.

I notice, with guilt, a redness forming on her neck where my stubble has punctured her skin. I was too rough last night.

She tries to look over my shoulder at the contents of the pan. "So long as it's not some weird Scottish haggis or black pudding."

"What did I say?" I warn, coming around her to squeeze her waist. "Less cheek, or you'll go hungry."

"You're such a grown-up." She exhales. "Look at all these gadgets. You have a juicer *and* a blender. And a pasta maker. Do you even know how to make pasta?"

"Not yet," I admit, pouring a cup of coffee and handing it to her. "Someday."

"I don't know what the hell those are for." She stares at my meat-shredding claws. "Like serial killer forks."

I chuckle, turning the bacon. "My meat shredders."

"Meat shredders." She repeats slowly. "I'm not sure I'm safe here."

I roll my eyes and set down two plates of sourdough bread, poached eggs, bacon, and avocado.

"Wait." Her eyes light up like she's been on a week-long fast. "Let me get this straight. You can give me multiple orgasms, and you can cook?"

"Glad I exceeded your expectations."

She loads up a massive spoonful of food. "Perhaps you're not the ogre I thought you were."

"I am," I reply, sitting down opposite her at the breakfast bar. "Don't let this fool you."

She shoves the spoonful into her mouth and starts spluttering, food spitting out. "My food usually gets a better reaction."

"Oh my god, Danny." She giggles. "There's a love bite on you."

I turn to the mirror to see a dark red bite mark on my lower neck.

*Fuck.* The threat of castration by Tristan looms.

# 23

**Charlie**

Ten miles down the road there's an elephant in the car called Tristan, now flashing on Danny's car display screen.

We are making our way to a lido near Richmond where Danny swims.

Given that it's fifteen degrees outside and I don't have his Scottish weatherproof skin, I'm a little apprehensive. Still, I said yes to save face rather than shatter the illusion of being young, adventurous, and carefree.

"Charlie." He looks over at me from the driver's seat. "I need to answer this."

"I'll be quiet." I roll my eyes. "Your dirty secret is safe."

"Tristan," he answers as he puts him on the loudspeaker.

"Mate," Tristan says through the speaker. "Did you get the custody form? You need to sign it as a reference."

"I'll do it this evening. I'm out now."

"Sure. Then hopefully she can't screw me over any longer."

I wince as I hear a darker, angrier Tristan than I'm used to. Danny gives me a sheepish sidewards glance.

"She can't leave the country with my son, Danny."

I stare aghast at Danny, but he ignores me. Gemina is trying to leave England? Why didn't Tristan tell me? He told Danny but not *me*, his own sister?

"We'll do it, Tristan," Danny says softly, bringing the Aston Martin to a stop. "She won't take Daniel." His voice is confident, but he fails to hide the concern on his face.

"Listen," Tristan starts. "Go easy on Mara, OK? She's working on a critical case, and I can't have her distracted. Don't turn her goo-eyed like all the others."

Mara. Perfect bloody Mara. I had forgotten about her. Her name does weird things to my stomach.

Danny visibly flinches beside me.

All the other goo-eyed morons *like me*. I squirm in my seat. How many does he have?

*You knew this*, a small voice chastises me. *Don't get emotionally attached.*

"Listen, I gotta go," Danny says hurriedly. "I'm running some errands."

Tristan's laugh booms from the speaker. "Since when do you do your own errands?"

"Bye, Tristan." Danny ends the call.

I plaster my big girl smile on. Mara might be the perfect match, but she's not here now. *I am.* I will get into this pond and show Danny Walker what a funtime girl I really am.

***

Swimming in a pond isn't as romantic and zen as it sounds. For a start, I've been here for twenty minutes, and I haven't managed to actually get into the water. I have gotten as far as my knees so far, and that took a lot of willpower and pain. Now I understand what Jack means when he explains to Rose about the water hitting you like a thousand knives.

Danny stripped off and jumped in as soon as he'd turned off the ignition like some kind of freak fish-boy and has been trying to coax me in ever since.

"Charlie, just jump in," he shouts from the water. "You're making it worse for yourself."

"No," I hiss at him.

There is sneering and snorts of laughter behind me. To top it all off, I'm being victimised by a gang of ten-year-old boys.

"What a wuss, lady!" the ginger one shouts at me.

I glare at him. "Go fuck yourself, dipshit!"

"Charlie." Danny shakes his head, laughing. "He's about ten. You can't say that to him. Anyway, you are being a wuss."

"Listen, Pamela Anderson," I snap back. "I don't need a few little pricks taunting me. If I'm doing this, I'm doing it my way."

"No, you're not," Ginger sings at me, inching forward.

"What are you doing?' I demand, flapping my

arms at him. "Don't come any closer."

Smelling my fear, his confidence grows. He waves his pre-pubescent army over.

"Come on, lads, let's get her!"

They advance on me like rodents on a dead bird. Pushing and shoving me.

"Get off, you little motherfuckers." My screams are smothered by high-pitched giggles and cries of 'get her.'

With a final shove, Ginger sends me flying into the lake, and I hit the water with force. A thousand knives immediately stab every pore of my skin from my toes to my ears. Jack from Titanic was spot on. I'm having a heart attack.

Strong arms pull me up, and as I hit the surface, my mouth lets out a scream so blood-curdling even the ducks do a mass exodus.

I thrash around wildly in the water, cursing, and I swear I've forgotten how to breathe.

The gang laugh from the riverbank.

"Assholes," I bellow, sticking my middle finger up at them. "I'll fucking murder each and every one of you."

"Easy, Charlie! They're just playing!" Danny wraps my legs around him so that he's holding up my weight. "You'll have a gang of angry mothers over here if you carry on like that."

I turn to him, spitting out water. "Don't you start," I growl with such ferocity that he cowers.

***

It's hard to stay mad with a man with a washboard stomach and a jawline that could cut glass. Especially since he is naked now, towelling himself dry in front of me, and even though he has been in freezing water, he's still huge.

We are in the outdoor changing rooms after my near-death experience. I'll admit I may have overreacted a tad, but I'm still freezing to the core.

"You are indecent in that string thing," he murmurs as he towels me dry. "The triangle barely covers your best bits."

"It's two sizes too small, remember?" We made a detour via a clothes shop before hitting the lido, but it was limited in choices. Of all the things to bring to Danny Walker's house on Saturday night, a bikini was not on my list.

"Good thing no other men were here to see you," he growls. "I would have knocked out anyone who looked."

"Except for that violent gang," I mutter as I turn around to hang up my wet bikini bra. "My bones have turned to ice with the shock of the attack."

"We can get you warm again." He grabs me from behind and pins me against the wall.

"What the hell are you—"

Before I finish my sentence, he has pushed my bikini bottoms aside and slipped a finger deep into my sex.

"Seriously?" I gasp. "Here?"

My body betrays me and my legs part to give him

more access.

The sound of him massaging my clit echoes around the cubicle and no doubt reaches the ears of anyone close by. My heart thuds. Will they know what's happening?

When did I become such a voyeurist?

"If we don't do it, I'm walking out of here with a raging erection." He groans way too loudly. "This bikini has me all hot and bothered."

"Keep your voice down," I reply, half giggling, half reprimanding him. "There are people in the other cubicles."

"Probably wishing they were doing this." He grinds his erection up against me, and the pulsing heat in my core grows.

Tugging my bikini bottom out of the way, he enters me from behind, hard and deep.

"Danny." I gasp at the sharpness.

He loses control and really gives it to me. His heat sears my cold skin, intensifying his thickness.

I clench tighter than ever and bite down on my lip, trying to stay quiet.

I don't know if it's because of the cold, the bikini, or the fact that anyone could hear us, but in less than a minute, I hear his laboured breathing behind me and know he's so close, he's not going to hold it.

"Damn, Charlie." He lets out a shaky laugh. "I'm not sure I'm going to be able to get it back out."

"Your problem." I breathe heavily, grinding into his rhythm. "You put it in. You get it out."

\*\*\*

We spent the last two hours drinking hot chocolate in the car with the heater on.

I'm not sure if it was triggered by the shock of the cold water or the sex afterwards, but I've entered a state of delirium where I have the giggles over anything and everything.

"This is how Danny the Destroyer, tech tycoon, spends a Sunday," I muse, blowing on my hot chocolate. "When he's not playing with his meat grinders, of course."

"Meat-shredding claws," he corrects, sliding his hands through my hair. "I'm not an abattoir."

"You have no clue what those things do, boy." I roll my eyes. "You made that shit up."

"I know exactly how to grind my meat, thank you very much." He grins. "I've had an enjoyable afternoon," he says with a lazy sexy smile on his lips. "Swimming with you was … entertaining."

A snort escapes me. "Dangerous, more like. I nearly died at the hands of those sharks."

"Pretty dangerous." He nods. "I almost lost my dick to a viper vagina. You used to love swimming. Remember when Tristan and I used to take you swimming when you were a kid?"

"Vaguely." I screw up my face trying to remember. "I was about seven, right?"

"And I was twenty," he chokes.

I arch an eyebrow in his direction. "The age difference doesn't matter now. I'm a grown woman if you haven't noticed."

"You make it impossible for me to forget."

My stomach rumbles loudly and reminds us of the fact that the day is creeping into late afternoon.

"I suppose I better ... drive you home," he murmurs quietly, looking at the car clock. "I have some work to look over this evening."

"Sure." I shrug, feigning indifference.

My night of fun is finally over.

A silence sweeps over us, and I can see his brain clogs whirling. He clears his throat. "Unless you want to come back to mine this evening so that I can show you my meat shredding claw in operation?"

I hide a smirk. "That sounds like something I need to see."

**Danny**

There is an intimacy I'm feeling that shouldn't be there and is giving me warning bells. Why did I invite her back tonight again? It was supposed to end this morning when I had fucked her out of my system.

Why am I playing boyfriend with her?

What the fuck am I doing?

I watch her as she stretches her long legs out on the sofa, her head resting against my chest.

She's back in that oversized sweater of mine that she belongs in and sprawled out like she owns the damn place. Her thick hair is spread out all over my chest and bicep.

She's wearing my boxers while she washes her

underwear which is a massive turn on, knowing her little cunt is rubbing against my fabric.

She has no idea how devastatingly attractive she is. I often wonder if she would be a different person if she realised. She does it effortlessly, minimal make-up, messy hair, frayed jeans. This is what sets her apart, her tomboy nature, not giving a fuck.

That bikini, I've never seen anything so sexual and sensational despite the fact she was thrashing about the pond like a mad bitch.

We had sex *again* after the outdoor changing rooms. I feel fucking spent.

We've been watching a movie for two hours, and neither of us is paying attention. We've been laughing, cuddling, and finding any opportunity to touch each other. I'm rubbing her damn feet, for Christ's sake.

*She's* the only thing I can focus on when she's in the room. This is why I need her to take voluntary redundancy before I plummet the company into negative equity. I've been shirking my responsibilities. It took all my willpower to force my eyes from her long enough to print and sign the form for Tristan. I am supposed to write my speech this evening for the annual security tech event in Canary Wharf. I guess I'm winging it again.

Something has changed in the space of twenty-four hours. This time yesterday, we were acting awkward and ignoring each other at dinner. Now? I'm staring at her like a love-sick teenager.

The film credits roll, and she sits up. "I need to

watch that again." She smirks. "Your amazing foot massage distracted me."

"Who knew I was a man of many talents? Cook. Lifeguard. Now masseuse, all in one day."

"Human dildo," she adds with a half-grin, rubbing her foot along my crotch.

"That's my favourite way to serve you." I smile, running my fingers over her foot.

"A multidimensional man," she says softly. She presses her lips together, looks at me then looks away.

"Spit it out, Charlie," I say, waiting.

"Do you think I'm stupid?"

I stare, puzzled wondering about the turn of topic. "Why on earth would you ask that? Where has this come from?"

"Come on, Danny." She rolls her eyes. "Most people in Nexus went to Cambridge or Oxford or Harvard or some other genius university. I went to Warwick."

"I'm not Cambridge/Oxford-educated. Neither is Tristan," I say, raising a brow.

"But you are highly successful. I know you think I'm not up to the Nexus standard. Don't bullshit me."

"Where is this coming from?" I ask, slightly thrown. "The truth is I think you need more experience. But I also think you are a beautiful, intelligent, sensationally creative girl."

"Girl?" She grimaces.

"Woman," I correct.

She stares at me, deflated. "I'm not a leggy blonde human rights lawyer. Why would you split up with her?"

"I wanted something casual; she didn't."

She clears her throat awkwardly, avoiding my gaze. "I get it; you don't do the commitment thing."

I expel a breath. I don't like where this conversation is going.

"Hey." I shake her ankle, forcing her to look at me. "We don't know what this is ... let's just enjoy it, OK?"

"Sure." She swallows. "I get it."

"Danny," she starts again. "Do you remember all those years ago?"

"I remember," I cut in.

Hurt flashes across her face.

"Why did you push me away?"

"You were twenty, Charlie." I sigh. "I was thirty-three. You were too young for me. You were blind drunk. Despite my reputation, I don't take advantage of young drunk girls. No matter how breathtaking they are."

"And now?" she whispers.

I reach over, scooping her up in my arms. "Now I'm well and truly fucked."

# 24

**Charlie**

The bed is cold when I wake up, running my hand over the spot where his body should be. My phone tells me it's 6 a.m. Monday morning, *yuck*.

The fantasy is over. Now I need to travel all the way across London to get ready for work.

The bedroom is eerily quiet. Where is he?

I peel off the bed covers and shuffle out of bed. Hmmm, the underfloor heating is on. No wonder he can wake up early.

There's no sign of him on the top floor.

Padding down the stairs in my underwear, his dry husky voice gets louder as I reach the bottom step. I follow the sound towards the kitchen.

"Write up the proposal and send it to me this morning, Michael." He has his back to me and his headphones in. "The deal needs to close tomorrow."

6 a.m. on a Monday morning, and he's already in work mode. I can barely muster the strength to brush my teeth yet.

He's wearing a black suit sculpted around his muscles, and as he turns around, I see that he's cleanly shaven, highlighting his razor-sharp jaw.

One glance at him in that suit, and I'm turned inside out.

There's a distinct slant to one of his eyebrows as he clocks my state of undress, making me self-consciously cross my arms over my chest.

He gives a brief nod of recognition and mouths 'five minutes.'

It must be the States if he's on this early. I can tell there's a number of them on the call from the names he's firing out, his commanding tone dishing out orders.

CEO Danny is *sexy as fuck.*

I sidestep him in the kitchen and grab a glass from the cupboard as quietly as I can.

When I'm at the tap, I jump slightly as his hand encircles my waist from behind, pushing me against the cloth of his tailored suit. "I need to go. I'll call you in the office."

"Good morning, beautiful," his commanding tone drops into a softer one.

He moves my hair and sends a trail of kisses down my neck, making me shiver.

"Morning," I say huskily, turning around to face him.

"This is a spectacular view to see first thing in the morning," he murmurs darkly, his eyes running up and down my body. "I hope I didn't wake you. There's coffee in the pot."

"No." I shift consciously from foot to foot. "I need to go back to mine to get ready."

"I'll call my driver."

I shake my head quickly. I don't need his driver knowing I stayed all weekend. "Public transport is quicker."

My eyes widen. "That love bite is still showing through your shirt."

He grimaces slightly, trying to pull up his collar. "I'll have to contend with the rumour mill on that one today." He gives me a half-grin as I flinch. "It was worth the rumours. Don't worry, they won't be able to identify it's *your* marking."

"I really am sorry." I giggle. "I got carried away in the moment."

His phone buzzes again.

"So, this is the life of a CEO, huh? Glad I'm just I.T. Support."

He shoots me an apologetic look.

"It's OK." I wave my hand. "I need to put some clothes on."

Fifteen minutes later, I'm back in my outfit from Saturday night. I've never had such a delayed walk of shame. Danny is resting on a bar stool, talking loudly into his phone with a frown on his face. Should I just sneak out?

I gave a slight wave from the kitchen door.

*Wait*, he mouths.

"I need five minutes," he barks down the phone then puts it on mute.

"I guess I'll see you in the office," I try to say breezily.

"The Nexus office." He walks towards me,

smiling. "You guys are moving into our offices today, remember?"

*Shit.* I had forgotten about that. I better get there early.

"Charlie." He frowns, staring at me. "Our secret, OK?"

I flash him my brightest smile. "Of course."

***

I walk through the ground floor lobby of Nexus, my trainers slipping on the tiled floor. This place is in a league of its own.

The receptionist looks like a hired model. I hand her my details, and she flicks through something on her computer screen, then smiles up at me, handing me a security pass. "Your team is based on the sixth floor."

Dunley Tech had two floors in our previous building. Nexus has all fifteen floors, with the top-level being the directors' floor.

As the Nexus employees line up beside me for the elevator, my stomach starts churning. Why didn't I put more effort into what I'm wearing today? I study myself in the mirrored elevator doors. I'm in my old jeans and sneakers that I always wear on a Monday. We became so complacent at Dunley, wearing jeans and T-shirts without anyone batting an eyelid.

Here, I stick out like a sore thumb in my rags. These coders, many aren't suited, but they are dressed sharply.

I get out on the sixth floor and stare straight out

at one of the tallest buildings in Europe, the Shard. What a backdrop for answering I.T. support calls.

Everything is shiny and sexy.

People are arranging personal items on their desks in an upbeat tempo. In the kitchen area, there is a crowd cooing at the coffee machine while Dan and Alex excitedly try out the bean bag chairs in the chill-out area.

"You're over there, Charlie." Jackie nods to a group of desks.

I don't know why everyone is getting so comfortable." Stevie comes up behind me. "Half of us won't have jobs soon."

"What's that thing Jackie is setting up?"

"She's setting up fucking lighting." He snorts. "So the light catches her at the right angle, she says."

"She's got competition," Stevie adds as we watch her fumbling with the lamp. "Some of the girls in this office are hot as fuck. I don't know how the blokes get any work done."

*She's* got competition? *So do I*, I think, feeling totally inadequate.

"I have to tell you something about the weekend," I say in a hushed voice. "Not here. Lunch."

"You had that dinner party on Saturday night. This better be a filthy story and not something your mother has done."

I flash him a grin. "The *filthiest*."

"This calls for an early lunch."

***

"Don't see this for more than it is."

We are eating burritos far enough away from the office so that no one will eavesdrop.

"I'm not." I tut.

Stevie looks at me wearily.

"Did he say he wanted to see you again?"

"No," I admit, biting my lip. "He asked if we could keep it our little secret."

Saying it out loud makes it sound seedy.

"Umm," he muses. "Just be careful, you have more to lose here than him."

I flinch. "I know, I know, he's the Casanova, and I'm the slut screwing her way to the top."

"You've got that look in your eye. Like you're ignoring all the signs."

"No, I don't," I lie. "I'm fine with a casual fling."

"Look, just let him contact you, OK?" he says firmly. "*Don't* run after him."

"I won't," I promise. "Besides, I've been holding in my farts all weekend; I need a break before my stomach explodes."

"Can you die by holding in your own farts too long?"

*Shit*. I better investigate that.

After lunch, I settle into the usual barrage of annoyed customers reporting failings in our software. I apologise profusely for our wrongdoings with each call.

"Look how fast this thing can go."

I look over, and Stevie is spinning around in his

chair.

"Stop that," I mutter, waving him away. "I'm trying to work here."

"Have you tried all these levers?" He rams his chair into mine.

"Argh! If I do it, will you piss off?" I move out from my desk and push my legs around. It does spin pretty fast. Trying out the new levers is more fun than dealing with angry customers.

"See?" Stevie laughs. "Best chair ever."

We spin around laughing until I feel really dizzy. A few people look up and roll their eyes.

"OK, it is fun," I admit. "I feel sick."

"Glad to see the new employees are enjoying their work," comes an icy female voice from the aisle.

I stop spinning, disoriented, and look up to see Cheryl, Nexus Head of HR, Danny, and some other upper management suits standing in the aisle.

Stevie flinches abruptly beside me, whacking into my chair.

In a cold, detached look of recognition, Danny's eyes meet mine, then a frown of disapproval forms over his face. How long has he been watching our stupid chair escapades?

He's different now. The relaxed Danny Walker rubbing my feet last night is gone. His eyes are dark as they flit between Stevie and me.

"Perhaps you can reshare the company code of conduct, Cheryl," his voice cuts through me, igniting a fire in my cheeks.

I shuffle back to my desk on my chair and hide

under my screen as they stride down the office.

Mature, Charlie. Really mature.

I swallow the lump in my throat and shift focus back to my screen. An email flashes up, and just as I'm about to hit delete, I re-read the title from Nexus HR.

Role opening: *Designer.*

*You will all have heard that we have recently taken over Dunley Tech. Now we are looking for a cutting-edge team to shape the future of these products. Do you have an innovative mind that can drive the future design? If so, read on. ...*

I scroll down, intrigued. After listening to a barrage of complaints for five years, I am brimming with ideas to shape these products.

Excitement swirls in my stomach.

*Submit a business case with three of your top ideas to apply.*

Dare I? It would be humiliating if Danny found out I had applied, but I wouldn't have to tell him. The applicants would never be shared with the CEO. It's way more senior than my current role so I have little chance.

My eyes light up as I scan down further. Two months working from the New York office.

I can apply, and they reject me; no harm done?

*Maybe I can show Danny Walker I'm more than a chair swinging buffoon*, the little voice in charge of hope says in my head.

# 25

## Charlie

Stevie was right. It's been sixty-four hours (yes, I'm counting) and no contact. Not a single text message and it's now mid-week. Clearly, my buffoon behaviour in the office put the nail in the coffin.

As each day passes, I grow more frantic and needy, analysing every minute detail about the weekend. Maybe the sex wasn't as good for him as it was for me? Was he just looking for some company, a playmate for a few days? Is he bored now?

One eye remains permanently glued to the phone, torturing myself. I turn it on and off again and check the coverage. I'm worse off than if the weekend had never happened. Now I've had a taste of how amazing he is. Literally, a taste. And it's gone, out of my reach.

Why did I build this up to be more in my head?

I'm mildly appeased by the fact that I get to spend time this evening with my nephew, Daniel. Daniel is Tristan's son from his toxic marriage to Gemina. I never liked the woman.

Both Danny and I are Daniel's godparents, which made for the most awkward christening ever. Every year Danny buys an obnoxiously expensive present, making mine look pathetic. I'm the fun godparent though.

Tonight, Tristan and Rebecca are going out for a firm event, so I'm babysitting. How he runs a law firm moonlighting as a socialite is beyond me. He's always at some gala or drinks event. The man never sleeps.

At least I can work on my business case for the role vacancy while Daniel is sleeping. If my rejected heart will let me focus on anything other than Mr. fuck-me-all-weekend-then-ghost-me.

"Hi, Natalia." I kiss the middle-aged Brazilian woman at the door. Natalia is Tristan's housekeeper. He's basically paying for a second mum; she does everything for him, from cooking to washing his underwear. The guy has no shame.

"Charlie, my darling." She pulls me in for a tight hug, and I come in, taking my shoes off. Tristan's place is always spotless, thanks to Natalia.

"Go right in. They're in the lounge area."

"They?" I ask, suddenly apprehensive.

"The boys, Rebecca, and her friend."

I hear Jack's loud laugh, then the dry, sarcastic Scottish voice, and girls laughing.

*Fuck.*

Sucking in a breath, I walk into the lounge area.

"Charlie!" Daniel runs at me, and I couldn't be happier right now for his unconditional love. I try to steady my rising heartbeat as I kneel and embrace him.

*He's here.*

Why didn't Tristan share these vital details?

"How's my number one nephew doing?"

"Your only nephew," Daniel scolds. "I'm not stupid, you know."

"No, you're the smartest boy I know." I ruffle his hair. "Are you going to beat me at chess tonight?"

He pushes his glasses up his nose. "Most definitely!"

"Charlie." Tristan comes over and hugs me. "You are a star."

I smile as I give him a kiss and cast my gaze around the room. Jack and Rebecca lean against the fireplace. Danny sits in an armchair with a hot redhead in a tight shift dress casually perched on his armrest. As if there aren't ample other chairs to sit on. She swings her legs in a deliberate act of seduction, giving him an excellent view of them.

In contrast, I'm in sweatpants with a bird's nest on top of my head.

While Jack and Rebecca greet me, my eyes collide with Danny's.

"Charlie, this is Mara," Tristan introduces me to the gorgeous redhead sitting too close to Danny.

Mara. My eyes go wide in recognition, and I look at Danny then quickly away. I notice with triumph that the love bite is still there.

*Don't pretend you aren't on a date, dipshit,* my inner voice screams at him.

I *hate* that he affects me so much that he controls my happiness these days.

"Hi Charlie." She beams at me. If only she knew. "Tristan said you work at Nexus."

"Lovely to meet you, Mara," I manage to say, my heart plummeting. "Yes, I do."

"Is Danny a friendly boss?" She giggles, giving him doe eyes. "I could imagine he'd be very demanding."

Woman, don't use me in your attempt to flirt.

"Very friendly," I reply, my frosty tone not matching my words. "I'll just go upstairs and get Daniel's bath ready, Tristan."

"Stay with us for a drink, sis?" Tristan shakes the wine bottle at me. "I haven't seen you in a few weeks. You've been ghosting me," he scolds.

"I came here to play chess in my sweatpants," I reply, half-smiling. "You never tell me when you have company."

I can't cope with this. I can't stay in this room to watch Danny Walker work his Casanova charm on another woman in front of me.

"Tristan, I'm going upstairs," I say. "All, have a nice night. Mara, nice to meet you. Enjoy your date with Danny."

The others chuckle, and Mara lets out a high-pitched giggle. She's nervous and excited.

*I've been there, girl.*

Danny glares at me, and I turn before they can see the tears forming in my eyes. I'm barely inside the bathroom when Danny storms in behind me and shuts the door.

"What the fuck was that?" he hisses. I stare at

him.

"What?"

"Your catty remarks down there." He moves towards me. "It's not a fucking date."

Anger swells in my gut. "I *know* it's a date. Asshole. Do I need to get tested for STDs? How many women *have* you had this week?"

The tension in his jaw tightens. "I'm here to see Tristan and Jack. I didn't know Rebecca was going to bring Mara. Don't give me this fucking shit, Charlie."

His dark eyes hold mine, and I fight back the tears. I can't cry in front of this bastard.

"Do you have a different woman every night of the week?" I cry. "Is that your tactic? I'm such a fool. Why did I ever go near you?"

"Fuck's sake." He glares down at me. "I don't need this emotional rollercoaster. I thought we had a lovely weekend, and now the mad bitch is back."

I slap him hard across the face. He stands frozen, taken completely aback before his eyes squeeze into thin slits.

"That better not have made a mark," he spits out. "When you're done with being a child, then we can talk."

I turn away defiantly. "Enjoy your date, Danny."

I hear him slam the door before I let the tears fall.

\*\*\*

Tristan came home around midnight, so I was in bed by half-past. I didn't ask him if Danny went home alone. I didn't ask Tristan much at all. I claimed to be tired and made a quick getaway.

Being in bed is pointless since I have no chance of falling asleep now, knowing some other girl might be lying in that giant bed right now.

In the dark, my phone buzzes and I pick it up, thinking it's Tristan checking if I'm home.

"Before you speak, don't fight with me," the familiar Scottish voice says hoarsely. "I'm outside."

All my muscles go rigid. "Give me a minute." I stare down at my old grey pyjama shorts and swear. I don't have time to fix my hair or my bloodshot eyes.

Throwing on a sweater, I sneak through the sleeping flat and down the stairs.

When I open the door, he is leaning against his car, his arms folded and a look of impatience on his face.

His eyes linger on my shorts for a moment before returning to my face. "Nice," he says softly as he walks towards me.

"I'm a bit worried you're going to ask me for a threesome," I grumble, looking around to see if Mara is in the car.

He cocks a brow in amusement. "I think the other girl would feel very left out if we had a threesome." He runs a hand through his hair. "Listen, I can't stay."

"I wasn't letting you in," I reply, my chin raised in defiance.

"This fighting between us needs to stop, Charlie. One day we're lovers, the next enemies."

I open my mouth to speak, then close it.

"I can't promise you commitment. But I'm not dating Jen or Mara or any other girl right now. The truth is I'm only interested in you." His eyes blaze as he waits for my reaction.

*Can I do casual?*

"I care about you ... a lot," he says softly. "I also don't want to share you with anyone else. But you have to stop bickering with me."

"You didn't contact me," I whisper. "I thought you were ghosting me."

He lets out a long sigh. "These past few days have been hectic. Just because I didn't message you doesn't mean I wasn't thinking of you."

I lower my eyes to his chest. "I thought you regretted it."

"Regret it?" he grins, forcing my face up again. "That was the most carefree weekend I've had in years."

His fingers sweep over my lower lip. "It's taking every ounce of self-control not to yank down these grey shorts and fuck you on the doorstep."

"You didn't even kiss Mara?" My eyes narrow at him.

"No," he says, taken aback. "Truth be told, I found her irritating. Now, will you give me something to hold onto while I'm in New York?"

"What do you—"

I'm cut off by his lips launching onto mine, and we kiss with such tenderness, my knees buckle slightly. His arms catch me, pressing my body tight against his.

My breasts brush against his lower chest, and I get on my tiptoes, desperately clawing at the back of his neck.

*I want this man more than I've ever wanted anyone.*

His tongue pushes between my lips, forcing himself deeper into my mouth, and I open to let him in.

I push a hand under his shirt wanting skin on skin and he holds me tight against his groin, his length hardening by the second.

"Fuck." His voice is low and gravelly as he pulls away from the kiss. "My driver's watching over the street. I need to go back to mine to catch a flight to New York early in the morning. I have to go."

"Ok," I reply through ragged breathing.

"Sleep well, gorgeous." He kisses my forehead, and I stare after the beautiful beast as he walks towards his car.

\*\*\*

"You can come in now, Charlotte." David from the Nexus HR team pokes his head out the door to where I'm sitting. I'm top of the line of five nervous looking Dunley Tech colleagues.

Statistically at least 2.5 of us will get the chop.

I stand up and shuffle into the room in my tight pencil skirt. How Jackie walks around in these all day is beyond me.

I thought rocking up to the meeting groomed and with my hair not looking like I had just rolled out of bed might support the fight for my job.

David takes a seat behind the desk and smiles, lifting his pen ready to write.

Even though this has been labelled a casual chat to talk through my options, my cheeks burn as the two of them watch me.

"Charlotte," David starts.

"You can call me Charlie."

He nods. "Charlie. I'm David and this is my colleague, Samantha."

Samantha stops writing to give me a curt nod.

"We want to make sure you are comfortable with the three options and what they mean to you."

I nod, rubbing my clammy hands on my pencil skirt.

"Obviously the first option is simple, your job remains as is and you continue as normal. This depends on how your job fits in with the direction of the company. Going forward, you'll be reporting to Janet Dixon as Mike is leaving us."

"Mike's gone?" I gasp, my eyes widening.

"Mike's position was no longer required," Samantha replies, deadpan. I make a mental note to ask Stevie what happened.

"The second possibility is redundancy, either voluntary or," David says, clearing his throat, "mandatory."

"We are looking to communicate with everyone as quickly as possible on this," Samantha says in a voice that tells me this is nothing new to her. "We understand how difficult this can be."

"When will I find out?" I ask in a strangled voice.

David smiles sympathetically at me. "We're still assessing your team. Circa two to three weeks I should think."

"The third option is where you move into a new role in the company," Samantha says in a mechanical way that tells me she's going through the motions. This is probably her thirtieth time this week. "We have advertised jobs internally first before going to market. I must stress it is a highly competitive market."

Way to go, sister, thanks for the vote of confidence.

"There is a position I'd like to apply for."

"Yes?" David raises his eyebrows.

"The Designer role," I say quietly, my knees jerking.

Samantha looks down at paperwork and frowns. "It's quite a senior role. Your experience doesn't seem to match?"

"But anyone can apply, right? Can I submit a business case with my ideas?"

"Yes." She shrugs, in such a way that says she thinks I'm wasting my time. "The deadline is next Monday. Be warned we've had twenty applicants already directly from *Nexus*."

I narrow my eyes in defiance. Fuck you, woman. I'll show you and Danny Walker that I can do this.

I have five days to write the best damn business case ever.

# 26

**Charlie**

My legs are shaking with the volume of caffeine pumping through me. Usually, on Saturdays, I am quivering under the covers trying to survive a hangover.

Today I'm *buzzing.*

I've worked all night and this morning on the business case for submission on Monday, and it's good. It's not just good; it's *great.*

After five years of listening to complaints across the globe and across the time zones, I know what this product needs.

I've been so focused I've barely thought of Danny. He messaged last night asking me how I was. Text banter isn't his strong point. His messages are to the point and with purpose, like a newsreader. As opposed to my messages with Cat, where we exchange fifty screenshots a day, even though we live together and sit on the sofa together.

I type the last point furiously and squeal to myself. I'm done. I can't give it any more than this. If they don't like it, I'll accept redundancy and walk away.

Shutting down my laptop, I bounce into the living room.

"Have you finished your paper thing?" Cat licks her lips nervously and darts her eyes between Julie and me.

"My business case." I grin like a lunatic and sink into the sofa. "Yes, I have."

"There is something you need to see," Julie says sharply, and my glow dims.

I look at her, alert. "What?"

She takes a breath and swipes her phone. "Look at this."

I take the phone and see a picture of Danny. I'm about to say I don't understand when I read the headline.

**Danny Walker leaves Lower East's side's hottest new restaurant with bombshell friend.**

My heart plummets.

The picture shows him in the back of a car with an attractive blonde. She is smiling directly at him, and he looks relaxed.

My mouth falls open. *He promised.*

"Maybe she's just a friend," Cat says hopefully.

"Friend." I snort. "How many guys just have friends that look like supermodels?"

I look between them both as their faces say it all and burst out crying. Big thick ugly tears stream down my face. Snot and liquid everywhere, I'm crying from my lungs. *From my soul.*

They leap up to fuss over me, and I sob into Cat's

chest as she rubs my hair.

"I swam in a fucking pond for that guy," I wail.

"You're too attached, Charlie," Cat says softly. "It's too soon."

"I know," I sob in broken breaths. "I can't handle this. My heart can't cope."

"Breathe," Julie says firmly. "Wait thirty minutes, then message him. Without emotion. Cool as fuck."

I look up through tear-stained eyes.

"You need to be a player, Charlie," she snaps. "Instead of becoming an emotional wreck each time you see him with another woman." She shakes her head at me like a schoolteacher. "It's unbecoming."

"Fine," I sniffle.

True to my word to her, I wait thirty minutes before picking up the phone. I'm breathing easier now, although the pain hasn't lifted. He's not mine, we aren't together, and I have no claim on him, so I need to stop acting like a needy, highly-strung bitch.

**Hi.** I type. **What have you been up to in New York?**

I stare down at the phone on the sofa like it's radioactive. The response sound beeps loud, and the three of us jump.

**Boring business meetings. You?** I read out loud.

"LIAR," Julie hisses. "Probe more."

**Did you get to do anything fun last night?** I reply, my hands sweating.

The buzz comes in instantaneously.

**Not really. Meetings went on late into the night.**

I read out loud again, this time in a higher pitch.

"Bastard!" I cry, firing the phone back on the sofa. "He thinks I'm a bloody mug?"

"He mustn't have seen the article." Cat frowns. "I mean, it wasn't hard to find. It came up on my feed, and he's not exactly an A-list celebrity."

I grab the phone, seething. I can't act like Julie. I'm not impartial. I'm *livid.*

**Business meeting with a blond on your cock?** I type furiously and hit send.

"Mature." Julie groans, looking over my shoulder. "You have blown it now, big style."

My phone vibrates again, but this time it's his name on my Caller ID.

"Answer it," she hisses.

"What the fuck was that?" the deep voice growls down the phone as I put him on speakerphone.

"Your business meetings," I burst out. "You hold your business meetings in the back of taxis with gorgeous blonde women? After dinner?"

There's a pause. "Actually, yes, I do. But how did you ..."

He trails off, and I know he's searching on the internet.

There's a long sigh down the phone. "She's my lawyer, Charlie. She's part of my legal team. I have a situation I need to resolve away from the office."

"I can see why you'd want to resolve that away from the office," I snap. "How many lawyers are you fucking? Do you have a conveyor belt of blonde lawyers ready to go?" How stupid does this guy think I am?

"I'm not sleeping with her."

"Really? Because we both know you like sleeping with blond lawyers."

I stick up two fingers to the phone in a silent curse. "I guess your talk about not seeing other women was time zone specific."

"No, we both don't know that. I finished with the last blond lawyer when you and I started something."

"Oh yeah," I reply, dripping in sarcasm. "Because leggy blonde lawyers aren't your type."

"No, I prefer hot-headed foul-mouthed brunettes who never run a brush through their hair, take mice to dinner parties and sleep in beds so damn uncomfortable and tiny, I have to go to a physio. You say I'm the moody one," he continues, "but you jump to assumptions and don't ask me. Then you act out."

"Act out? I'm not a child," I snap. "Stop patronising me."

"Then stop acting like one," he grits out. "Look, I'm giving you more than I've given anyone in years. I'm putting my closest friendship on the line here for you. What more do you want from me?"

"How am I supposed to feel?" I grumble. "You don't show me any emotion. You never message kisses."

"You want me to message a kiss to you?" he sighs impatiently. "*That's* what you're pissed at?"

"The *bombshell* from the article is really your lawyer?"

"Yes, Charlie. My happily married lawyer."

There's a long pause.

"I'm sorry." I exhale heavily. Getting involved with someone as successful as Danny is making me irrationally insecure. "You get so much attention from women everywhere you go. It deflates my poor ego which is already battered since I don't have my shit together. I mean, you're a millionaire tech tycoon, and I take calls from angry clients who can't reset their passwords."

He chuckles. "If you don't reset those passwords I won't make any money from the angry clients."

"I'm serious, Danny," I whisper. It's the first time I've confessed my insecurities to him.

"You have no need to be insecure, sweetheart." His voice softens. "I happen to consider myself very lucky. Are you going to be in the flat between 4-5pm today?"

"Why?" I ask curiously.

"There's a new bed arriving. I'm not lying on that heap of planks again."

"You bought me a new bed?" I splutter.

"Don't get excited," he shouts over some type of announcement like he's in a train station. "It's not as big as mine. I'd never get that into your flat."

There's more background noise.

"Where are you?" I ask.

"Heathrow."

He's back? He's in the UK?

"Why? Weren't you supposed to fly home tomorrow?"

"I changed my flight," he says. "There's a new bed I need to try out."

***

"Hey." I tilt my chin up to meet his gaze.

There are bags under his eyes, and he has that dishevelled plane hair and clothes thing going on. My grin widens. *He looks like shit, and it's because he flew home early for me.*

"I was forced to fly standard class," he mutters. "First class was all taken. So you better take care of me now."

"Poor baby." I roll my eyes unsympathetically as we walk up the stairs to my flat.

"That new bed better fucking be here. Or I'm turning around and walking out that door."

"Am I not worth lying on broken planks of wood?" I pout.

"I've lost a full night's sleep," he growls. "No, Charlie, not even you are worth that tonight."

I hit him. "It's here. Come have a look."

We walk into the bedroom where Suze, Cat, and Julie are sprawled across the new bed.

Danny releases a soft groan beside me. "Ladies."

"This bed is amazzzzzzing." Cat rolls around on it, and Danny curses a bit louder.

"I searched for this bed online." Julie eyeballs him. "These beds cost two grand."

"Two grand?" I shriek, turning to him. "You did not pay two grand for a new bed for me?"

"I thought I was buying it for you." He eyes them.

"Didn't realise it was actually for the whole flat."

"Feel free to kit the whole house out if you want," Julie says wryly.

"You better not let your mother into your bedroom again, Charlie," Suze says. "Or Tristan. They'll be at you like hawks wondering why you forked out on this luxury."

"Damn." Danny flinches. "I didn't think this through."

"Your dirty little secret will have to come out sometime." Julie smirks, and I glare at her.

"Can the three of you fuck of now?" I mutter, shooing them off the bed like geese.

Two hours later, we are sitting in my favourite Indian restaurant around the corner.

I love this place, but I'm usually in elasticated trousers ready for a food coma rather than a leather pants and bra number.

As soon as we heard Danny was flying home early, Julie forced me to up the antics. I'm wearing a leather ensemble that Stevie forced Cat to buy.

She says she hasn't worn it yet, and I really hope she's not lying because the leather is chafing so high up my crack, I think it might slice me in two.

"It's good, right?" I say, shoving more korma into my mouth. "I know it's not your typical exclusive Mayfair restaurant where the food is telescopic portions at shameless prices. This place is inclusive. Sweatpants, PJs, anything is allowed."

He chuckles. "I'm not a princess, Charlie. I go to

expensive restaurants if the food deserves it, for no other reason. I grew up in a country that eats deep-fried pizzas, remember."

I roll my eyes. "I don't believe that for a second." I shuffle my backside on the chair to dislodge the leather. This stuff is *really* itchy. In hindsight, I could have put it on after the meal; it's not like I was planning to strip down in the restaurant.

"You OK?" he asks as I cross and uncross my legs in an attempt to scratch the itch. Argh.

"Great," I mutter, resisting all urge to take my fork and scratch my inner thigh until all leather has disintegrated.

"Is deep-fried pizza actually nice?" I wrinkle my nose.

"Delicious. Although with Mum being a vegan nut, it was a rarity when I was allowed it."

"I never hear you talk about your parents," I say softly, reaching across the table to take his hand.

His breath catches. "When you stop making new memories, you find yourself talking about the person less."

"What was she like?" I ask tentatively.

His face sags, and I instantly regret pushing him out of his comfort zone.

"It's OK," I say quickly. "We can change the subject."

He gazes out the window for a minute, then he turns to me fully. "You two share some similar traits." He lets out a short sad laugh. "What does that say about me, hey? Mammy issues. She was creative, fun, the life and soul of the party," he continues. "She loved to sing. She used to sing in a band around the pubs in Glasgow." His tone darkens: "Until that prick stopped her."

"Your dad," I whisper.

"I don't call him that," he replies gruffly, staring into his beer.

"She would have liked you."

"I'm pleased." I smile. "Do you think that's what made you so determined to become successful? The … accident?"

"It was no accident," he mutters darkly. "I became successful because I didn't have anything else going for me. All I had left was my grandmother and Karl."

I nod. "That's why Tristan means so much to you."

He laughs again. "Yes, for some reason, Tristan took a liking to me. I wasn't like you in uni. I didn't drink. I was reserved and sullen, I stayed away from people. But he stuck with me regardless. So yeah … I'm worried about how he'll react if he finds out … about us."

He closes his eyes with a dark exhale.

"I could count on one hand how many people care about me, and he's one of them."

"That's not true," I say softly. "You need one more finger. I care about you too."

When he opens his eyes, a private, unspoken emotion passes between us, one I never thought I'd see on Danny Walker's face.

He shifts uncomfortably in his seat, and I decide

I've pushed him enough for one night. "How's the jet lag? Since you had to fly with the *normal* people, Princess?"

He grins, taking a swig of his beer. "Fair enough, I deserve that. The truth is I'm absolutely shattered." He looks it.

"We can have an early night."

"This is officially our first date." He gives me a lopsided smile. "I'm supposed to be sweeping you off your feet. Showing you that I can keep up with a twenty something."

Groaning, he grasps a hand on his pocket. He takes his phone out, and I see Tristan's name flash across the screen. "He thinks I'm still in New York." He frowns. "I won't get it."

*Part of hiding our dirty little secret.*

"Danny," I start, trying to sound light-hearted. "Why are you so worried about Tristan knowing about us? Are you embarrassed?"

His forehead creases into a frown. "No, Charlie, I'm not embarrassed. Tristan made me promise I would never go there. He's very protective of you and Callie, you know. After he witnessed how your mother was treated by your father. He used to go out for days and come back, and she'd hear he was with some other woman. Tristan used to hear her lying in bed crying. He doesn't want anyone to hurt you. You're his baby sister."

"I know all that," I say, frustrated. "I might have been younger, but I still witnessed it. That's not a reason to mollycoddle me. I'm a grown woman now.

Not to get into Sigmund Freud theories, but you are not my father! Just like I am not your mother. Do you treat women badly?"

He gives a soft laugh. "No, I've always been very straight with women. I rarely want to jump into something serious. Sometimes they ignore that and get hurt when it ends badly."

*Like I will.*

I wither a little as his hurtful words sear my ears. If he notices, he ignores it.

"Tristan knows me. He knows I've been with a lot of women. He doesn't want that for you."

"What about what I want?" I ask. "Doesn't that matter?"

"You're younger than me, Charlie. You're in a different time of your life. What you want will change."

I stare at him in disbelief. "Don't patronise me, Danny."

He takes both my hands. "Let's not fight. I can't tell you what's going to happen in the future. All I can say is that I'm taking a big risk now because to walk away would be worse. That's all I can give you right now. Is that enough?"

There's a pause.

"Yes," I say at last.

He gives me a look of relief. "Now, what's good for dessert?" he asks, opening the menu and turning to the back page.

Damn, I was hoping we could leave after the main course so I could scratch the leather. He's here for the long haul. For Fuck's sake, who orders dessert after scoffing two naan bread, a whole bowl of rice, and a large meat stacked Jalfrezi?

I can't take this.

I use my elbow to subtly stroke back and forth between my legs. Nearly ... nearly ... ooh, it's not enough. I need this damn contraption off.

"What are you doing?" His eyes are wide, watching as I dig my elbow in further. "Did you just try to scratch your Nether region with your elbow?"

I snort. "It's the leather."

"The leather?"

"I'm wearing a tight leather bra and pants ensemble. It was supposed to be a surprise."

He gives me an amused smirk. "God, give me strength. You take out the leather after I've sat squashed against a fat man and a baby for eight hours. Are you trying to murder me through exhaustion?"

"You look like you have fleas."

"That's not the look I'm aiming for," I mutter.

He lets out a snort of laughter and finds my hand across the table. "Let's get the dessert to go."

***

Back on my new luxury bed, we rip at each other's clothes like bears trying to maul the other. It's only been a few days, but it's been too long since I saw him naked. I'm panting hornily as he tugs my sweater over my head to reveal the leather bra.

I fumble with his jeans like an amateur. There's

no time or desire for foreplay tonight.

I push him down onto the bed and climb onto him, my legs straddling his hips.

"It would be a shame to waste the leather," he says gruffly, pushing a finger inside the leather bra to circle a nipple.

I hover just above him without touching him as he pushes the leather cups down so that my breasts spring free. His length stands up straight, thick and impatient.

"Stop teasing me," he growls. "Get on my cock."

I smirk down at him and reach between my legs to pull down the zip of my leather pants, exposing my crotch.

"Zipped," he hisses. "Very efficient."

His hands tighten around my hips, and he lowers me down so that his head is rubbing against my wet slit.

Then he impales me onto him, filling me so deeply I cry out.

"Easy," I breathe, rotating my hips to stretch my core out so that I can take his size.

"Sorry," he replies gruffly. "It's been a week."

I start to gyrate gently on top of him, thrusting my hips, reaching the spot that I know will bring me pleasure.

"You're so deep." I moan, looking down at him. "Do you know how good you feel inside me?"

I thrust, increasing the tempo as my pleasure dictates, and his breathing becomes laboured, louder.

"I'm going to come." He closes his eyes, groaning. "If you keep doing that, I can't stop."

I don't want him to stop. I want to prove I can make him come hard and fast. I control the movement; I'll control when he comes.

I slam my hips into his groin and widen my legs deeper, so he is buried to the hilt.

He lets out a strangled growl. "Fuck, I'm coming. Now. Now."

I feel it like it's part of me. He explodes into me, filling me with his come as I watch his handsome face twist and contort with a mixture of pleasure and pain.

"Did that help the jetlag?" I ask breathlessly, holding him inside me.

When he opens his eyes, they are swimming with tenderness. "Yes, Charlie, I'll have the best sleep of my life now."

# 27

**Danny**

We watch the ball fly past the eighth hole and disappear into a bed of grass.

"Shit form today, Walker," Jack calls out, laughing.

"I'm tired."

"You mean your dick is tired."

I look at him wearily. "What's that supposed to mean?"

"You're too cheery. Smiling at us like a fucking schoolgirl all day even though you're playing a shit round of golf and even Karl is trouncing you, and he really is shit at golf. Who is she?"

I roll my eyes. "I'm happy; therefore, I must be getting some?"

"Precisely," Tristan says as he lines his ball up. "You've been AWOL all week. She must be hot if you missed our Wednesday man date."

Jack pretends to cry. "We were devastated you blew us off for a woman, Walker."

Tristan hits the ball, and we watch as it smacks down close to the eighth hole, much closer than my pathetic attempt. I couldn't care less if I won this round of golf today.

"That's how you do it." He smirks. "So?"

"So what?" I reply, exasperated.

"So who is she? Why are you being so cagey about this one?"

I stiffen, focusing on my golf club. I'm on shaky ground.

I give a sideways glance at Karl, who is trying to hide a smirk. He's the only one that knows everything.

*Don't fucking say anything.* I glare the unspoken words at him.

Since I returned from New York two weeks ago, Charlie has been in my bed every night, give or take a few.

I've finally settled down into a routine of being able to let us both sleep by midnight rather than fuck her persistently into morning time.

"I've been on a few dates with someone I met at a tech event." I give my best casual shrug. "No big story."

The three of them grin at me.

Tristan's eyebrows raise. "She must be sensational to turn down Mara."

"She is," I respond in a low voice as Jack takes his shot. It lands just shy of Tristan's.

"Well, what's she like? Give us some details, for Christ's sake. How old is she?" Tristan asks.

"Twenty-eight."

"Same age as Charlie," Tristan muses.

Fuck, I shouldn't have revealed that.

"That's a great age," Jack says. "Everything is still nice and tight. Pert. Nipples facing outwards, not downwards. That's why you look exhausted." He grins. "Trying to keep up with a twenty-eight-year-old in the sack."

"Is the sex good?" Tristan asks.

I flinch. "The best," I say through gritted teeth.

"That's it?" Jack looks at me curiously. "That's all you're going to give us?"

I fold my arms. "I didn't think you needed me to educate you on how a dick worked, Knight."

He whistles loudly. "So rattled. I swear you get grumpier as you get older."

"Come on." Karl chuckles, changing the subject for me. "Let's get moving. I don't have all day."

"Maybe you can help me figure out what to buy a twenty-nine-year-old for their birthday," Tristan says as we pick up our golf bags. "It's Charlie's birthday soon. She wrote the song for my birthday; how the hell do I compete with that?"

I frown. I had forgotten it was coming around soon.

Jack rolls his eyes. "You'll throw money at it like you always do, then she'll get annoyed and make you return the obnoxious gift that you bought her."

"What date is it?" I ask as we make our way to the buggy.

"Two weeks, Thursday," Tristan replies. "She's having birthday drinks with a few of her friends. I'm going to swing by."

"Maybe I'll keep you company," I say casually as

Karl cocks a brow at me.

Yes, Karl, I know I'm a fool that's going to get caught.

## Charlie

"These people." I scowl at the screen. "Look at this imbecile."

"Your software is not working on my computer," Stevie reads out loud over my shoulder. "It's vague, but what's the issue?"

"The issue is that he's not a customer of ours. He doesn't even have the software installed. So, of course, it's not working."

Stevie and Alex laugh behind me.

"You can have fun with this one."

"These calls cost us twenty-five quid each time, you know." I start typing a sarcastic reply as they both watch over my shoulder, guffawing loudly like a couple of idiots.

"Uh-oh." Alex stops laughing abruptly, jumping back into his seat. "Boss guy is here."

I look up to see Danny and Karl talking by the elevator flanked by the Nexus CFO and Head of HR. Towering over the others, he's hard to miss. *Delicious.*

Danny has his sleeves rolled up to his elbows, and his arms crossed over his chest.

My breath hitches as it always does; dating him these past few weeks hasn't tamed the flutters in my stomach that happen whenever he enters the room.

Here, he is CEO Danny, not my lover, or dare

I suggest, boyfriend, although I know to stay well away from *that* conversation.

They advance down the aisle, and I watch with amusement as, row by row, postures straighten, conversations stop, flirting ceases, and online shopping carts close.

His eyes are stormy as Damion, the CFO, talks intently, meeting him stride by stride.

When his eyes seek out mine, every hair on my body stands to attention. I smile back, and his expression softens for a fleeting second before he returns his attention to Damion.

We rarely talk in the office. He resides on the top floor making the million-pound decisions, whereas I'm down here hand-holding people through the harrowing experience of resetting their password.

I stare dreamily after him as he marches down the office turning heads. His presence takes up so much space, despite the size of the floor.

People are either trying to escape his line of sight or falling over themselves to get a hello. All *man*. All *mine*.

Knowing that I'm the only one in the office that has seen those broad shoulders under that sculpted shirt makes me shiver with pleasure. The other girls can fantasise, and I know they do from all the conversations in the kitchen, but I've got the *real* thing between my legs when I go to bed at night. It's fucking awesome.

Karl catches me staring and winks.

I avert my gaze quickly back to my screen.

How much does Danny tell him, I wonder?

These past few weeks, I've been floating through life, high on daily orgasms and the drug that is Danny Walker.

I've spent most nights with him, and on the rare nights we've been apart, he's called me from his bed before I go to sleep.

He's not officially my boyfriend, and we are still a secret, but things are changing. He has non-dairy milk stocked each time I come round because he knows I prefer it. I have jumpers there and a few swimsuits for the swimming pond. My make-up remover wipes are in his bathroom. He's given me a bathroom shelf. It's an unwritten rule that the right side is my side of the bed because I like to face the door.

I'm wrenched out of my daydream by Jackie standing in front of me.

"Hello? Anyone there?" She waves her hand over my face.

"Yes, Jackie?"

"Janet wants the report. Now."

"I've already emailed it to you," I snap back. "Check your inbox." I look at her, confused. "Why do you have a full-body spray tan done?"

"Because," she lowers her voice and moves closer to me. "I've been taking minutes in meetings for Danny Walker, and he is *all* over me."

Pain shoots through me. "Oh, really?"

"*Really*," she emphasises. "Tonight's the night I make it clear I'm interested. The drinks, remember?"

That's right, there are free drinks on the top floor bar this evening.

For the umpteenth time since I entered into this thing with Danny, I am crippled with insecurity. Jackie looks a million dollars and me? I'm still wearing my sneakers to work.

He's not mine. It's been four weeks, and I'm falling head over heels for him. He has every woman in the goddamn city of London after him. Can I cope with this? What happens when I'm no longer flavour of the month?

An hour later, I'm still on edge, replaying Jackie's comments in my mind. *He's all over me.* Work is piling up, but I'm too upset to focus.

That's the curse of Danny Walker. He seems to control everything these days, even my productivity.

Mindlessly, I log into OpenMic. I've been watching it a little over the past few weeks, and my views are creeping up.

Then I see it.

Two stars.

*Worst song ever. Cats fighting in an alleyway would be easier on the ears.*

The words jump out and spear me like a knife. No, I'm not built for rejection, either by Danny Walker or some random stranger on the internet.

***

Why is it that the floors get sexier the higher up you go in a building? We are in the top floor cocktail lounge admiring the 360-views over the London skyline. There's even an outdoor rooftop garden terrace.

The newbies from Dunley Tech are easy to identify. We gawk like we have just landed on the moon.

It's a free bar, and I'm standing in a group with Stevie, Alex, Jackie, and Aldus, one of the Nexus developers.

Truth be told, the Nexus coders intimidate me. They all come from the same brainiac factory with IQs off the scale, but they all lack the chip that allows them to talk about anything other than I.T.

Aldus is talking about cryptocurrency, and I understand a few words out of every sentence.

"It's basically the single-best asset that gives the diversity of exposure to crypto," he explains.

"Really?" I nod, pretending to know what he's talking about.

Please don't ask my opinion.

The elevator opens, and out walks Danny, Karl, and the rest of the executive board located in London.

He's talking to a woman that looks familiar. Where have I seen her before?

It takes me a minute to register that she's the lawyer from the news article in New York.

They don't look like they are talking business. She touches his arm, and he throws his head back in laughter.

"Who's the bitch?" Jackie mutters under her breath as we watch him deep in conversation, enthralled with whatever his female friend is explaining.

"Save me," Stevie hisses in my ear. "Before Aldus figures out how stupid I am. Bar. NOW."

"I'm coming too," Jackie huffs.

As we approach the bar, Dylan the sleazebag is there with other coders. There are twenty shots on a tray beside them, some empty, some spilled, some full.

"Charlie." He beckons us into the circle, as Rory in his team passes us shots.

"I'm not drinking this stuff," shrieks Jackie. "Can someone get me a proper cocktail, please?"

"I'll drink it," I sigh, taking the sticky shot glass. I'll need it if I'm going to witness Danny get mauled all night by beautiful women. Besides, the pain of the internet stranger roasting is still too fresh.

Dylan strategically places himself between Stevie and me. "That's the spirit." He places his hand on my lower back, too familiar as usual.

"Stop being so handsy, Dylan," I grumble. "And your bloody hand is sticky from that shot!"

"Ah, come on, I saw you on Tinder, Charlie. Why won't you let me take you out?"

"No, Dylan." I snort. "*Not* happening."

"What about the date with the doctor?" Rory asks me.

I draw my lips into a thin line. "That didn't end so well. I'm not even sure he was a doctor. My mate Cat stalked him online."

"Isn't that catfishing?" Rory asks.

"No." Dylan laughs. "All guys do it. We can be whatever the girl wants us to be." I glare at him. "And that is why we aren't going out."

"I'm on the elite singles site," Jackie informs us. "You have to be invited. You wouldn't catch me being catfished."

"What fishing?" a low voice says behind me.

I move over to make room for Danny, who has come up behind Dylan and me. His arm brushes against mine giving me goosebumps.

"Hi, Mr. Walker." Jackie beams at him.

"You can call me Danny." He smiles back.

"Danny," she repeats in her huskiest come-fuck-me tone. "We were just laughing about Charlie getting catfished. It's when someone creates a false identity to lure you in."

My cheeks flame. "He lied about his job. I wouldn't say he took on a separate identity."

"Do you have an online dating profile, Danny?" Jackie asks, all flirts and smiles. "I'm part of elite singles."

"No. I'm seeing someone."

I shoot a sideways glance at him, but he's smiling back at Jackie politely.

He's talking about me, right? It's the first time he has acknowledged us in public.

Her face drops in devastation. "The woman over there?"

He frowns, running a hand over the stubble of his jaw. "Martina? No, absolutely not, she's my lawyer. We work closely together. I've known her and her husband for fifteen years," he elaborates.

"What's the company policy on office romances?" Jackie giggles, eyeballing him suggestively.

"There's no policy. As long as it doesn't affect your working relationship. We treat our employees as adults."

"That's good because Dylan and Charlie matched on Tinder," Rory chimes in. "A new office romance."

"Is that so?" Danny says, running his tongue over his teeth.

"We did not match!" I gasp. "I'm not even active."

"You were active three days ago." Dylan takes out his phone. "It says so on your profile." He turns his phone around to show the group my profile.

My eyes dart sideways to Danny. With an unreadable stare, he studies the phone.

My cheeks burn a hot molten. "I think profile shaming a work colleague is against the rules of online dating," I grit out. "We did not match, Dylan."

I cross my arms, tutting loudly, as they swarm around his phone.

Dylan swipes through each picture in turn then sucks in sharply. "You look sexy as fuck, Kane. You polish up nicely. Why don't we see you in those heels and little red dress at work?" He catches himself realising he probably overstepped the mark in front of the boss. "Sorry, Mr. Walker."

"Put it away!" I yell.

Danny hangs back, raising his eyebrows at me.

"I'm not online dating right now," I say sternly, addressing the group but looking at him.

He finishes the last of his beer and sets it down on a table beside him. "Look at your messages," he says in a low voice as he brushes past me to get to the bar. "Unless you're too busy swiping."

Confused, I reach into my bag and get my phone. There is a message flashing.

**You have Friday and Monday authorised as leave. Tell Janet tomorrow.**

I don't understand. I type **??** and hit send.

He hears a beep and takes it out immediately.

Shit, this is so obvious, but the others are thankfully too busy laughing at my profile.

My phone beeps. I should have put it on silent.

He looks at me impatiently as I turn to talk to Stevie. I'm too paranoid to check it yet. After two minutes, I read the message.

**I'm taking you to Scotland this weekend. Keep it between us.**

I've no chance of playing hard to get or pretending I need to consult my social calendar. Before I can stop it, I'm smiling so wide it reaches my ears.

"See?" Dylan says. "She *is* happy we matched."

# 28

**Charlie**

When we arrive at Gatwick, I find out that we are flying to Aberdeen. Danny hasn't told me where exactly we are going or what we will be doing.

Honestly, I would board a flight to hell if he asked me to.

The cold Aberdeen air hits my face and neck like needles the moment the plane doors open, and I curse my lack of preparation.

Besides a few jumpers and scarves, I mostly packed for a sexy weekend. This cold is *not* sexy. We flew business class on the two-hour flight, which was a complete waste of time as the only differences I could see were three inches more legroom and a complimentary bottle of water.

"I told you to dress for seven degrees," he chides, watching me shiver.

"That's very precise," I mutter. "I'm not a meteorologist. Your instructions should have been to dress for arctic conditions where my bones will be replaced with ice."

He takes my bag down from the overhead locker. "It's going to get a lot worse."

"How?" I stare aghast as I gather up my belongings from the plane seat.

"We have one more flight." He grins down at me. "A short one."

"We're not staying in Scotland?"

"We are technically, but further north. The Shetland islands."

I'm halfway to standing, and I stop in my tracks. Is he taking me home?

"That's where you went to live with your grandmother when ..." I trail off.

"When the brute killed my mum. Yes. My grandmother is still there."

I suck in sharply.

"Don't worry, our first dirty weekend away isn't with my grandmother listening in the next room." He grins. "We're staying somewhere else."

"Your grandmother will have nothing to listen to," I grumble. "If you think you're getting an inch of clothing off me in this cold, you have another thing coming." I wrap my useless scarf around me as we disembark the plane.

*****

"We are flying in this thing?" We are at the foot of the steps of a small private jet.

"This *thing* is one of the best small planes made today," he says as he beckons me to ascend the steps. "It's a twin-turbocharged aircraft that can go up to 280 knots."

"You think I know how many knots we need?"

I step onboard with the grace of a rhino wearing stilettos. The interior looks like a flying luxury city apartment with white leather seats and sexy lighting. I count eight seats, not including the cockpit.

"It's just us?" I ask, twirling to face him. "Are we the only passengers?"

"Yes. It's my plane."

He opens the door to the cockpit, where a million lights, buttons, levers, and screens are flashing. I peer in. It's my first time seeing a cockpit up close.

"Take a seat, co-pilot."

"I get to sit beside the pilot? Cool!" I step inside, and he follows me into the compact space. "When are they arriving?"

Danny reaches up, lifts a pilot's hat from the top shelf, and puts it on. "Oh, silly me, I forgot my uniform."

"OK, very kinky, mister, but are we really going to play dress-up with the cabin crew right here?" I ask, confused. "I'm not joining the mile-high club on this. It's a small plane, they'll hear everything."

"No mile-high club on this flight. I'm good at multitasking, but I can't pleasure you and fly the plane at the same time."

The corner of his lips tug into a grin as he watches my brain misfire.

"*You are flying this thing?*" I draw in a stuttered gasp as I stare at the complicated dashboard. He better be joking. "How are you going to watch all these flashing lights by yourself?"

"Don't you know I've got my pilot licence?"

"Are you … Can you … Is there another pilot with you?"

A laugh breaks from his chest. "Thanks for the vote of confidence."

"But aren't there usually two pilots?" My voice increases two octaves.

"Only for commercial flights," he says with a chuckle as he does a thumbs up to someone outside on the steps. "Relax, Charlie. I've flown hundreds of times, maybe over a thousand. I've been flying for over a decade."

"But … what if you die?" I cry. "What if you have a heart attack in the air?"

"Don't worry, this thing can fly itself. You can drive a shift car, can't you? It's very easy to pick up."

"This isn't funny, Danny." I want to throttle him. "Do you have anything in your medical records I need to know about? When was the last time you had your heart checked? Eyes checked?"

"No illnesses in the family. Just murderers. We go through medicals to keep our license. I'm as robust as Superman."

I'm entirely unconvinced.

"What if there is an engine failure?"

"It's just a big computer. You work in I.T. Turn it off and on again." He bites his lower lip, trying not to laugh.

"Ha, bloody ha. I think I'm going to be sick."

"All clear, sir," a guy shouts from the steps outside.

Danny nods at him. "Thank you."

Then he twists the massive lever of the airplane door and bangs it shut.

I let out a weeping sound.

"It's OK, sweetheart. I promise."

He steps into the cockpit, guiding me into one of the seats with both hands.

When he leans over to attach my seatbelt, my breathing is so shallow I can't speak. He yanks hard on it to ensure it is secure, then kisses me lightly on the lips.

I sit stiffly like a human doll watching the graphs, flashing lights and other gadgets do strange things.

"Is that bad?" I point to a flashing red light on my side of the panel as he flips buttons and switches.

Danny waves his hand at me dismissively, and I resist the urge to smack the man.

"Safety checks done." He looks over, expecting me to be reassured. I'm not religious, but I'm quietly praying to Jesus, Mary, Joseph, *and* the Holy Ghost, as he buckles himself in.

"Taxi to runway two-seven right via alpha two, bravo," a voice booms out over the speaker. He talks back to someone in equal gibberish as I make whimpering noises in the corner.

Then we are moving. The plane slowly creeps forward and arrives at the start of a runway.

He flicks more buttons up and down when the deep voice announces, "Piper two-zero, cleared for take-off runway zero-one."

"Cleared for take-off runway zero-one, Piper two-zero," Danny repeats in a calm voice.

My hands grip the seat in a death grip as he accelerates at power down the runway, and I feel every bump like I'm on a bicycle cycling over a crowd of hedgehogs rather than sitting on a plane.

A strangled moan escapes from my throat, like a trapped animal dying slowly. He doesn't hear it over the roar of the engine.

We tilt upwards and climb so steeply I feel like we are going to slip back down again.

My head shoots back against the seat, and I close my eyes. Sixty minutes, he said. Maybe I can ask him to knock me unconscious then wake me up when I get there. If I get there.

"You OK?"

I open one eye to peer at him. "Fine besides the raging panic attack."

Then the roar stops, and we tilt back horizontal.

He looks at me, concerned. "I never realised you were so scared of flying. I'm sorry, Charlie."

"I'm not," I say through gritted teeth. "If I'm in a Boeing triple 7. In this thing, I feel like Mary bloody Poppins on a bicycle. Like we are just going to drop out of the sky at any time."

The plane shakes, and I let out a deep-rooted scream making him flinch.

"It's just a little turbulence. You feel it more on the smaller planes."

"Sure." I blow out through my cheeks.

I stare at him as he simultaneously monitors screens, checks gauges, and listens to air traffic control. It's the sexiest yet most terrifying visual of my life. My life is literally in his hands.

*I want this man so badly.* I want him to be mine, only mine. If we make it to the ground alive, he is going to get the best sex of his life. Right now, airborne, I'm fucking furious that I was never consulted in this life-threatening expedition.

There's another jolt, and the plane drops a little as we travel through thick clouds. Rain spills down in sheets against the windows. I can't see anything out the window, so he must be flying this thing blind.

The muscles clench so hard in my stomach I think I'm going to throw up.

"Bag. Need bag." I scramble to get my handbag from the floor, then take out the bottle of red wine in there. Thankfully it's a screw cap.

"Sedation," I explain as I take a large gulp from the bottle. "How do you have time to do all this?" I look at him in wonder. He's as cool as if we were on cruise control down the motorway. "You're a CEO, a cook, a pilot, a sex god. Seriously, Superman?"

His sharp gaze lands on me, and he chuckles. "Superman. Let's keep that name. I've got at least a decade on you, remember?"

"That's right, I keep forgetting I'm dating an old bloke," I say as I put the wine bottle to my lips. The bottle is emptying rapidly, and I've thirty-five minutes to go.

We screech to a halt on the tarmac, and I breathe properly for the first time since we left the mainland.

"Not so fast," he says in a sharp tone as I grapple with taking off my seat belt. "Safety first, I'll tell you when you can unfasten your seatbelt."

"Bossy." I stare over at him as he slows the plane to a complete stop, trying to figure out if he sounds sexy or scary.

Maybe a bit of both.

"*You*," I start as he leans over to undo my belt, "are the sexist pilot alive. But I've never hated you so much."

I fling the belt off me and stand up on shaky legs.

"I said not so fast."

His arm snakes around my waist as I step out of the cockpit, and I feel his warm breath on my cheek as he presses himself into my back. "You need to earn your plane ticket."

"Yes, captain?" I whisper, tilting my face back to see him, my arousal going from zero to one hundred in seconds.

"Face the wall and take your clothes off."

I pull my sweater over my top then follow with my tank top until I'm in a bra.

The sound of footsteps circles the plane outside. "Danny, there's—"

"Ignore them," he says gruffly as he unfastens my bra. Behind me, he grunts in appreciation and swipes a large hand over my left breast before he pinches the nipple.

"Everything needs to come off."

I unbutton the top button of my jeans and

shimmy the jeans down past my hips. I hear him unzip his jeans behind me.

I pull down my panties and step each leg out of them. As my ass arches backwards, he jolts me against him, and I feel his erection press hard against my buttocks.

He reaches a hand around my waist and slides a finger deep inside me. "Hands up against the wall."

I place my hands on the wall, and he pushes them higher up with his right hand while his left-hand thrusts in and out of me.

I moan against the wall and jolt upwards as he pushes in deep.

"Spread your legs."

People talk in hushed tones outside the airplane.

I move my legs apart, and my bare breasts push against the wall as he leans into me, stroking circular motions against my clit.

"Wider," he commands, and I do as I'm told.

"You like people listening, don't you?" he whispers in my ear. His hands circle my ass roughly then he boldly reaches one finger down there, circling my rim.

I inhale sharply. "Danny, I've never …"

"Soon, baby, not now," he shushes me, moving his hand back to my hip. Without warning, he slams his length into me hard and aggressively, and I cry out.

With one hand, he holds my wrists on the wall above my head, so I can't move them, and he uses the other to keep my hips tight against his erection, thrusting in and out of me, grunting.

The sound of my skin slapping against his grows louder and quicker. I cringe slightly at the thought of the people outside, waiting for us to open the doors.

"So good, Charlie." He pounds faster until he loses control and unloads inside me, growling loudly.

I feel every drop as he fills me.

"You're mine," he whispers in my ear as he pulls out. Wetness drips down my inner thigh.

I collapse against the wall as there is a timid knock on the airplane door.

"Mr. Walker?" a bodiless voice asks. "Are you ready to disembark?"

# 29

**Danny**

"We are staying in *that* hotel, Danny?"

We are parked outside the gate of my mansion. A stillness washes over me as it always does when I set eyes on my gothic beauty after time away. The panoramic and uninterrupted elevated sea views were the reason I sunk a lot of money into this place.

I made an offer twenty minutes after walking into it and outbid the other bidder by an obnoxious amount to seal the deal.

Watching the stormy sea with the waves crashing against the rocks as music while the wood burner roars in the background? Priceless.

"It's not a hotel," I explain as I wind down the car window. A gust of icy air hits us and she screeches in retaliation. "It's a home away from London."

"This is all yours?" Her breath comes out in small puffs of cold air. I can't wait to get her inside into the heat.

Fuck, what's the code? I always forget this.

I reach my arm through the window and press a code into the keypad.

Nope.

Try again.

The black wrought iron double gates automatically open. I coax the car up the windy hill in second gear until we creep to a stop outside Sumburgh Hall.

"Are we the only ones staying here?" She turns to me with her smouldering green eyes, and my heartbeat does that erratic little beat it does every time she gives me her full attention. Does she not notice the effect she has on me?

"Danny?" Charlie repeats.

"Besides the ghost and the gargoyles." I grin as we get out of the car. The two leering gargoyles on either side of the door stare down at us.

"Built in 1867," she reads the placard on the wall. "The place will be crawling with ghosts."

I fumble with the keys. The wooden door is so large it makes even me look puny. A few hard shoves, and we are in.

"Wow." She does a 360-degree turn in the hallway. "This place is magnificent." Her voice echoes through the hallway. "But so haunted, Danny. You cannot leave my sight even when I go to the toilet. Also, just to set expectations, we won't be having sex again because I'm not removing any clothes until we are back in England. It's too cold."

"Come on." I put my hand on her lower back and lead her down the hall, our footsteps clicking on the stone floors. "That's why I have a massive fireplace. I told you it was cold," I berate her like a scolding father as I take her into the sitting room.

She hesitates at the threshold, mouth dropping open. "Danny, this place is like a fairy-tale."

I gaze around the vast rustic area with its cathedral ceiling, seeing it through her eyes. It really is spectacular.

"Are these walls stone?" she asks, trailing her hands along them.

"Yup. All the original features are preserved."

She looks at me intently, those green eyes burning into mine. "It's beautiful. This mansion ... this life. It doesn't even faze you anymore, does it?"

"They're just possessions, Charlie," I reply simply. "Things to be appreciated, treasured ... but disposable. I've had real loss in my life. These things? Don't even register on the scale."

I turn on the open gas fire, standing nearly as tall as me, and it roars to life.

It was the only thing I compromised on by tweaking from the original feature; fumbling about with coal and sticks every night wasn't my idea of a relaxing holiday.

She plants herself cross-legged right beside it.

I hunker down on my knees to unzip my travel bag and rummage through it. "Here, take this."

Her eyes are wide as she inspects the thermal jacket I hand her. "This is for me?"

"Well, I doubt I'll squeeze into it."

"You bought this for me? It's even in my size!"

"Don't forget these." I wrap the thermal scarf around her neck and fasten the hat on her head. "You look cute." I grin.

"I'm so warm!" she shrieks, wrapping her arms around my neck. "How did you have time to get this? How are you so thoughtful? It's making me horny."

"Good." I lift a brow. "Because as soon as you are warm, I'm going to strip you naked."

\*\*\*

We finish dinner beside the fire.

Scotch in hand, I watch her sleeping face and the movement of her chest as it rises up and down on my lap.

The red wine topped with the cold air has her out like a light. I brush a finger down her sharp cheekbone, careful not to wake her.

Her eyelids flutter indicating she is dreaming.

Watching her will never get boring. Her breath falls out softly from her full lips. If I have to sit like this all night, I will, just so she can sleep here, peaceful and protected by me.

I need to bite the bullet and tell Tristan. I'll make him understand that it's serious, that it's not like the other flings. I know now it's not.

Losing Tristan would be something I couldn't recover from. I don't have many friends, not ones I can trust. I can count them on one hand—Tristan, Jack, Martina and, of course, Karl.

But giving up Charlie now? It's not an option. I realise that now, as she sleeps in my lap, her long brown hair draped over my knees. Even the *thought* of losing her sears me with pain.

Her eyes flit open, and she smiles lazily up at me.

"Hey, you. Are you being creepy and watching me sleep?"

"Guilty," I whisper as I run a finger over her bottom lip.

"I'm sorry for calling your plane chitty chitty bang bang."

I let out a chuckle. "That's good because you know that's how we're getting home?"

Her eyes grow wide. "Shit. I forgot about that. Am I the craziest bitch you've ever had in the air?"

"Maybe," I say softly. "I took Jen to the South of France. That was quite a turbulent flight."

Her face sags, and I try to recover my faux pas. "No one has been here with me."

She gazes up at me, letting out a small laugh. "You are trying to kill me, so you don't need to tell Tristan. Haunted house on a hillside with gargoyles overlooking sea cliffs. Small plane in thunderstorms. This weekend is a horror cliché."

I raise a brow. "You're the first person to call a million-pound plane small. Truth be told, I don't share this place often. I come here alone or occasionally with Karl. I'm pretty private, Charlie."

She lifts herself off my knees so that she's facing me, a beautiful crush creeping across her cheeks. "You've never taken another woman here?"

"No." I frown. "Only you."

She inhales softly and cups my cheek in her hand. "Thank you for sharing it with me. Does that mean," she asks quietly, "that I'm your girlfriend?"

My eyes hold hers as a barrage of emotions flood

me. Fuck this. For the first time in years, I know what I want.

If I could stay in this moment forever, I would.

With this girl.

My girl.

Leave London, my company, everything behind and become hermits on these cliffs.

"Yes, Charlie. You most certainly are."

She rests her head on my shoulders, and I inhale deeply into her hair.

So this is what content feels like.

## Charlie

It's a contender for my favourite day on the planet so far.

I woke up to a morning coffee overlooking the sea then we spent the morning hiking across miles of breathtaking coastline. Despite the brutal winds punching me repeatedly in the face, I'm starting to understand why Danny loves it so much here.

We've walked for miles without seeing another person; in fact, it feels like our own private island. Just us, the sheep, and puffins.

The 'Danny up a mountain trying not to step in sheep pellets' versus 'CEO Danny negotiating acquisitions'? Like chalk and cheese. Here his smile reaches his eyes, and the deep-set frown has all but vanished.

"I told you my grandmother lives here." He squeezes my hand as we meander down the cobbled streets of the main town, window shopping the thrift shops. "We're going to her house for lunch."

"What?" I stop short, filled with sudden panic.

My hair is wild, and I'm wearing so many layers of clothing I look like I've been bubble-wrapped.

"I can't meet your granny!" My arms flap wildly to highlight my wild sheep farmer look. "Like this!"

"You look beautiful," he says as he pulls me down another pedestrianised side street. That's the lovely thing about the Shetland islands, there's hardly any traffic.

"She's from Shetland, Charlie. Do you think she's expecting you to rock up in a designer frock?"

"A bit of warning would have been nice," I grumble. "So I could have at least brushed my hair."

He stops outside a small cottage at the corner of the street.

"Nervous?" he grins, kissing my forehead.

"Terrified," I hiss as I try to flatten down my hair. "What if she hates me?"

He raises a brow. "Why the hell would she hate you? She'll love you as much as I do."

My eyes search his.

"As much as you do?" I whisper, watching him.

He smiles softly but evades the question. "Come on. Get ready for the interrogation."

He knocks on the door, setting my pulse racing. This is more than I had signed up for today. On the flight, I pretty much downed a bottle of red wine to calm my nerves, so I'm not on my A-game with conversation today.

"Danny!" The door opens, and a bohemian-looking lady, probably in her 80's at a guess, reaches up to hug her handsome grandson.

Her body is draped in colourfully patterned clothes, mismatched with vibrant chunky jewellery dangling from her neck and arms. She's got a hint of the Walker dark features showing through the grey.

I look down at my own attire, more akin to living rough in the woods, and silently curse Danny.

His large biceps curl around her frail ones. I wonder if this is his grandmother on his mother's or father's side. Surely his mother's side?

"Hello, my dear, so lovely to meet you." Her accent is strong. I have to focus on every word to keep up.

"Charlie, this is my grandmother, Edme."

She smiles at me warmly as she reaches for a hug, giving me a strong whiff of sherry.

"So lovely to meet you, Edme," I say. "Your cottage is truly beautiful."

She bundles us into the cottage, as quaint on the inside as it is on the outside, a world away from Danny's luxurious gaffs. I expect she's never wanted to move even though he has offered.

"Sit down, sit down!" she fusses. "I've just made tea and lunch for us. I hope you are hungry!"

My stomach growls in response.

We hiked for hours without a cafe in sight. I realised I've been living in London too long when I asked where I would get a flat white coffee with almond milk, only to be given a look of disapproval by Danny.

"Look, you don't need to eat it if you don't want

to," Danny murmurs as she goes to the kitchen.

"Why wouldn't I eat it?" I frown.

"You'll see." He smiles.

"Do you need any help?" I call into the kitchen.

"No, dear." She comes through the door carrying a tray with three bowls on it.

"Danny said you liked fish," she declares, setting down the tray on the table.

I peer in horror at the massacred hollowed out fish heads staring up at me with their glassy eyes.

"It's called crappit heid," he explains to me, holding back a smirk.

"Some would call it fish haggis," Edme explains proudly to me. "We ram the fish with oats, suet, and onions. Then we sew the head shut again and boil it in our seawater. It's very healthy."

I pick up the bowl of steaming fish heads and plaster on my lying happy face. "Sounds yummy."

"Here." Danny leans in, watching me trying to spear a fish head with my fork. "You open it from this end."

He levers my fork in, and the head opens.

I tentatively gather a small sample of food onto my fork and take a bite. It's not bad. If I don't think too much about what it is, I can cope.

I nod a sigh of relief at him as he chuckles.

"Would you like some sherry in your tea, dear?"

"Sure!" I giggle, thinking Edme was a bit of a good time girl in her day. "I've heard some of your songs, sweetie. They are beautiful." She takes my teacup and adds a generous amount of sherry.

My eyes pop wide. How would she have heard my songs? Surely she's not on OpenMic?

"Danny shared them with me years ago," she explains, her eyes twinkling at my surprise. "He talked about Tristan's sister who was a singer."

"It's just a hobby." I blush. "I'm not an actual singer." I turn to Danny in disbelief. "I didn't think you liked them. You seemed so distant at all of my gigs."

He cocks a brow. "Seriously? It's called self-preservation, Charlie. Can't you read me at all?"

"I knew back then that he carried a torch for you." Mischief dances in her eyes as she looks between us both. "I knew I would meet you one day."

"Careful, Grandma," Danny scolds gently. "Don't scare her away."

"I'm not scared," I reply, deadpan. And for the first time in my procession of flings and relationships, I mean it.

I stare at him, and he holds my gaze, a recognition passing between us.

If Danny Walker wants me to move to the Shetlands, live on a sheep farm, and make him fish haggis every day, then sign me up.

# 30

**Danny**

"Mr. Walker, Charlotte Kane is here to see you. It's an unscheduled meeting. I said not to disturb you."

The disapproval of Michelle, my PA, is apparent over the intercom. Why is this girl expecting to see the CEO unannounced?

Michelle's right. I have the board of directors meeting in fifteen minutes.

But my curiosity is piqued.

She's never been brave enough to arrive at my office uninvited before. In fact, when I see her in the office, she turns in the opposite direction, afraid people will smell the sex hormones fuming from both of us if we stand too close.

And of course, it's her birthday today.

"Send her through," I confirm.

There's hesitation on the other end. "The board meeting, sir."

"Yes, I know," I reply sharply, irritated at being challenged.

"Yes, sir."

There's a soft knock. "Come in."

She enters, and I stop typing, leaning back in my

chair.

"So you knock now?"

Her hair is messily bundled in a bun on top of her head, hair escaping everywhere, and she's wearing her reading glasses. A fitted white shirt that needs an iron run over it is rolled into figure-hugging jeans showing her long legs.

She's beautiful. Without fail, I feel a pulse of desire between my legs.

Will I get used to this? It's becoming embarrassing.

"Charlie?" I question. "As much as I want to see you, and believe me, I'd prefer to spend the next hour with you rather than old men in suits; I have a director's meeting in ten minutes."

"Hey," she says, and my expression softens. "I wanted to thank you for the nice flowers."

"You're welcome, beautiful. Happy birthday."

Her lips part, and she looks unsure of herself.

My intercom buzzes, and I press to talk.

"Mr. McMillon is in reception. Shall I get him escorted to the boardroom, sir?"

"Yes, please," I confirm to Michelle as Charlie walks around my desk.

I push my chair back, thinking she's going to kiss me. Instead, she sinks to her knees in front of me, pushing my legs apart.

An involuntary rush of breath escapes my lips.

What the fuck?

Here?

Now?

"What the fuck are you doing, Charlie?"

She puts her hands on my knees, looking up at me with fake innocence knowing *exactly* what she's doing.

My dick betrays me, and the blood pumps through it, anticipating what might happen.

Pulling down my zipper, she takes the base of my shaft in her fist and wraps her mouth around my cock.

I close my eyes, gripping the desk.

I should push her away.

I can't.

I don't.

She moves her mouth around my cock like she's sucking a piece of candy.

"Baby," I say in a strangled voice watching the swallowing action in her throat.

My intercom phone buzzes, and I jab it on mute.

Her bright green eyes stare up, equally wanting to please me and own me.

My hips buck up to sink deeper into her mouth, and she uses the excuse to wrap her hands around my buttocks.

Fuck, now she has me in a hold.

I grasp her hair harder than I mean to, and she yelps a little, the humming around my cock only bringing me closer.

My teeth bite down hard on my bottom lip to stop my groaning from reaching my PA's ears. I'm not going to last.

"I'm close," I groan, my breath so ragged it's

embarrassing.

She picks up pace, thrusting my length in and out of her mouth, staring up at me with those earnest eyes.

"I'm coming ... I'm coming in your mouth."

Both my hands grip the desk as she sucks harder, faster.

Moaning loudly, I spurt into her mouth and watch her swallow every drop, never breaking her gaze with me, before releasing me from her mouth.

"That was unexpected but amazing," I rasp out, adjusting myself back in my underwear, willing my cock to calm down.

She looks proud of herself, and so she should. "You're welcome."

I pull her up to standing and kiss her softly on the neck. "Tomorrow," I whisper in a daze. "We finish this tomorrow."

"Do you have the board meeting now?"

We both look down at the tent in my trousers, and I curse.

Never mind Tristan. HR and the board will break my nuts.

How is it that I own the company and can still get into trouble with HR?

### Charlie

"So don't mention anything?"

"No, Suze," I repeat for the twentieth time. "Keep your mouth shut. Tristan doesn't know yet."

"If I keep my mouth shut, will you buy dinner?"

I glare at her. "It's my birthday, but yes, if that is the only way I will have an easy life. Keep your gob shut, and I'll fill it with food."

"This is ridiculous." Julie snorts. "It's been two weeks since you went away for your dirty weekend. You'll have to tell Tristan sometime."

"We're planning to, just not tonight," I explain. "We're going to his house for dinner at the weekend and will tell him then. We want to get him alone."

We are drinking cocktails in a sexy bar nestled in a basement in Soho. It's Tuesday but looking around the heaving bar, you would be forgiven for mistaking it for a Friday. Every night is Friday night in London.

"I'm going to freshen up," I say, standing up. Danny, Tristan, and Jack will be here any minute. "I'll go to the bar on my way back."

"Ladies first."

I look into an extremely attractive face as I queue at the bar. The smirk on his face says he knows I think he's gorgeous.

"Thanks," I say, flustered, giving my order to the bartender. If I wasn't with Danny, I would be delighted at being in the presence of this godlike creature.

"What's your name?" There's a slight American twang to his deep raspy voice.

"Charlie." I smile. "Short for Charlotte." "It's your birthday today?"

I do a double-take. "How did you know that?"

He nods in the direction of the table, and I glance over to find Suze, Cat, Julie, and Stevie watching me like hawks. "The presents on the table. I saw you unwrapping them."

I whip round to face him, lifting a brow. "Someone's observant."

"You caught my eye, Charlie." He says my name like he's trying it on for size. He's confident; I'll give him that.

"Need a hand with the drinks?" a steely voice says behind me.

I turn around to see an annoyed Danny watching my exchange with Sexy Stranger.

He leans over to reach the bar, strategically placing himself between the guy and me, taking two of the cocktails.

I take the others.

"I have to get back," I say to Sexy Stranger in a strained voice as we walk away.

This is awkward.

"I'd like to take you out, Charlie," he calls loudly after me.

"I don't fucking think so," Danny growls back.

"Who the fuck is that?" he fumes, his eyes firmly locked on me.

"Just some guy that started talking to me at the bar."

"Fuck's sake."

"Tristan will hear," I say in a loud whisper. "Behave yourself."

"You behave," he snaps when we are within

earshot of the table.

"Hi Tristan, Jack," I say loudly.

Tristan and Jack turn to greet me.

"Happy birthday, sis." Tristan sweeps me up for a hug, and Jack reaches in for a kiss on my cheek.

The waitresses circle, shark-like. *Before*, we had to wait ten minutes for someone to approach us, *now*, they are giving us more attention than any other table in the bar.

Typical. The Tristan, Danny, Jack effect.

I sit down on the barstool, and Danny takes a stool opposite me, sitting beside Cat.

"Thanks for dropping by." I turn to Tristan and Jack.

"I'm sorry we can't stay," Tristan says. "I can't get out of this law dinner. I had to stop by and give you your present."

"Although you probably don't want three old blokes cramping your style." Jack raises a brow. "Who's Mr. handsome at the bar? Is he your date?"

I dart a glance at Danny. A frown creases his brow as he processes Jack's words.

"No!" I say quickly as the waitress brings three scotches for the men.

She looks at Danny and does a double-take, recognising him, then her eyes light up like she's won the jackpot. "Here's your drink." She puts a hand unnecessarily on Danny's shoulder, making me want to scrab her.

"Mr. Walker," she purrs, giving him sex eyes as Jack chuckles beside me, muttering 'every time' under his breath.

Annoyed, I divert my attention from the flirty waitress.

"Where is your law dinner?"

Tristan brings the scotch to his lips, smelling it before knocking it back. "Mayfair. It's the annual dinner for the law society. I'm speaking at it."

"Are you two going?" I ask Jack and Danny.

"To listen to Tristan talk?" Jack lets out a laugh. "God, no. I'm meeting a lady for dinner, and workaholic Walker is working tonight."

I look at Danny, slightly disappointed. I wanted him to stay for my birthday and go to sleep with me tonight. That's the only gift I wanted. But Danny staying behind when Tristan and Jack left would look suspicious.

"It doesn't beat having a song written for you." Tristan smiles, handing me an envelope.

"You can't sing." I roll my eyes. "That would have been the worst gift ever."

"Tristan, this is too much," I scold, scanning the paper. It's a weekend in the South of Italy for me and three others.

Julie whoops beside me. "Yes! Holiday!"

"Nonsense," Tristan scoffs. "Right, I *really* need to go now. I'm already late."

He knocks back the rest of the scotch and slams down the empty glass as Jack and Danny follow suit. "Ladies and Stevie, it's been a pleasure. Charlie, enjoy the rest of your birthday."

"I will," I smile, hiding my disappointment as

Danny puts on his jacket and leather gloves.

He turns when Tristan steps away from the table. "Before I forget." He hands me an envelope, and our hands touch. "Happy birthday, Charlie. It's just a card. Open it when we are gone."

Confused, I feel something lumpy in it.

His eyes have a glimmer of reluctance, but he nods his goodbye and follows Tristan and Jack out the door.

I rip open the envelope, and something sparkles up at me.

"Oh my God," Julie shrieks as we all stare open-mouthed at the exquisite diamond pendant necklace.

"Is it real?" I gasp.

"Of course, it's real!" she hisses. "And clearly wasted on you. It's from Tiffany's. That necklace costs about five grand."

"That's more than six months' rent!" I choke. "I can't accept this."

"Wow," Suze says. "This thing between you two is clearly more than sex."

I swallow the lump in my throat. Yes, this isn't just sex. This is in a different league to anything I've ever experienced.

I am hopelessly, utterly irrevocably in love with this man, but I can't admit it out loud.

I want this man from my very core. I've never wanted anything more, and that thought terrifies me because to love this deep means I have so, so much to lose.

# 31

**Charlie**
**One week later.**

"Charlie?" Someone cries my name as I enter the flat after work on Thursday. The voice sounds strange, like they've been crying.

I take my shoes off and pad quickly through the hallway to the living room.

Julie sits slumped on the sofa, her face flushed.

"Julie?" I drop my laptop bag and run to her. "What's happened?"

Tears slip from the corner of her eye. "Charlie." She starts howling again. "Sorry ... accident," is all I manage to decipher from the sounds she is making.

I'm freaked. I've never seen Julie like this.

"Julie?" I shake her hand softly, trying to break her hysterics.

She lowers her head to the ground, not looking at me. "Charlie, our emails." She swallows a sob.

"Emails," I repeat, confused. What is she talking about?

"Our emails about getting revenge on Danny, way back when things were weird between you two."

I remember.

"Yes?" A sense of dread hits me.

"They were on my work email server and ... and some of the media team found them."

I sit up alert. "And?"

"And," she wails. "There's a story ... I couldn't stop it. I begged them." A large grunt escapes her. "I'm so stupid, Charlie," she whispers through tears. "And so sorry. Please forgive me."

"A story?" I ask, my heart in my throat as my brain tries to understand what she is saying. "Show me," I add, breathing hard.

She nods, wiping the wet from her cheeks, then takes out her laptop. "I see all the articles before they go live."

She turns the laptop to me and inhales sharply.

The large font headline hits me.

**Nexus CEO Danny Walker rocked by sleazy office sex scandal.**

With every word, my skin crawls like insects are running over me. "He's been seeing someone else?" I whisper.

"Wait, no," she says. "It's *you*. The article is about you."

I scan the lower font below the headline.

My name. Everywhere. His name. Our secrets are laid out in black and white but distorted through a sleazy exaggerated lens.

**Danny Walker, 41, reportedly offered employee Charlotte Kane an undisclosed sum to perform sordid explicit sex acts.**

**Danny Walker has long been dogged by allegations of womanizing.....**
**...exposing himself and making indecent propositions....**

The blood drains from my face, and the words dance in front of my eyes.

"But that's not why he offered me a buyout," I cry. "This is all wrong. All fucked."

I stare at the screen, no longer reading it.

That cannot be happening. I'm a lowly I.T. Support person in a mouse-riddled flatshare. I'm not newsworthy.

*But Danny Walker is.*

Searing pain shoots through me. There's no return from this digital footprint, this slander. I'll lose my job. Even if I don't get fired, I'll have to leave. Would anyone hire me after this?

A million images race through my head. Tristan's furious face, Alex, Jackie, all the techies, everyone at work laughing and whispering about the office slag, Mum's mortification and consequent hibernation, another family shame, but the image that sticks in my head the most and stabs at me is Danny ... Danny's fury, Danny's disgust, Danny's hatred of me.

I inflicted this on him.

The article is a poor reflection of me, but Danny? Danny's reflection is on another level. It's so sensationalised. They make me sound like a gold-digging slut and him, a creepy Casanova preying on staff.

"Charlie? Please speak to me."

"Is it live now?" I sob.

"No," she says. "But it's going to press on Saturday."

"Can we stop it? Can I talk to someone and say it's bullshit?" I glare at her. "This can't be fucking legal. It's not true."

"You can try to sue for libel afterwards," she says in a small voice. "But you can't stop it in time." She swallows. "Do you hate me?" she whispers.

I breathe out heavily. "No, Julie. But I know someone who will hate me."

She nods. "Are you going to invite him over?" She lets out a joyless laugh. "He'll strangle me."

"No." I shake my head. "He's swamped. I need to tell him now. Over the phone."

I stare at my phone, inhaling a deep breath.

Julie asks me something, but I barely hear it over the sound of my pulse in my ears.

Taking the phone, I walk down the hall into my bedroom and shut the door.

I jab the buttons with my trembling fingers, and his name flashes on the screen.

"Charlie." I know from his voice he is smiling.

"Danny," I reply shrilly, choking back tears.

"Charlie?" his tone becomes alert. "Are you OK?"

I have to make him understand I didn't mean for any of this to happen. He has to forgive me. I can't lose him.

"I'm sorry," I whisper. "There's an article coming out ... it's terrible ... it's about us."

"How do you know this?" he asks, his voice sharper. "It's OK, sweetheart."

"It's not," my dry mouth spits out the words. "It's my fault. It's from Julie's media company. It's from emails between Julie and I about … us."

There's silence.

"Send it to me," he replies grimly.

I open my laptop again and, with shaky hands, forward the email from Julie to his personal email. It's an attachment of what the actual article will look like.

"Have you got it yet?" I whisper.

"Not yet … Yes, it's come through."

I hold my breath as I hear his brain chugging at the other side, and curses escape from his throat. Why isn't he talking to me?

"I'm so sorry," I sob. "I never meant this to—"

"Leave it." His voice comes low, cold, making my eyes fill with tears.

"Can I come over?"

It takes a long time before he replies.

"That wouldn't be advisable," he responds, monotone. "I need to go. Don't talk to anyone about this."

The phone goes dead, the silence crushing me like a vice.

I can't breathe.

I sit on the bed, not moving, staring at the wall.

It'll be there forever. My name, his name, our relationship tainted on the internet.

It's all over.

I've ruined my reputation and my relationship. I've ruined everything. Tristan will be devastated and fall out with Danny, blaming him for this. Mum will want to move houses again. The second disgrace of the family. I'll never be able to walk into work again.

At 11 p.m., I haven't moved from my position on the bed, and I message him.

"Please talk to me. I'm sorry. I'm scared."

I wait. And wait. And wait.

At 1 a.m. my phone buzzes. "Don't go into the office tomorrow."

That's it.

Tears pour down, and I am sobbing so loudly that Cat comes in, gets on the bed, and embraces me in a hug.

***

Things always look better in the morning, they say.

I call bullshit. In my case, the pain is worse. I've rolled around the bed all night, waiting for a text that never arrived.

I go through the day in a zombie state, not eating, barely drinking water, pacing around the house. There's no point getting dressed.

I tried his number a few times, only for it to go to voicemail.

He never refuses my calls, once he even stepped out of a board meeting with the entire board of directors to talk to me.

Cat didn't want to leave me alone, afraid I'd slash my wrists or something, but I was better alone. I logged on at 9 a.m. to send an email saying I was sick. Only to find an email saying I was being offered the Solution Architect role. I had managed to wrangle myself the role. I'm going to be part of the team redesigning the products. It meant relocating to the New York office for three months, and they wanted to know if I wanted to find my own place or live in their Manhattan apartment for staff.

It's a bittersweet victory. It wouldn't matter on Monday; the offer would be null and void. I was never going back to the office once this story hits.

There is still one person I have to tell, and it will almost be as hard as telling Danny.

I have to tell Tristan. Black fear takes over me.

## Danny

"You fucking asshole."

I'm jolted backwards against the door as his fist connects to my jaw.

A stream of blood flows from my nose.

"My sister," Tristan snarls, his face twisted in anger. I've seen him this angry once before, over nearly losing his son, but never with me, never because of something I've done.

I back away as he launches another punch at me.

"You could have any fucking girl. You chose to fuck my sister?"

"It wasn't just a fuck," I whisper hoarsely. "I care for her."

"Care for her enough to drag her name through the mud?"

"Can you come in so we can talk about this?" I ask in a low voice, holding the door open. There's blood trickling on the floor.

"If I come in, I'll smash every damn thing in your house. What was it, the thrill of going after someone you shouldn't?" he shouts, his face inches from mine. "You just couldn't keep your dick in your pants? Explain to me why shagging my sister was worth fucking up our friendship."

"I meant what I said, I care about her."

"Bullshit," he hisses, his face twisted. "If you cared about her, you wouldn't have taken advantage in the office. You wouldn't have allowed this seedy story to come out."

"I'm dealing with it, Tristan. I'm sorry," I say hoarsely. "I'm sorry I went behind your back. I would never deliberately hurt Charlie. I took her to the Shetlands," I add.

He does a double-take. "Why?"

"I told you why. She means something to me."

"You look like shit." He laughs without humour. "I hope you're not fucking sleeping over this either."

"I haven't slept since I found out about the story."

He looks mildly appeased.

I stare at my oldest, closest friend, my eyes begging forgiveness. "Can we recover from this?"

"Look, just stay away for now. Stay away from me. Stay away from Charlie."

"How is she?" I ask tentatively.

He narrows his eyes. "How do you think she is? She's in fucking bits. Crying all the time."

I close my eyes and breathe out. The thought of Charlie in pain is killing me.

# 32

## Charlie

D-Day.

There's a dull unease lying permanently in my stomach, waiting to rise. It's Saturday morning, and I can say I haven't slept a full hour since Thursday.

There's been no contact from Danny. Zero. Nada. No matter how many times I checked my phone and my emails just in case he happened to email my work email.

I've almost gnawed my fingers off. My nails are bitten down to a stub. I haven't showered in two days, and I've barely slept. I'm a walking zombie.

How do I prepare for the melodrama that is going to unfold? Do I warn my Mum and Callie? Do I deny it? Is it true what they say—today's news is tomorrow's chip paper? That was fine in the world of print; now, our digital footprint stays with us for life. If anyone searches for me, they'll see it time and time again.

My brain floods with the worst scenarios. Will it get nasty? Is Danny so angry he will sue me for libel?

I need to see his face, for him to hug me and tell me it's going to be OK, that we are stronger than this.

It's minutes until Julie's media department upload their new stories. Cat and Suze are sitting on either side of me on the sofa.

Julie is on her laptop pressing refresh every ten seconds, waiting for the site to release today's articles. She's going to screen how bad it is for me as we thought it best that I don't see the trolling comments immediately once it goes live.

"It's been released," she says in a high pitch, and I close my eyes and summon a deep breath.

Cat and Suze grab my hand on either side.

"I don't understand," Julie says.

I open my eyes.

"What?" I snap. "What do you not understand?"

Her eyebrows knit together as she studies the laptop screen. "It's you, but it's not you."

"What do you mean?" I lean over and grab the laptop from her.

"Your name, I can't see it."

I speed-read the article, which I know by heart. It's the same article I've read a hundred times in two days. Trying to find a positive spin.

But something's wrong.

I read it again. And again.

"Read this," I say to Cat and Suze. "What the hell is going on?"

His name is everywhere on it. But me? I've become this nameless, faceless employee.

"Oh my God." Julie slaps a hand over her mouth. "He's found a way to keep you out of it."

"No-one knows it's me?" I blink. "How? How did

he do it?" Relief floods through me like someone turned on a tap.

She pauses. "It makes no sense. It's a more lucrative story with you named."

Her eyes widen. "He must have paid them a lot of money to keep your name out of it."

"He protected me?" I ask in a small voice. "But why didn't he stop the story completely?"

"I dunno." She shrugs. "He obviously used himself as a bargaining tool. Run the story but without you in it. It's near impossible to stop a story in its tracks unless there is a threat to life. All you can do is deal with it afterwards."

I collapse back onto the couch as two days of heart-wrenching emotions and tiredness floods me.

The ugly, scandalous story is still out there for all to see with his name in it. He'll never forgive me for this. I'm never going to be held or kissed by him again.

**Danny, I know what you did for me. Please talk to me.**

The read message appears, and I wait.
No response.

***

I know the code to the gate, so I enter it rather than buzz him to let me in. Since we started dating, he gave me the code, and I would just let myself in whenever I visited.

Now, I'm not so sure it's the right thing to do. It's

Sunday afternoon, a whole twenty-four hours since the article has come out, and he hasn't responded to any of my messages.

But I don't want to have the conversation through the intercom. What if he doesn't let me in? No, I need him to see my face, to see how sorry and upset I am. To see how broken I am.

So here I am, outside his door, sick with fear and nerves.

I inhale deeply and rap on the large knocker.

I'm expecting a dry husky Scottish voice, but the familiar female voice I hear from the hallway is ten times more terrifying.

"Is that the takeaway, babe?"

My blood runs cold as I realise whose voice I'm hearing.

Footsteps come closer to the door.

Panic rises in me, and I sprint down the steps, across the driveway, and out of the gate, the stones flying over my feet. Breathing hard, I lean back out of sight, hiding behind one of the large pillars.

Peeking out, I watch my worst nightmare as she stands in the doorway wearing Danny's T-shirt and a pair of shorts. A T-shirt he's given me to wear.

She looks around, confused.

"Who is it?" says the familiar Scottish voice approaching the door.

I slap a hand over my mouth to stifle my cries.

"No-one." She shrugs, turning to smile.

The door closes, and for a moment, I'm frozen, unable to process the memory of what's just happened. Then something snaps inside me, and I collapse to the ground.

The air I'd been holding escapes my lungs in a gargle. It's over. We can never recover from this, never go back. It all meant nothing. He has moved on.

I start to sob uncontrollably, sitting on the street.

Danny Walker has opened me up and sliced my heart down the middle.

***

I sit on the sofa with Cat, Suze, and Julie watching me. Because I was in such a state, Cat collected me from Richmond and escorted me back to the flat.

"Jackie." Cat's shocked eyes find mine.

"Yes."

"Seriously, Jackie?" she repeats an octave higher. "I know she's beautiful, but she's just so annoying. I can't believe he went there."

I shrug, wiping my tear-stained face. My cheeks are red and sore from crying so much. Suze stares at me from her position on the floor.

"He was so into you. He had such an issue with dating people that work for him so he does it again? It doesn't make sense."

I let out a joyless chuckle. "He's the CEO. He can do what he likes. He sees something he likes, he takes it. I knew. I saw the signs. I'm so stupid."

I let out a sob, and Cat puts her arm around me. "He had a new girlfriend every two months. What was I expecting? That he would sit around and pine after me?"

"This is all my fault," Julie whispers from the corner, her eyes to the floor. "The story, your break-up. I've fucked up everything."

I lean over and take her hand. "No, Julie, it's not. You didn't make him move on with Jackie. If he can move on so quickly then it wasn't what I thought it was. You need to get back to normal." I laugh at her through tears. "This being nice to me is freaking me out. You're supposed to be telling me to put my big girl pants on and deal with it."

She flashes me a small, relieved smile.

"What will you do?" Cat probes gently. "Are you going to turn down the job in New York?"

I pause. "I think I'm going to take it. The time away will be good."

"By yourself?" Her eyes widen. "Is now the best time?"

I look between them. A part of me wants to leave Nexus so I'll never have to see Danny Walker again. But a part of me wants this job; I worked for it. It's mine. Just because he has cast me aside doesn't mean I should give up on everything else.

"I'm saying yes." I nod firmly. "My name didn't come out in the article. In fact, it could easily be Jackie. People would believe that. This feels right ...a new start. Three months away to clear my head."

"I just don't like the idea of you being by yourself right now. I'm worried about you. You're so ... distraught." Cat stares at me. "I've never seen you like this."

"I'll be OK." I smile sadly. "This will be good for me."

She nods, unconvinced. "When do you leave?"

"I need to work through the details with them, but they say I can come over in the next week. I'll work from the New York office and start part-time in the design role while I do a transition plan for my current tasks. They are going to merge my role into the Nexus team, so this suits them perfectly."

I give a joyless laugh. "Turns out Danny was right. They would have chopped my role and made me redundant. Maybe he was trying to do me a favour."

Later that night, I decide there's something pressing I need to do if I have any hope of recovery.

**Danny, I want to apologise for the embarrassment I've caused you through this article. None of this was my intention. I sincerely hope you and my brother rebuild your friendship. The last thing I wanted was to come in between that. We made a mistake, but I'm sure you will agree that for the sake of Tristan, we must be civil and learn to be OK with each other ... perhaps even someday we can be friends. I'm taking the job in New York, so you won't have to see me.**

**We are both moving on, and that's for the best. I hope you will still let me take the position regardless of all the drama I've caused. I won't be the brat I used to be. When we meet again, it will be as if things never happened.**

I send it to his personal email address rather than his phone. That way, I won't know when he's read it.

It's done.

Then I lie back in the bed and stare lifelessly at the ceiling.

I was lying in my email. I'll never be able to move on from him. From us.

# 33

**Charlie**
**One month later.**

"These are what the core features will look like,"
I explain, proudly tracing my fingers over the
whiteboard. "We will need to do user research with
our existing customers, but I know some that would
love to be involved. They'll give us honest feedback
then we can refine the prototype."

I look down at Joe and hesitate.

"Brilliant," he says, giving me the full force of
his pearly smile. How is it that every American in
New York has a Hollywood smile? It's giving me a
complex.

He gets up from his seat and studies the
whiteboard. "Seriously, Charlie, they are brilliant.
Solid visions for the product."

I beam up at him. Joe is classically tall, dark, and
handsome. I've met a lot of those types in New
York. It's a sausage-fest of pearly white square-jawed
muscular men. Nice to look at for a fleeting second,
but they did nothing to mend my shredded heart.

It's the first smile that has reached my eyes in
weeks. Since before the night I found Julie crying on

the sofa.

"Will you be able to do a prototype with these?"

"Absolutely. We'll work on them tomorrow and showcase them to Karl on Thursday?"

"Sure." I smile happily at him. "It's wine time now, isn't it?"

"I sincerely think so." He grins back. "I'll go grab the others, OK?"

I nod as I clear up in the room and put my laptop away. I look at my watch and see it's 7 p.m. It's nearly midnight at home, probably too late to call Tristan back. This past week, we have missed each other's calls.

I walk over to the wall-to-ceiling windows as I do every night and stare out.

It's my evening ritual. It doesn't matter how late I work, I always have time to finish the workday with this. It's the only time I feel a sense of stillness.

We are on the twentieth floor, and I'll never get used to the Manhattan Skyline in the dark, the colourful lights of the skyscrapers dancing off each other. In the distance, I can see the iconic Rockefeller Center. Apparently, in a few weeks' time, we'll be able to see the Christmas tree. Working here every day with this background? It never gets old.

"Are you ready, Charlie?" Joe puts a hand on my shoulder and drags me from my daze. "We're heading to Dead Rabbit."

I nod, put on my coat, and then pick up my hat and scarf. I hesitate as I always do, smelling the hint of the scent there before. The smell of our weekend beside the fire in Shetland. I wear them every day here, not just because the New York winters are brutal, but because, in some far-fetched way, they make me feel close to him.

"What are we eating?" I hesitantly ask.

He shrugs. "We'll eat at Dead Rabbit."

I let out a groan. "Look, I know New York is a foodie heaven but these portions ... I'm growing a snout and a tail."

*\*\**

Dead Rabbit is heaving as we walk in, and I spot at least five of the team in one of the corner booths whilst a few others are playing darts.

I love these American-style bars with their old-school sawdust floors and prohibition-era style bar booths. Sometimes on Saturdays, I go in by myself and spend hours writing the lyrics of songs, chatting to the bartenders. Here in New York, bartending and waitressing are art forms; the bartenders are counsellors, and the waitresses are mind readers, knowing exactly when to approach you and when to give space.

We squeeze our way through the crowd to the booth.

"Charlie, Joe." Karl grins at us, beckoning us over. "What are you having?"

"Two Old Fashioneds please, boss," Joe says.

He looks around the group. "Two Old Fashioneds, two whiskey sours, G & T coming right up."

"Do you need a hand, Karl?" I shout over the

music.

"Sure." He smiles, putting his hand on my lower back as we make our way to the bar.

"How are you, Charlie?" He looks genuinely concerned. "Are you enjoying New York?"

"I love New York." That wasn't a lie. I do love New York. I've walked every inch of the glitzy concrete jungle and its parks. My distractions.

"You seem to have settled into the design team shockingly fast." He looks at me, and I glow at the compliment. "I'm sorry I haven't been around to make sure you're OK this past week."

I heard he was in Singapore for a tech conference.

"You don't need to make sure I'm OK, Karl." I frown. "You've got hundreds of people in the office to look after."

His eyes flit from mine as he starts to say something but holds back.

*He thinks he needs to watch out for me after what's happened with Danny.*

There's been an unspoken rule since I landed in New York. We don't talk about Danny to each other. Karl took me out for lunch a few times during my first few weeks. We only ever crossed paths at Tristan's parties before, so I never got to know him well. We had only ever scratched the surface, but here in New York, I've been able to spend time with him. We talked for hours about the new plans for the Dunley products.

"What are your weekend plans?" he asks as he hands the bartender his card.

"Actually, I'm going to do some work on Saturday," I admit sheepishly.

"Work on a weekend?" He raises a brow. "Are we working you too hard?"

"No." I smile. "I just want to finish some design ideas so Joe can build the prototypes."

He tilts his head to the side, studying me. "You are really flourishing in this role, Charlie. It's a good fit for you. I never realised you had such a creative streak."

"Thanks, Karl." I blush. "That means a lot coming from you."

"Look, don't spend all weekend working, though?" he asks as he hands me the whiskey cocktails.

"I won't," I promise. "On Sunday, Joe is taking me to the Brooklyn Museum."

Karl lifts a brow. "Joe, huh? Doesn't he live in Brooklyn?"

"Yes," I reply with a hint of irritation. What's he insinuating?

"He's been showing me around the city."

"You know he is interested in you?"

"Nothing is going on, Karl." I frown.

Interest flickers in his eyes then disappears. "I'm glad you've got someone showing you around. Do you know anyone else here?"

"No." I shrug.

And that's fine with me. Because when I stop pounding the streets going to museums, art galleries, comedy clubs, and burger joints, I close the door to my beautiful loft apartment and can be alone to cry.

"Let's you and I go out for lunch soon, ok?"

"I'd like that." I nod at him, smiling. I take a large slug of my Old Fashioned. It burns going down my windpipe, but it might help me get to sleep quicker.

Huh.

So this is how you become an alcoholic.

\*\*\*

It's midnight by the time I get back into the apartment and throw my shoes off. Too late for a school night with the amount of work I need to do tomorrow.

Although I miss Cat and the girls, I love living alone in this beautiful apartment with its exposed brick and high beamed ceilings that I'd never be able to afford if Nexus didn't own it.

I turn on the heating, get into my sweatpants, then sit cross-legged on the sofa with my laptop resting on my legs and my herbal sleeping pill dissolving in hot water.

Then I flick to the photos I'd taken with my professional camera and allow the tears to fall. We looked like the happiest couple in the world; like we belonged together.

For four weeks, I've done this ritual.

Fun times, I think sarcastically to myself.

During the day, I'm 'happy go lucky' Charlie exploring the best of New York but at night, alone in my apartment, I allow myself to mourn.

I replay every interaction we've ever had in microscopic detail, then torture myself with scenarios of the present. How many times has he slept with Jackie? Is it just sex, or does he like her? Does he love her? Is he going to take her to Shetland? That thought makes my heart freeze.

Stevie gives me snippets of what's happening in London. He's been told he can keep his job. He said Jackie has been out on sick leave, and Danny is walking around in a permanent bad mood. Julie says he's suing her media company for defamation of character.

At work, things are back to the way they were before, he's the CEO, and I'm just an employee. I get my paychecks, I get his company-wide emails of motivation, and once a month, I painfully listen to a live video he streams with all employees.

I exit my photo collection and click on the music software.

I've been writing new material the past few weeks, much darker than my usual upbeat tunes, because writing lyrics about pain brings back the pain, and the sadistic side of me wants to wallow in this darkness as long as possible.

I upload them to OpenMic. These ones are building traction and the views are creeping up daily. I guess there are a lot of mourning, brokenhearted people out there.

A message flashes in my Inbox.

*Samantha Dalton, Creative Director, DreamWorks Pictures*

Samantha wants to talk about using my music ... sure, Samantha, if that's your real name.

I get flooded with these every day. Samantha will market my songs at a mere five grand cost to me, making me millions!

*\*\**

I tilt my head to the side, studying the screen. "They're amazing, Joe."

He grins. "I know, right? The board is going to be blown away."

I flinch. In a week's time, we will present our roadmap for the products to the Nexus board of directors. There is a possibility that Danny will attend, although his schedule is never confirmed until a few days in advance when his team decides what are the most important events for him to attend. Since he is usually quadruple booked, this won't register as high on his priority list. Karl already confirmed that his presence is unlikely.

We've worked day and night for this presentation for three weeks, and I'm determined not to fuck it up. It's funny how a broken heart turns you into a workaholic.

"Just a minute, Joe." Tristan's name flashes on my phone, and I walk over to the side of the office for privacy.

It's 10 p.m. London time.

"Hey, sis," his warm voice floods the phone.

"Hey." I smile at the view, happy to hear my big brother's voice.

"You've been ignoring me again," he scolds.

"I know, I'm sorry. I've been swamped with the new roadmap. We're presenting to the board next week, and the design has taken up so much time," I say excitedly.

"I'm glad to hear the passion in your voice again. I'm worried about you, Charlie. You've been distant since you've been in New York."

"I'm sorry for being distant." I swallow the lump in my throat. "I just needed some time ... after everything."

There's a long pause.

"Maybe you should look for another job? There are some I.T. positions in my firm we need to fill. It's not healthy working for Danny after what happened. It's not normal."

"I never see him. It's fine. Right now, I love the role. When I get back to London, I'll look for another company."

"Charlie, he's going to be in New York next week."

*Fuck.*

The presentation. I was banking on him not attending. I draw in a breath. "How do you know? Are you talking again?"

"No." He sighs. "I need time away from him. Jack told me."

"I wish you would speak to him, Tristan. I've done enough damage without wrecking your relationship."

"None of this is your fault," he retorts. "He's older, wiser, he's the CEO, for Christ's sake."

"What else did Jack say?" My stomach churns.

He lets out a long sigh. "Jack says he is in a bad way."

"The stress of the article?"

"No," he says slowly. "That washed over him. He's not telling Jack much, but we think it's related to you."

I stiffen. "I doubt that, Tristan. He got over me quickly."

"How do you know?"

I don't want to have this conversation with my brother.

"He slept with our receptionist three days after it happened," I choke out. "Jackie."

The blood leaves my face as I say her name out loud.

He curses under his breath. "Fucking asshole, I'll slaughter him. Still, you must have affected him since he paid half a million to keep your name out of the article."

"He did what?" I ask loudly.

"He paid to keep your name out of the article," Tristan repeats. "I thought you knew that. He paid the reporter something between half a million to a million."

"I didn't know that," I whisper, my mind whirling.

"He did the right thing," he adds begrudgingly. "I'll give him that."

"It must have been for you," I say in a small voice. "For your friendship."

He snorts.

"Please, Tristan. The relationship between Danny and I is ruined. But you owe him twenty years of loyalty. Think about how he was there for you through all the drama with Gemina. The article wasn't his fault. It was mine," I continue. "I'm a grown woman, and it took two of us to get into that mess. You can't keep punishing him."

"I need time. He went behind my back."

"He made one mistake."

"What happened between you two?" he asks softly. "He's never taken a girl to Shetland before."

I sigh. "I thought it was special. I misread it. Listen, I have to go," I say as another call comes up on the screen.

"Bye, sis. Next time, answer my call."

I press connect on the unknown number; it's not a New York area code or a UK number. "Hello?"

"Is this Charlotte Kane?" a female American voice drawls down the phone.

"Yes?"

"Hi, Charlotte, this is Samantha Dalton from DreamWorks Pictures."

# 34

**Danny**

"Send them in." Laura, our Head of Product, nods to Tracey.

We are sitting in the twentieth-floor boardroom waiting for Charlie and one of the designers to pitch their ideas for the next generation of Dunley products.

I tap my fingers against the desk, and Karl raises his eyebrows at me to stop.

I keep on tapping.

Tracey comes back into the room flagged by Charlie, and a Ken Doll look alike with white teeth. Joel, I think.

My entire body hardens in response. She is wearing a tight royal-blue dress that accentuates the blue/green of her eyes.

*Dear God, she's breathtaking.*

I fold my arms across my chest and try to hide how unhinged I am by her presence.

Her eyes flit to everyone in the room but me as they introduce themselves.

"Mr. Walker," Ken Doll addresses me excitedly. "It's such an honour to have you listen to our pitch today."

"I always take an interest in the new features being pitched," I reply dryly, ignoring him and staring at Charlie.

She has her back to me now, fumbling with cables between the laptop and the screen. I see her hands tremble and realise that she's nervous.

"Can we get someone to help with this set-up?" I ask, irritated. "I have thirty minutes here, counting down."

She turns, her eyes widening in horror as Ken Doll snaps to attention and helps her. He leans over her to take the cable and puts his hand on her lower back, murmuring something in her ear. She gives him a soft smile, and jealousy surges through me.

Way too fucking over-familiar, boy. Get your greedy little mitts off her.

I let out a heavy sigh as Karl flashes me a warning look to behave.

Charlie clears her throat and straightens her dress with long, nervous strokes. "I'll explain first our approach for developing the roadmap. We conducted user research with ten of our existing customers and some larger companies that don't use the software. We analysed the customer satisfaction results over this past five years but also, importantly, we devised a vision for the direction of the product that tells us where we want this product to be in five years' time."

Karl gives her a big thumbs-up, and she flashes a full-voltage smile back at him.

I shift my glare to Karl. Is every man in this bloody room under her spell?

She flounders a little, I suspect from the low growl that involuntarily erupts from my throat.

"This is what we propose for year one for a minimum viable product." She talks through the visual with pride in her voice. Given her experience, it's a big role for her. Karl said she's been working long hours and weekends.

It looks like it has paid off; the ideas and strategy are concise, achievable, and innovative.

"Good," I reply as she finishes, and her gaze finds mine for the first time, causing her cheeks to flush.

She looks like someone just walked over her grave.

"So next ... Here are ... These are the features," she stumbles through her words, flipping to the next slide.

I know my eyes devouring her are putting her off, but I can't wrench my gaze away.

Her face flushes scarlet as the team drills her, dissecting every detail of her pitch.

They're ruthless, I'll give them that. Even as she reels in shock at some of the abrasive comments, she attempts to hold her own in an inexperienced yet determined manner.

I get a vision of her on the boardroom desk, dress bunched around her waist, legs wide and her soft pink flesh wet and ready for my tongue, begging me to fill her.

I miss those moans.

My cock twitches in response.

*Down, boy.*

"Danny, you're very quiet. Do you have any questions?" Laura raises a brow at me.

I hesitate, bringing myself back to the presentation. "Your ideas are good, solid. But your delivery needs work. The pitch was choppy, rough, and immature."

Charlie physically flinches, taking a step backwards.

"It's got promise," I add, levelling my tone. "You've got the go-ahead to continue. Laura will guide you with the next steps to proceed to alpha."

"Thank you." She nods awkwardly. "Mr. Walker."

So I'm *Mr. Walker* now.

"That's all the time Mr. Walker has," Laura says. She turns to me. "Danny, you have a call with Senator Williams now."

Fuck Senator fucking Williams.

I watch Charlie and Joel packing up their equipment, and I hear her giggle softly at him as he says something. He leans over and rubs her arm.

My hands ball into fists. This Joel guy is fucking pissing me off. Just how close did they get working on this pitch?

We pile out of the room into the hallway, Charlie and Ken Doll turning left while I turn right with the rest of the team to head to the elevator.

Laura talks to me about the NextGen launch of one of our crypto products, but I'm too rattled to focus.

"Charlie." I turn around and call her back.

Everyone stops walking, waiting for me to speak.

"It's OK." I wave a hand to dismiss them. "I'd like a moment with Charlie."

Her eyes widen, but she nods and stops walking.

I pace towards her until we're a metre apart.

Ken Doll remains by her side like a lap dog. Who does this guy think he's up against?

"Alone." I glare at him.

"I'm the designer, sir. I'd be happy to answer any questions."

The guy has guts, I'll give him that.

My eyes narrow on him. "Did you not hear me?"

"Of course, sir." He looks upset but reluctantly scuttles down the hall.

I turn my attention to the breathtaking creature destroying my sleep. Her eyes reluctantly lock onto mine.

"Danny," she says, her voice barely above a whisper.

My cock twinges as those big green eyes stare up at me.

I want to sweep her up in my arms and never let her go.

*Focus, Walker.*

"How are you?" I ask softly. "Is the apartment OK?"

"It's beautiful." Her face lights up as she speaks, and I resist the urge to take her cheeks in my hands. "I love the high ceilings and the exposed brick. The gym, the wide street lined with trees, the coffee shops nearby ... it's amazing."

"Glad you approve."

She launches into a nervous chatter. "When I was asked if I wanted a company apartment, I never in a million years thought I would be staying in this luxury. Every day I come home, I still can't believe there is a doorman to open the door for me. I feel like I'm in a movie. I can't believe employees get to stay there for free."

"They don't," I admit, trying to keep my gaze from dropping down to the V line in her dress. "The apartment is my personal one, not the company's."

She twirls her hair around her fingers, something I recognise as her nervous twitch. "I ... I never realised it was yours," she stammers. "That makes sense why it's so nice. I inconvenienced you. I would never have said yes if I realised that."

"You could never inconvenience me, Charlie." I frown, holding her gaze. "Besides, Karl's place is big enough for ten people."

"How is Jackie?" The words tumble out of her mouth.

I give her a double-take. "Did Karl tell you?"

"Yes," she says with a brittle smile.

"It wasn't planned, obviously, but out of mistakes come good things. We're excited. It'll be the first Walker baby in the family."

She jolts backwards with such force I step towards her and grab her wrist.

"Are you OK?"

"She's pregnant?" she chokes out.

"Yes. I thought you knew that."

She bites her lip and looks to the floor. "I thought it was just sex."

"That's generally how you make a baby." I smile dryly.

"I have to go, Danny." She tugs her wrist out of my grasp.

"Just a minute." I raise my voice. "Are you dating that guy with the teeth?"

A flicker of a smile passes across her face. "All the guys I date have teeth. I have some standards."

"You know who I mean," I growl. "Ken Doll."

Damn, that was unprofessional. He's a member of my staff, for Christ's sake.

"You mean Joe?" she asks, taken aback. "No, of course, I'm not dating Joe."

Good. Then that son of a bitch better back off before I reassign him to a different department.

"But I am dating," she adds, staring at my feet. "I'm really happy. Maybe I should stay in New York. Nothing is keeping me in London."

My jaw clenches. "I guess not. Perhaps you should move to the New York office then. I'm sure the team could facilitate that."

When she looks up, I think I see the start of tears pooling in her eyes.

"Bye, Danny, take care of yourself."

I watch her walk away, and something inside me breaks into a thousand tiny pieces.

# 35

**Charlie**

If I thought I was in pain before, then I was kidding myself. Now I am drowning in pain.

I've never felt so low. It's like my heart has been ripped out of my chest. Even Dad leaving us pales in comparison to this.

For the last seven days since I found out about the baby, I've been having this recurring nightmare where I'm in London, and Jackie and Danny are there with their kid. Then I wake up in a cold sweat, and for seconds I relax, realising it was a nightmare only to be jolted back into the crushing reality that it's all true.

Sometimes it starts as a happy dream. I'm the one pregnant with his baby, then the baby morphs into a sack of air.

Sometimes, I wake up sobbing. Huge body-shaking sobs that keep coming in unstoppable waves.

During the day, it's no better. I don't let the tears fall, but the dark cloud follows me no matter what I do.

In work, my designs are going from strength

to strength. The project has moved into the alpha stage, and development teams are being selected to start working on the new software in the next few weeks. I have the choice of relocating to New York if I want to. I should be happy. Except the feeling of pleasure has been sucked out of everything. Now I'm just going through the motions of life.

I'll never get to kiss him again. Or touch him again.

I'll never get to call him mine.

I'll never get to carry his baby.

*It should have been me.*

A yellow taxicab pulls up outside the flat, and a tall agitated blonde girl steps out with two suitcases.

I smile and bounce down the steps. "Julie."

She does a low whistle. "Fuck me, girl, this is a nice building."

"Of course, it is, it's *his*." I pull her in for a massive hug. "I've missed you."

"Oh." She grimaces. "He must have a guilty conscience if he's putting you up here. Can we vandalise it when we leave?"

"No." I roll my eyes, lugging a suitcase up the steps. What the hell does she have in here? "I still work in his company for now, remember? How was your flight?" I ask, pushing open the revolving door.

"You have a bellboy?" she says too loudly as Tom, our doorman, greets me.

"I don't think bellboy is the right term." I frown. "Isn't that someone who does errands?"

"I dunno." She shrugs. "I thought bellboy was an

American butler."

"Tom's not a butler either, Julie." I snort as we get into the elevator. "This place is so amazing." I laugh. "You haven't even seen the apartment yet."

"*Apartment* is it now, what's wrong with flat?" she complains as we reach my floor. I turn the key and push the door open.

"Holy crap!" she screeches, dumping her luggage in the middle of the floor and running circles around the open plan room. "This place would cost a bomb to rent. Like thousands a month!"

She runs so fast towards the window I worry she's going to burst through it. "Holy fucking shit, this view!"

"Yeah, it's amazing," I agree. "Except now it's tainted because it reminds me of him."

Her lips draw into a thin lip. "We need wine. Wine is your medicine."

"Believe me, I've tried that. I'm at risk of becoming an addict," I say, lifting a bottle of red from the wine rack. "All I do is drown myself in work and drink away my sorrows. Everything I use in this apartment, every mod-con in this kitchen, the bed, the bath."

I laugh dryly. "I'm thinking about how Jackie will be using it when the three of them come here to play happy families. In my mind, there is a family of three sitting beside the fire in matching Christmas jumpers with easy listening jazz in the background. He likes jazz. Then they return to their beautiful mansion overlooking the Thames, and occasionally they'll vacation in the Shetlands."

"You have their lives all figured out." She stares at me, concerned. "Charlie, you need to stop torturing yourself."

I hand her the glass of red and pour my own generous portion. "It's good to have you here." I clink my glass with hers.

"I'm glad to be here," she says. "We are so worried about you at home. Your messages ... you just seem sad all the time."

I muster a small smile and look away. "It'll get easier."

She takes a sip. "Nice wine. How was he? When you saw him last week?"

I pause. "He just seemed so unaffected. So normal. He was keeping to his schedule so he wouldn't be late for his next meeting with some senator. Meanwhile, I was a pathetic wreck." I fight back the tears. "I craved his approval, wanting him to say my ideas were good. He just sat there, deadpan. Then afterwards he casually told me he is having a baby."

I let out a half snort, half cry. "He didn't even notice the moment when he tore my heart into a million tiny little pieces. He said it like it was the most casual thing in the world." I sniffle. "Like, *hey, they made my coffee wrong, but I kind of like it.*"

"Oh, Charlie." She sets down the wine and pulls me for a hug. "I know it's awful. But don't leave London because of that asshole."

"Sorry," I sob, wiping my tear-stained cheeks. "You visit me in New York, and I just sit here blubbering. Hardly the holiday you wanted. I'm so goddamn sick of crying."

"I hope you haven't spent every night blubbering over Danny Walker."

"Of course not," I lie, looking away. "I've seen a lot of New York. It's magical. Honestly, Julie, it's amazing here."

"How long do you have left?"

"Just one week," I calculate. "I've been here seven weeks. Then I'll have to return to reality."
I don't want to think about my return to London, to the city of Danny, Jackie, and her unborn baby.

"Let's get dressed up and get something to eat, OK?" I brighten up.

She nods. "You've lost a lot of weight. You need feeding. I mean, you look fantastic, but you are skinny. If you don't start eating, you'll have pimples for tits."

I let out a short laugh. "With all the despair gnawing at my guts, they've stopped working. Food is just a chore now."

"Enough sorrow." She slaps her hand on the table. "Let me see this contract that DreamWorks has sent. One hundred thousand pounds. Is this for real?"

I grin and pull open my laptop. "I'm hoping my hotshot lawyer friend can help me figure that out. It's likely a scam, so I'm not getting my hopes up."

"Does he know?"

"Danny? Of course not." I shrug. "He's got no reason to know. We don't talk now."

She cocks a brow. "He would be impressed."

"It's irrelevant." I shake my head. "It's pointless trying to impress him. What good would come of it? A child is ... irreversible."

"Here." I turn the laptop to her, and nerves flutter in my stomach. The moment of truth.

She puts on her glasses and starts reading.

"There must be a catch?" I ask tentatively, watching her. It read too good to be true. DreamWorks want to buy the rights to use one of my songs in a movie.

She keeps reading, and I wait with bated breath.

The silence breaks with a half-laugh, half-screech. "No catch. Charlie, this is fucking legit."

We stare at each other for a moment then the silence is broken with hysterics.

"My song? My song?" I shout as we dance around the kitchen like idiots.

"Fuck Walker!" Julie shouts, splashing wine all over his expensive floor.

"Charlie, after this movie comes out, you'll be dating movie stars."

I grin back. Danny Walker can go to hell. I don't need him. All he ever brought me was pain.

*∗∗∗*

Christmas time in New York is magical. It's five days before Christmas, and I know I'm going to be getting on that return flight home kicking and screaming.

Julie flew home this morning, and we've done everything from visiting the winter villages, skating around the Rockefeller, watching Broadway shows, to sitting on sexy Santa's knee at a late-night club in Greenwich, telling him to forgive us for being naughty girls this year.

I could write a best-selling guide on what to do in New York if you are a heartbroken tourist. Most of it involves hard liquor.

Tonight is my leaving party from the New York branch. I'm heading back to London for the Christmas break to mull over whether I want to relocate here. I'm conflicted, to say the least.

We're making real traction now, development has started, and we think we will have the first version out for beta testing with a few selected clients in six months' time. This is the most excited I've ever felt about a work project, and for the first time, I feel valued. Laura is a fantastic boss; she's the type of woman that builds you up and encourages you to be brave about your ideas. I can't believe I tolerated working under dickface Mike for so many years.

I haven't seen or heard from Danny since, except for the all-staff conference calls.

The pain is slowly but surely fading; I guess what they say about time healing everything is true. I'm finding more things to distract me and replace the sorrow with some happiness.

I've even been on a few dates, but I'm too raw to do anything more than mildly flirt. If I tried to have sex, I think I'd start sobbing my head off. Any sight of a rogue dick, and my body would physically reject it. God damn Danny Walker for giving me the best orgasms of my life. I might as well be celibate from now on in.

The Dead Rabbit is heaving. It seems like every office in New York decided to have a Christmas party here tonight. We are crammed in like drunken, sweaty sardines.

There are people I don't know, friends of friends, and those who wanted to jump on the free drinks' bandwagon.

I'm doing shots with Laura, Joe, and some of the developers. The shot size is so much larger in New York than in London, and I'm ramming them down my throat as fast as oxygen.

It's a good thing I've booked a few days' holiday. I'm flying back in two days, so I should have recovered from my hangover by then.

"Are you going to stay with us, Charlie?" Laura shouts, trying to be louder than the entire bar singing along to Fairytale of New York by The Pogues.

"I'm definitely considering it." I grin at her.

"Good." She hands me a green shot.

I smell it and grimace.

"Because you fit in so well here. You're sailing towards a promotion. I don't want to influence your decision, but I'd love it if you stayed in New York."

"Jesus." Karl leans in behind me, sniffing the tray of green shots.

"Karl!" I swing my arm around his neck, a little too drunk.

"Easy, girl." He laughs. "If you vomit that green stuff over my shoes, I'm not allowing you back in the country."

"You two knew each other before, didn't you?" Laura looks between us curiously.

"That's right," I shout over the music. "He's my brother's friend."

"Danny and Tristan, Charlie's brother, are closer. They've been close friends for twenty years ...." Karl's voice trails off into nothingness as he realises what he's saying.

Are they still close friends? I managed to ruin that.

I swallow the green shot and shiver as the liquid hits my stomach. The mention of Danny still makes me react physically. At least here, I can hide it with shots.

"What have you told the team, Charlie?" Karl turns to me as Joe starts a conversation with Laura. It's too loud to have a conversation in a group.

I chew my lip. "I'm deciding over Christmas. It's so difficult because I can do the role from London or New York. I love both cities. New York would be a fresh start."

He nods, his eyebrows knitting together. "So it really is over between you and Danny, huh?" He shakes his head. "I thought you would go the distance."

I stare at him in disbelief as I double-check his words in my head. "Seriously?"

"Why not?" He shrugs. "You seemed good together. He was so happy when he was with you. You could have worked through the news article. I guess you're just not interested?"

My eyes pop like saucers. Is he for real? Is he actually asking me this?

"I can work through a news article for sure. I can't work through a *baby*." I roll my eyes at him like he's a moron. "What?"

He gives me a quizzical look. "Why would the baby change things?"

"Why would Danny having a baby change things?" My voice goes up an octave. "Karl, are you trying to be funny?"

He looks at me for at least a minute. "Charlie, are you serious?"

This is the strangest conversation I've ever had. Is it these green drinks? Do they have some sort of hallucinogenic drug in them? Is my brain misfiring this conversation?

"Fuck me." He slaps a hand over his mouth. "You're not joking. Why do you think it's Danny's baby?"

"What? How drunk are you?" I shoot him a look. "He told me, Karl."

"Are you sure about that? What were the exact words he said to you?"

"I don't remember," I grumble. Why does it matter how he told me?

"You're being very weird, Karl. Look, I saw Jackie at his house." I feel stupid now admitting it, in case he tells Danny.

"When?" A deep line forms on his forehead.

"After the news article. I wanted to apologise in

person, so I went to his house and rang the doorbell," I say, flustered. "But then ... I heard a female voice and legged it behind the gate. Jackie came out wearing his T-shirt. I disappeared when I heard his voice."

Karl stands very still, staring at me like I'm an alien. "When you heard *my* voice Charlie, you heard my voice."

I open my mouth to speak, but the muscles in my mouth are paralysed. Is he trying to be funny?

"I'm the one having the baby." He gives me an incredulous stare. "That's why I've been in London so much these past few weeks. Jackie and I had a one-night stand. I'm not proud of it ... but I'll look after the baby. It's mine. I took her back to Danny's that night. He was bloody furious with me for it."

Now all my muscles are paralysed. The baby is Karl's? Danny is not with Jackie. Danny is not having a baby. He didn't move on like I thought ... at least not with Jackie.

My head spins as my brain tries to compute this new information.

*Oh shit.*

"Excuse me!" I rush out of the bar, shoving drunken people out of the way, and hit the fresh air just in time for the green projectile vomit to hit the pavement.

Karl is close behind me. "Sorry," I say, sheepishly wiping green dribble from my chin.

I plant myself down on a step beside an open discarded kebab.

He tentatively follows suit. "I'm fine, Karl. You don't need to sit. I don't want you to ruin your outfit. I just need a minute."

"Bit late for that," he chuckles, nodding to his vomit-stained shoes.

"Oh." I flinch. "Sorry about that." I pause trying to take in the news. "He said he was excited about the baby." I stare blankly across the street.

I try to remember our exact conversation. How did I get this so wrong?

"He is. We both are now we've got over the shock and come to terms with it."

"He's not going to be a dad."

"No."

"All this time, I thought he had moved on." I pause. "It's too late, isn't it? I ask in a small voice. "He was so cold and detached at the presentation. He doesn't care if I return to London. He pretty much said so himself."

"I'm not sure that's true." Karl pauses, and I turn to face him. "After the news article and Tristan's reaction, he wanted to give you time and space so that you could decide what you wanted. Honestly, I don't know if it's too late. Once you told him you are dating and staying in New York ... he seems to have closed the door on it."

"Charlie." Joe runs out of the bar as people yell at him. "They're playing an ad for the movie on the big screen. They're playing *your fucking song*. Get your ass in here!"

"Huh?" Karl looks at me, confused.

My mouth twists into a stupefied grin. "DreamWorks have bought the rights to one of my songs for their movie."

# 36

**Charlie**

Three flights, four whiskies, two crying babies, six airline meals, five movies, and not a minute of sleep later, I land in Sumburgh airport. The cold, harsh reality of my knee-jerk decision hits me.

I stare up at the sign. "Welcome to Shetland."

*What am I doing?*

This is the stupidest idea I've ever had. It was just a short romance, and then it ended. Now I'm travelling halfway around the world like a bunny-boiling crazed stalker?

He's going to think I'm a nutcase. Who turns up uninvited two days before Christmas? Karl said that the door had closed. What did I think I was going to do? Knock on it and say Santa has a special surprise?

I fucked it up, and I can only blame myself and my damn insecurities. Tristan always teases me about being too hot-headed. The three flights gave me a lot of time to think. I was too caught up in believing Danny the tech tycoon persona and I failed to listen to Danny the man. Danny the boyfriend. I've learned my lesson, and I may have paid dearly with my heart.

Ho Ho bloody Ho.

If this backfires, I'll have to spend Christmas alone in a holiday rental apartment surrounded by sheep, with no turkey, just that weird fish haggis.

Mum, Tristan, and Callie think I'm flying to London tomorrow from New York. I'll have to make something up like I've gone to a retreat in Bali to find myself so I don't have to tell them the truth.

Maybe it's not too late to back out? I'm still at the airport so I could book the first flight back to London.

Although they are turning off the lights now … What is going on? I thought airports never closed.

I haven't ironed out vital details past disembarking. Now I'm standing at a deserted airport twenty miles from the main town and there isn't a single taxi office in sight.

"Hey," I greet a man mopping the floor. "What's the quickest way to get to town now?"

He nods to the exit. "Number six bus goes to Lerwick. Stay on until the end."

"Great." I sigh with relief. I'm not walking twenty miles in arctic conditions. "When's the next one?"

He checks the big clock on the wall. "You're in luck, about fifty minutes."

This man has clearly never used a metro system if he thinks a fifty-minute wait is 'lucky.'

"How long does it take?"

"It's got a few stops. About an hour."

"Thanks."

*Damn.*

It's so slow, Karl will beat me to Lerwick at this rate, and he doesn't depart New York until tomorrow.

It looks like I'm going to have to go straight to the pub, which was not the plan. I wanted to freshen up first. I have that exhausted, dishevelled look you get on long-haul flights. The build-up of dribble stuck to your chin after sitting in a zombie-like state tilted forty-five degrees for hours.

I smell like a zombie too.

Ho Ho bloody Ho.

It's definitely longer than fifty minutes by the time the bus arrives, and I'm the only person on it. I do my make-up in the dark and apply layers of deodorant to mask the odour of aeroplane sweat.

The closer the lights of Lerwick loom, the sicker I feel. Not only will he reject me, knowing Danny, he'll also feel obliged to look after me in Shetland until he can send me back to London. That's all I need; his pity and concern.

Then he'll message Tristan, who will also become really concerned and will no doubt stage an intervention. My moment of madness will be a point of embarrassment for the next decade until I do something even stupider, of course.

Way to go, Charlie.

"Last stop." The bus pulls to a halt a few doors down from the location of my demise, 'The Lounge.'

It's a small-town bar with live music and open mic nights, one of the only bars in the town. It's not expecting a guest appearance from a transatlantic visitor.

I haul my two suitcases and guitar case off the bus and hover outside the bar.

"Do you need help?" The guy doing the door stares dubiously at my homeless chic look.

"Is it Open Mic night?"

"Yeah," he says, looking at the suitcases. "Are you part of a band?"

"No. It's just me, I've come from ... New York." I hesitate. "I'm here to surprise someone."

He laughs at me like I'm a lunatic. "Holy shit! You've literally stepped off the plane?"

I grit my teeth. "I couldn't risk not getting a slot. So?" I ask. "Can I have a slot?"

"All the way from New York? Sure!" He grins. "You can go on after Timmy has finished."

Timmy must be the one making the awful sound with bagpipes.

"Five minutes?"

Panic seizes my heart.

"We don't get too many requests," he explains, staring at me as if I were an imaginary person. "Timmy and the band from Unst mainly." He pauses. "Everyone will be shocked at you all the way from New York!"

"Uh-huh," I rasp. "Look, can you sneak me through the back? It'll ruin the surprise if I come through the front door."

He grins. "Follow me."

He turns suddenly, causing me to collide with

him. "You're not famous, are you?"

"No." I look around the paint-chipped walls of the pub. Why would I be playing here if I was famous?

I drag the suitcases and the guitar down the alleyway to a back entrance bashing the guitar against the wall as I try to manoeuvre all my baggage.

"Wait here, Timmy will be off in two minutes."

Nodding, I peer around the door to the bar.

*He's here.*

Danny is here.

I try to breathe but it feels like someone is clutching my throat and stopping my airflow.

I rub my throat. My mouth is so dry and tight I can't speak, never mind sing.

I can't do this.

I'm going to be sick.

I'm going to pass out.

My heart is going to explode in my chest.

*I'm having a full-blown panic attack.*

Again, I peek inside. The shock of his life is coming; I just hope it's not a nasty one.

He looks the picture of serenity as he leans against the bar, perched on a bar stool. Edme sits beside him. He's got a week's worth of stubble and is wearing a wool jumper with holes in it. He could pass for a sexy sheep farmer.

For the forty thousandth time since I landed, I wonder how I could be so ridiculous to think this would be a good idea.

They are laughing and drinking scotch together.

Edme is covered in mismatched jewellery like a Christmas tree and claps her hand out of rhythm to the bagpipes.

"Who's the request for?" the barman asks as Timmy lets out one final painful blow.

"Danny," I choke, "and Edme."

He nods. "And your name?"

"Charlie."

He scurries to the small stage area where Timmy is packing away his bagpipes. "Next up, folks, we have someone all the way from New York! This is a very special request for Eddie and Tammy."

What!? No, you fool!

"Please give a welcome to Charlie!"

As he claps me out, the twenty or so people in the pub join in half-heartedly.

I take a deep breath and walk out into the light.

# 37

## Charlie

He sits still as though someone has turned him into stone, his expression unreadable.

Beside him, Edme shrieks. "Darling, it's Charlie!"

"Hi Danny, Edme," I say shakily into the microphone.

"Danny," I hiss at the bartender, and he shrugs his shoulders. "Not Tammy. Is Tammy even a name?"

As I wrap the guitar strap around my shoulders, my head yanks back. My hair is tangled in the strap. I fumble with it for a painful amount of time and hear people getting restless.

I can't look up again. If I look into his eyes and see horror, pity or embarrassment, I'll never be able to deliver this song.

"I, uh," my voice breaks, and I clear my throat. "I wrote this song to explain how I feel about a recent romance."

There are a few murmurs around the pub. They aren't bothered. Can't blame them really.

"This is called 'You're gone,'" I rasp out. It was written in the dark in my New York apartment over the past few months.

My version of a diary.

No one has ever heard it. I've never played it outside the apartment.

No one was ever meant to hear it.

Not OpenMic.

Not Julie, Cat, Stevie, Suze.

Especially not Danny.

Yet here I am.

Singing my lowest moments to a group of sheep farmers, the love of my life, and his eccentric granny.

I burst out into the first verse, and it's raw, so raw, I feel like I'm standing in front of them, naked and crying.

My bittersweet lyrics loaded with heartbroken emotion surge through the bar. My voice is loud and fierce, demanding to be listened to.

All eyes are fixed on me and my pain.

Including his.

The chorus is high pitched, even for me, but every time it comes around, I hold the note for so long, there are gasps and whoops throughout the pub.

With every breath I expel, every note I hold on to, I let out more pain.

Then I'm done. I have no more air left in my lungs.

Nothing more to say.

There's a high-pitched whoop from the bar stools. Edme jumps up and down excitedly, trying to put her fingers in her mouth to whistle.

"Wow." Barman's eyes are wide. "Got a real Amy Winehouse thing going on there, haven't you?"

I don't wait around to see *his* reaction. I just can't.

I grab my guitar and leg it out of the bar through the front door.

"Your luggage!" Barman shouts after me.

The cold air bites into my lungs, and I walk out onto the street.

"Where the fuck are you going?" the low husky voice demands behind me.

I turn to meet the dark eyes that have haunted my nightmares and dreams for weeks.

We stand frozen, two metres apart. I don't trust myself to move towards him.

"I'm sorry," the words stumble out of my mouth. "It was a stupid, crazy idea. I must still be drunk from my leaving party. I'm sorry I embarrassed you. I—"

"Shush." He strides towards me, closing the gap between us. His body overshadows mine as those startling brown eyes stare right into me, demanding my full attention.

I had forgotten how nervous he made me.

"No more games, Charlie. This thing between us has been full of incorrect assumptions, jealousy, stubbornness. You thought I was the father of Jackie's baby, for fuck's sake. Karl told me yesterday. Is that what you think of me?"

My stomach sinks as I hear the evident fury in his words. He's pissed.

"I understand," I whisper, studying my feet. "I get it. I'm sorry for assuming you impregnated the receptionist. I'm an ass."

"No, you don't get it," he growls, putting his hand

under my chin. "Look at me."

His eyes lock on mine, his demanding gaze softening slightly. "I'm wiping the slate clean. I love you, Charlie. I've never loved anyone like this before. I want you to be my girlfriend; I want you to be my last girlfriend. I've never been so sure of anything in my life. I've wanted you for ten years. I'm forty-one. Someday in the not-too-distant future, I want us to live together. I want you to be my wife and the mother of my children someday."

He draws breath.

"So there it is. I'm not expecting you to want all these things right now, but I'm hoping since you travelled halfway around the world that you want something too. All my cards are on the table." His voice breaks low and gruff. "You have my heart. Do with it what you want."

He stares at me, waiting, his arms slightly open.

Every neuron in my head fires at once.

"Danny." I choke back tears and rise on my tiptoes to meet him. "I love you too. I love you so much."

As his arms enclose my hips, he pulls me flush into his warm body. The arctic Shetland conditions have suddenly disappeared. His mouth comes down onto mine and he kisses me like a man who hasn't been kissed in years. Desperate. Tender. Urgent. Like two people who might die if their bodies don't touch.

All the pain, all the ups, and all the downs were worth it. For this. For now.

He pulls back to meet my eyes, smiling softly. "Good, that makes life easier for both of us."

I bury my head in his chest where I belong.

"I'm sorry I stink," I mumble from his chest. "Can I go have a shower now, please?"

## Danny
## Christmas Day

"I know what I'm fucking doing, Danny. Stop treating me like an imbecile." Tristan's eyes blaze as he blocks my right of passage.

Anger bubbles through me. "Are you joking?" I sneer. "Natalia does everything for you, including wiping your ass. If you think I'm letting you manage this operation, you have another thing coming."

He shoves me a little as he moves to open the oven door.

I inhale sharply. This guy is fucking infuriating.

"Daniel, this is what is called peacocking," says a sarcastic voice from the doorway.

My jaw tightens as we both turn to glare at her.

From the kitchen doorway, four women watch us nervously. Christmas jumpers and tinsel wrapped around their heads make them look ridiculous.

Shockingly, they agreed to the last-minute change of plans to join Charlie and me for Christmas at Sumburgh Hall.

Charlie hugs young Daniel like she's protecting him from wild beasts. He looks up at her, confused.

"When two turkeys fight over a turkey," she elaborates. "As demonstrated here."

She turns her attention back to us, and her jaw slackens. "You know it's on the grill setting? Has it been like that the whole time?"

What?

My eyes snap back to the oven.

"Fuck!" I yell, shaking my hands at the ceiling, then catch myself and shoot an apologetic glance at Grandma and Mrs. Kane. I'm not exactly covering myself in glory here.

Their faces collectively fall.

"Useless gobshites," Grandma mutters. "I should have eaten before I came over."

Charlie's eyes flit between us. "I guess dinner's going to be another few hours."

Behind her, Callie sighs in disgust.

"Move!" Grandma charges ahead with Mrs. Kane hot on her heels. "Out! Out!"

"I think you should do as they say," Charlie muses.

I look at Tristan, and he exhales in defeat.

"Fine." I roll my eyes as we are shooed to the other side of the kitchen.

Charlie smirks between both of us. "I'm glad you and Tristan have something else to fight about instead of me."

"I could have managed the damn turkey," Tristan grumbles, pouring two glasses of scotch and handing one to me.

I take the peace offering and raise my glass to him. "You've never cooked a day in your life, Kane."

"Doesn't mean I can't," he mutters back.

Soft arms curl around my waist, and I grin at Charlie, pressing her closer. I'm head over heels, utterly in love with this woman. There's no one to hide it from now. There's no reason for us not to be together, except the talking to I received from my head of HR, Cheryl, of course, but she came around eventually.

"Woah." Callie giggles. "That's a hot look."

I turn to see my brother standing in the doorway with his hand on his hips, basking in attention as the women swoon over his kilt.

Grandma wolf-whistles loudly, and I feel a pathetic pang of jealousy as Charlie blatantly ogles Karl.

"Careful," I growl, prodding her ribs. "Wrong brother."

She whips her head around, her bright green eyes flashing up at me. "If you want the same attention you know what to do. Get into your own kilt."

"Please don't," Tristan interjects as my phone beeps loudly in my pocket.

Her forehead creases. "Seriously, today? Christmas day?"

"Just one work call, I promise," I attempt to appease her, stepping out of her embrace.

If I settle this issue, I can relax for the rest of the day. The company will IPO from private to public in a few days, and the stock market doesn't wait for Christmas turkey. I need to make sure we have our shit together.

My fingers type back quickly to Martina, my head lawyer, telling her I'll be calling in two minutes.

She responds immediately, being the same type of workaholic I am.

"Martina?" I say, taking the stairs two at a time.

"Danny. I need you to sign forms for the underwriters," she says. "I'm emailing them over to you now." She pauses. "Oh, and happy Christmas."

I smile at the afterthought. "Happy Christmas, Martina. Send them over. I'll sign them now."

"Thanks, boss."

The phone goes dead, and I flip open my laptop, giving it some power juice.

There's a soft knock on the door.

I'm unable to hide the goofy smile that plasters my face every time she enters the room, despite being under pressure. "Sweetheart, I have a critical job to do."

"Yes, you do."

She walks forward and wraps her legs around me, removing the laptop from my reach before I can protest.

My gaze drops down to her full luscious lips, then lower to those gorgeous breasts being paraded in my face. She knows exactly what she's doing, exactly how to push my buttons.

"Charlie—"

"Just five minutes." She brushes her lips against mine, and I succumb, widening my mouth to taste her fully.

My hands roam across her buttocks, then forward, finding the hem of her soft yoga pants, and she moans softly like her skin is hypersensitive to my touch. The kiss becomes impatient, more demanding.

I'm a goner.

My cock instantly stands to full attention.

I delve into her soft wet flesh, groaning at how wet she is already. Her body trembles against my touch, driving me so fucking horny, but I know we don't have time, not with everyone waiting downstairs, not when Martina is having kittens across the Atlantic.

Fuck them all; they can wait. This can't.

With efficiency, I pull down her yoga leggings and soft lace underwear so that she's naked from the bottom down and pull down my own trousers with speed. With short moans escaping her, she pushes me down onto the bed, taking my shaft in her fist and pushing herself down onto me.

We both groan in ecstasy as I fill her deep.

Our mouths hang open as she rides me, holding her legs tight so she is entirely in control.

"I love you, sweetheart," I say in broken chords as she looks down with so much emotion it wipes any remaining breath from my lungs.

My hands tighten around her hips, and I can tell by her face that I'm grinding against her clit with each thrust.

Fuck, she wants it so badly. It makes me want her even more.

I cry out like a schoolboy as I spurt furiously into her for what seems like an eternity.

Pulling away, I attempt to catch my breath. "Now, will you let me finish this critical work that the success of the company hangs off?" I ask, tilting my head back to kiss her.

There's a mischievous gleam in her eye. "Only if you wear the kilt like a true Scotsman."

"Not a chance," I say firmly. "My grandma, your own mother, and your younger sister are downstairs. Underwear stays ON."

"Three flights I travelled to be here with you, Danny." She pouts. "That's what you are worth to me. What am I worth to you?"

This woman will be my undoing.

"Fine." I exhale. "No underwear."

I'm suffocated in a massive hug. "This is the best Christmas ever."

# EPILOGUE

**Charlie**
**Eight months later.**

My phone flashes angrily as Laura chats over the video call.

I jab at the phone, sending the automated notification, **sorry, I can't talk right now**.

He's going to be furious.

I'm not trying to antagonise him despite what he thinks, although part of me is turned on by that clenched jaw, nostril twitching, eyes blazing Walker stance.

I am genuinely busy. We have a launch in five days of the NextGen products, and I've worked too hard all year on this to scupper it now.

Considering it's his company, you'd think he'd understand.

Before I look up, I know he's approaching. The shift in the atmosphere is a giveaway. The entire floor appears to sit straight in their seats and pretend to be model employees.

"What's he doing on this floor?" someone mutters behind me.

He stops beside my desk and clears his throat.

Eyebrows raised, I look up to see him glaring at me. He's wearing his trademark dark blue suit and brilliant white shirt, but I don't have time to swoon right now.

"I'm on a work call," I mouth, stating the bleeding obvious. I know he's the CEO, but doesn't he realise the rest of us have work to do as well?

He exhales loudly, dangling his arms over my desk.

"Laura?" he asks, irritation evident in his voice.

I nod.

"Tell her you'll call her back. You've been summoned."

"You're summoning me?" I repeat loudly, looking at him in disbelief.

The nerve of this guy.

I bite my tongue to refrain from unleashing all fury on him in the open-plan office.

"Danny's beside your desk, isn't he?" Laura laughs over the video link.

"I'm so sorry, Laura. Yes." I grimace.

"Can I—"

"Yes, go, it's fine." She waves her hand dismissively. "Let's pick it up in an hour."

I stand up, ignoring the floor full of eyeballs staring at me from all angles.

"Start walking," I mutter, striding down the aisle.

He follows behind me.

"What the hell are you playing at?" I grind out, fixing my fake smile on my face for the benefit of everyone else. "Springing up at my desk making demands. It's irrational."

Our relationship is still on the down-low, mainly because I want to keep it that way. Besides disclosing it to the Board of Directors and, of course, Stevie and the team, to everyone else in the company, I'm just the scruffy Solution Designer who may run a brush through their hair on a good day.

Not the girlfriend of the CEO.

We stop at the elevator, and I stand apart from him, deliberately creating distance.

He stares at me, arms crossed. "I wouldn't need to act irrationally if you let me see you."

"I'm sorry." I sigh. "It's just this launch. I want to make sure everything is perfect."

His stormy eyes hold mine. "I haven't seen you in three days, and I leave for New York tomorrow," he replies, his tone laced with irritation.

"I'm sorry, Danny, it's just a busy period. Aren't you overreacting just a little?"

His jaw twitches like it always does when I insinuate he's being a drama queen. "No, I'm fucking not. If you moved in, we wouldn't have this problem," he barks. "We would see each other every night."

"I have enough cash to buy my own flat now," I tease. The pay-out from DreamWorks equates to a nice healthy deposit.

"Quit fucking teasing me, Charlie," he growls. "You can buy a flat and rent it out. I need you living with me."

In the last three months, he has persistently

asked me to move in with him. He was overreacting a tad, I made sure to see him at least three times a week.

I do want to move in with him soon. What girl wouldn't want to live with Danny Walker?

Right now, I have one foot in the doorway of the beautiful Richmond mansion on the hill and one foot in my mice infected flatshare, the place I spent the best years of my twenties.

He's right. I need to let go of my days of flat sharing with friends. Because this isn't just about me now.

My stomach lurches.

"There is something I need to talk to you about, and I really didn't want to do it here, but I can't miss Stevie and Cat's engagement party later," I whisper up at him.

"What is it?" His voice is steely. "Let's go to the office."

The elevator pings open, and two developers walk out, cutting through the strange atmosphere.

He puts his hand out to usher me into the elevator first, and our eyes lock in the mirror before we turn to face the door.

It stops at nearly every floor between the sixth and the fifteenth floors as people come and go, with everyone addressing Danny.

In the elevator, he shoots me a sideways glance. He knows when I'm nervous.

Panic rises inside me. He's got no fucking clue what's coming.

We walk in silence down the aisle to his office, then he bundles me in and closes the door.

He stands frozen, his dark eyes searching mine. He doesn't like surprises. It's a control freak thing. "What's going on, Charlie?"

Biting my lip, I stare hesitantly into his eyes. I've been over this scene in my head a hundred times. I intended to wait until he got back from New York so I could tell him in the house with an entire speech rehearsed. Now I'm going to have to improvise.

Here I go. I decide to do it efficiently and bluntly.

"Danny, I'm pregnant."

I wait with bated breath as his jaw hits the floor.

"No joke?"

"You think I would joke about this? Are you mad?" I chew on my lip. "I must have missed a pill. Or when I was sick or something. I'm so sorry."

Immediately, his expression softens, and a bright smile spreads across his face. "Why on earth would you think I would be mad?"

"Thank God," I cry out. "I know we didn't plan it, but—"

He moves towards me, locking me in an embrace and tilting my head up so that our eyes meet.

"Shush, sweetheart," he murmurs. "This is the best news of my life."

Happy tears fall from my face, and I gaze into his ridiculous grin.

"I love you so much, Charlotte Kane," he whispers, taking my wet face in his hands. "Thank you for making me the happiest man alive."

His lips take mine like he has forgotten he's in the office, or maybe he no longer cares.

Excitement surges through me as his hand drops protectively to my stomach. "How long?"

"Just a few weeks. It's still early days."

He nods. "You know this means that I insist you and bump move in immediately."

"I know." I giggle, pressing my head against his chest.

"Shit." He takes a deep breath. "Mrs. Kane is going to murder me. Getting you knocked up before marriage."

When I look up, he seems genuinely fearful, as he should be.

I let out a laugh. "Don't forget Tristan. And you can tell HR you've got your employee pregnant."

He pulls me closer. "I think it's time to retire to the Shetlands."

# ABOUT THE AUTHOR

## Rosa Lucas

Rosa writes steamy, contemporary romance novels featuring feisty heroines and sexy alpha heroes. She likes her characters to be relatable, flawed, and have real-world issues and insecurities, but all have a happily-ever-after.

Printed in Great Britain
by Amazon